D0775745

Ace titles by Robert Asprin and Eric Del Carlo

WARTORN: RESURRECTION
WARTORN: OBLITERATION

WARTORN
OBLITERATION

ROBERT ASPRIN
and
ERIC DEL CARLO

ACE BOOKS, NEW YORK

THE BERKLEY PUBLISHING GROUP
Published by the Penguin Group
Penguin Group (USA) Inc.
375 Hudson Street, New York, New York 10014, USA
Penguin Group (Canada), 90 Eglinton Avenue East, Suite 700, Toronto, Ontario, M4P 2Y3, Canada
(a division of Pearson Penguin Canada Inc.)
Penguin Books Ltd, 80 Strand, London WC2R 0RL, England
Penguin Group Ireland, 25 St. Stephen's Green, Dublin 2, Ireland (a division of Penguin Books Ltd.)
Penguin Group (Australia), 250 Camberwell Road, Camberwell, Victoria 3124, Australia
(a division of Pearson Australia Group Pty. Ltd.)
Penguin Books India Pvt. Ltd., 11 Community Centre, Panchsheel Park, New Delhi—110 017, India
Penguin Group (NZ), Cnr. Airborne and Rosedale Roads, Albany, Auckland 1310, New Zealand
(a division of Pearson New Zealand Ltd.)
Penguin Books (South Africa) (Pty.) Ltd., 24 Sturdee Avenue, Rosebank, Johannesburg 2196,
South Africa

Penguin Books Ltd, Registered Offices: 80 Strand, London WC2R 0RL, England

This is a work of fiction. Names, characters, places, and incidents either are the products of the authors' imaginations or are used fictitiously, and any resemblance to actual persons, living or dead, business establishments, events, or locales is entirely coincidental. The publisher does not have any control over and does not assume any responsibility for author or third-party websites or their content.

WARTORN: OBLITERATION

An Ace Book / published by arrangement with Bill Fawcett & Associates

PRINTING HISTORY
Ace edition / February 2006

Copyright © 2006 by Bill Fawcett & Associates.
Cover art by Duane O. Myers.
Cover design by Judith Lagerman.
Interior text design by Kristin del Rosario.

ISBN: 0-441-01347-3

ACE
Ace Books are published by The Berkley Publishing Group,
a division of Penguin Group (USA) Inc.,
375 Hudson Street, New York, New York 10014.
ACE and the "A" design are trademarks belonging to Penguin Group (USA) Inc.

PRINTED IN THE UNITED STATES OF AMERICA

10 9 8 7 6 5 4 3 2 1

RAVEN
(1)

IT WAS SHOCKING to be alive. It filled Raven with such a strange, overwhelming feeling of happiness that she barely knew what to do with herself. She wasn't used to being happy.

As yet, she hadn't actually done anything at all. She hadn't even opened her eyes. She was lying prone, and it felt like others were nearby, gathered around her. She knew something had happened to her, and it was something bad.

But she could feel her lungs working, drawing in air, and her heart beating in her chest. She was alive! And the fact that she was so amazed to be alive made her realize that she hadn't expected to be. That was right, wasn't it? Whatever bad thing had happened to her, she had thought it was going to kill her, right? It was hard to organize her thoughts. Her memories were a jumble.

But there was something very wrong about all this.

Suddenly, Raven's eyes sprang open and she lurched

upright, her left hand grabbing for a spot on her back, at the base of her neck, just above her right shoulder. There was some vague, frightening, urgent memory of trauma there. Something had struck her from behind, violently, with deadly force. Struck her just as . . . as she was running to protect General Weisel.

"General!" she cried out, in a strange voice.

Calm down, Raven. Lord Weisel is quite well.

Her eyes were wide open but her vision was blurry. She felt very strange, and the happy thrill of being alive suddenly evaporated. Something was indeed very wrong. The voice she had just heard seemed to have come from inside her own head.

Who . . . who is that? Raven felt foolish, like a child scared by a noise in the dark. But she asked the question silently anyway, in the confines of her own thoughts.

She was answered. *My name is Vadya. Welcome to my body.*

Maybe she'd gone insane. That would certainly explain the extra voice in her head.

What . . . what are you doing here? Raven asked.

Actually, you're the guest. I am the host. We're going to get to know each other very well.

This isn't real. Raven raised her hands to her face.

Oh, it's very real. Why don't you take a look at yourself? Examine your new lodgings. I'd like to know what you think.

Raven's hands rested oddly over her face. She moved her fingers. Something wasn't right about the shape of her face. It wasn't as full as it was supposed to be. The bones were sharper, more pronounced.

Her hands were shaking as she lowered them. Her eyes were still unfocused. She couldn't see where she was. She had the dim impression of two or three figures standing nearby, watching her, but she couldn't make out any details. She was in a room or a tent, some enclosed space.

Look at yourself, the voice in her head said, more forcefully.

Raven found that her immediate field of vision was functioning better. She was able to focus on her hands as she dropped them from her face. Her fingers were long, elegantly narrow, the backs of her hands graceful. Her fingernails weren't chipped or bitten, like they were supposed to be.

These weren't her hands.

Even so, they moved as her mind commanded them to. She waggled her thumbs experimentally, and the strange hands obeyed without hesitation.

She was sitting half-upright on a bed. A dark blanket covered her. With a sense of awe, fear, and curiosity, she reached for the top edge of the blanket. She could feel that she was wearing no clothing. She slowly peeled the cover away, letting it drop to the floor.

Raven looked down in absolute wonder at her new body.

It's so beautiful, she whispered inside her own thoughts.

The strange occupant in her head let out a happy burst of laughter. *I knew you'd like it.*

Raven more than liked it. She adored it, immediately and completely. She gazed down on her naked flesh. Her breasts were firm, nicely rounded, not too small, but not so big they were awkward. Her belly was smooth, not protruding at all. Her hips curved perfectly. Her thighs were molded as an artist of pornographic illustrations would make them, taut and supple. Where they joined her slim, sleek, beautifully healthy body was a thatch of golden curls.

"Raven? Are you there?"

She blinked. This voice had come from outside the borders of her skull, and it sounded somewhat familiar. But Raven couldn't yet tear her gaze away from the spectacular sight of herself. She raised a hand and touched herself here and there, testing the impossible flesh. Incredibly, it all felt real.

But it *couldn't* be. She didn't look anything like this. She was shapeless and heavy. Her body didn't curve this way, or have this sculpted tone. This was the body of someone beautiful, someone ideally feminine, one of those females who had total confidence in their physical selves. Raven wasn't one of those.

She was ambitious. She was a fledgling wizard. She had been assigned by Lord Matokin himself, leader of the Felk Empire, to spy on General Weisel in the field. It was a hugely important duty.

By the madness of the gods, she wasn't even a blond! Her hair was dark and stringy and as unsightly as anything else about her. What was happening here?

"Raven? Bah! This is foolish. How are we supposed to know it's worked?"

"Have some patience, General," said another voice. "And some faith. *You* certainly should trust the process."

Raven thought she recognized this voice as well as the first. She blinked more, rubbing her eyes, tearing her stare away from further study of this body.

She looked around. She was indeed inside a room, one with stone walls, and there were three others with her. Two wore the dark robes of mages, and the other was dressed in military garb. A sudden burst of modesty overcame Raven, and she grabbed up the blanket from the ground and covered herself.

"I imagine by now your new host has introduced herself," said one of the robed wizards. "You will get to know Vadya very well. I have only this to say about her. She is a loyal subject of the empire, and she didn't hesitate when called upon for this duty."

"Lord Matokin!" Raven said, finally recognizing the man. He was short and heavy, with lively eyes and hair as dark as hers was supposed to be.

"Yes. And you are Raven."

"Am I?" She felt profound doubt about that. Again she had to wonder if she hadn't gone insane.

"Yes, you are. But you now live inside the body of another, the aforementioned Vadya."

"But that's . . . impossible."

"It's not," said the second mage. This one looked drained, wiping sweat from his forehead, his face colorless. "Lord Matokin, if I may go . . . ?"

"By all means, Mage Kumbat," Matokin smiled. "You have our thanks for a staunch effort."

The one named Kumbat exited the room. The figure in the military uniform stepped forward. This, of course, was General Weisel himself. What a mighty pair they made, Raven thought with some amazement. The ruler of the Felk Empire and the commander of its army, both standing side by side at the foot of her bed, both apparently here to see her. It was a fantastic honor.

Yes, I'm honored as well.

The voice leapt unbidden into Raven's thoughts. It was not quite an intrusion, at least not an aggressive one, but Raven found herself unsettled by it. If she was indeed sharing this body with its original owner, how exactly were they supposed to share the mental space of one mind? Would their thoughts and memories and personalities somehow meld together?

No. Kumbat explained it. It won't be like that. We will have a certain privacy from each other but we will be intimate as no two other beings can be. You'll see.

Very well.

Raven returned her attention to her two distinguished visitors.

"General Weisel," she said, still disturbed by how strange her voice sounded, "I am glad to see you are well. I remember . . ." But she couldn't remember yet, not quite.

"You remember saving my life?" Weisel filled in, offering her a smile. "You stepped in front of a crossbow bolt meant for me. That was valiant. I shall reward you for it."

Raven tilted her head. Crossbow bolt? Yes. That was right. She had seen it from the corner of her eye, falling toward the general.

She reached again toward the place at the base of her neck.

"There's no wound there, Raven," Weisel said. "That was another body. You'll get used to it. I feel sure you'll develop an appreciation for this new form you're wearing."

"But does that mean . . . ?" she tried to ask, barely able to consider the concept.

"It means," Matokin put in, quietly, "that the body you knew, the physical person you remember as Raven, is no more. But the essence of that being, everything that made her who she was, all of that crucial substance remains. It has been reborn." His dancing eyes settled on her. "You have been resurrected."

Raven started to shake, and then couldn't stop. Her whole body trembled, this new, wonderful but totally alien body. She wasn't herself anymore. She was someone else. Actually she was *sharing* someone else's body.

Obviously, this was magic. But it was magic of a magnitude that she'd barely suspected. She had traveled through the portals, hurtling across distances in a few steps that would take days to traverse on horseback. And yet, this was even more amazing.

Portals . . . ? The portals! Yes, she remembered now, Weisel's daring and unorthodox plan to use the portals in the invasion of the city-state of Trael. Rather than using those magical portals to transport the army's troops, Weisel's scheme was to simply open them around the target city, allowing whatever creatures dwelt within that otherworldly realm to roam freely into this world, and straight at Trael.

When Raven had been shot—and apparently *killed*—by that crossbow, Weisel had been on the cusp of giving the final order to open those portals. She didn't know if he'd gone through with the plan.

Raven pulled the blanket tighter around herself. Neither man came forward to physically comfort her, but that would have been unseemly anyway, considering their elevated positions. It didn't even matter that Lord Matokin was her father. Raven was the daughter of one of his retired mistresses, but such a thing might actually carry very little weight. Regardless, she had yet to tell him of her identity.

"Are you all right, my dear?" It was Weisel, peering at her closely.

With an effort of will, Raven brought her shaking under control. "Yes, General. It's just all . . . a bit of a shock."

Weisel gave her a droll look. "Yes, isn't it just? Well, you'll need a little time to recover. Perhaps, Lord Matokin, since we have this rare opportunity to meet face-to-face, we should discuss the progress of this great Isthmus campaign."

Matokin turned with a look that was just slightly cool. He said, "General, I am satisfied with your very able handling of the Felk army. But that army needs you now. Surely you see that you must return to the field immediately. We have used up critical time seeing to this . . . indulgence."

Weisel didn't wince. He gave Matokin a hard little smile, glanced again at Raven, and exited the room.

Raven's thoughts and memories were still somewhat jumbled, but things were gradually clearing. She had remembered her spying assignment for Lord Matokin. Now she also remembered what she had learned from Weisel. The general had taken her into his confidence and had told her he suspected that Matokin was deliberately sabotaging the war effort. This was a war of magic, at least in part, and Matokin, the empire's greatest mage, was withholding vital information from Weisel about the army's magical faculties.

Matokin, Weisel claimed, wanted the war to go on indefinitely, so as to keep his position as emperor secure. It was a heinous, treasonous accusation.

It was also something she had never reported to Matokin.

"My Lord?" Her voice had an odd purring quality to it, a kind of casual sensuality that went well with this body.

"What is it?"

"Could you tell me where I am?"

"You're in the city of Felk, in a room of the Palace we had prepared for you. A great deal of effort has been expended in this venture, but General Weisel was very insistent that you be recalled to the living. Still, there's no getting past the unsettling effects of what you've been through."

The general must have transported here via portal magic from the southern part of the Isthmus, where the Felk army was in the field.

"You will adjust to your new condition," Matokin continued. "Recovery will depend on how strong you are, physically and mentally. And how eager you are to resume your work."

"I am very eager, my Lord."

"Good. I want you back at Weisel's side. It may just be that he'll find your new shape a pleasing one. You may in fact become something more than his confidant. Are you prepared for that?"

"I am prepared to serve you any way I can, Lord Matokin."

"Good." Matokin smiled. "I wonder if the general is truly aware that we have the power to snuff out his life any time we choose." He shrugged. "Rest now, Raven." He turned and left the room.

Yes, Raven. Rest some. And I'll tell you about myself.

Raven lay back on the bed, which was very comfortable. *Go ahead, Vadya,* she said silently to her host. *I am listening.*

RADSTAC
(1)

IT WAS A game of dressing up, of make-believe, of playing their roles as surely as actors played theirs on rude
creaky stages. In Radstac's judgment she and Deo were
currently enacting a farce. But, like most comedies she'd
experienced, she didn't think this one especially funny.

She crossed the open ground toward the squad circle,
steps measured, unhurried. But not so slow as to draw the
interest of a supercilious junior officer looking for a sub-
ordinate to reprimand or order about for sport. There were
significant differences between serving in a national military, such as this one made up of the Felk and conscripts
from the states they had conquered, and serving in a mercenary force, which was Radstac's true element. Merce-
naries weren't required to do anything but fight on behalf
of their employers. They needn't waste faith on foreign
causes, and the code of discipline they adhered to did not
include servile fealty. One need only go through the mo-

tions of loyalty when one was a mercenary. And what was more, nothing greater than that was expected.

Masquerading as a Felk soldier, however, meant that Radstac had to submit to all manner of affronts, to personal offenses she would not otherwise have tolerated longer than an eye blink. This army's hierarchy, its complex chain of command, was quite annoying. She had thought several times of appropriating an officer's uniform for herself, even if it meant bodily removing that uniform's rightful occupant. But, no. She and Deo needed to maintain a minimal visibility. Going about this huge encampment in the trappings of a typical Felk foot soldier was the smart thing to do.

Radstac wasn't a member of this particular squad, but she slipped casually into the meal line with a tray and waited until she'd reached its head. The squad circle's cook dully scooped out a load of the hot, not particularly appetizing food.

"Put a second portion on top of that," she said quietly.

The young cook blinked, as surprised as if his ladle had started speaking to him. "What?" He sounded utterly mystified.

"Double the portion." Radstac gave him a meaningful gaze from her colorless eyes in her scarred face. It seemed to convince him that the easiest thing to do would be to just dump another share of the stewed meat and vegetables onto her plate and let her be on her way. Which is what he did.

Rations of course were just that—rationed. No soldier, at least none in these lowly ranks, was permitted additional servings. If you wanted extra food, she knew, you had to be lucky and skillful enough to forage it on your own.

She still possessed all her familiar accoutrements of

combat, despite the Felk costume she was reluctantly wearing. Leather armor, bracers, kidskin boots, and the finely balanced throwing knives tucked therein, hidden from view. Naturally her left hand still wore the weighted leather glove. A weight of gears, of twin recessed prongs that she could extend with a sharp snap of her wrist. And, just as naturally, she retained her faithful combat sword, a companion through more battles than she could bother herself to number.

It was when she was almost out of sight of the squad circle that a voice rose behind her. She took two more steps, past the corner of a storage tent, and halted. This, of course, was the game of it. If anyone *did* confront her, question her, discover that she wasn't a legitimate member of this army, it would be the end of the whole farce.

And such so-called comedies, she understood, tended to conclude in hilarious tragedy.

A sergeant followed her around behind the tent. He had a thick face, a neck that swelled the collar of his uniform. His eyes were noticeably tiny but highly alert.

"What entitles you to a larger meal than the rest of us are enjoying?"

Radstac balanced the tray on one hand, her right. She was already planted into a ready stance. It was still possible that with enough groveling soldierly behavior she could extricate herself from this. .

The sergeant's tone was surly; but there was something else playing beneath his voice and a particular glint in those minute eyes.

"I asked you a question."

Which was significant in itself. Though this man was of rank, he wasn't yet enforcing that status. He was *asking* her a question.

"I'm especially hungry," Radstac said, lacing something tacit into her voice as well.

A small stub of tongue came out of that thick face to lick the sergeant's lips. "Are you . . . ?" They were unseen here, behind the tent.

Now it *was* almost comic. Radstac shifted her stance just slightly, still balanced but now posing herself provocatively. She let her mouth move slowly, sensually. It was all caricature. But evidently effective.

The sergeant's breath caught. Then he heaved his heavy chest. "I could overlook this."

"You could," she agreed.

"But I need something to make me forget."

"Show me what I need to do."

He did, eyes widening in surprise at the ease of this. His hands moved hastily, and he drew himself out of his trousers, holding his hardening shaft proudly and nervously.

It wouldn't be so much to do this thing. But Radstac had no assurances that this would be the end of it.

"Why," she said, eyes lowering, then lifting, "I see I've mistaken you for a man. How embarrassing."

That thick face reddened. It was a trite vulnerability she'd targeted, but this sergeant was acting out the cliché perfectly. Trying to hold up his undone trousers with one hand, he snatched a knife from his belt. It fumbled slightly clearing the sheath, but he swung it, a fast arc for Radstac's throat.

She was faster. Elbow moving, hand flashing upward. She batted the blade cleanly out of his hand, reversed the movement, and pounded her open gloved palm hard across his mouth.

"So, you try to rape me, then kill me. An interesting use of your authority, *Sergeant*. But not, I think, something

your superiors would approve of. Why would they believe
me, you ask? All I need do is give you a hard shove, and
you'll stumble back into sight of that squad circle with
your trousers dropped halfway down your legs and your
lip bleeding. I'll follow, calling out for help. Then . . . well,
then we'll see. Maybe you'll emerge the hero after all."

All the while she was twisting her left fist where she'd
seized the front of his tunic. The fabric wound tighter and
tighter, and his face reddened more. It would have been
easier just to have loosed the prongs from her glove and
have done this annoyance. But easier only in the simplest
sense, in the shortest term.

Very quickly the sergeant saw reason, and Radstac went
on her way. She had spilled nothing from the tray.

SHE TURNED PAST a row of stationary wagons, their
beds loaded with standard ordnance and guarded by a disinterested unit of Felk. Nevertheless, a few of the male
soldiers eyed her as she went by. With her chopped short
hair the color of spoiling berries, the white scalp scar
across the back of her skull and the two other scars mark-
ing her bronzed face, she didn't represent the unimagina-
tive man's ideal of womanhood. Not that she cared a
bugger. Sex was a sport in which one seized one's prizes,
and playing that sport violently and decadently was perfectly within the rules. In her life she'd had her share of
playing.

As she walked, Radstac let out a low tuneless whistle.
She paused, then repeated it an octave higher. As she
neared the flap of a tent, the same atonal melody was returned. Dusk was making pink of the west, where full surg-
ing clouds were rallying. It was already too chilly for her

Southsoil tastes. Among this Isthmus's many failings was its inhospitable climate, particularly now that autumn had taken firm hold. She slid a hand inside the canvas flap and, sweeping her small eyes behind her a final time, stepped into the tent.

"Ah, supper! My savory fowl, so delicately sautéed, spiced with flavors exotic and perhaps narcotic—here at last!"

Deo smiled up at her. He was cross-legged on the canvas floor, sword arranged beside him, tunic undone to the middle of his breastbone, exposing the stitches that held together the precise shallow wound across his nicely molded chest. Radstac had given him those stitches. It was only fair. She'd given him the wound as well.

"And if you don't want that," she said, flourishing the laden plate, "there are these slops instead."

"Now, it doesn't look so bad as all that, does it? Give it here. See, it appears thoroughly edible. By which I mean, of course, that neither of us shall die from eating it. The fowl I was talking about? There's a dining hall in Petgrad that serves it. A very choice bird. Difficult to hunt. Even harder to cook properly. But when it's done right—and oh, it was done so *very* right there—then it was a meal to rhapsodize over. A culinary joy better than your average buck and cork. In fact, better than your *better* than average—"

Radstac squatted opposite Deo. "Food and sex. Weaknesses of royalty."

"Of all creatures walking about on two or more legs, I should say."

"Indeed. But it's only the lofty that can so completely confuse the two."

"Nonsense. To compare is not to substitute. Thus"—Deo picked a sliver of moist meat from the plate, popped it in his mouth, swallowed—"and thus." He leaned and planted his lips smartly and briefly atop hers. "There. Two categorically different experiences. But both of the senses."

She let a small droll smile tighten a corner of her mouth. "And how do they compare?"

"Oh, you are decidedly the more rewarding weakness."

"Most kind."

They ate off the plate together, without utensils, sitting with their legs folded beneath them, their knees touching. Radstac didn't bother telling Deo about the incident with the sergeant. This tent was not being used at the moment and so was their temporary hiding hole. But even its dubious safety wasn't something they could allow themselves to enjoy for long. Over the past days they had ranged furtively across the massive encampment, alighting here and there, stealing water, stealing food, snatching a watch or two of sleep. It was relatively easy to go unnoticed amidst all these units. As with any undertaking of such scope, some disorder must result. For her and Deo it was a matter of stealth, of diligence. It wasn't a difficult thing to be just two more soldiers among so many others, among this grand Felk host.

But, of course, they were not Felk, nor captured soldiers inducted into the ranks. They were the two who had attempted to assassinate this army's topmost commander, General Weisel.

Actually, Radstac conceded, credit where credit was due. It was Deo who had fired that crossbow bolt that—so the avid scuttlebutt went—had so nearly found its target. Truly it had been a magnificent shot. Miraculous. Or . . . almost so.

"It looks like time to take that thread out. You haven't been scratching at it?"

"In the noble family of the premier of Petgrad," Deo said, fastidiously licking his fingers clean, "we learn not to scratch our wounds from a very young age."

"How very wise. Unbutton that tunic the rest of the way. I'll barely be able to see what I'm doing as is."

It wouldn't do to light a lamp in here. Nights were safer for them than days in this camp, but every caution had to be strictly observed. Radstac peered closely at the line of gashed flesh. She had inflicted it and done so neatly. A cosmetic wound. It had served to fool the searching parties that were hastily mounted following the failed assassination of Weisel. Deo had pretended to be a scout, newly returned from the field and wounded by bandits. The Felk searchers had found Radstac tending to that very convincing wound. Then, during the ongoing commotion, the two of them had slipped away.

She snipped the stitches one by one, removed the bits of thread. Deo was admirably stoic about it. Nephew of Petgrad's premier he might be, but he was no coddled noble; so she had concluded some time ago.

"Radstac," he said when the last binding thread was cut. The wound had closed tidily. The light inside the tent was almost gone. They were shadows to each other, familiar hinted shapes. She had her ungloved hand to his chest, atop the healing slash.

"What is it?" she asked.

"We have to get out of here. Out of this camp."

"You don't want another shot at Weisel, then?"

"I do. I do. But I won't get it. Not now. He'll be guarded. It'll be impossible."

In truth this whole venture had been impossible, Deo's self-appointed quest to assassinate the Felk war commander. It was vastly improbable that they'd made it as far as they had. Deo's bolt had almost caught the general. *Almost . . .*

"I agree," she said.

"Then we must go."

She lifted her shoulders, a silhouetted fatalistic shrug. "That's a nice thought. But I don't think we can simply stroll our way out."

"No. We go out the way we got into this camp."

"By being Far Moved? And how do we convince one of those Felk wizards to accommodate us?"

Her hand was still to his bare chest. One of Deo's hands rose now and closed gently over her fingers. "I think we might find a willing accomplice."

THE LEAF WAS gummy, blue, and it came away from the wax paper in a slow peel. A moment after her teeth had bitten it through a third of the way up from its stem, pain— intense and expected—flared through those same teeth. Radstac bore it. She could not imagine ever not being able to handle that special pain. But if ever that day came, if ever she was tempted, as longtime addicts oftentimes were, to have her teeth pulled from her skull in order to eliminate that initial discomfort, that was the same day *mansìd* would have defeated her, the day she would have lost her will, her strength, her dignity. If it came, her life as a professional *mansìd* addict was done. All that would remain ahead would be the squalid, pathetic, debased existence of any hopeless amateur leaf user.

But, coincidentally, on the arrival of that hypothetical day, Radstac would open the veins down both her arms and have done with it.

She wasn't careless. She wasn't stupid. She respected

her particular addiction, and she had sufficient faith in herself to cope with the powerful needs roused by the stimulant. *Mansìd,* after all, brought clarity. She was very clear about its purpose and capacity in her life.

She was even clear that she was now consuming two-thirds of a leaf, when a quarter-lune or two ago she'd only needed half. Bodies contrived to build up tolerances. She understood this. There was a mathematics about it, a physical equation. It was one she'd worked many times before.

The pain had left her teeth. The other initial disorienting effects had passed. The clarity was enveloping her. *Mansìd* grew only on the Isthmus, and so Radstac came to this wretched land, to fight its wars . . . and to find her leaf.

She pressed the remaining third of the blue leaf back onto its paper and made to tuck it into the pouch under her armor.

"No . . . no . . . *no* . . . please—I—I'll—I—"

Radstac hadn't needed the preternatural clarity of the *mansìd* to see the need riding this Felk wretch so earnestly. Yet she would be hard pressed to identify the specific telltales. This soldier certainly appeared functional. He wasn't one of those toothless horrors that lay under a blanket out of the light and gummed leaves, with no other purpose left in life. But something in his comportment, in his eyes that focused intensely on irrelevant objects, in the slow gliding shadow of his being . . . something gave it away.

Nonetheless, she might have been wrong. But she wasn't wrong. And here was the proof. Dangle a leaf before a creature who desires its effects more than air to breathe, and watch the response. How entertaining. And tritely predictable. Amateur.

This was one of the units assigned to transporting food and equipment. Supplies were Far Moved, quite an expedient method of keeping an army provisioned. Actually, with that advantage alone, the Felk were fairly godsdamned overwhelming. It was such a mammoth undertaking. Full conquest of the Isthmus. But if weapons and rations and probably even fresh troops could be instantaneously conveyed to the field, to *any* place the active army might be, then the Felk's mobility became an unchecked force.

The odd thing about that, however, was that this army had for the past three days been standing fast. No movement. It remained in a state of readiness, as if anticipating the order to mobilize, but no such word had come. Both Radstac and Deo had eavesdropped on and interacted fleetingly with these Felk soldiers, enough to garner the rumor that General Weisel, following the failed try on his life, had either gone into hiding within this camp or quit it altogether. Certainly the Felk war commander could have had himself Far Moved to wherever he liked. It would be the prudent action, at least until his would-be assassins were apprehended.

Radstac had stalked and separated this soldier from his fellows. He wasn't one of the robed wizards, just a regular troop member, one of this army's list makers and invoice checkers. The two of them were huddled behind a great stack of sacked grain, received through one of the portals and not yet distributed to the mess corps. They were out of sight. She had lured him along with a few obvious seductive flourishes. But, having brought him here, she had used the *mansìd* leaf rather than the promise of her body to capture his full attention.

She certainly had it now.

"Oh?" she murmured. "Did you want a nibble?" Her smile, she knew, was unnerving. She treated him to it, there in the murky diffuse glow of the camp's many cooking fires.

"I do." There was terrible longing there, worse than the desire the most foolish romantic felt for his object of affection. It wasn't properly said that one could love *mansìd*. Addicts didn't love their narcotics. But need, if it wasn't purer or truer than love, was at least occasionally more damningly powerful.

"I could give you a taste," Radstac said.

"Please."

"But why should I? Can you answer me that?"

"Because—because . . ." Desperate search for words to express that great need.

"No, none of that. Not why you want it. I know why. Tell me why I should give you what you want."

He was two tenwinters old, thereabouts. He was slim, slightly spindly, a callow face, anxious eyes. He licked his lips repeatedly as his mind worked.

"What can I give you?" he finally asked, fairly panting it.

Radstac nodded.

He gushed with increasing promises of money he didn't actually have on his person at the moment. She gave him free rein, letting him wear himself out. His desperation mounted as each of his offers was met with silence. She still held the bitten-off piece of leaf in view. The soldier's eyes were fastened to it. He gave a last rasping sigh of frustration, then asked, "What do you *want*, then?"

"Transport."

"What?"

She again made to tuck the leaf away.

"No! Right. Right. Transport. What and where?"

"Myself. To someplace other than here."

"That can't be done," he breathed.

This time she reached into her pouch beneath her

leather armor, extracted a full intact leaf. Turned it in the weak light.

"This is quality you dream about," she said. "This isn't weak marketplace rubbish. This is the real stuff. A full leaf of it? Of real quality? Imagine how long this would last you."

He was doing the arithmetic as she watched, nervous eyes fixed intently. "But—it isn't—I can't . . ." Heartbroken voice, forlorn gaze.

Radstac brought out a second leaf.

Something was strangling inside him. "We . . . we transport out the wounded. After an engagement we're very busy. But right now, when it's quiet, we just receive supplies. There's very little going out."

"Someone will be traveling with me," she said as she took out a third leaf.

His gnawing aching need was almost palpable. But it took a fourth leaf to finalize the arrangements for her and Deo's escape.

IT WAS A matter of clever official lies. But in the end, it was only a matter of that one Felk soldier's vulgar want.

The wizards paid them no mind, other than to perfunctorily instruct the two of them on the proper procedure while moving between the portals. Walk a straight line toward the far portal exit point. Do not deviate. Do not linger. Keep eyes focused ahead and ignore the disorienting surroundings.

Radstac couldn't remember if she'd visited the Isthmus city before. It was in the northern reaches, but it was entirely possible that at some stage in her mercenary past she had either fought for or against the city-state.

It wouldn't have been her first choice of destination.

And it certainly wasn't Deo's. This magic-abetted excursion would put them deep inside Felk-held territory, far behind the southward advancing lines. But they didn't have the luxury of choosing where they went. Staying here meant risking, at every moment, being discovered as impostors. Or, much worse, as the ones responsible for Weisel's attempted assassination. Better then to *go*. Go anywhere.

Deo gave her a furtive assuring nod, as they stood side by side, waiting for the magicians to coordinate their efforts with their distant counterparts. Deo was affecting confidence and ease, for her benefit and probably for his own, a means of bolstering himself up for the unknown perils ahead, for whatever they would find when they reached the occupied city of Callah.

The watch was late. Night was heavy over the camp, overcast obstructing the stars. It was cool enough to bring out gooseflesh on Radstac's arms.

"Are you ready?" Deo asked her unnecessarily, his voice a whisper.

"I am." She frowned. Then understood. Deo knew what this jaunt was costing her. She had paid in the only currency possible. Deo was accustomed to wealth, to access to vast resources. But coin wouldn't have brought them this passage. Only an addict's cravings could have persuaded a member of this Felk army to arrange for an illegal transport, all while a search was still in progress for whoever had tried to murder this same army's general.

Still, it was quite a fee she was paying. Those four full *mansìd* leaves were her last. All she had now was that last pitiful little piece . . . and the effects from what she'd chewed earlier. The fantastic clarity of that was still with her, but it was lessening incrementally, wearing off.

She would be facing quite a challenge in the days ahead if she didn't manage to find more leaves in Callah, a Felk-controlled city.

Deo gave her another nod. There was warmth in his blue eyes, understanding, sympathy. Radstac had stood by him, her employer, when he'd gone off on this mad endeavor. Though she wasn't one to make such assumptions, she felt sure he would stay with her through whatever hardships were still to come.

The Far Speak mage had completed the necessary communications. The Far Movement mage, matching the efforts of his complement in Callah, now opened the portal. It was a wavering breach, a hole torn through the air, through the substance of what Radstac had always understood to be reality. She was from the Southern Continent, a far more civilized place than this Isthmus, where magic wasn't regarded with the same cultural fears. Even so, it was an act of unsteady faith to step inside that hole, into a world of milky uneasiness and chaotic perceptions.

PRAULTH

(1)

THERE CAME A winking impression of speed and danger, a quick whisk of wind across her nose. Then a hard *chunk* sounded from the tree trunk on her left, just off the road, and a single leaf, brittle but still a spectral green in the autumn climate, detached itself from an overhanging limb and twirled to the ground.

Praulth, her reaction delayed and exaggerated and unproductive, seized her horse's reins violently and yanked with all her muscle. This succeeded only in causing the animal to make a frightened noise and rear, which consequently dumped Praulth off the saddle and onto the road.

Around her was a suddenly terrifying confusion of hooves. These were Xink and Merse's horses. Both men were still in their saddles. Praulth put her hand to her nose, quite certain she'd been struck there, by whatever that thing had been, whatever projectile . . .

She looked to the left and saw the arrow embedded in

the tree. Her hand came away from her nose unbloodied. The feathers on that arrow must have brushed her. It had been *that* close.

Xink was hastily swinging down from his mount. "Praulth, are you hurt? Are you—are . . ." His normally handsome face was a rictus of concern as he knelt over her.

She nearly shoved him away as he helped her sit upright. She gathered what breath she'd had knocked out of her by the fall.

"Tend the horses, you two!" Merse called angrily, reaching over to grab up the loose reins of Praulth's mount. Xink's horse was shuffling about skittishly.

Now Praulth did give Xink a shove. "Get the beast before he tramples me to death." She was more confident on horseback now than when they'd left the University at Febretree, bound for Petgrad, but she was never going to be an accomplished rider. Merse had set the punishing pace. It was urgent they get where they were going.

As Xink wrangled his horse to a standstill, Praulth realized for the first time the true peril of this situation. That arrow! It had nearly taken her nose off, yes. But who had fired it? Was their party being . . . being *waylaid*?

She scrambled to her feet, heart pounding. Merse was still atop his horse. He now had a knife in hand. He would surely laugh at her for her slow reflexes—if they had occasion later to reflect back on this incident. Merse was the Petgradite messenger who had fetched her from the University.

This stretch of road was abutted on either side by dense foliage. But the arrow was sticking in that tree on this side; so it had to have come from *that* side of the roadway. Praulth peered into the woods. The day was early—Merse had barely permitted a watch of sleep—and there was a maze of shadows amongst those trees.

"Do you see anything?" she asked.

"By the madness of the gods," Merse hissed, *"quiet."* He too was studying the woodland, eyes narrow in his aging leathery face.

Praulth took her horse's reins from him but didn't climb back onto the saddle. She patted the creature's sides, and it quieted. She listened, intensely aware now of every sound that emerged from the surrounding trees.

Perhaps later she would laugh, too. Her expertise was military history, the study of the strategies of the grandest wars, but that did not include knowledge of something so base and coarse as *banditry.*

"Are we in danger?" Xink asked. This time Praulth hissed for silence.

She heard movement. Her heart beat even harder. There were deliberate footsteps approaching, leaves crunching. She peered deeper into the thicket.

She saw movement. A shape appeared beneath the interlocking branches, amidst the complex shadows.

"Come, then!" Merse cried out. "You won't have an easy time of it." He slashed the knife through the air.

The figure paused. At the same instant another arrow sprang from the woods, faster than the eye could completely follow. This one whipped past Merse's cheek and struck the same tree as before, a mere handsbreadth above the first arrow.

"Godsdamnit, Frog! Stop showing off!"

A female voice. She emerged into view, walking as steadily as before. She was short and extremely muscular.

"Keep the blade in hand or put it away," she said. "Makes no difference. Obviously you won't get to use it." She had halted just beyond the trees, at the roadside.

Praulth gazed at her. She looked . . . rugged. Someone who spent her time out of doors, on the move.

"You sound confident of that," Merse said, voice stony, betraying no fear. Praulth wasn't sure she would even be able to form words at the moment. But she made certain her face didn't reflect that fear. She was a personage of importance, and her dignity mattered, even now.

"I've got cause to be," the bandit said. "My archer could put shafts in both your eyes before you got off your saddle." She held up a hand, shook her head. Her tone softened. "But—but that's how we *used* to do things. The truth is, we're no longer in that business. We only want one thing."

Praulth held her horse's reins in a fist. She held herself still, very still. She didn't glance behind her, at Xink, didn't seek comfort there. What did their party have that these bandits could want? What was of value?

The answer was manifest. They must want *her.* Someone somehow had set this band after her, to capture her, to—

"This isn't our territory," the bandit woman said. "We're looking for the city of Petgrad. Where is it?"

Atop his horse Merse cocked his head, as if wondering if this were a joke. Finally his mouth twisted, just slightly, and he said, "Petgrad's along this road."

The bandit shook her head again. "We don't take roads. It's a bad habit. Just point it from here."

Merse appeared to orient himself, looking up at the early sun, nodding, muttering a few barely audible words. At last he lifted the knife and pointed. It was off at an angle from the road.

"Our thanks," the bandit was saying, already turning away, disappearing back into the trees.

Eventually, when all had been silent for several moments, Merse returned the knife to his coat and looked down at Praulth.

"Back on your horses, you two. That's going to count as our morning rest stop."

Praulth struggled and scrabbled back up into the saddle, silently glad she hadn't said anything aloud.

When they were moving once more, she glanced back over her shoulder and saw someone tall emerge from the woods to retrieve the arrows from the tree.

SHE UNDERSTOOD, HALFWAY up, the true and implicit meaning of this summoning. Cultat wanted to see her, yes. That was understandable. But their meeting was to take place on his ground. It was the fact that the premier's "ground" was so very high in the sky that gave the occasion its unspoken significance.

Praulth, on arriving in the huge bustling city of Petgrad, had been awestruck by many things. The scope of the place was amazing, the number of inhabitants, the very *noise* of it all. Really, it was a frontal assault on her rural sensibilities. But dwarfing all else, literally and mentally, were Petgrad's mighty towers.

They were improbable, fanciful, magnificent, dominating. They reared into the sky higher than anything Praulth had ever seen in her life. They were level atop level atop level of stone construction materials that somehow didn't fall over when the wind blew. They were spires as a child might imagine them to be, impossibly grand; but these had been made real. In the city's heart they rose like trees in an ancient woods, where the eldest timbers rose regally above the younger.

Praulth now squelched her earlier fancy with much

darker thoughts. It even annoyed her that she had resorted to similes about trees, knowing that it no doubt related back to her girlhood spent in the timber town of Dral Blidst. Her family had thrived in that particular industry, the same family that had drubbed her with their scorn and ignorance until she had fled to the University at Febretree, there to embrace her true calling of a life in academics.

"Can I lend you a hand?" Xink asked as she sagged against the wall of the apparently endless stairwell in which they had been trapped for what felt like days.

"And what do you intend?" she returned tartly. "Throw me over a shoulder and carry me the rest of the way up?"

Something flickered across Xink's face. "Is that what you want?" He might have asked it sharply, sarcastically, but he didn't. Instead, it was meek, submissive. He didn't have the will to defy her. Or perhaps his feelings for her were so genuine that he couldn't bring himself to speak a harsh word to her.

At the moment, either way, Praulth didn't care.

This climb was murderous, and it was supposed to be so. That was the great revelation she was having, halfway up this monstrous tower, this insane architectural feat, which was a monument better observed than experienced, she judged.

But as drained as she now was, as heavy as her legs felt, she was also determined. Cultat wanted to see her. That was fine. She was ready to prove herself at any time.

Merse, when he'd arrived at Febretree, had told her she was needed in Petgrad. Her talents at predicting the movements of the Felk invaders, as led by the commander they called Weisel, were crucial to the alliance that Cultat meant to build. Praulth understood the history of warfare as perhaps no one else alive did . . . no one, now that her mentor

Master Honnis was dead. She comprehended tactics; she grasped battle strategies that belonged to conflicts hundredwinters old. She had identified the swift and sure hand of Dardas the Conqueror in the movements ordered by General Weisel. She had thought him a brilliant imitator, one shrewd enough to have studied and absorbed the skills of the Northland's most successful war commander.

But Honnis had corrected her assumptions. Imitator? No. Weisel *was* Dardas. It was almost impossible to accept. Equally impossible was the explanation for it, a thing Honnis had called resurrection magic. Dardas had been reborn somehow within the body of a Felk noble named Weisel.

Praulth believed it, though. She believed all of it. Master Honnis had been an irascible creature of vast knowledge. He had also been possessed of magical abilities that she had known nothing of until the University's war studies head was lying on his very deathbed.

Cultat had called her to Petgrad, and she had come, inviting Xink along with her. Now that she was here and settled into her new quarters, Cultat was summoning her to his royal presence. Again she was acquiescing. The premier had charged her with devising a battle scheme to resist the seemingly implacable Felk advance. She had proposed a reenactment of an ancient engagement, the Battle of Torran Flats, one of Dardas's many celebrated victories some two hundred and fifty years ago. Her version of it, of course, had Dardas/Weisel falling into a cunningly constructed trap. That plan could still work.

She was sagging against the wall again. Her legs were like iron, inhumanly heavy. She was spent. This wasn't possible, this stupid climb to the absurd top of this ridiculous tower. It was simply beyond her endurance to keep going like this, to ascend to heights that humans patently were not meant to reach. Was the air up here . . . scarcer? It certainly felt like it. Her lungs were laboring painfully. Her heart was working faster than normal. She felt as if both her knees were about to give way. She closed her eyes, rested her head against the cool stone wall. Cultat was just going to have to see her some other time . . .

"Beauty?"

A line creased between her closed eyes as she felt a new sharp surge of annoyance. "Beauty" had been Xink's affectionate name for her early on in their relationship, before things had turned so disastrous, before she'd learned that the handsome sixth phase University Attaché was just Honnis's tool. The war studies head had put Xink deliberately on to her, and like a blithe virginal fool she had fallen hopelessly in love with him. It had all been devised to keep her singularly focused on analyzing the Felk advancements. It had worked. She had neglected her normal studies at Febretree, and Xink had filled her innocent heart with love and her nights with untold sexual ecstacy.

Oddly enough, despite seeing her lover in this new, much less flattering light, she did still feel love for him. And he professed to have legitimately fallen in love with her.

"Don't call me that," she muttered.

"Praulth," Xink said, with some insistence, "we're here."

She opened her eyes. The two of them had been searched for weapons by a contingent of guards at the foot of this tower, then passed on to the stairwell, and told simply to climb until there was nowhere else to go. No guards had accompanied them on their ascent into these implausible upper reaches.

Without her noticing, the endless stairs had finally played out. They had reached a broad landing, the floor a dark red stone polished to a high gleam. Another contingent of guards was here, their uniforms lustrous, their bearing formal. Praulth pushed herself off the wall with some effort as one approached.

"You may come this way," he said.

"Oh, *may* we?" she grumbled. Sarcasm was still new to her, but she found herself employing it more and more often. Before, she had been timid in all things that didn't relate directly to her studies. Now she was becoming assertive, testing out the trappings of aggressive behavior, as a young girl would try on her first adult frock.

They entered a chamber, and whatever scornful retort Praulth might have made when their escort told them to wait died on her tongue. The room was barely furnished, though it had an elegance lent it by a few tastefully placed fixtures. What drew Praulth's total attention, however, was the wall composed entirely of glass, which looked out over the immense vista of the city.

It wasn't that Petgrad was magnificently large and sophisticated. It was that; but after two days here she was already acclimating. What pulled her toward the glass was the fantastic height of this vantage. She had understood, intellectually, that climbing to the top of this tower, all the way up to where it was capped by a metal cupola, would take her far into the heavens, virtually up among the clouds. But to *see* it, to look out from this summit, it was . . . it was . . .

She was still walking toward the glass, the view broadening and deepening with every step. It was approaching sunset, and lights were appearing among the array of buildings below. It all looked so small! Up here she felt enormous, aloof. It was intoxicating.

Too much so. Before she had reached the glass wall, hearing Xink trying to get her attention again and ignoring him, Praulth's limp legs finally did give out. As she dropped toward the floor, it felt as though she were falling into the incredible panorama before her, falling from this vast height, falling toward the streets of Petgrad, waiting far far below.

A frightened cry was just tearing from her throat as a strong hand caught her, stopped her, drew her gently back onto her wobbly feet, and held her there until she could stand without aid.

"There, Thinker Praulth. You're not the first to swoon at the sight."

She blinked rapidly. The vertigo was passing. How strange. The view had seemed to physically *pull* her.

"I'm all right, Premier," she said. This wasn't how she'd wanted to present herself before Petgrad's ruler. It was the second time she was meeting the formidable royal personage, the first having taken place at a secret gathering at the University, the same night she'd learned such terrible secrets about Honnis and Xink.

"Once you get used to it, though, it's really quite soothing," Cultat said. He let go of her, and she tottered a few steps back.

Petgrad's premier was as fearsome as she remembered, hair a thick red and gold, a greying beard of the same colors dressing a craggy face, where harsh blue eyes burned. He was tall, broad of shoulder, perhaps fifty years old or more.

Praulth had been made to climb the arduous outrageous height of this tower to see him, and what did she do when she was finally here? She fell to her knees. Obviously the climb had symbolic value. It made one a supplicant before one ever arrived. It drained one of physical energy. On every slogging riser of this upward journey Praulth had promised herself she wouldn't let the trick work. She was no longer the unassertive University student. She, by dint of her value as an expert war strategist, was someone to be reckoned with. Cultat would have to learn that.

"It's a pleasure to see you again. Your quarters, they're comfortable, I hope?"

"I . . . yes, Premier."

"Good. You have my heartfelt appreciation for agreeing to come to Petgrad on such short notice."

"It's, uh, my honor."

A smile touched his worn, weary but ferociously alive features. This was no doddering elder. This was a vital leader of a great state, the largest the southern half of the Isthmus had to boast.

And with those few rumbling words and a supporting hand he had disarmed her completely, robbing her of the necessary heat of her self-righteousness.

"I've gathered a conference," Cultat said. "It's been very loud, very contentious, and so far has accomplished very little beyond the fact that we've all come together in a single room, without anyone seizing anyone else's throat. These are representatives and consuls from the states and lands unconquered as yet by the Felk. My hope . . . our only hope . . . is to turn this alliance from an admirable notion into a functional reality. We are ready now, Praulth, for you."

He was gesturing toward a set of doors. The wood, Praulth noted, was blood-oak. She was hesitant.

"Your messenger," she said. "The one who came to Febretree. Merse. He said your neighboring states were all agreeing to the alliance, ready to pool resources and manpower against the Felk."

"See the ease with which the words are said? Yes. It's a sensible plan. It's the *only* chance the free lands have against the Felk. But details kill sensible plans. Niggling and old grudges cloud otherwise rational minds. We states, we cities and townships and peoples, we've had our strifes in the past. Waged little wars against each other's borders. Spoken unforgivable insults. All that must be set aside, but it takes great effort, even in the face of so overwhelming a threat as the butchering Felk and their diabolical wizards. Since your arrival you've received all the current field intelligence regarding the Felk?"

"Of course, Premier."

"That's fine. Your aide can wait here. Come in now, won't you, and show these squabblers the excellence of your abilities."

HER HESITANCY HAD been a simple case of stage fright. Her academic life hadn't prepared her to face a roomful of people who were hanging on and judging her every word. Her years at the University had been ones of private efforts and solitary studies, of judgments rendered by individual instructors. One could pass an entire lune at Febretree, if one tried, without having direct spoken contact with anyone.

But the maps spread over the large table were so irresistible, so familiar. She had seen them before, renderings delivered to her by Master Honnis. These were a comprehensive history of the Felk war, so far. And *history* was most certainly what this was. However this war was resolved, it would alter the future of the Isthmus for hundredwinters and more.

She didn't now entertain these grand thoughts. Her mind was occupied with the meat of it all, with the movements and maneuvers of the Felk army, with the tactics that belonged only to Dardas the Butcher and no one else.

She orally reenacted the war for the assembled notables and envoys. The early Felk conquests of Callah and Windal. The brutal slaughter of U'delph, which was preceded by the Felk's first wholesale use of Far Movement magic in the field. Then the surrender of Sook, followed by the army's southward move toward the city-state of Trael.

Praulth illuminated it all, the military designs, the logic of warfare, the peculiar marks of Dardas's brilliant strategies. She answered questions when they were put to her. She didn't hesitate now. She felt no misgivings, no self-doubts. She was equal to this task. Xink was waiting outside, but she didn't need him for this.

Finally someone, a figure in much finery who, if Praulth recalled correctly, was from Ompellus Prime, said, "Impressive. Now, will you deign to tell us why the Felk have halted cold only a day or two from Trael? It seems to me they might be considering a new course, toward, say, the city of Grat. Or, worse, my own state."

"You would rather the Felk monsters crushed *us*? What a miserable, selfish creature—"

"Don't pretend to parts you can't play. By the sanity of the gods, how often have you kindhearted ones of Grat wished for our downfall? How often have you poisoned our crops? How—"

"As a response to the abduction of our beloved Jade Priestess!"

"She *wanted* to leave, fool! She had found love with our prince."

"If it's crop poisoning, I'd like it explained how the river that irrigates our fields turns black twice a lune with filth dumped in it by you people upriver in Hassilc."

"It's not your river when it flows through our lands."

"Fiend!"

"Imbecile!"

By now the exchange had five or six participants. It was quite a vehement display. Praulth felt she understood now the genuine reason for holding this conference here atop this tower. It was so no one could easily storm out of the room, not unless he or she meant to make that entire long and steep descent.

Cultat rose from his seat, an expression of put-upon disgust on his face. He drew a short—and presumably decorative—sword from his belt and banged its bejeweled pommel three times on the tabletop, hard enough to leave an indentation.

"This is precisely what I mean," he said, addressing no one in particular in his robust voice. "Something intelligent is said, and the price we pay are ten useless outbursts. *Silence* . . . please. Now, Praulth, our esteemed delegate from Ompellus Prime raises a good point. Our intelligence informs us that the Felk remain encamped a short distance from Trael. They've been stalled thus several days now. Why would they do this?"

"Yes, girl, why?"

"Oh, do tell us."

These last were sarcastic mutterings from among the nearly twenty members assembled. Praulth found she didn't like their offhand scorn. They didn't appreciate her. Her analytical abilities were a marvel. No one else could have predicted the Felk movements so far in this war so accurately. Honnis himself had said so.

The field intelligence to which Cultat referred was thanks to a secret elite unit of Petgradite wizards, a small force literally bred for their abilities to use the Far Speak magic. Honnis had relayed their war news to her at the University. Merse himself belonged to the family of gifted nobles.

This inner chamber appeared to be a formal dining hall converted for the occasion into this conference site. Lushly woven tapestries adorned the walls. Each one appeared to display multiple pictures or abstract motifs among its fabulously intricate threads, depending on at what distance one stood to view it.

Praulth hadn't taken a seat at the table. She'd stood, ignoring her tired legs, indicating this map and that, lecturing this body on the war's history, revealing its secrets. Now she straightened, folded her hands, and asked coolly, "Why is there no representative from Trael here?"

Cultat's blue eyes flickered away, came back to her. "That diplomatic mission failed," he said bluntly.

Praulth knew that meant a member of the premier's family had been lost. Cultat had used his own kin to deliver the initial proposals for an alliance.

Her eyes swept the assembly. Finally she said, "I don't know why the Felk have halted their advance."

Someone laughed, a short unkind burst, and the chamber erupted in protest. What good was this girl, then? What sort of military expert was Cultat trying to foist on them? Praulth stood and weathered it stoically, while anger bloomed hotter inside her. She would explain in detail to these fools her scheme to use the Battle of Torran Flats against the Felk general.

While this was happening an attendant entered, went quietly to Cultat's side, and spoke urgent words to the premier. Praulth, ignoring the assembly's ignorant barbs— how *much* they sounded like her family just now—for the moment, watched surprise spread across Cultat's craggy face. The attendant presented a sheet of paper.

Once more Cultat brought the hubbub to an end by banging his pommel on the table.

"I may have an answer as to why we've no delegate from Trael here at this table," Cultat said. "A small party has just arrived in the city bearing *this*." He held aloft the paper, a densely printed document of some sort. "It's a government promissory note, for an extraordinary amount of money, which I have no intention of honoring during this crisis, and it is signed by my nephew. Why is this of interest? Because the little band that presented this—bandits, I believe—tell a tale of my nephew abandoning his mission to Trael in order to pursue a goal of his own choosing. He meant to infiltrate the Felk horde and assassinate its leader. Now, if he succeeded in this grand ambition, might that not explain why the Felk army has remained immobile these past several days?"

Cultat smiled, proud, even smug. Once again the room came shrilly alive with overlapping voices.

Praulth's first thoughts were to wonder if those were the same bandits they had met on the road, those who had seemed intent on taking the slower clandestine woodland trails to Petgrad. But these thoughts were deliberate and momentary distractions.

She felt a cold and heavy sinking in her chest. It took her a moment to identify the feeling as disappointment. Dardas . . . assassinated? It couldn't be. It was too haphazard, too *unworthy* of the great Northland war commander. That some minor relative of the premier had snuck into that camp and murdered the host body of Weisel, killing the brilliant military mind that lived within . . . it was almost offensive. She couldn't absorb it.

After all, *she* wanted to be the one who defeated Dardas.

AQUINT

(1)

"WHAT DO YOU mean, they're gone?"

Cat regarded him with a withering, disapproving stare. "I'd think that's a simple enough sentence to have penetrated your hangover."

Aquint made an effort not to groan out loud as he pushed up onto his elbows. This bed was big and soft, and he remembered having at least one soft companion in it last night. Now, she, or they, were gone, and there was just his young confederate here in the room.

He'd had a lot of wine last night. It was easy to have a lot of wine when you didn't have any worries about being able to pay your tab. He was enjoying this luxurious apartment and the generous stipend he was collecting as an agent of the Felk Internal Security Corps. The fact that, as a native of this conquered city of Callah, he still regarded the Felk as basically evil wasn't interfering noticeably with his performance in their service.

Aquint ran a hand over his bleary face.

"The rebels?" he asked, focusing. "You're talking about the group that's holed up in my old warehouse?"

Cat continued to stare with those judgmental eyes. The boy had never approved of any of Aquint's recreational habits.

"*Was* holed up there."

"When . . . when did they go?" Aquint sat up straighter, his head whirling, but determined not to let it show.

"Sometime between the last time I checked up on them and just half a watch ago."

"You're sure?" Aquint asked.

Cat looked offended by the question, and rightly so, Aquint thought. The boy moved like a shadow and was as good a spy as any Aquint had ever known.

Aquint reached for his scattered clothes. As he did he felt his gorge suddenly lurching dangerously. Cat wordlessly handed him a big cup full of cool water. Aquint drank it down, gratefully, feeling it restore him somewhat.

His mind was slowly starting to churn. If what the lad said was right, and the rebels had vacated their lair, then it did indeed mean trouble. As an Internal Security agent he was charged with rooting out traitors and revolutionaries here in Callah. He had already had some real success in that duty. He had broken a clever counterfeiting scheme that had flooded the local economy with worthless duplicates of the Felk-issued scrip.

He had also, with Cat's inestimable help, tracked a bona fide group of rebels to the same warehouse where he had once run a freight hauling business, before this war. He had also done some smuggling and black marketeering on the side, but that was neither here nor there.

Aquint had planned to feed those rebels one by one to

his superior, Lord Abraxis, head of the Corps. Job security was important, especially since if Aquint was hunting rebels in Callah, he got to stay in Callah and enjoy all the benefits of his position.

Of course, as far as rebels went, this was a motley bunch, hardly worth anybody's effort to arrest. Aquint, however, preferred that nobody knew that but he and Cat. He had even picked out their first trophy catch, the man who had been behind that counterfeiting operation, the Minstrel. That one, at least, had committed a real crime. Besides the forgery business, he'd killed a Felk soldier, which had brought the wrath of the garrison down on all the people of occupied Callah.

Aquint dressed, drank more water, and gathered himself together. Cat waited patiently. Aquint combed his fingers through his hair as he thought.

"I waited too long," he finally said, fatalistically.

"You're just realizing that?"

"Forgive me, lad, my mind's still somewhat adrift."

"On a lake of wine," Cat scowled.

"I waited too long to start turning them over to Colonel Jesile's troops," Aquint said, repeating himself with great self-recrimination.

"This isn't going to help us," Cat said.

Jesile was the Felk governor of the city-state. As far as occupiers went, he was a sane and sensible man, not a sadist, not a barbarian.

"Do you have any idea where the rebels went?" Aquint asked the boy desperately.

"Don't you think I might have mentioned it by now if I did?"

Aquint still wasn't sure he wasn't going to vomit. Having that group hiding in his own abandoned warehouse had been like holding a pair of Headsmen cards when one was playing Dashes. It was a great secret advantage.

He had been too smug about it all, he realized. He thought he'd had the game all sewn up.

He shook his head several times, determined to clear it. Cat was right. This wallowing wasn't going to help anything.

"All right. This is bad but not catastrophic. I want those rebels found, and I want to do it without any help from the Felk garrison. I still want us to come out of this looking better than them, for when I report to Abraxis. You got a look at their faces, the night you spied on the rebels, right?"

The boy shrugged. "Sure. But this is a big city. Finding a handful of individuals—"

"Now, don't get pessimistic on me, Cat. We've got other things in our favor. Remember those circles with the slashes through them? The ones that appeared all over the city during the Lacfoddalmendowl festival? I think we can finally use that to our own advantage."

EVERYONE OF FIGHTING age had been absorbed into the Felk army when that force had overrun Callah, several lunes ago now. Aquint wore his arm in a sling to maintain the pretense that he had been wounded, and thus was currently on soft duty here in Callah. So far, the disguise was working.

Callah was a beautiful city, to Aquint's eyes anyway. Even occupied as it was by these Felk bleeders, it gladdened his heart to be home. He hated this war. It was a big messy waste. Sure, it was affording him opportunities to skim and scam monies out of the Felk coffers, but he had been doing just fine before, with his legitimate and illegitimate businesses.

How many had died on battlefields since this thing began? It was a lot, to say nothing of the absolute atrocity that had been committed at the city-state of U'delph, when the Felk had butchered and burned until the place was nothing more than a corpse-filled ruin. Aquint had been a part of that terrible carnage, and it had sickened him. It sickened him still to think about it.

The sun was peeking out from the clouds, bright enough to make Aquint wince every time he fell under its direct rays. That really had been an awful lot of wine, but he was collecting good wages these days, on top of the walking around scrip Governor Jesile's office had issued him. He couldn't help but spend a little on the pleasures of life.

That scrip had been rendered effectively worthless by the flood of phony notes that had apparently gotten into circulation. Aquint had heard that Jesile meant to combat this by imposing severe taxes in an effort to rebalance the local economy. The thinking was that it was more efficient than a complete recall of the paper money.

Good luck with that, Aquint thought. Further oppressing these conquered people with heavy taxes wasn't going to help pacify them. Quite the opposite, it might create more rebellious attitudes.

But that debacle with the Felk scrip wasn't Aquint's problem, not directly, at least.

He walked the streets, enjoying the cooling autumn breeze. He could almost imagine, at moments like this, that the war had never happened, that the Felk and their soldiers and their magicians had never poured south out of the Isthmus's northernmost state.

Someday, this war was going to have to end. But what if the Felk won it? And considering how powerful they were, the betting man's odds were with them. That would mean things would be like this forever, Callah occupied by a foreign force. Callah *owned* by the Felk.

Aquint shook his head, snapping himself out of the gloomy reverie. He could brood the next time he had a belly full of liquor. Right now, he had work to do.

He entered a café and ordered a light breakfast, bland foods he thought his stomach could handle. It was a busy eatery, and he was inevitably recognized and greeted. He still had quite a number of acquaintances here in Callah, among those too old or too infirm to have been drafted.

"Aquint, if I didn't know better I'd say you were playing up that wounded arm of yours just a bit," said a large elderly man named Gownick, whom Aquint had invited to join him at his table.

"You can imagine how anxious I am to return to the fighting," Aquint said, ruefully. He ate his eggs and biscuits slowly, careful not to upset his stomach.

"What's it like working for the Felk?" Gownick asked. He was drinking a large cup of tea. It was a blunt question, with confrontational undertones.

Aquint set down his fork. Gownick had been in the hauling business, too, before the Felk arrived and conscripted his wagons and horses.

"It's like being apprenticed to a master you despise," Aquint said. "You wish him dead every day, but you're stuck with him until your term of service is up."

Gownick nodded, grimly. "That's how I figured. If you'd been smart enough to have been a tenwinter or two older you never would have gotten into this mess."

"Next time I'll know." Aquint smiled.

They chatted amiably after that, while Aquint finished his meal. He felt better for having the food in him, soaking up last night's dregs.

"Gownick," he said suddenly, in a low voice, "can I trust you?"

The older man blinked. "We were rivals in the old days, Aquint, not enemies. We're not enemies now."

"I'll take that to mean you won't go blabbing what I tell you."

"You may take it as such," Gownick said, but there was eagerness in the old businessman's eyes.

Aquint looked around the café. Then he huddled closer to the older man, opened his jacket, and removed a swatch of coarse cloth.

"See?"

"What am I looking at, Aquint?" Gownick frowned.

"This was nailed to the door of the garrison barracks this morning."

"So?"

"So? Look at it, man. That pattern. It doesn't look familiar to you?" Aquint asked in an urgent whisper.

"It looks like a stain on the cloth," Gownick said, confused.

"It's not, for gods' sake! The circle, with the line through it. Don't tell me you don't recognize it."

"Should I?" Gownick asked.

"It doesn't mean anything to you?" Aquint feigned a dumbfounded expression.

The large elder was starting to look a little flustered. No one liked being left out of things. It was a childish impulse people never outgrew completely.

Aquint made to put the piece of cloth back into his jacket.

"Wait," Gownick said. "You say you found that on the Felk barracks door?"

"I had to report there early this morning. I saw it before

anyone else did. I removed it, and didn't tell anybody about it."

"Why not?"

Again Aquint gave him an astonished look. "Because if I did then the whole garrison would know that the rebels are bold enough to leave their mark right on their very door. It would send soldiers into the streets, into people's homes. We don't need another shakeup like that last one."

He was referring of course to the garrison's violent response to the murder of one of their own by that Minstrel. But by telling Gownick this, he was siding himself with the Callahans, not the Felk.

"No," Gownick said, gravely, "we certainly don't need that." He frowned again. "Let me have another look at that."

Aquint showed him the mark on the cloth again. He himself had drawn it, naturally, using a stick of charcoal. This same slashed circle, which had been branded on numerous walls and doors throughout Callah, was, so Aquint had told Jesile, the emblem of the rebel underground.

Actually, he hadn't known if that was true or not. But at the time it was an expedient ploy, one that had helped firm up his position as an Internal Security agent fighting a real rebel network here in this city.

"I think I've seen this . . ." Gownick finally said.

It was quite possible he had. Whoever had been responsible for those strange brands had done a thorough job of spreading them throughout Callah. Jesile's troops had since eradicated the marks, removing doors and defacing walls where necessary.

"Well, I'm keeping it," Aquint said, finally stuffing it back into a pocket. "Hopefully, one day soon I'll make contact with someone in that rebel underground. When I do I'll use that symbol on that cloth as a kind of credential, to show I know who they are."

Gownick shook his head. "Why do you want to contact them?"

Aquint blinked at his former business rival. "To join them, of course."

With that he got up from the table, and left the café.

BY THE TIME he rendezvoused with Cat later in the day, Aquint was feeling much better. His mood had improved as well.

"You look pleased with yourself," the boy said, as they ducked beneath the flamboyant eaves of a building.

"And why not?"

"It went as you planned?"

"It did." Aquint nodded. "How about you?"

Cat shrugged. "Tracking is time-consuming work. There's lots of places that group could've gone, if they didn't just scatter individually."

Aquint was feeling magnanimous. "There there, lad. We'll find those motley rebels, one way or the other."

The boy shrugged again.

They stood there a moment, watching the foot traffic pass. Occupied or not, life still went on in Callah for its native inhabitants.

Aquint was indeed pleased. He had confided in three others besides Gownick, all just as big-mouthed. Word would get around about both the rebels nailing their mark on the barracks door, and about Aquint wanting to contact the underground. The first gambit would lend even more credence to a potential rebel uprising, which would secure

Aquint's position even further, so long as he eventually turned the culprits over to Abraxis.

The second ploy just might put him in contact with the rebels. It depended on how seriously they took themselves. They had started as a sort of semifictional group, which Aquint himself had encouraged the Felk to believe in. Now, they might just become real, and might start accepting recruits.

If that happened, then they could be infiltrated.

Aquint was smiling, but his smile faded after a moment, as he considered the bigger picture. Suppose these ragtag rebels did rise up against the Felk. Suppose, somehow, they defeated Jesile's troops here in Callah. Did Aquint really want to be responsible for undoing a rebellion like that?

"What's wrong?" Cat asked, as always sensitive to Aquint's mood.

"Nothing." Aquint waved dismissively. "Tell me, do you think it's too early for a drink?"

DARDAS
(1)

THE MILK-WHITE UNREALITY played havoc with one's senses. It moved like a fog and offered no convenient points of reference. It left one without any sure sense of distance or depth. But the instructions of the Far Movement mage were clear. Walk straight ahead and don't linger.

Weisel acknowledged the wizard's warnings. They were in a chamber of the Palace. He waited patiently for the spell to be completed. It had to be coordinated with the mages at the far end, via Far Speak.

This portal was being opened between the city of Felk and the army in the field near Trael. Matokin had ordered Weisel to return to his troops, now that the matter of Raven's resurrection had been settled. That girl had sacrificed herself for him, and he had demanded that a host body be found for her, and her spirit returned to life. Matokin had complied.

I think, Lord Weisel, that you find this type of journeying just as unsettling as I do.

I don't recall saying I found it unsettling.

You needn't say it, of course. Thinking it will do.

Ah, but we can't spy freely on each other's thoughts. There are limitations.

It was a stunning reversal, and Dardas was still adjusting. Just a few days ago, he had been the one operating this body. He had been the dominating personality and will. Then, unexpectedly, Weisel had seized control. Now Dardas was the one pushed to the remote mental corners, unable to move these limbs, or work this mouth. He was, effectively, disembodied.

It was a sorry state of affairs. He hadn't been reborn after two and a half centuries just to ride around passively in this effete Felk nobleman's skull. No, he must have an active role again. He was a general. He was meant to lead an army.

Limitations? I suppose, Lord Weisel.

It's interesting you refer to me as Lord, since you demanded to be addressed as General when you had full use of my identity.

Do you fancy yourself a general? Do you really intend to lead the Felk army on your own?

I'm not on my own.

You still expect me to help you? Dardas was shocked.

That was what you were resurrected for. To instruct and assist me in the techniques of warfare.

It was almost beyond belief. Could this fop be so deluded? Those had been the terms that Weisel had originally agreed to when Matokin arranged for Dardas's resurrection. But it seemed evident that Matokin had expected all along that Dardas would swiftly assume control of the host body, which was what had happened.

Then again, Weisel *was* the one holding sway now. Maybe he was in fact in a position to dictate terms.

"The portal is ready, General Weisel," the Far Movement mage said.

"Very good."

Weisel stepped into the breach that opened before him.

See? That wizard isn't too proud to call me General.

You may have a point.

Dardas sensed surprise. It wasn't as easy to detect emotions as it was to hear deliberately directed thoughts.

I'm glad to hear you finally talking some sense.

I have always been a man who could adjust to new situations.

From what I know of history, that's always meant trouble for your enemies.

They were past the portal now. Weisel obeyed the instructions and put one foot in front of the other, aiming for the exit portal, which was just visible in the misty distance.

Tell me something.

Yes? Weisel asked.

If you are so eager for my advice and expertise, why did you thwart my strategy of opening those portals around the city of Trael?

Quite suddenly, Weisel stopped walking. He stood still, deliberately, hands on hips.

What are you doing? Dardas asked.

But Weisel was silent, directing no thoughts Dardas's way. This wasn't a Weisel that Dardas was familiar with. This was some different version, someone other than the weak-willed Felk lord that Dardas had once so easily overpowered. This Weisel seemed confident and decisive.

Maybe Weisel had been taking lessons from *him,* Dardas thought wryly. Then he considered the thought more seriously. It had some plausibility. It might be that Weisel, during that time when Dardas thought him completely suppressed, had instead been learning how Dardas conducted himself. Dardas was an assured, resolute leader. It was what Weisel aspired to be.

Why have you stopped? Dardas felt a twinge of unease now, on top of the general anxiety of traveling by way of this portal. He had been honest earlier when he'd said this type of travel unsettled him.

Wait. Listen. Watch. Weisel's thoughts were composed.

Dardas could only borrow Weisel's senses now, not direct them in any way. Through the Felk lord's eyes, he scanned the surrounding fog as it eddied and flowed according to no perceivable pattern.

With Weisel's ears, he listened. Suddenly, he heard something, or thought he did. It was as vague and ill-defined as everything else about this terrible place. As Dardas tried to sort the sound he became aware of a growing feeling of being watched. He tried to dismiss it as childish, but it wouldn't go away. In fact, it got worse. At the same time, the sound was getting louder . . . or getting nearer.

Actually, *sounds* was more like it. Dardas was nearly able to pick apart the individual parts of it. It was almost like they were voices!

It was an awful thought, one that chilled Dardas's disembodied being.

Let's get going, he urged.

Are you in such a hurry? Weisel asked archly.

Let's get to the exit, Weisel!

Amid the roiling mist, Dardas thought he perceived shapes now, just the vaguest silhouettes. The voices were definitely louder.

Whatever point you mean to prove, this isn't the way to do it.

Oh, I think it's a very effective means.

Enough. Please. We have to get moving.

Weisel at last relented, and moved with hurtling steps toward the far portal. Dardas felt certain that whatever was gathering in the fog would seize this body before Weisel could get to the exit. He was happy to find himself mistaken when they charged through the second breach, into a large tent where two mages waited.

The magicians were startled to find the general bursting through so suddenly.

"Are you all right, sir?" one wizard asked.

"Was there any difficulty in the transit, General?" asked the other.

Weisel drew a calming breath, smiled, and said, "Nothing to speak of. You both did your jobs just fine. Dismissed." He waved.

They exited the tent.

What was the meaning of that? Dardas demanded.

Meaning of what? Weisel mentally retorted.

That misguided display back there. People who put themselves deliberately and uselessly in jeopardy aren't heroes, you know.

Were you frightened? Because I was. What do you imagine those things were, moving so eerily in that white mist?

I don't know, Dardas admitted.

Neither do I. That's the point. They might be illusions. They might be creatures. They might be gods know what, considering how strange that place is. They might even be the restless spirits of the dead.

That gave Dardas pause. He had extracted information about the nature of portal magic from one of the mages in this very army. He had been compelled to do so because of Matokin's orders regarding secrecy about all things magical. The Felk leader meant to keep Dardas ignorant about such matters, probably so the general wouldn't become too powerful.

What Dardas had learned was extraordinary. It seemed that all magic in this world was derived from *another* world, the same alien plane of existence that the portals employed. This, Dardas was told by the Far Movement mage he'd questioned, was called the Wellspring. It was a sort of antireality, a metaphysical opposite. Where this world was life, that place was death.

Dardas had had to conduct his questioning at knife-point. Afterward, he'd also had to kill the mage. Such necessities didn't bother him.

But he hadn't known that Weisel was aware of the episode. At the time, the nobleman's consciousness had seemingly disappeared altogether.

Yes, Dardas finally said. *It might be that the dead would have emerged and overrun the city of Trael.*

What powers would they have possessed, do you suppose, once they were loose in this world? And what would they have done when they'd finished with Trael? No, General Dardas, it was too risky. In fact, it was insanely so.

Dardas didn't mind the barb. He was actually somewhat moved that Weisel was addressing him by his rank.

It was a calculated risk. We take those in wars.

Weisel said, *I don't see that it was calculated. Too many unknown factors. The potential for disaster was too great.*

So you decided to . . . intervene. Dardas still had no clear idea how Weisel had managed to completely overthrow control of this body.

I am the one who will be remembered as the leader of this army, regardless of what assistance I've had. I do not wish the name of Weisel to be synonymous with a cataclysm as huge and historic as the Great Upheavals that toppled the kingdoms of the Northern and Southern Continents.

I think I can understand that.

Do you? I hope so. Because we are very literally in this together. Now, if I can rely on your good counsel it's time to gather the senior staff and discuss strategies. When I was in Felk, seeing to Raven's resurrection, I tried to get Matokin to confer with me about the war's progress, but he wasn't interested.

He's a wily wizard, that one. You never know for certain what he's thinking.

I agree. So, General Dardas, will you help me win this war, and unite the Isthmus forever under the rule of the Felk?

There was of course only one answer.

I will . . . General Weisel.

HIS DETOUR TO the city of Felk had had the effect of stranding this vast army here in the field. Weisel had ordered that they remain at this position, while he had himself Far Moved to the north.

Now it was time to get this war moving again.

The senior staff was visibly relieved to see him. Weisel assembled them in the tent.

"We shall move on the city of Trael," he announced.

The officers grew excited and agitated. At present, the army was only two days or so from Trael, if they were to march there.

"Will you be ordering the use of the portals?" one of his officers asked.

The senior mages were present at this meeting as well. The regular officers eyed them askance. The tension and prejudice between the two groups was a problem through-out the ranks, one that needed correcting.

"Yes," Weisel said, "we will use the portals."

Some among the regular officers looked uneasy at the thought.

"But not to Far Move the entire army," Weisel smiled.

Dardas, observing the proceedings through Weisel's eyes, watched the reactions. Weisel had learned some-thing, evidently, about showmanship and panache.

"I want an elite unit assembled," Weisel said. "Special troops who can work stealthily and efficiently. The rest of our forces will surround Trael. Meanwhile, I want one of our scouting squads in the field, one outfitted with a Far Speak and Far Movement mage, to infiltrate the city. Mage Limmel, you'll pass on the order. When I give the signal we'll transport through the elite unit inside the city limits. They will locate the city's ruling council and take them hostage. We'll take this city without wasting a drop of blood on either side."

They gaped at him. Weisel was still smiling.

Well, whatever else, they're impressed, Weisel said silently.

As I promised, Dardas said.

The plan was actually a compromise between the two men. Dardas had meant for Trael to be another example, like U'delph had been when they had razed it to the ground and slaughtered nearly every inhabitant. Weisel, however, favored a less violent approach, though he had still wanted to demonstrate his tactical flair and military abilities.

"If I may say so, General," another of the officers said after a long shocked silence, "that is a brilliant plan, sir."

For a moment, Dardas thought the group was going to break into applause. Weisel beamed.

See how well it works when we cooperate?
I do. I most certainly do, said Dardas.

IT WAS NIGHTFALL. They would move in the morning. Weisel's aide reported, rather contritely, that the assassin with the crossbow had still not been located, despite every effort. Weisel dismissed him and lay down to sleep, exhausted by the events of the past few days.

Weisel slept. Dardas did not.

His consciousness was effectively held prisoner inside this body now. It wouldn't do. Weisel had been correct earlier when he'd pointed out that they couldn't directly spy on each other's thoughts. That was good. Dardas certainly didn't want Weisel knowing about his intention to prolong this war, to create a perpetual state of warfare, in fact.

To maintain that, one naturally had to have an enemy. As yet, the sorry peoples of this Isthmus had offered only the most pathetic resistance to the Felk. The massacre at U'delph had had real purpose. It wasn't just random bloodshed. Dardas meant to *provoke* resistance.

Now he was hampered in his plans not only by Matokin, but also by Weisel.

Dardas concentrated. He remembered how it had felt to control this body. He tried now to imagine himself once more in command. Memory mingled with his desire. He exerted himself, while Weisel's consciousness continued to sleep.

Suddenly, the little finger on Weisel's left hand wiggled. It was a small movement, barely noticeable. But Dardas was certain he was the one who had initiated it.

Victories could be large or small, he knew from his long career as a war commander. But almost any victory was sweet.

BRYCK
(1)

"YOU THERE!"

The sudden cold had nothing to do with Callah's autumn weather, a harsher season apparently than it was in U'delph, to the south. Instead, this was a shock-chill of fear.

Bryck had the collar of his coat raked up, shoulders hunched. He had just been starting to feel assured about this little excursion out of doors. The early morning sun, where it found its way through the clouds, felt good. The air was certainly sweeter than that in the rooms he was sharing with the entire complement of the Broken Circle.

He had skulked along unobtrusively, gaining confidence with every unmolested step. He had traveled one street, then two, away from the relative safety of those rooms.

The voice had called from behind. It had a hard authoritative ring to it. Bryck didn't doubt that when he turned,

he would find a Felk soldier there, one who had just recognized him as the murderer of one of the garrison.

The members of the Circle didn't know about this jaunt
of his. He had slipped out while most of the others were
still sleeping. Today was going to be a busy day for the
group, and he had advised everyone to rest up properly.

He was at the edge of the street, which was just stirring
with activity. He looked furtively and hurriedly for escape
routes. He was near an alleyway's mouth. Casually he si-
dled toward it.

"*You.* Hold. Hold, I said—"

But it wasn't a proper alley, just a niche between buildings where debris had accumulated. The three walls en-
closing it were too high to scale.

The Broken Circle had a small arsenal of mostly improvised weaponry—hammers, cooking cutlery, and the
like. Bryck was unarmed. Still keeping his manner nonchalant, he finally turned, as if just becoming aware of the
hail.

He expected a uniform, armor, a sword. Instead, a man,
Bryck's senior by a tenwinter in a once-fancy merchant's
coat, was stalking toward him. His face was tightly drawn,
and his eyes moved a little wildly in their sockets.

"Don't you hear?" the man demanded.

Bryck barely lifted his face from the circle of his coat
collar. "What do you want?" he asked, voice pitched softly.
He didn't recognize the man.

"I want to know what's become of your *promises.*"

It occurred to Bryck then that this might merely be
someone mad, mistaking him for some bygone acquain-
tance who had wronged him and unable to realize he had
the wrong individual, even now, when they were this close
to each other.

"I made you no promises." Bryck turned. He would simply and quietly go back the way he'd come.

But the man seized his shoulders and spun him back. He had some strength to him. "Now you make your lies worse! Haven't you a shred of honesty?" His coat appeared to be loosening at every seam, and it was generously stained.

There were just enough people in the street by now for this commotion to be drawing attention. It was the last thing Bryck needed. He wrenched his shoulders out of the man's grasp.

"You are mistaking me," he said, enunciating it clearly, concisely, hoping against all reason that this would penetrate.

The man's eyes went a bit wilder. "In the tavern . . ."

Despite himself, Bryck asked, "What tavern?"

"Those beautiful, beautiful words. In the tavern. The songs. Then . . . then your words. About rebellion. About people rising against the Felk in Windal. Godsdamnit. *Godsdamnit.* Why did you tell such lies?"

The man had heard him some night, when Bryck had been going from tavern to tavern throughout Callah, posing as a troubadour and spreading the gossip about an uprising that hadn't occurred (at least to his knowledge) and a rebel underground here in Callah that didn't exist (or hadn't at the time).

Bryck looked beyond the man, saw watching eyes in the street. None of them belonged to a Felk soldier, but one might come by at any moment.

He had to end this. Now.

Bryck edged once more toward the litter-strewn alcove. The man grabbed for him a second time. Bryck sidestepped, drew him farther within the fetid recess.

"You'll pay for your lies," the man said. His teeth showed. His hands rose, fingers spread and claw-like. He lunged, this time catching Bryck's coat as he tried again to dodge. Bryck's heel slid in something damp, and he found himself suddenly tipping backward. He clutched the man's tattered merchant's coat and pulled him down as well.

They crashed together among the refuse, a board splintering across Bryck's back. He had pivoted so that the man's weight didn't come down entirely on top of him, and also so that his elbow struck the man's chest with a good thump.

Bryck turned farther, throwing off the body, scrabbling for the broken length of wood. His searching hands snatched it up. He spun around on one knee, raised the board and swung it.

It broke into two even smaller segments, this time across the man's temple. It had been a powerful blow; but unlike that time he had killed the Felk garrison soldier, he knew that this wasn't a fatal strike. The man slumped down heavily in the garbage, but his chest was still rising and falling. Bryck had knocked him unconscious.

He came back out onto the street, brushing hurriedly at his clothing and hiding his face down in his coat's collar once again. He met no one's eyes and, thankfully, heard no one else hail him as he made for the Broken Circle's refuge. Whatever else, this early morning outing had taught him that staying put was the wiser course.

IT HAD BEEN a jolly household in which he'd spent his childhood, his young impressionable years wrapped in a fondly remembered familial warmth. He recalled with a distinct immediacy, even now, songs sung around the great dining table, his mother's lilting laughter, his father's wit and ribald dash with a vox-mellifluous.

Good days. They were, Bryck realized, the foundation stones on which his own character had been built. He had chosen laughter over tears, humor over sarcasm, a jolly disposition over a sour one. These choices had served him well; and when he eventually found himself wed and with a family of his own making, he had done all he could to impart these same gifts to his children.

Of course, it had helped that as a wealthy noble and successful playwright he could also provide comforts and luxuries beyond the grasp of most people.

As an outgoing gregarious individual, Bryck had felt free to indulge his appetites for life. Sometimes these were in mild excess. Sometimes he gambled a bit too much or drank an inordinate amount. But these were simply expressions of his basic character and a desire to live to his fullest.

Despite his propensities, however, he had never performed in one of his own works. While he was perfectly at ease entertaining friends at a celebration or comrades at a tavern, the notion of reciting words before an audience and acting out some spectacle was, frankly, terrifying. He couldn't imagine how the actors did it, night after night.

But it didn't matter now, none of it. The extrovert was dead. As dead as U'delph, the city where Bryck had been all those things—husband, father, playwright, noble. He retained only one facet of his original character. He was still able to work his very minor feats of magic, an innate ability.

"I still don't understand. Why're we doing this? You said this dye won't poison the water. It wouldn't even change the taste."

This undertaking, Bryck supposed, was a sort of magic.

Not the mystical breed. More the obvious magic of turning whimsy into believable fiction.

He regarded the adolescent girl. A frown creased a very adult line between her brows. Tyber had finally made her wash, scrubbing the scabs from her fingers and the lice from her hair. She looked fairly presentable now. She also, unfortunately, looked too much like recruitment age.

"We don't want to poison the water, Gelshiri," he said. "We have to drink the water, too."

"But who's going to want to drink it? Especially when it's *that* color."

"Just keep going with that thought. You'll figure it out in the end." Bryck didn't say it condescendingly, and the girl didn't take it wrong. She was at that age when emotions were their liveliest and their hardest to manage. But she was also a full-fledged member of the Broken Circle, a group of rebels dedicated to the overthrow of the Felk here in Callah.

Gelshiri scampered off—or went as fast as her "missing" leg would allow. She wore a long coat, with her left leg folded up behind and secured with cord. It had to be quite uncomfortable, but she didn't complain. She worked the crutch they'd found for her like she'd been born to it. When people saw her, they saw someone crippled and ineligible for service in the Felk army.

She had her packets of dye and had memorized her assigned itinerary. Bryck had no doubts she would visit every one of the public cisterns. If she wasn't as bright as she could be, she was certainly single-minded.

Bryck examined the marked map. Callah's reservoirs were indicated. Four other members of the Broken Circle were on similar errands today. It was the first united organized effort for this group, and Bryck was pleasantly surprised how smoothly it had all gone. So far. The results of this operation, of course, were yet to be seen.

Bryck, after his morning adventure, had returned stealthily to these rooms, which were behind a row of metal- and woodworking shops. During the day there was a steady clangor and also the seeping heat of furnaces, which Bryck enjoyed. Winter in this northerly state, no doubt, would be quite harsh. He didn't know if he would still be in Callah then. His work might not yet be done. Also he had to wonder where he would go from here.

The rooms weren't too squalid. They certainly weren't worse than the cheap lodgings he'd taken when he first arrived in the city. Still, this was a step up from that dilapidated and deserted warehouse where they had been holed up. Bryck had relocated the group here. As enticingly clandestine as that warehouse had appeared, he had deemed it better that they base themselves somewhere where they could come and go without drawing notice. This was a busy district. Despite the shortages pressing on Callah and an announcement of new severe taxes, these craft workers remained active.

Bryck had ordered the move, and the others had heeded the order. It was still a strange—and yes, admittedly thrilling—dynamic. He wasn't accustomed to being in charge, to making command decisions. His previous life as a noble hadn't really prepared him for it. Even his status as a playwright was more a matter of celebrity than authority. Bryck had always been content to let his affairs more or less run themselves. If a problem came up, there was always enough money around to salve things. Also, his wife, Aaysue, had an organizational knack and kept the household orderly.

Aaysue, besides being his first line of defense against the pressures of being a noble, had also willingly served as Bryck's first—and perhaps most important—audience.

He kept his plays secret until he'd penned enough pages to get the gist of the story across. Then he would take Aaysue aside, after the children were asleep, and read her what he'd concocted. He would enact the various roles with amateurish glee, knowing even as he capered and gibbered that he could never do this in front of anyone but his wife.

And she laughed or didn't laugh. She was surprised by the twists that devotees of his work had come to expect. Or she wasn't surprised. She was delighted, or merely and mildly and insufficiently amused.

That was how he judged the initial value of his work. If Aaysue responded well, the play was worth finishing. If she didn't—and she was kind enough not to tell him sweet lies—then he either repaired the piece or, more often, fed the pages into a fire. Revamping a mediocre work was usually more trouble and more demoralizing than creating something entirely fresh.

Bryck's theatricals had made him famous in a way that being a mere noble with money and lands never would have. It was odd that he had stumbled into the profession at all, since it normally attracted men and women of gloomily serious bents.

Maybe that was why he had succeeded so well. What he wrote were shameless comedies.

He wondered, as he continued to brood over the map, what Aaysue would have made of *this* work. It was ironic that she wasn't here to give her opinion, since this was most certainly dedicated to her. And to their children. Bron, Cerk, Ganet, little Gremmest. He was doing all this in their memories.

It was vengeance. Vengeance against the Felk, who had destroyed Bryck's family, city, people. Who had destroyed his life.

Now he had assistance, it seemed. The Broken Circle. It was still difficult to think of this group—fourteen, including himself—without feeling the impulse to roll his eyes. Had he still had a jolly disposition, he might even laugh aloud. It was all so improbable. These people were, almost literally, the products of his imagination. In his guise as a minstrel he had spread rumors throughout Callah about the Broken Circle, a clandestine rebel ring bent on overthrowing the Felk. His aim was to incite rebelliousness among these Callahans, if not an outright uprising.

The paradox was that at the time there had been no such thing as the Broken Circle! Bryck had further enforced the illusion by branding that slashed circle sigil all over the city. Only then, after the fable was in place, had a "real" Broken Circle formed; and Bryck, through a series of misadventures, had found himself joining the group. More than that: He had been automatically appointed their leader. They had only the urge to rebel. They keenly needed direction, leadership.

He had occasionally met devotees of his theatricals who thought that the comedies he wrote were somehow real. These people could be comical themselves . . . or most unsettling. But this was the first time reality had truly sprung from something he had conceived.

Perhaps he should be proud of what his creation had accomplished. But as yet, the Broken Circle had done nothing to threaten or upset the rule of the Felk here in Callah. Bryck at least had violently disturbed the local economy with that counterfeiting scheme. And he himself was personally responsible for the murder of a member of the Felk garrison. But he wanted to do more. He had to do more. The Felk had to pay.

He finally set aside the map. He could gain nothing

from staring at it. He had devised this operation and dispatched his agents. It was in their hands now. He sat on his bunk and gazed about at the small dimensions of this room, solemnly noting the bangs and clangs that came through the walls from the bustling workshops.

Bryck, he now had to truly acknowledge, was effectively confined here. The garrison had a description of him, and they were very interested in locating the man who had killed one of their own. If Bryck wanted to play it completely safe, he would have to remain in these rooms day and night. It would be possible, of course, to direct the Circle from here, to continue giving orders and sending the others out.

But there *had* to be other ways, surely. This confinement rankled him, despite this morning's misadventure. He was a creative individual, even though his days of writing plays were, like so much else, forever behind him. He contemplated the problem as he waited for word of the water-dyeing project's success or failure to come back to him.

HE KNEW IT had succeeded even before Gelshiri and the four others returned one by one to the set of rooms that were the Broken Circle's headquarters. The news spread boisterously through the streets. There was a satisfying edge of hysteria to it that Bryck could hear even through the walls.

His fellow rebels arrived in the last watch of daylight. The others of the group assembled as well. Among this band only Tyber was also restricted to these rooms, owing to his having tried to bribe a Felk officer into setting up a contraband operation. Tyber was currently wanted by Colonel Jesile and the garrison, though certainly not with the same vigor with which Bryck was sought.

"Success! Success!"

"Nobody ever even noticed me when I—"

"—slipped that packet into the pipe—"

"—didn't even loiter around to watch the first reactions, though I *dearly* wanted to."

They were all uproariously pleased with themselves. Each member had been assigned several targets, all publicly accessible, all well trafficked. It really required nothing more than simple sleight of hand, but there was still potential for danger, even disaster.

It was Quentis who gathered up the individual reports, questioning each Broken Circle agent to be certain that no one had been seen and all precautions had been observed. Quentis had a cool nature. Bryck owed her much. She was the one who had given him shelter when he was first on the run from murdering that Felk soldier.

She was a capable woman, a street vendor with a cart. Her face was somewhat weathered, but not so much as some who were nearing their fortieth year. And what age and wear were there was tempered by the softness of her amber-colored eyes.

"The disruption has by now reached all of Callah, I think it's safe to say." She gave Bryck a nod.

"So I've been hearing." He waved, indicating the busy street beyond the shops, where for the past watch he had heard cries and panicky shouts.

"People are . . . very upset," Gelshiri said, excited and confused all at once. She had done her job well but still hadn't figured out what it was all about.

"Godsdamned right they are," Ondak, Quentis's cousin, said happily. "When water turns to blood, you have to guess that *some*thing's amiss!"

Everyone laughed merrily. They made quite a crowd in

these undersized rooms. But they were still so few, Bryck couldn't help thinking. So very few, compared with the Felk occupying this city.

It was Ondak who had explained which powders were needed to create the transmutation of the water. Others in the group had procured the substances from bakeries and restaurants around Callah that were still operating. Ondak had mixed the packets, which, when put into a water supply, would change the color and viscosity of the water without adding anything harmful. The blood-water now flowing from Callah's cisterns and reservoirs might be unpleasant to look at and pour too thickly, but it was perfectly fine to drink.

"Those buggering Felk might have magic on their side," Tyber pronounced as he filled glasses for everyone, "but I'll wager they still carry their superstitions about the gods."

"*Oh,*" Gelshiri suddenly cried out, a light coming into her eyes. "This is supposed to scare the Felk, isn't it?"

Tyber, who had a face of blemished skin and a mouthful of unhealthy teeth, threw an arm around the girl's gaunt shoulders.

"Girl, if you were a creature of more interesting gender, I'd make you fall in love with me. Lift your glasses, my fellows. We drink to the Minstrel."

It was wine that had been poured, not the newly transformed Callahan water. Bryck dutifully took a swallow. Once, he'd taken real pleasure in drinking and in the carousing and camaraderie that went with it.

He hadn't divulged his name to the members of the Broken Circle. He hadn't even given them the alias he had lived under when he first arrived in Callah. And so he had become the Minstrel. That was fine. There was an anonymity about the sobriquet that he appreciated. After all, he wasn't doing this for glory.

They all continued to congratulate one another, and Bryck did nothing to interfere with their celebrating. As Gelshiri was finishing her glass, she asked, frowning as she concentrated, "If we do scare the Felk, won't we be scaring everybody else, too?"

Again Bryck didn't patronize. "But we can spread the word that this is the work of the Broken Circle. No Callahan need fear the water." It would have been a nice final touch if they could have left the Circle's sigil at each water site. But that would have called attention to them and lessened the chances of success for the operation dramatically. It was too bad Bryck couldn't follow each of them today and brand the slashed circle at each target, using that trick of magic that allowed him to make fire from nothing.

Bryck settled back and sipped quietly at his wine. He had plans for the days ahead. This band had performed successfully. He could have a little confidence in them; they'd earned it. But greater challenges and much greater dangers were ahead.

Tyber, Bryck noted, had a curious charisma about him, particularly since he was such an unsightly fellow. Yet, as Bryck watched, the celebration seemed to slowly gravitate toward him. He laughed and made the others laugh. He had a cheerful air, a winning self-assurance. He was the point of focus, the same position that Bryck had once so naturally and ably held whenever people gathered and the wine flowed.

It was when Tyber grabbed up three empty glasses and started deftly juggling them, as everyone applauded, that Bryck got the idea he'd been waiting for. Afterward, he pulled the man aside and asked, "Tell me, Tyber, do you know any magic?"

RAVEN
(2)

HERE HE COMES! Vadya said unnecessarily.

Raven could actually feel her host's excitement. She shared in it. The two of them had developed quite an affinity in a very short time. They shared thoughts easily. Now, they were occasionally sharing emotions, especially when both women were excited about the same thing.

Stepping out into the corridor, moving this new body with sensual ease, Raven glanced casually and "noticed" Lord Abraxis approaching. He was tall, lean, and had exceptionally long fingers.

"My Lord," Raven said, bowing a greeting.

He slowed, frowning, then halted. Next to Matokin, this was the most politically powerful mage in Felk. He was also said to be head of the Internal Security Corps.

"Who are you?" he asked, curtly.

"I am Raven, Lord Abraxis." She fluttered her eyelashes a bit. Vadya had already taught her many of the

tricks of this shapely body and how to get the most use of
her attractive face.

Surprise showed in the wizard's normally inexpressive
eyes. Then he nodded, "Yes, Matokin mentioned he'd had
you resurrected. Quite an effort. It was at Weisel's request,
I understand?"

"Yes, Lord," Raven said.

"Well, that at least means you've succeeded in getting
near him. Good work. When do you return to the field?"

"Soon." She was feeling better almost by the watch,
adapting to her new form, and recovering from the physical and psychic shock of being resurrected.

"Good. You realize you're still under the constraints of
the assignment Lord Matokin and I gave you?" Abraxis
asked pointedly.

"Of course," Raven said. "Lord Matokin has already reminded me."

"That's fine then."

Raven had worn a gauzy gown for this stroll through
the Palace corridors, picking a time and place when she
knew Abraxis would be passing. The garment offered teas-
ing peeks at her body. She knew just how pleasing a shape
it was. She had studied it thoroughly in the mirror in her
room, marveling at its perfection. Vadya had been only too
happy to point out its many attributes, assuring Raven that
she would have a power over men like nothing she had
ever experienced before.

Judging by Raven's first experiments with the guards
and messengers of this Palace, Vadya hadn't been lying.

"You're very kind to take such an interest in me,"
Raven said, moving a step closer to Abraxis and speaking
in that low purring voice.

Again, reaction showed in Abraxis's apathetic eyes.

"I . . . that is, Lord Matokin and I . . . we only want you to perform to the best of your abilities," he said, somewhat haltingly.

"Oh, I'm happy to *perform*," Raven said, trying not to overplay it. Seduction was new to her, though certainly not to Vadya, who had cheerfully shared her experiences in detail with Raven. They were very exciting tales.

"Well, that's good . . ." Abraxis's eyes now moved down the front of her gown.

Raven pushed out her firm breasts. She moved even closer and brushed a lissome thigh against him. There was no one else in this stretch of corridor.

"Tell me, Raven," Abraxis said, his voice a little hoarse now. "Whose body were you reborn into? This face looks familiar."

Raven smiled, and it was a smile that was luscious and appealing and natural, very unlike when she had been in that *other* body, her original fat and awkward body. She found herself gladder by the moment that she was rid of it.

"Lady Vadya was generous enough to receive me into herself," Raven said. She lifted a hand and stroked Abraxis's forearm with her fingers, slowly, provocatively.

This time Abraxis's look of surprise was total.

"Vadya?" he gasped. "Why, she is the most renowned courtesan in all Felk!"

Raven smiled. "Did you ever wonder why she was so famous?"

"I . . . I have," Abraxis said.

"Then let me show you," Raven said, taking his arm, leading him back toward her room. Inside, Vadya was wild with glee.

· · ·

RAVEN HAD, AT first, been quite shocked when Vadya revealed those details about herself. Why, Raven wondered, had Matokin arranged for her to be resurrected within the body of such a woman? But the question answered itself.

Matokin had no doubt seen the situation as an opportunity to make her, Raven, more appealing to Weisel. It would certainly make spying on him easier.

Raven stretched her supple body the full length of the rumpled bed. Abraxis had excused himself, a bit dazedly, and gone off to what he claimed was an important council meeting.

It had been the single best sexual experience of Raven's life, which wasn't saying too much, considering the two previous trysts she'd had, both fast and unpleasant. It wasn't even that Abraxis was so much better a lover than either of the other two. More, it was that his excitement over her body filled her with a reciprocal excitement.

"It's amazing how different a man treats you when you're pretty," she murmured languidly out loud, stating the obvious.

Yes, it is, Vadya added, silently.

I feel wonderful, Raven said, now communicating on the same subvocal level. She rolled her naked body on the covers and giggled.

That's good. Bask in it. But don't take all day. It'll be time to get moving soon.

Raven stopped laughing. *Where are we going?*

Why, back to the field of course, to General Weisel. You've obviously recovered enough to travel.

For some reason, the thought of leaving Felk dampened Raven's spirits a bit. Strange, since she had felt no attachment to the city before. Then again, those years had been spent at the Academy, Matokin's school for magic training, a place of harsh authority and brutal discipline. Raven had still been learning the basics of magic when she was reassigned to General Weisel.

I'll be sorry to go, Raven finally said. *Where else but at the Palace can you meet one of the most powerful men in the empire just walking down a corridor?*

And where else can you drag him off to bed? Vadya asked wryly.

That, too. Raven giggled again. It was a new thing for her.

Vadya was right, of course. It was time to get back to work. She hopped off the bed and went to the mirror, pulling a chair up to it. As always at the sight of her new body, she smirked and ogled. Then she snatched up a brush and started combing her full, silky blond hair.

Have you spent a lot of time here at the Palace? Raven asked.

A lot. Yes.

Did you sleep with a great many men?

Well, not all at once . . .

Raven barked a laugh. Vadya was smart, and witty, and she acted very kind to Raven, instructing her in the ways of her new body. Mostly though, she treated Raven like an equal. She didn't talk down or make Raven feel bad about the graceless figure she used to have, or her social awkwardness.

Suddenly, Raven set down the brush. She stared into the mirror, into eyes that were bewitching and that were feeling more and more like her own. Really, though, they were Vadya's. Lady Vadya, renowned courtesan.

Tell me something . . . Raven hesitated.

Yes?

Did . . . Lord Matokin ever take you to bed? Raven's throat abruptly tightened.

I won't tell you that, Vadya said after a pause.

It wasn't an answer Raven had been expecting. *What do you mean you won't tell me?* She frowned.

Just that. And, guess what? You can't force me. Now, don't get upset. I'm still on your side. But I know who you think Matokin is. You think it often enough and "loud" enough that I couldn't help overhearing. He may very well be your father. I don't personally know. But I'm not going to spoil anything by letting you even entertain the idea that this same body has . . . has been . . . well, you know. So put the thought out of your mind.

Raven tried to do just that. Vadya was right. It seemed she was right a lot of the time.

Clothes had been fetched to the room. Raven sorted through them, picking the most practical items. One didn't wear diaphanous gowns in the field. She chose boots, a warm coat, but sensible as her choices were, she noticed that they still flattered her curvaceous figure.

Tell me something else, Raven finally said.

If I can, Vadya said, a bit cautiously.

Had you ever gone to bed with Abraxis before?

Old slim and sour? Vadya asked, amused. *No. He never requested my services, and I certainly was never personally attracted to him.*

But you encouraged me to seduce him, Raven said.

And it was fun, wasn't it? Confidence-building. It may also give us an edge with Abraxis if we ever need it in the future.

An edge? Raven asked, unsure.

Raven, Vadya said, *I am a loyal subject of the Felk Empire. I believe in Matokin's plan to unite the whole Isthmus*

*under one rule, to create one great land where there will
be no further need for war.*

I'm glad to hear it.

Yes, Vadya went on. *But I'm also an intelligent, independent, and very experienced woman. I know politics as
no other civilian can. I have seen firsthand how things are
done, how decisions get made. I understand power and
what it can do to a person. Abraxis is the head of Internal
Security. It is a very important post. It will become more
and more important as this war progresses and more lands
fall under Felk rule and require internal policing. Abraxis
is a man to watch.*

Do you mean . . . he's a threat? Raven asked, astonished.

All power is a threat.

Raven absorbed that. It made her head whirl a little.

*Matokin and Abraxis assigned you to watch over
Weisel. They never said why. A good guess is that they are
merely playing it safe, making sure the general doesn't ex-
hibit any signs of disloyalty.*

Raven swallowed. Weisel had, of course, already spoken treason against Matokin, to her.

It is sensible that we play it safe, too, Vadya continued.
*Abraxis is the number two man in Felk politics. Maybe he
has secret thoughts of being number one.*

What makes you say that? Raven asked.

*Because of the human nature I've observed in my time
here.*

I have one more question, Raven said.

Go ahead, Vadya said, with no obvious sign of im-
patience.

Why did you agree to this?

This . . . ? Vadya seemed confused.

Being my host. Letting my resurrected being inhabit

your body while you remain passive. Obviously, you had a thriving career in Felk. Why give that up to allow me, a total stranger, the privilege of using your body?

Vadya was silent a moment. Then she said, *Because Lord Matokin asked me to.*

Raven sighed, *I think it must have been something more than that. You're too intelligent and cunning a woman not to think how you could benefit.*

I thank you for the compliment, Vadya said. *But for the moment you will have to do with the answer I've given you.*

It seemed plain that she would speak no more of it, no matter how much Raven prodded. She decided she would trust this woman to reveal everything later on.

Now, Vadya said, *we really should get going.*

Go they did. Raven brought along a small bag of field gear. She reported to one of the chambers where the Far Movement mages were transporting people to and from various points throughout the growing empire. She had already informed Matokin, via messenger, that she was returning to the field, after having received an authorization from one of the Palace physicians.

Vadya had never been Far Moved before. Raven rather enjoyed having had an experience her worldly host had not. She went through the portals quickly, without incident, glad not to have a recurrence of that one strange episode, when she had heard voices and had felt something closing in on her.

The army was on the move when she arrived. Luckily, Raven had been transported while the troops had stopped for a midday meal and rest period.

She presented her orders to an officer, who didn't try hard to hide the fact that he was more interested in her body than the scroll she'd handed him. Raven soaked up the attention.

This was far more effective than when Weisel had ordered her groomed and put into more attractive attire. Now she was drawing stares from virtually every male.

This time, though, she had Vadya telling her how to best react, how to use her femininity and sensuality to her advantage. It was quite a game, with feints and ploys, veiled glances and cold silent dismissals.

Raven was enjoying it, immensely. Now she had the power of beauty, as well as the authority of her status as General Weisel's liaison to the magic-using units of this army. It was a position he had created just for her.

"The general wants you to report to him," the officer said. He pointed. "He's back that way."

"I'll find him," Raven said, and set off.

The sights and smells were definitely different from those of the Palace. A few more days there, and she would have gotten too used to its luxuries.

General Weisel was encircled by a squad of watchful guards when she located him. She knew that the assassin who had tried to kill him, and who had succeeded in killing her instead, was still at large. If the culprit hadn't been found yet, Raven guessed, then he or she had probably managed to flee.

It might have been an action on the part of the enemies of Felk. That assassin might have been an agent sent to kill Weisel, so as to slow the army's southward push. It was also possible, and more disturbing, that it had been done on the inside. Maybe some disgruntled Felk soldier had taken it on himself to murder Weisel. Maybe the assassin was from among the conscripted troops from the cities the Felk had already conquered.

Whatever, Weisel was being scrupulously protected now. Raven's identity was checked a second time, before she was passed through the vigilant circle surrounding the general.

"Raven!" Weisel said, in what sounded like a sincerely happy greeting.

She saluted. "General, I'm reporting as ordered."

Weisel was dressed in his riding gear. He took a sip from a cup of water, gargled, spat, and handed the cup off to one of his retinue. He waved her nearer.

"You're recovered?" he asked. "I understand the experience can be . . . unsettling."

"I've been cleared for duty, General," Raven said.

"That's good." He took a moment to look her over. "I must say they certainly picked a pleasant body for you. Are you enjoying it?"

"I am," she smirked, unable to hide the expression.

Weisel laughed. "I thought you would be. Raven," he said, more serious now, "there have been some changes in strategy since your . . . leave of absence. We're no longer going ahead with the portal operation. You remember it?"

"I do, General."

"Instead, we're going to do something safer and perhaps a bit less flamboyant," he shrugged.

Raven knew enough not to ask why the operation had been canceled. If Weisel wanted her to know, he would tell her.

"But that's not why I wanted to see you," Weisel went on. "I know you had your position as a liaison thrust upon you without any notice—"

"I was honored to be selected," Raven burst out, then sucked in a startled breath at her own impertinence at interrupting the general.

Weisel ignored it. "But you've served well. And it makes me think you can handle even more responsibility."

This time she waited, to make sure he had really paused. Then she said, solemnly, "I am humbled, General Weisel."

"I promised you a reward for saving my life. This might not qualify, precisely, but I need someone I can trust who can handle a serious task. As you may know, my assassin or assassins have not been found. My senior staff has saddled me with this special guard, to keep me protected. But that doesn't solve the problem. One way or the other, a failure in security is responsible for that assassination attempt. It can't be repeated. I will tell you in confidence that I believe the one who fired that crossbow to be . . . Felk." His eyes bored into her.

Raven gasped almost inaudibly.

"That makes it a matter of internal security, within this army," Weisel said. He was speaking intently but softly, too low for his guards to overhear. "Do you understand?"

"Yes," she said. "Are you going to contact Lord Abraxis and have him send in some of his agents?"

"*No*," Weisel snapped, looking suddenly annoyed. "I don't want that shifty mage meddling with my troops here in the field. No. What I need, Raven, is an internal security force of my own, one that will police this army. I need to be assured that these warriors are loyal. For that, I need someone in charge of security whose loyalty is unquestioned."

The full weight of it descended on Raven. She nearly staggered.

"I will make you an officer and appoint you to the head of the force," Weisel said. "Will you accept?"

She didn't hesitate. "I will serve you in any way I can, General Weisel."

"That's good." Weisel nodded. "We'll be bivouacking in a few watches, then moving into position around Trael early tomorrow. This evening, come to my pavilion. We'll discuss the details."

"Yes, General!"

"Dismissed."

Raven slipped away, her head whirling. This was a remarkable turn of events. Head of internal security for this army. The implications were stunning.

She had made the right decision. How could she have possibly turned Weisel down?

I will serve you in any way I can, General Weisel.

It was, she realized, almost exactly the same thing she had said to Matokin.

RADSTAC
(2)

IT WAS LIKELY the Felk officer with the bored, irritable, bureaucratic air would never know how near death had been in that room. He was not interested in faces or personalities. Identity, to this meticulous creature, meant verifiable paperwork.

He was interested in official traveling orders, which neither Radstac nor Deo possessed. They had been Far Moved from the active ranks in the field to this occupied city of Callah; and the arrangements had been decidedly unofficial.

This didn't sit well with the officer, who seemed to take their appearance here as a personal offense. So be it, Radstac had thought. But the officer, an undersized man with lips evidently permanently pinched, made the error of approaching Radstac, of waving a finger under her nose, of barking unpleasantries and finally—and most seriously—of jabbing that same finger into her chest. He poked her once, and every instinct called for her to unsheathe her combat sword and proceed with a fast but messy disemboweling.

It was almost beyond her to control the response. As the officer was making to stab that finger again into Radstac's leather-armored chest, Deo, surely understanding the direness of the situation, intervened.

"Sir, if there's some problem, perhaps we could speak with someone with the authority to decide what to do with us." Deo said it with perfect ingenuousness.

It earned him a pinch-mouthed sneer; but it also made it apparent that this officer did *not* have that authority. This was a functionary who collected and filed papers. He didn't make decisions. What authority he exerted was a bureaucrat's fussiness.

And so Radstac and Deo were led from the room where the Felk mages, who'd immediately excused themselves, had created the arrival portal.

It had been an experience like no other. Radstac didn't fear magic, but this was magic of a scope that was unfamiliar. That foggy world . . . it was so alien. She was a mercenary. She relied on her senses, on the power and coordination of her body. She wondered how those traits would serve her *there,* if she ever had to engage in combat in that deranged environment.

She further wondered what it would be like to travel under the full influence of *mansìd.* Surely it would be a memorable experience, as the clarity that the blue leaf brought met the profound murkiness of that realm.

Radstac turned away from any thoughts of *mansìd.* She did not even have a full leaf in her possession now, and that lack set her addict's heart speeding slightly. It made for a seeping anxiety. A buzzing background of anticipatory uneasiness. But her professionalism would see her through.

Of course it would. And this was still the Isthmus, after all. It didn't matter that they were now deep inside Felk territory. She would find more leaves.

This building, they learned, was called the Registry, and the Felk garrison had evidently commandeered it. It was a place of finished stone, high-ceilinged chambers, and it exuded a sort of official atmosphere, as if it had been some local governmental seat before the arrival of the Felk.

Radstac and Deo were deposited in an empty office. The door was closed, but at least one guard was placed outside it.

"Do you—" Deo started, but she silenced him with a cautious flick of her eyes. This could all go very badly for them. It depended on how reliably these Felk could trace her and Deo's journey back through the portals. If they eventually laid hands on the leaf eater who'd arranged their escape, it would mean disaster. Arrest. Possibly execution.

All for the want of a few convincing documents.

Radstac looked around the office. There were scrolls, loose papers, writing implements. But she put any thoughts of forgery out of her mind. Falsified documents were surely worse than none at all. Besides, she had no idea what a Felk travel order looked like.

It was a windowless office, and she and Deo exercised their only option; they waited silently. She imagined someone of higher authority—and thereby, more of a danger—was being informed of the situation.

Deo remained cool during the wait. Eventually the door was opened. The man who entered was in civilian dress, of a sort apparently peculiar to this city. But he was no civilian himself. Radstac recognized something glinting in his deceptively mild-looking eyes. There was swift calculation there. It was reflexive, the kind of fast sedate judgment a professional gambler would employ.

He eyed the two of them, closing the door behind. After a moment he said, "Deserters get executed, I understand."

"That would be the tradition," Radstac said neutrally.

It quirked the man's brow. He seemed to find it amusing. He nodded. "All right. Are you two deserters?"

"Certainly not."

"Does he speak?"

"We're not deserters," Deo said, his tone as calm as Radstac's. Perhaps he, too, sensed that any show of fear before this man would be disastrous. Or maybe he was just following her lead.

"There," the man said. "You're not deserters. See how simple that was? Deserters don't get themselves Far Moved to an occupied city. They sneak off in the night. And they don't abandon an army that's winning fight after uncontested fight." He no longer seemed to be addressing them. He was of medium height and build.

Was he a Felk officer? Radstac wondered. Then why no uniform? He didn't seem like the type of ranking soldier she had encountered in that Felk camp.

"Lieutenant Wesbecht was most upset that you arrived here without orders."

"He's the one with his mouth in a pinch?"

"He is. Wesbecht is an orderly individual. And you two are a couple of untidies. Why is it that you don't have any traveling orders, anyway?"

"We were never issued them," Radstac said.

"And there again. Simplicity. You were verbally ordered into the portal—"

"We were."

"—and in you went. You don't question an order, do

you? Of course not. And so you arrive here in Callah without the niggling credentials you need, and whose fault is that? Not yours, obviously. Unlucky circumstances. And worst of all, you've personally done nothing wrong."

The man crossed the office, around the desk, and dropped into the chair. He casually put up his feet, folded his hands over his middle. Radstac and Deo watched and waited.

Finally he spoke again. "I like it. It requires no proof on your parts at all. You were told. You obeyed. Paperwork? You don't know anything about paperwork. I can only guess why a soldier would want to leave the field of action. Wait. That's a flagrant lie. I was in the field. I hated it. I got myself transferred to Sook, and I was much happier there. Had a bed to sleep in, decent food. No marching, no fighting. Callah's far from the action, isn't it?"

"Actually," Deo said, "I for one am not quite sure where this place is."

"This is the empire." Something dark moved in the man's voice. "That's all you need to know."

"Yes, sir."

The man said, "You both give convincing details about troop units and commanding officers. It's a pity you can't name the one who ordered you to be Far Moved."

"She never identified herself," Radstac said.

"Well, that was her prerogative, wasn't it?" The man sighed. "You understand, of course, that *some*thing must be done with you. We can't just let you take up space here. Colonel Jesile . . . he's the governor here . . . he has handed the matter over to me. He's got enough on his hands. Coincidentally, so have I. I don't really have time for this. The easiest thing to do would be to send you right back where you came from."

Radstac didn't wince. They hadn't been relieved of their weapons. This office had no windows, but if they killed this man, then overpowered the guard or guards outside—

"I could also have you executed. The court-martial would consist of me signing an order. There would be a certain neatness about that. Whatever trouble you've aroused in the smooth running of operations would be over."

Deo nearly spoke up. But he caught himself, shook his head minutely, stayed silent.

"It's really all up to me. And since they've deposited this matter with me, I see no reason why I shouldn't take full advantage of it and benefit myself as best as possible. I haven't introduced myself. Now that I've made up my mind about you, I shall. I am an agent of the Internal Security Corps. It is entirely possible you have never heard of that branch of our empire's operations. I like that anonymity. But it doesn't negate the authority I bear. My job is to sniff out treason and unrest. My methods are up to me. I report to the head of the Corps. This eliminates a great deal of the fuss and nonsense of military life. Currently, here in Callah, I'm on the trail of a group of rebels who I believe are responsible, among other activities, for tampering with local water supplies. It's an important task I have. I intend to be successful at it. I have one other agent presently working with me. It occurs to me that I could use more. Say, two more."

He smiled now.

"My name is Aquint, and this is an opportunity you can't afford to pass up."

CALLAH DIDN'T LOOK familiar. Then again, Isthmus cities had a dreary sameness about them, so it was remotely possible that Radstac had visited here before. The air was decidedly chilly, and the wind stung her face.

Radstac and Deo had been relieved of their Felk uniforms. She had also given up her sword. The one called Aquint had arranged for it to be stored at the Registry. She still had her boot knives, however; and certainly no one was going to take away her left glove with the two recessed prongs. She had surrendered her leather armor, which was being kept with her combat sword. Coats had been found for her and Deo, civilian wear.

It had all been organized in the space of a single watch, and this was convincing testament of Aquint's authority. None among the Felk who issued her and Deo the proper credentials questioned Aquint's actions. Actually they seemed to regard the Internal Security agent with a certain apprehension.

Aquint had led them, in their new garb, out of the Registry, into Callah's streets. Radstac was perplexed when the agent put his arm into a sling before they departed.

"We'll need cover stories for both of you," he said now as they strode along. There was traffic in the streets, people going about their business. But there were Felk, too, here and there, armed and armored, watching these citizens. Radstac noted a wariness in their eyes, their postures.

"Cover stories?" Deo asked. He, like Radstac, had agreed immediately to Aquint's proposal to join him as agents under his authority. Plainly they'd had no choice.

"You're of fighting age," Aquint said. "Both of you. Why aren't you off at the war?"

Radstac suddenly understood the reason for the sling. They were supposed to blend with this conquered population. They needed plausible grounds for their exemption from conscription.

"You"—Aquint glanced back at her over a shoulder—
"look like you've seen a good amount of combat in your day.
Can you fake a limp? With those facial scars that might be all
you need." He turned round the other way. "But you . . . I
don't know about you. You're the kind of prime meat they
like to put straight into the infantry. Do you have any
thoughts? You're being paid to *think*, not just do."

Radstac looked sidelong at Deo. This had all happened
with such improbable speed.

Deo mulled it a moment. "How about this?" he suggested. He let his features go slack, his lips part. His blue
eyes dulled. "It'sh a cold day today, ishn't it?" He spoke
with a childish slur.

Aquint halted. He faced Deo directly. "You think you
can keep that up?"

"Ash long ash I have to."

Aquint nodded. They turned down another street, nar-
rower, less trafficked. Radstac tried out the limp, hitching
her right leg slightly. It wasn't much of a chore. Like Deo,
she figured she could maintain it indefinitely.

They came to a large ramshackle building that, like
many others Radstac had noticed, had flamboyantly constructed eaves. Must be an architectural affectation, she
thought. This Callah appeared to be a fairly sizable city, at
least by Isthmus standards.

Aquint led them into a front parlor, where he haggled
briefly with a plump aging woman with whom he was apparently acquainted. It didn't stop either of them from angling for the best price. When they were done, Aquint handed
over a small batch of curiously colored bits of papers, which
the house's proprietress accepted as if it were money.

She recited the house rules in a foreboding tone, then
told them where they would find their room.

It was a rambling affair of staircases and corridors, much of it in shabby repair, though the beams appeared solid. They found the room on the third story, a nondescript little hole that nonetheless looked clean enough to inhabit.

Aquint came inside with them and closed the door. Radstac had the impression that a number of the rooms here were unoccupied.

"This room," he said, taking up a chair, "has some significance. It belonged to the Minstrel, who is a man we are seeking and who we will find."

At that moment the door opened. Radstac turned sharply, ready to free her prongs from her glove with a snap of her wrist. It was a boy who entered. He was thin and moved in a kind of quiet glide. His hair was softly colored, and his eyes didn't seem to look directly at anything. It occurred to Radstac how near to invisible this boy would be in a crowd.

"These are Radstac and Deo," Aquint said, pointing. "Ah, you have it," he added as the boy silently handed over a sheaf of papers. "This is Cat. He is also an Internal Security Corps agent."

"I don't much like you calling me that," Cat said in a soft voice.

"You can call a cat a dog, but he still won't bark at the moon. Isn't that the saying? Doesn't matter. Come now, Cat, let's be a good example to our new recruits. They were wily enough to get themselves Far Moved here, out of harm's way on the field of battle. That's admirable. And someday, over a hardy drink, maybe they'll tell us how they managed it. In the meantime there's work for all of us. This is a good job, as far as working for the Felk goes. Neither of you comes from Felk. Correct?"

"Correct," Radstac and Deo said in unison.

Aquint nodded. "I was sure of that. Native Felk, they've

got a look about them. An unpleasant zealousness. Hard to describe. Can either of you read?"

"Yes," they said, again simultaneously.

Aquint blinked. "*Both* of you? That is impressive. In that case, here." He tossed the sheaf toward Radstac. She caught it and glanced at the papers, turning them so Deo could see. "Read that."

They read. It was a report on rebel activities here in this Felk-occupied city-state of Callah.

"So," Aquint said, after they'd finished the pages, "it's that Minstrel and his merry bunch we want. They're here, in Callah. I don't know about the Far Movement mages in the field, but here you need documents and authorizations and reauthorizations before you can get near one of those wizards at the Registry. That's where Colonel Jesile keeps them, incidently. He doesn't like them much. Doesn't want them wandering around his city. So the Minstrel, if he's fled, hasn't gotten himself Far Moved anywhere. And Jesile's garrison has got Callah locked up tight. I don't believe anyone could get out."

"You're convinced these rebels will cause trouble?" Radstac asked. The report hadn't made a very persuasive case. Vandalism, counterfeiting, assembling after curfew and tampering with the water seemed to be the extent of their "rebel" activities. That last operation did show a real organizational talent, though, and even some flair. Changing water into "blood" had done no physical harm to anyone, but it had doubtlessly disrupted things in this city.

The most serious offense was the murder that had been committed by the one referred to as the Minstrel.

"They're already causing trouble," Aquint said. "Just by existing. But remember something"—his eyes shifted—"while we're hunting this group, we are doing important work for the Felk Empire. We have Lord Abraxis's sanction to conduct ourselves however we see fit. We have autonomy. That's something rare during wartime." He pushed up from the chair. "Settle in here. Take this. It's scrip. You're drawing pay now as Internal Security agents. I or Cat will contact you soon, when I have specific assignments for you."

He had handed over a small bundle of those same colored papers he'd given to this house's proprietress.

"Remember—you've got a maimed leg, and you're a dullard. Behave accordingly in public."

With that Aquint exited, Cat sliding out with him. Deo looked at Radstac, his features tight with tension. Suddenly his lungs emptied, and he looked like he was about to collapse to the floorboards. Radstac felt a similar surge of emotion, as the stress of this adventure finally eased a few degrees. She felt and contained the urge to burst into wild laughter.

First she went to the door, checked the corridor outside. Empty. Nobody listening in on them. Then she sat on the room's bed.

"Did you get the feeling our new friend, Aquint, isn't entirely interested in catching these rebels?" she asked.

Deo was blinking, shaking his head. "I . . . I'm not sure what to think just now," he said dazedly.

"I think he's more concerned with maintaining his position here. He must have it good. If we go along with this, maybe we will, too."

Deo took three staggering steps, then flung himself down onto the bed, alongside her.

"I have to say," he murmured, "that my first thought is that I *am* interested in these rebels. And we might just be in a truly unique position to help them against the Felk."

PRAULTH
(2)

SHE WAITED FOR the summoning. She waited with much self-righteousness. Cultat had been so smugly pleased at the news of his nephew, at the possibility that his relative might have succeeded in his apparently wholly independent mission of assassinating General Weisel.

But Praulth had seen the latest intelligence. The Felk were moving once more, closing on the city-state of Trael—just as she had predicted some while ago.

The quarters she and Xink had been appointed were very comfortable, certainly by University standards. Praulth hadn't stirred from these rooms for the past day. In that time she'd barely spoken a word, despite Xink's efforts to engage her in activities. She was even disinterested in sex. She could not accept, on a fundamental level, the prospect that Weisel—and thereby, Dardas—had been defeated by a single assassin.

Now, however, the Felk were on the move, indicating

that *someone* was leading the army. Praulth could only hope that it was still Dardas.

"Do you want anything from the shops?" Xink asked. "There are these sweet pastries I found I think you'd like—"

She turned cold eyes on him, and he ceased his prattling. Really, he could be such a blathering fool. Why hadn't she seen it before? That was obvious, of course. She, too, had been a fool. Naive. Virginal. *Blind*. Well, that time had passed and was gone forever. One lost one's virginity once. It remained to be seen if one could recapture any trace of innocence, ever. It occurred to Praulth in a distant corner of her brooding mind that this newfound cynicism wasn't a very enjoyable state. But enjoyment wasn't important, she reminded herself immediately. She had a real purpose in this world, and no indiscriminate assassination of her worthy nemesis was going to end that function.

She was going to defeat Dardas. Therefore, Dardas still had to be alive. If he wasn't . . .

It went around and around in her head, as it had since Premier Cultat had temporarily adjourned the conference. The many representatives of the various threatened southern states remained here in Petgrad. Praulth had waited, watch after watch, until finally the fresh war news had been relayed here by Cultat's Far Speak wizard spies. There was not enough intelligence yet to determine if Dardas was still guiding the Felk army, through the guise of General Weisel.

During the past day Praulth had had enough time to entertain every unpleasant probability. Dardas might be dead. Cultat may have decided to proceed without her aid as a military strategist. This Felk war might simply sputter into nothing; maybe the Felk had determined that they'd conquered enough new territory and had quit their campaign.

No and no and no. The Felk were heading for Trael. By now they might even be in sight of it. This war, whatever else, wasn't over. She was sure of that much.

She also knew, logically, that Cultat and his burgeoning alliance still desperately needed her help. All she had to do was wait for the summons.

She had been pacing a great deal. Now she put herself firmly into a chair, one that was patterned in a decorative design. Xink had gone off without further word to the shops that this district of Petgrad had to offer. Praulth continued her wait.

It ended a few moments later, with a sharp rap on the door. It startled her, as anything which arrives after being so long anticipated will do. Without rising she bid her visitor to enter.

Amidst her brooding she had also entertained the delicious fantasy that Premier Cultat himself would come calling, contritely, begging her forgiveness for any slight she may have incurred, beseeching her to take up her rightful place as the de facto leader of the alliance.

It was, of course, instead a messenger who entered the rooms. A girl, younger than Praulth, her brow damp with sweat and her undeveloped chest rising and falling.

"The premier . . . requests . . . your presence." Panting. She must have run full out.

Praulth stood, taking up her coat. There were other clothes here in the rooms, but she hadn't bothered changing out of the traveling garb she'd worn when they left Febretree. Perhaps she should dress in something a little more . . . urbane. Something to emphasize the importance of her status. As it was, she looked no better than Merse, the uncouth messenger who had fetched her from the University.

"Is it to that tower, then?" she asked. She wasn't looking forward to climbing those stairs again.

"No," the girl said, still catching her breath. "Somewhere . . . else. I'll show you."

"I'm not going to run with you, girl," Praulth warned darkly, as she followed the young messenger out the door. It was typical of Xink that he'd managed not to be here at just this precise time. The irritation she felt was becoming reflexive. Xink need do very little to annoy her lately, it seemed. She shrugged. Now wasn't the time to examine personal relationships.

They came out of the apartment compound, with its landscaped court and ornamental columns. It was another overcast morning. Petgrad's streets were alive with what seemed like routine commotion.

The messenger pointed. "It's just two streets that way."

"Two? Then why're you so out of breath, girl?"

"I've been informing all the delegates."

"A full meeting, then? Good. Next time, though, you'll inform me *first*. Understood?"

"Yes. But the premier wanted me to guide you there personally."

Praulth feit a thin smile brush her lips. Cultat still recognized her importance. "That's good, girl. Now lead the way."

ACTUALLY, AS IT became apparent during their short walk, the bustle in the streets was not routine. The intensity of movement, the volume of the voices, clued Praulth that something extraordinary had occurred. She hadn't noticed it earlier, sequestered in her rooms.

"What is your name?" she impulsively asked the messenger.

"Taff." She was leading Praulth toward an edifice of stone, great blocks of it, stacked precisely into a squared shape, the shades varying, creating a pattern that was pleasing to the eye.

"Tell me, Taff, what is going on out here?" Praulth indicated the milling ruckus.

"The refugees."

"Refugees?"

"Yes. They've been arriving for days. But now the numbers are growing quite high. Some people are worried about food supplies, about housing. There's talk about calling on the Noble Ministry to seal the borders."

The refugees could only be those fleeing ahead of the Felk. Word of the war had spread throughout the Isthmus by now. Panic had evidently taken hold; and with good cause, Praulth judged. Obviously those people worried about food and shelter that Taff spoke of were the Petgradites themselves. These prosperous people wouldn't want their city flooded with copperless rabble who would only be a drain on local resources.

The building that was their destination was fronted by a grand stairway that ran the full width of the structure's exterior. It was another architectural feat that seemed to have been committed for no reason other than impact, like this city's towers.

"We're meeting here?" Praulth asked, halting at the foot of the stone steps.

"Yes," said Taff. She was pleasingly obedient.

"I'll find my way in alone."

Praulth left the girl there and started up the stairs. It was much less of a climb than going up in that tower. Figures scurried to and fro on either side of her, but she kept up a measured pace. She meant to arrive with more decorum than last time, when Cultat had had to catch her from falling at the sight of that vertiginous view.

She entered a huge lobby, beneath an ornate arch. Inside, there were uniformed soldiers, armed. One stepped up to Praulth as she started across the finely surfaced floor. His uniform was spotless.

She didn't wait for him to speak. "I am Praulth of the University at Febretree."

The man saluted, and Praulth liked that. He indicated the way toward a large auditorium deeper inside the building. Praulth continued on at her studied pace, setting her features, letting her eyes settle into a more imperious cast. She had made an effort to alter her walk. Less of a scurry now; more a chopping stride that neither slowed nor sped for anyone. She was no student any longer. She didn't obey the dictates of masters and mistresses less astute than herself. Her fixed future as a permanent academician at the University had been spoiled by this war. But she was glad of it. Without this vast Felk aggression she would never have found herself. Without Dardas to pit herself against . . . what identity would she have?

So it was that she entered the auditorium in full confident stride. There she halted. It was a scene much different from the one she'd found at the top of that tower.

Upon the broad central dais tables had been gathered. These were overflowing with maps and intelligence reports of a kind with which Praulth was very familiar. Around these tables delegates—she guessed they were all delegates, anyway—moved about in a formalized chaos. However, there were many more representatives than previously. Forty now, at least. Some were in uniform, and those uniforms plainly belonged to disparate militaries.

Out in the space that surrounded the dais was a fantastic

company of people. They wore cloaks and gowns that were
at once glamorous and cabalistic. They carried themselves
with a strange air, circulating only among themselves. They
spoke little, watching the proceedings on the stage with an
interested wariness. Each had a stick in hand, each stick elab-
orately carved or jeweled or trimmed with feathers.

Praulth moved down the aisle now, realizing her appearance here was making no impression whatsoever. On
the dais the delegates spoke with great animation, but the
tone wasn't argumentative this time. Praulth recognized
what was happening as she approached. Plans of action
were being made, finalized. Troop numbers were being
committed. The war now was truly *on*. The Felk had an
enemy. And it was this alliance.

Cultat suddenly mounted the dais from the far side. He
was dressed in military regalia, in the red and gold that
were the colors of Petgrad's standard. He called for quiet
in a voice that didn't order, but that also would brook no
defiance.

"Esteemed consuls," he said, coming to the fore of the
dais, "as you can see, we are stronger now than we were even
two watches ago. With every arrival of a fresh delegate, rep-
resenting a land and a people—be it state or village—we
gather against a common foe, one we all have reason to
dread. I welcome also to this conference Thinker Praulth,
learned war tactician from Febretree. It's my further privilege
to receive here the Noble Ministry of Petgrad."

Cultat swept a hand over the cloaked and gowned ap-
paritions. They murmured amongst themselves, remaining
aloof. A few eyes fell on Praulth. She made certain her posture was stiff, expression firm.

No applause or cheers came at this pause in Cultat's
speech. The atmosphere was absorbingly serious here in

this auditorium. This, Praulth noted, was most definitely a moment of history. War against the Felk was going to be made official. Evidently when the Felk had decamped after several days of inactivity and moved toward Trael, it had convinced these delegates that the intruders from the north had no intention of giving up their plans for full conquest of the Isthmus.

The words that were spoken here today would be chronicled in history texts and read by fascinated scholars a hundredwinter from now. It was a staggering thought. Praulth knew a thousand episodes in history, momentous and pivotal moments; knew these occasions as if she had lived them herself. But she *hadn't* lived them, none of them. She had read of them and imagined herself there.

This was categorically different. Here she was a living witness. It was remarkable. Yet . . . it was insufficient. She had to be a participant. More, she wanted her name to be the first one thought of by those future scholars who studied this event.

"Our time is short," the premier went on, a rumbling inspiring voice, the voice of a great statesman and natural leader. Plainly, though, this wasn't some rehearsed bit of oratory. Cultat was simply saying what needed to be said to get this alliance under way. "We don't have the luxury of squabbling any longer. The city-state of Trael is about to be captured by the Felk. It may happen within the next watch. Trael has no adequate defenses. They also have no representative here. We have had reliable notice for some time now that Trael would next fall to the Felk. That knowledge, obviously, has done little good. But it *could* have served. Had we gathered sooner, set aside our petty differences quicker, perhaps we could now be safeguarding Trael from harm. And, not incidently, protecting the as yet unconquered southern half of this Isthmus. We still have the source of that knowledge. A reliable predictor of the Felk's military movements."

He gestured to Praulth, and she felt more eyes on her. This, she realized, was her moment to speak up. She could interject her own words here, something meaningful, something memorable. A poignant quote to be passed down through the ages. A maxim of her own devising, one that would perhaps seep gradually into common usage but still be attributed to her . . .

"Since this great conference is taking place here within the borders of Petgrad," Cultat continued, "I *must* ask the endorsement of the Noble Ministry." The subtle emphasis indicated the premier's displeasure with the formality. Nonetheless, he said without a hint of irony, "Lauded members of the Ministry of Petgrad, it is self-evident that the greatness of our state rests on your shoulders as well as mine, and that all of you serve the greatness of the Noble State of Petgrad with a humble devotion that cannot be measured by . . ."

It went on in that vein for a while. Praulth had let her opportunity go past, of course. She hadn't really believed she would interrupt the premier's speech, after all.

Eventually Cultat reached the end of the ceremonious petition. He was asking this oddly appareled Noble Ministry to officially commit Petgrad's military forces to the alliance. What followed was a curious ritual unto itself. The ministry milled and murmured more, circulating among themselves. They tapped their totem sticks together. Cultat's craggy features were somewhat strained as he watched. This was an effort of patience on his part. The other delegates watched the exhibition with expressions ranging from wonder to bafflement.

When the ceremony was done, the premier had the sanction he needed. He then proceeded to call for the formal declarations of all the delegates present.

Praulth watched it happen. She had a role here. Obviously. Hers was a crucial part. This league of free armies, both large and minute, was an impressive assembly. The numbers represented here might indeed be quite substantial, enough perhaps to stand against the Felk—*if* they were properly directed. That was her role.

But would she be remembered as ardently and vividly as, say, Premier Cultat?

History was occurring here. But that history hadn't yet been written. No documents chronicling the matter could yet have been assembled by eager war scholars. The page was blank.

Praulth, even as she meticulously noted the details of this scene, considered the great war memoirs that had been penned by commanders throughout the ages. Even the least of these, even the most fragmentary and crude journals, were fairly revered by academicians who made warfare's history their study. Imagine, then, a chronicle written by one with insight not only into military strategies, but insight into a war's proper historical context.

Imagine a person writing such a history of *this* war. A memoir authored by someone aware of each moment's overall significance. This was a war like no other. It deserved to be chronicled as a war never had been before.

"We are now, comrades," Cultat pronounced when the formalities were through, "united in purpose as in action. We are now truly . . . the Alliance."

At last it did bring forth cheers. They were words to remember. Praulth duly noted them.

Later, after the Noble Ministry withdrew from the

auditorium, she came up onto the dais and once more explained her plan to re-create the Battle of Torran Flats. It
was foregone that Trael was lost. But the Felk army would
encamp while the occupation of the city was seen to. If this
Alliance could muster its collective forces quickly enough,
Praulth's plan could go into effect on the southward
prairies outside Trael. Someone mentioned that these were
called the Pegwithe Plains.

Of course, Dardas still had to be in command of that
army for the scheme to succeed.

The conference lasted into the evening, but before the
day's light had even started to wane, wine and spirits appeared and it became a celebration that grew in volume
and jubilation. Praulth didn't join in with the gaiety. Instead, she observed.

SHE PULLED XINK'S face tighter against herself,
seizing a handful of his long dark hair. Her disinterest in
sex had vanished. She put back her head and ground her
pelvis at him, thrilling to the warmth of his mouth, the spry
movements of his tongue. He, of course, had introduced
her to this act, as he had every other sexual deed. She particularly enjoyed this one, even though it left her feeling
somewhat guilty—or *used* to. Before, she had always been
concerned that Xink was receiving no stimulation himself
while performing so. Now, she took her pleasures shame-
lessly and didn't waste time worrying about Xink.

Who, after all, was more important—herself or him?

The pleasure was building steadily. He really was quite
talented. Groans turned to growls in her throat as he panted
and labored between her spread thighs. She was sitting on
the foot of their bed. He was kneeling before her.

"*Do* that!" she heard herself suddenly cry. "Do that. Godsdamnit, that's good! Lick me, you . . . you . . . you insignificant *fucker!*"

And the pleasure flooded through her powerfully, intense enough to burn red shadows across her closed eyelids. When she'd finished, she put a foot to his shoulder, pushed him away, crawled up the bed, and fell into a deep satisfied sleep.

AQUINT
(2)

"I HAVE TO trust my instincts . . . to a point."

"And this isn't *past* that point?" The boy frowned.

"Cat, when Abraxis appointed me to this position he showed a certain amount of faith in me. Maybe you could—"

Cat cut him off. "I was afraid all this would go to your head, in the end. You really think you are an Internal Security Corps agent." The boy sounded incredulous.

Aquint was getting annoyed. "By the madness of the gods, lad, I *am* an Internal Security agent! Whether I want to be or not. Whether I wish the Felk would just bugger off back to where they came from or not. I've been given this job as sure as a horse gets a saddle put on it. And I might add that I am very constrained to do this job well . . . or suffer the consequences."

When Aquint had accepted this assignment from Lord Abraxis, the Felk mage had made a cut on Aquint's thumb and taken a drop of his blood. Abraxis had blotted it onto a piece of cloth, and put it into a red bag that he said remained on his person at all times.

Abraxis had claimed that with that blood sample he could administer disciplinary actions without needing to track Aquint down. That faraway threat was nagging and unsettling. Aquint didn't have any reason to doubt Abraxis's powers. The wizard had also said that similar samples had been taken from every student at that Academy in Felk, where magicians were trained, and from anyone in the empire who held a position of power.

Aquint wondered if that meant that Abraxis had a sample of General Weisel's blood.

"You told me about Abraxis," Cat said, sounding uncharacteristically sullen.

"Then what's the problem?" Aquint asked, trying not to let his irritation show.

They were in their apartment. Cat had been dutifully trying to locate the rebels' new retreat, to no avail. Maybe the boy was just frustrated, Aquint thought. Cat had at least learned that the group was being called by a specific name now. The rebels were the Broken Circle, so went the whispers on the street. A fitting name, thought Aquint, recalling the symbol of the circle with the vertical line through it.

"I just don't know about that pair you recruited," Cat said, shaking his head. "Something about those two . . ."

He was talking about Deo and Radstac. Aquint admitted he had acted somewhat impulsively in hiring the two on as Internal Security agents, but he had that privilege. Besides, like he'd told Cat earlier, he had to trust his instincts.

"What is it about them you don't like?" Aquint asked, seriously interested. The boy had a nose for trouble.

"Well, for one thing, I hope you don't believe that horseshit about them being ordered through the portals without traveling orders."

Aquint blinked. It was very unlike his young, somewhat prudish friend to use obscenities.

"Of course not," Aquint said.

"They're on the run from something."

"Like the war?"

"Maybe something more," Cat said.

"You have any ideas?" Aquint asked.

Cat shook his head.

"Then what're you . . ." Aquint started, and trailed off. Could it be that his young associate was jealous? Was that possible? He and Cat had had a partnership since before this war broke out. By now, they had covered a lot of territory together, literally and figuratively. Maybe the boy simply didn't like the idea of anybody else intruding on their association.

Aquint of course didn't voice any of these thoughts. It would only embarrass Cat.

"I wouldn't worry about our two new recruits, Cat," he said, adopting a jollier tone. "We'll keep an eye on them. If they give us any trouble, I can just have them arrested. They're under my direct authority, after all."

"That's good," Cat nodded.

"Besides, I'm only going to use them as bait anyway."

"All right." Cat suddenly shook himself and hopped nimbly to his feet from where he was sitting. "I better get back out there."

Without another word, he slipped out of the apartment, off to roam Callah's streets and alleys, looking for any hint of the rebels.

Aquint sighed. As if he didn't have enough to deal with,

now he had to be sensitive to Cat's feelings. Sometimes people and the strange complexities of their emotions could surprise you.

He shrugged and went to grab his coat and arm sling. Cat, whatever else he was, was also Aquint's friend, though their relationship was certainly an unconventional one. If he had to make allowances for the boy's unexpected moods, so be it.

Aquint did in fact have an idea of using Radstac and Deo as bait. He could circulate them through Callah's marketplaces and taverns, posing as people eager to join the Broken Circle's rebel underground. It might work. It was also possible that those rebels, if they got wind of it, might just come down on the two of them, suspecting a trap. But that would at least draw the rebels out.

It struck Aquint, however, that such a plan was a waste of potential talent. He had been favorably impressed by those two. The female, in particular, moved like a fighter of much experience. And they had both somehow finagled their way into being illegally transported to Callah. That took sharp wits and cunning.

Suddenly Aquint came up with another plan, a way to use those two new agents as something more than the meat you laid out in the meadow to entice your prey into range of your bow.

He smiled to himself and exited the apartment.

CALLAH'S NEW TAXES had been officially announced. From the grumbles Aquint overheard as he made his way, they were being received about as enthusiastically as he'd expected.

The panic that had erupted the day Callah's water

turned inexplicably into "blood" had died down. For that day, though, a great unease had come over the city's inhabitants, native and Felk alike. Some people called it a sign from the gods, though exactly *what* the sign meant varied from individual to individual.

Colonel Jesile had grudgingly set his mages onto the problem. They had determined, using the same divining magic that had uncovered the counterfeiting ring, that the water was perfectly safe to drink, despite its unwholesome appearance.

The water supplies had since been refreshed and guards put around the reservoirs, but during those first days it had taken some courage to swallow that thick, red water. Aquint had stuck mostly to wine.

The sights and sounds and ambience of Callah were still a great pleasure to him. This grand city held memories for him in almost every quarter. As a youth, younger even than Cat, he had spent his days running errands for his father. Aquint's father had been a man given to extremes of behavior. When he was happy, which was usually when he had money, he could make everyone around him deliriously happy as well. When he was angry, he was a great storm of rage, fearsome and dangerous.

Aquint had started in the freight-hauling business as just another strong back moving cargo on and off wagons. He wasn't as big as some of the other workers, but he never shirked, never missed a day of work for any reason. That fact impressed the owners of the business. They gave him a little more responsibility, and he proved himself able to handle it.

Actually, he demonstrated that he was quite intelligent, in a shrewd sort of way. With no formal tutelage, Aquint was good with numbers—especially when it came to ledgers and invoices. He had a knack, which his employers soon discovered to their delight, for hiding overages and shortages. These were discrepancies that wouldn't be appreciated by the governmental agencies that handled levies and special export fees.

It got Aquint out of the heavy lifting tasks and drew him ever deeper into the managerial ranks of the enterprise. Soon he was keeping the books for the whole company and also drawing better wages.

Unbeknownst to his employers, he was also paying himself a *second* equally healthy wage. In all honesty, Aquint judged that he deserved it. He was also in a position to route the monies invisibly to himself. He wasn't greedy in his embezzling, recognizing that such behavior led inevitably to disaster. He kept things fair, accumulated his brasses and bronzes, and bided his time.

Eventually, he had secured enough capital to go into business for himself. He had advantages that others new to such undertakings didn't. He understood the basic deceit of employees, even the most seemingly loyal, the smilingest, the most dependable of the bunch ... they could well be the ones shafting you worse than any of the others.

Aquint's personal business philosophy allowed for his workers to help themselves, here and there, now and then, to a little extra something for their troubles. Sometimes merchandise "fell off the wagon" and sometimes payroll was slightly inflated. But as long as none of it got too far out of hand, Aquint had always been willing to turn a blind eye.

He was also equally sincere about punishing those who abused that rare and special privilege.

He'd had a fine business, hauling freight and moving

smuggled goods on the side. Sometimes one line did better than the other, but on the whole he probably made as
much money doing legitimate business as he did in crimi-
nal ventures, though he was loath to admit it.

And then, one day, the Felk had decided they wanted to
rule the entire Isthmus, and they came and conquered
Callah just to get things started, and that was that for
Aquint's business, his personal life, and the sovereignty of
his city-state, which hadn't been compromised in many
tenwinters.

These people had all suffered the same fates, he thought
as he continued through the streets, eyeing merchants and
workers. Many still had the same livelihoods as before the
Felk had come, true, but whatever monies they'd saved up
had been confiscated and replaced by what had turned out
to be truly worthless pieces of colored paper. The *real*
money had gone into the Felk war chest.

Callah was conquered . . . and it felt conquered. Aquint
tried not to dwell on it, but it was almost impossible.

He turned in at one of the smaller marketplaces. He
sought out a particular stall. He knew the man's goods by
reputation, but not the man himself.

"You honestly dare to sell such an indecent implement?" Aquint asked.

"At the price I'm giving you, I will probably have to
starve myself for a quarter-lune," the dealer said. "Don't
you have eyes to recognize a bargain?"

Aquint held the instrument and fingered its strings, trying to appear knowledgeable. It certainly seemed serviceable. He and the dealer haggled awhile more. The price the
man was quoting really was quite high, but Aquint worked
him down a little, mostly for the sport of it.

Finally Aquint handed over a fistful of notes and carried

away his purchase. The dealer had never questioned how Aquint planned to play the thing with one arm in a sling.

Aquint crossed over several winding, disorganized streets into a shabbier district of Callah. Even these environs, however, were a pleasure to him. He had spent many happy times as a boy capering on these particular streets.

So many familiar faces were gone, sucked away by the war, but here and there he still saw people he recognized. He entered old lady Laina's hostel. She was among those people he knew.

Aquint climbed to the third floor. It had been somewhat whimsical to lodge his two new recruits in the room the Minstrel had occupied. But maybe it did have some purpose. It was nonsense, that old saw about the thief returning to the location of the crime. A thief treated his occupation professionally. Fools who committed crimes impulsively, or for reasons other than profit, however, *might* return.

Who knew? Maybe the Minstrel would return to this room someday.

Aquint knocked on the door. He had gotten the impression that his two new agents were something more than mere comrades to each other. He didn't want to walk in on them if they were frisking about on that bed in there.

While he waited for someone to answer his knock, Aquint acknowledged that the pair might have fled since he'd installed them here yesterday. He had recognized this risk from the start. They would find it difficult to get out of Callah though.

But the female, Radstac, answered the door. She was, in her way, a very striking woman, even with those scars on her face and her short, choppy hair. She was alluring in the way that snakes were, with their sleek shapes and gliding movements.

"Ah, Radstac." Aquint smiled. "You're finding the room comfortable?"

"I've slept in far worse places," she said. There was some trace of an accent there that Aquint couldn't quite place.

"And you, Deo," Aquint said, looking past her shoulder, "did you get a good night's sleep?"

He nodded. "I did."

"Fine. Now that the pleasantries are done, does anybody know what this is?" Aquint held up the instrument he had purchased at the market.

Deo shrugged. "Looks like a stringbox."

"And so it is," Aquint said. "Do either of you know how to play it?"

Radstac just gazed flatly, but Deo said, "I had a court tutor—uh, I've had some training."

"Then take this."

Aquint held it out, and Deo came forward and took the instrument into his arms. He examined it, flicked a few strings, turned the knob at one end, and nodded.

"Well," Aquint said, a bit impatiently, "let's hear a little something."

Deo took a seat, wedged the vox-mellifluous against his fit body, and rang out a ditty. He faltered a couple times but recovered quickly, picking out a fast tempo. He got more confident with it as Aquint watched.

Finally Aquint lifted a hand. "Enough. That's good. Do you know a lot of songs?"

"A fair number, I guess," Deo said, looking a little confused. "Why?"

Aquint ignored the question. "Can you sing?" he asked.

Deo frowned, then shook his head and sniffed a small laugh. "Actually, no. That they couldn't teach me, no matter how hard they tried. But if you want me to make noises like a wounded dog I can do that." He gave Aquint a self-deprecating smile.

The man had a certain charm to him, Aquint acknowledged. He turned to Radstac. "Can you?"

"Can I what?" she said.

"Can you *sing*?" Aquint asked sharply, though he didn't really imagine that this woman, so obviously built for battle, would have wasted her time learning to sing songs.

Radstac's eyes were almost free of color. They bore into Aquint a moment, then, quite suddenly and unexpectedly, she drew in a breath and sang out.

> *Moonlit, your face becomes another,*
> *A memory sweeter, now torn asunder.*

Aquint blinked. Deo, too, was visibly taken aback. Radstac's voice was surprisingly gentle. Into that brief verse she had poured a tenderness that reached Aquint's heart. It was a skilled voice, nicely modulated.

"That was . . . impressive," he finally said.

"Radstac," Deo said, "I had no idea—"

"You don't really want to know everything about me, do you?" she retorted. "How boring would that be?"

Aquint again noticed the connection between the two. Yes, these two were definitely lovers, whatever else they were to each other.

"Now," Aquint said, pleased with the unanticipated success of this, "you play something on the stringbox, and you sing along."

They consulted briefly with one another, settled on something they both knew, and launched into it. It was a somewhat solemn tune, sounding a lot like the traditional ballads Aquint had heard all his life. That was perfect.

He put his hands together, applauding.

"This is outstanding." He smiled.

They halted the song. They were both looking at him, perplexed, surely wondering what all this was about.

"This is how it's going to work," Aquint said. "You two are going to go around the city, playing and singing. Our Minstrel, the rebel, was probably spreading dissent the same way. I want you to concoct some anti-Felk songs. Just take some other song you already know and swap in some new words. I've written down some ideas for you. Here."

He handed over a couple pages of fragmentary lyrics that he had cobbled together in a café after leaving the apartment. He was no poet, but the words put across the point.

"I want these new songs to vilify the Felk," Aquint continued. "I want them full of protest and rebellion. The people of Callah have no love for their conquerors. But I want to draw out those Callahans that have gone to the extreme and thereby made life tougher for everybody else. I want them to rally around these songs."

Deo appeared to be considering the scheme from every angle. "And the garrison won't give us any trouble?" he asked.

Aquint barked a short laugh. "We're Internal Security. We don't have to worry about any of that. I could order Colonel Jesile himself arrested, if he was guilty of treason."

Deo and Radstac both looked impressed.

"Look, you two were smart enough to get yourselves away from the fighting," Aquint said. "Now I'm counting on you to go on being smart, and clever, and wily. You're going to be a pair of . . . of rebel bards! And, hopefully, you'll draw the Broken Circle to you. After all, who doesn't like a good song?"

Radstac asked, "Do you still want me to fake that limp? I've been practicing it." She demonstrated with a few lurching steps. It was convincing.

"And do you shtill want me to shpeak like thish?" Deo asked, imitating the speech patterns of an imbecile.

"Yes," Aquint said to him. "You're not the one singing. Sometimes a simpleton will have prowess in unexpected areas, like with a musical instrument. Radstac, keep up that limp. We don't want anyone thinking you're working for the Felk. Your ruses will allay suspicions. All I want you to worry about right now is putting together a repertoire of persuasive revolutionary songs. Got it?"

"Yes," they both said.

"Good. Get to work." Aquint exited the room. It was a somewhat unconventional plan but Abraxis had, after all, given him full leeway. All the mage wanted were results, and Aquint was going to have to produce some, soon.

The plan was also very likely going to encourage rebellious thought in Callahans that might not otherwise have considered the notion of rising up against their Felk oppressors. But Aquint decided not to worry right now about such fine points.

DARDAS

(2)

"COME IN, MY dear." He smiled, gesturing her into the pavilion.

Raven looked comfortable in Vadya's body as she came inside, and Vadya's body looked good in the officer's uniform. She pulled closed the tent flap. Outside was Weisel's special guard, always on duty.

"Care for a drink?" he asked, solicitously.

"Thank you, General Weisel," Raven said.

Dardas chuckled soundlessly to himself. This was, of course, still Weisel's body. But, for the moment at least, it was Dardas who once more had complete control of it. He had discovered that when Weisel slept, he, Dardas, could assume command of the body. It had taken some practice, but now he had full power. Even now, pouring a drink for Raven and one for himself, he was aware of Weisel's slumbering consciousness.

Weisel had control while he was awake in the daytime.

But the night, it seemed, belonged to Dardas. He was pleased with this new development.

Today, the army had moved in around Trael, surrounding it. The city had no defenses that could begin to stand against the Felk forces. The elite guerrilla squad had been Far Moved inside the city. Their goal was to take Trael's ruling council hostage and force a surrender. By morning, Trael would probably do just that.

It was a rather unassertive way to fight a war, Dardas thought. But it was what Weisel wanted.

"I appreciate you reporting here so late," Dardas said.

"I am happy to be of service, General . . . anytime." A small sultry smile just curled her lips as she sipped her drink.

Dardas eyed her. He had learned that this Vadya, whose body this was, was a courtesan back in Felk. She certainly was a beautiful woman. Yet, Dardas still had the instinctive impression that this was Raven, the plump girl from the Academy who had put herself bravely in harm's way to save Weisel from assassination.

"How do you like being an officer?" he asked.

"I am still absorbing that fact, frankly."

Dardas laughed. "You'll get used to it. Remember, as chief of Military Security you'll have a kind of ecumenical authority."

They had reviewed the details of the new position last evening, while Weisel was still awake. Military Security was going to be for this army what Abraxis's Internal Security Corps was for the rest of the empire.

"You understand that I don't wish to create a climate of fear among my troops," Dardas said.

"Of course, General. We discussed that at length," Raven said.

"But I do need to know if anyone in the ranks is discontent or disloyal enough to try to kill me."

"In general, you're very popular with the troops, according to my own observations," she said.

"The regular troops, yes." Dardas nodded. "But what about among the wizards?"

"Actually, from what I've seen and heard traveling with that company of magicians, they respect you. You don't treat them with the same severe discipline that we all knew at the Academy."

Dardas had learned from Raven just what conditions were like at that magic training school, where students had to swear constant allegiance to Lord Matokin and were encouraged to denounce each other for any disloyalties. Whatever else such treatment did, it had the effect of turning out paranoid, anxious magicians.

"I have respect for those wizards," Dardas half-lied. He still wasn't entirely comfortable having so many of those magic-users under his command. "I respect my regular troops, too. They've proven themselves in battle. We've come so far in so short an amount of time."

"History will remember this time," Raven said, smiling again. "And remember you."

"Bah!" Dardas threw up his hand. "Being remembered by history isn't so great a prize, I can tell you."

Raven frowned, though on her new face it was more of a coy pout. "How can you say that, General? You'll be remembered for hundredwinters and more as the greatest, most successful war commander since . . . since . . ."

"Since Dardas the Invincible?" he asked, wryly.

Raven blinked. "Well, yes."

"Child, one day I may tell you a story, and we will sit and laugh till tears run from our eyes," Dardas said. He was looking deep into her eyes now. Really, she was quite a gorgeous creature.

Weisel, it seemed, had no interest in the women that Dardas had once regularly sent his aides to fetch. Lord Weisel was single-minded in his determination to master the art of warfare. He didn't distract himself with the pleasures and frivolities of the flesh.

Then again, Weisel's consciousness was currently fast asleep.

Dardas moved toward Raven, setting down his drink. He raised a hand and stroked her soft blond hair. She turned slightly away.

"Do I make you uncomfortable?" He frowned.

"I . . . General . . . should we?" Raven asked in a small voice that was nonetheless a sensual purr.

"Life is for living, Raven," Dardas said. "You have a new life. Don't waste it."

His fingers brushed her cheek now. She turned back to him, moved against him, and their mouths met, hungrily. He moved her toward the bed. It was nighttime, *his* time, and he would do what he liked with it.

WOMEN CONVINCED OF their own beauty were, so went the rule, almost always the worst lovers. They entered into a tryst with the belief that the other party must feel supremely privileged to be allowed this intimacy with such grace and loveliness. Men of especially good looks, Dardas mused, were probably the same way.

But Vadya, while undeniably beautiful, was also a professional when it came to the use of her body. And Raven, who was in control of that body, made up for her inexperience with an eagerness and an exhilaration that were charming. She made for quite a delightful lover, actually.

Afterward, Dardas dismissed her, though not in a callous manner. He simply told her she needed her rest, and sent her off. He, too, had to sleep. Weisel's body wouldn't be getting much rest if Dardas appropriated it every night while Weisel's consciousness slept.

Still feeling the luscious afterglow of lovemaking, Dardas fell asleep in his bed.

He awoke when Weisel did, in the early morning. The Felk noble started out the day with a few limbering exercises, then called for his current aide. He was still following Dardas's routine of rotating his junior officers through the post.

I think it's time you settled on a permanent aide, Dardas ventured.

Why do you say that? asked Weisel.

The whole idea was to familiarize oneself with one's junior officers. Since the start of the war they've all served in the post at least once.

So, I should pick the best? Weisel asked.

I recommend Fergon, said Dardas.

He struck you as the best of the lot?

The most loyal, anyway. I understand you knew his father.

Fergon? Weisel considered a moment. *Of course! Fergon's father is a nobleman in Felk. We used to meet at the social clubs. A fine man.*

Dardas said, *Then perhaps his son would serve well as your permanent aide.*

I wonder if you have any other motive for recommending him.

General Weisel, as you've pointed out, we are in this to-

*gether. It's in my interest to provide you with the best coun-
sel I can.*

Weisel pondered it. *Very well. I'll make the arrangements later.*

Weisel's current aide stood in attentive silence during
the wordless debate. At last, Weisel called for the morning
reports. There had been no word from the elite unit that
had infiltrated Trael, despite the fact that they had a Far
Speak wizard with them.

"That is disquieting," Weisel muttered, throwing aside
the scroll. "Assemble the senior staff," he ordered his aide.

Weisel stood brooding. He didn't venture outside the
pavilion, not even to take a breath of fresh air. Dardas
knew that Weisel had been quite shaken up by that assassination attempt. Dardas, too, had been alarmed, but he
was more familiar with danger, with the immediacy of
death. The constant circle of bodyguards had been
Weisel's idea. Frankly, it was getting on Dardas's nerves.

*I thought the guerrillas would have captured Trael's
ruling council by now,* Weisel said, with some anxiety.

The mission may have failed, Dardas said.

What? Weisel's heart beat hard in his chest.

*Come now, General Weisel. It was a good plan, for
what it was. You were concerned with taking Trael without
taking any undue risks. We hatched this scheme along
those lines. A minimal risk of manpower with a maximum
result, if the operation was successful. It is possible it was
not.*

Weisel wrung his hands. *You're very matter-of-fact
about it.*

Dardas felt a surge of disgust. *This is war! Every plan
isn't going to go off without a hitch. There will be mistakes.
You may lose troops due to errors beyond your control. Or*

you may lose them for blunders you and you alone are re-sponsible for. But that's the point. You are responsible!

Weisel drew a deep breath. *You're telling me I should act like a general.*

If Dardas still had control of Weisel's facial muscles, he would have sneered. He said, *Yes.* Act *like one.*

Because, Dardas added in the privacy of his own thoughts, no matter how hard you try you will never be the military leader you so ardently wish to be. You simply do not have the gift.

But Weisel heard none of this last.

The senior staff came into the pavilion. There was much debate, but it was based more on opinion and intuition than any verifiable facts. All anybody could tell Weisel was that no communications had come from inside the city, via that Far Speak wizard who was with the unit.

"Perhaps the mage has been killed," suggested one of the officers.

"If the mission was successful," said another, "we would know by now. Trael would have surrendered."

"Maybe taking their rulers hostage wasn't enough of an incentive for the people to give up their city," said a third officer.

"Enough!" Weisel said sharply. The senior staff fell silent.

It's time for action, General Weisel, Dardas advised.

Weisel evidently agreed. He said, "Trael is ours to take. We certainly have the manpower and resources. We will invade the city. I want operations to commence within the watch. We shall lead off with a barrage from our archers, then send in the infantry. We will hit them from four sides, simultaneously. I want to know the best points of incursion. Resistance will not be tolerated. Every citizen of conscription age will be rounded up. All monies will be confiscated from the city. I expect the fall of Trael to occur before the sun sets. See that it happens!"

It was a forceful performance. Even Dardas was impressed. The senior officers scurried away to see to the invasion.

That is how you command an army, General Weisel. You may make the wrong decisions, but it's important that you do make them.

Even if they are wrong? asked Weisel.

Even so. Your troops want decisiveness. In my day, I had the absolute loyalty of every man and woman under my command.

No need to gloat, General Dardas.

Dardas was amused.

Trael's falling was predetermined. The city-state simply couldn't muster anything to stave off the invasion. This was to be the fifth city to fall to the Felk, Dardas noted. Where was the opposition? Where were those of this Isthmus who wanted to preserve their independence against the onslaught of total Felk rule? It was discouraging.

Do you think we'll lose many troops here? Weisel asked.

Some, probably. If Trael was going to surrender of its own volition they'd have done it already. That means they intend to fight.

Weisel sighed. He called again for his aide.

"Tell the senior staff I want to know what happened to our guerrilla unit. If possible, I want whoever in that city is responsible for their fate brought to me."

"Yes, General." The aide saluted and hurried out.

You're taking it too personally, Dardas observed.

How should I take it? Weisel asked darkly.

Like a general. So the mission failed. That doesn't mean you failed.

But you said I was responsible, said Weisel.

You are. You take on the burden of making the final decisions. But you succeed when you accept that hardship, regardless of the relative success or failure of an individual operation.

Weisel put a hand to his head. Even with his newfound confidence, this was evidently quite a lot for him to handle.

For a fleeting moment, Dardas almost pitied the man. He was after all not built for this sort of thing. He was a noble who was playacting the role of a general, something far beyond his abilities. He had agreed, at Lord Matokin's request, to serve as the host body for Dardas. Weisel could really only hope to achieve a reflected glory, a surrogate fame. Certainly *he* didn't have the talent to lead an army, no matter what bits and pieces of command stature and military strategy he'd managed to garner from Dardas during their cohabitation of this body.

But Dardas's pity quickly evaporated. Weisel was vain and weak. If Dardas had faced him on the field of battle, with both men commanding their own armies, Weisel wouldn't have survived. He was a fraud.

And Dardas was committed to helping him maintain that facade.

"I wish I wasn't so tired," Weisel said out loud, stifling a yawn.

Perhaps you didn't sleep well, Dardas suggested while he secretly laughed.

The senior staff reported back individually. Weisel, at Dardas's prompting, approved the incursion routes. Really, they could hit Trael any way they liked and the invasion couldn't fail.

All the while Weisel remained inside the pavilion, while his guards kept the tent encircled. It was, in Dardas's opinion, a very unexciting way to conduct an invasion, not the sort of thing Dardas would have done in his time as a Northland war commander. It occurred to him quite abruptly that he very much missed those days, his original life, when war was a way of daily life and his victories soon became uncountable.

War was, in fact, his natural element.

Soon, the invasion was under way. Reports came back to the pavilion that the archer companies had launched their salvos, picking off a number of Trael's defenders. Then the infantry was moving in, storming the city's streets. Weisel received fresh reports throughout.

As expected, there were light casualties for the Felk. They were very light actually, the sort of numbers Dardas or any other seasoned officer wouldn't have been concerned about for longer than a moment.

Weisel, however, was agitated. This was, after all, the first invasion he was ostensibly commanding. Dardas had decidedly been the prime mover behind the assaults on Callah, Windal, U'delph, and Sook.

I'm losing brave men and women, Weisel said mournfully.

Soldiers fight and soldiers die, said Dardas. *Bravery figures into it less often than you imagine.*

That's rather heartless, General Dardas.

It was yet another example of why this man was so unfit for the role he had assumed. Dardas said, *It is a bloodthirsty business. There's no escaping it. But did you imagine the Isthmus could be captured for Lord Matokin by peaceful means?*

Weisel, examining the latest field map, said, *No. Or if I ever did, it was a foolish mistake, right?*

Right.

Trael did fall before sunset, as Weisel had commanded. The Felk cut down the city's defenders until the few that remained surrendered. The members of the ruling council were ordered brought before General Weisel, but the order could not be obeyed. Those council members, four in all, had drunk poison, apparently just before the invasion commenced.

The bodies of the Felk guerrilla unit were discovered. The report Weisel received was sketchy. No witnesses to or perpetrators of their murders had yet been found.

"They died bravely," Weisel pronounced to his senior staff, on receiving the news.

Careful, General Weisel, Dardas cautioned. *You don't know that. They might simply have bungled the mission.*

Later came the business of occupying the city. As mammoth an undertaking as this was, this army had performed the feat before. The various specialty units moved in to do their jobs.

Eventually, when Weisel's direct input was no longer needed for the business at hand, he summoned Fergon and explained that he was to be the general's permanent aide.

"I'm very honored, sir!" said the young man with freckles.

Weisel nodded. "I will be allowing my officers to make a few personal communications with Felk via Far Speak. Do you think you might be contacting your father?"

"Most definitely, General. I can't wait to tell him the news!"

Weisel smiled. "Then be so good as to tell him, from me, that when the red grass turns green, the dogs will come home." He gave the junior officer a wink. "Your father will know what it means."

Fergon looked delighted as Weisel dismissed him.

Dardas, too, was pleased. It had gone as he had hoped. The last time Fergon had served as aide, back when Dardas still had exclusive control of this body, the freckly fool had used that same cryptic phrase from his father on him, expecting Dardas to know the proper secret response. Dardas, of course, hadn't. He had worried that Fergon might become suspicious about "Weisel's" behavior. Now, Weisel himself had smoothed everything over.

You know, General Weisel, you are right. Things are better when we cooperate.

BRYCK
(2)

THE CONSISTENCY HAD taken some while to refine. At first it had caked, then flaked; then it was too runny, sliding off Bryck's face at the least suggestion of body heat. With a little help from other members of the Broken Circle it was correct now.

It was still uncomfortable, provoking a maddening urge to itch, but as a disguise it was impeccable. Also simple. It appealed to Bryck. There was a certain bold panache about it. The Felk garrison was still searching for him, and he was now walking about in the daylight, unmolested, undetected.

Tyber gave him the sly nod, and Bryck concentrated, expecting and feeling the pressure around his skull and the mild wave of feverish chill. Tyber was juggling the three leather balls with a brash dexterity. He was competent enough keeping the trio of objects skipping through the air, but what held their audience was his accompanying patter, a mixture of ribald witticisms and fast awful puns.

Tyber's hands were gloved. Of a sudden one of the three balls erupted into flame, followed just as inexplicably by the second, then the third. The audience, a crowd of about twenty by now, sucked in a collective breath. It was a good trick. Good because as impressive as it was, everyone watching it no doubt thought it *was* a trick. Sleight of hand. Fakery.

They would think it magical, not magic. That of course was how Bryck wanted it.

Tyber kept the flaming leather balls, which had been treated so to resist melting, moving through their patterns. It made the juggling that much more impressive, as the spheres left behind trails of fire.

"My own balls have felt like this sometimes after a particularly harsh fuck!" Tyber cackled, and the crowd laughed along with him.

Bryck, in his time around various theatrical troupes that had put up his works, had occasionally met types like Tyber. Big, brazen, loud. More exhibitionist than actor. Such a variety of performer actually suited some of the roles in Bryck's plays, characters whose function it was to draw the audience's attention, to entertain in a broad way while subplots with more substance played out around them. Bryck had often found these "buffoon" parts useful.

Sometimes, though, in his better theatricals, when he was actually making an effort at what he was producing, sometimes those large and audacious characters themselves had a deeper purpose. Sometimes they turned out to be the heroes.

Tyber's face, too, was painted. One half yellow, the other blue, which were traditional carnival colors. It had the effect, at least, of covering over his many unsightly blemishes. Physical appearance, however, often meant nothing to personalities like Tyber's. They got by on the bluff and bluster of their deportment. Tyber's carnal tastes ran toward males, the younger the better, and Bryck had no doubt that the plump man with the bad teeth still drew more than his share of willing partners, presuming there were still enough young males in Callah for him to hunt among.

The Broken Circle's water-dyeing campaign had been successful, at least in that they did manage to transform all of Callah's public water supplies. The disruption during that first day, when everyone found the cisterns full of what appeared to be blood, had been exceptional. Commerce and all other activities ground to a standstill. The garrison hastily investigated. A fear overcame people, dread that the gods were intervening in a way that they were always rumored to do, but of which nobody ever had any proof.

The Felk remedied the situation with admirable speed, even as Bryck's fellows in the Broken Circle circulated the word that the water was safe for any native Callahan to drink.

In the end, Bryck conceded, the disorder it had caused probably didn't amount to much in the way of effectiveness. It hadn't tangibly loosened the Felk's grip on Callah. But perhaps it gave some among the occupiers real pause. If the water could be tampered with, next time it might be poisoned. Or maybe these rebels would do something else equally widespread but more destructive. Perhaps Governor Jesile himself had been disturbed by the possibilities the operation had raised.

As with everything else Bryck had done to undermine the Felk since arriving in Callah nearly two lunes ago, he had no reliable means to gauge the impact of these activities. He simply had to hope that these deceptions and confusions were adding up to something.

That required faith. Absent that, he always had his hatred. For the Felk. For what they had done to U'delph, to his people, to his family.

"This is impossible, you say?" Tyber grinned, exposing those awful teeth. "How did these balls light with fire? It can't be done. We were all watching. We saw nothing!"

The crowd was mesmerized, watching the flaming trajectories of the juggling balls.

"But obviously it *is* possible! You see it happening! Watch close . . . and you'll see even more."

With that he altered the pattern. Two of the balls he kept moving in a circle, one chasing the other, around and around. The third, he tossed straight up so that it came down in exactly the same place, bisecting the circle; when it did, he caught it and tossed it straight back up, all the while keeping the other two going in their circular course.

Juggling was strictly a matter of timing. It looked beyond human capabilities, which made it a fun spectacle to watch, but Tyber had explained that you just had to keep it moving. Once you learned the pattern, it became relatively easy.

This particular pattern had purpose. The crowd, gathered here at this street corner, continued to watch. As they did, Bryck detected the first sharp inhalations. He saw recognition light the eyes.

"Nothing is impossible!" Tyber cried.

Bryck gave him the signal, and he let the leather balls drop one by one. It had rained earlier, and the ground was still damp. The juggling balls extinguished themselves with tiny hisses.

The audience cheered and applauded. Tyber took a great exaggerated bow, grinning happily, soaking up the adoration as if it was his unquestionable due. Bryck took the jauntily feathered cap from his head and circulated through the crowd. The faces were astonished, and those who hadn't noticed the Broken Circle's sigil traced out in flame were being eagerly told what they'd missed by those who had seen it.

A few people tried to put money into Bryck's cap.

"Save it," he said softly. "Taxes are bad enough. The Broken Circle works only to rid Callah of the Felk."

He came back around to where Tyber was retrieving his gear.

"Time to go?" the older man asked.

"Yes, it is," Bryck said. A policing squad of Felk was moving toward the corner, though their manner wasn't outright hostile. Still, Bryck thought he saw an anxious tension in those faces.

But the assembly was already dispersing on its own. Bryck and Tyber, in their half and half painted faces, couldn't just blend in with the crowd. The whole idea of this disguise, of course, was to hide in plain view. Bryck turned deliberately toward the patrol. His clothes were as festive as the feathers he'd added to his cap.

With the same studied flourish he'd seen Tyber use, Bryck gave the Felk soldiers a grand bow. They ignored him and passed on by.

Tyber tapped his shoulder. "We were going?"

"Yes. We are." But Bryck felt a small hard smile move his lips. None of those Felk had recognized him, had given him any attention beyond the flamboyancy of his appearance. This had been a fine test of the disguise's effectiveness. Now that he had freedom of movement throughout Callah's streets once more, he would have to make use of it.

HE HADN'T PERFORMED magic since the Lacfoddalmendowl festival, when he'd seared those sigils all over the city. This episode didn't strain him so severely as had that previous occasion, which had bedridden him with fever for two days.

Bryck was suddenly hungry, and they stopped at a tavern. When the proprietor told him how much a meal would cost, however, Tyber burst out, "That's outrageous! For that price my friend should get a sweet damsel kneeling under the table and sucking his stump while he eats."

The proprietor shrugged blandly. He looked tired, without the spirit to argue. The tavern, Bryck noted, was nearly empty.

Tyber was evidently annoyed by the lack of response to his vulgarity. He made a final stab. "Make it your daughter, and we'll think about it."

Bryck hauled the man out of there.

"It's the taxes," Bryck said as they moved along down the street. Their colorful faces drew passing attention. "They're going to inflate prices. Goods and services are going to become rather dear in Callah, I'm afraid."

"And how will people pay for them?"

"With their money. With that scrip the Felk issued everyone when they confiscated all the hard currency. Only, they're being heavily taxed now as well, which is draining off the access paper currency already in circulation."

"Paper you're responsible for creating," Tyber said quietly.

Bryck gave a shallow nod. He accepted that responsibility. He had known his counterfeiting scheme, which had flooded Callah with false notes, would have consequences. That was the aim. But it was going to be a burden for more than just the Felk. These Callahans would suffer. But they were already suffering, Bryck noted. The sovereignty of their state was gone. They were a conquered people. If they wanted to change that condition, they had to risk what little comforts they had left. They had to be willing to sacrifice it all—

"Not that any of us in the group blames you," Tyber

went on, interrupting Bryck's thoughts. "Frankly we applaud you. In my time I've been involved in quite a few, oh, less than legitimate undertakings. Some extremely profitable. Those were also, however, the same ones that were the riskiest. What my fellow Callahans have to eventually understand is that risk and reward go hand in hand."

Bryck blinked. Tyber had just voiced Bryck's very thoughts. It was like the routine of a true carnival huckster, mental games meant to awe an audience.

"I was just thinking that," Bryck murmured.

"Were you? Well; just shows that the minds of the magnificent all flow in one direction. Still, I must defend my fellow Callahans to some extent. They've been beaten, and had their sons and daughters conscripted into the same mighty army that conquered them. There is a loss of identity for us. Who are we now? Not the Callahans we were, living securely, prosperously, within the inviolated borders of our state. Now . . . we are some other people."

This did not move Bryck. In fact, it had the effect of chilling his feelings of sympathy. True, these Callahans had fallen under the unwanted rule of the Felk. But they were still *alive*. Their city hadn't been burned, destroyed. Not like U'delph.

"It's time for your people to decide who they are, then," Bryck said. "Permanent subjects of the Felk . . . or men and women with the determination to overthrow that rule."

They continued on in silence.

At another intersection they paused briefly to again perform. Bryck had procured a tinny whistle and now blew a repetitive tune on it, something catchy and fast. It drew enough interest for Tyber to once more launch into his act.

As Tyber performed, Bryck realized that many of the seemingly spontaneous comments he was making were ones he'd used earlier. Well, one didn't have an endless supply of wit. Bryck himself acknowledged that in his days of carousing at pubs and being the reliable wag at every gathering, he would often tell the same jokes and stories incessantly. They were always amusing, though, and few people were graceless enough to point out that they had heard this or that one before.

They enacted the flaming sigil again, and again there was scattered response throughout the crowd. The Broken Circle's members had been spreading the word. Bryck himself had been responsible for those twenty-eight sigils burned onto doors and walls during Lacfoddalmendowl. The Broken Circle was a rebel underground intent on over-throwing the Felk here in Callah.

It was a fiction. It had begun, just as all those theatricals he'd penned, as an idea in his mind, a fancy. But now it was being played out in reality, not on a stage. Even the players—Tyber and Quentis and Ondak and Gelshiri and the rest—weren't aware they were enacting predesigned roles.

In the past Bryck's contribution to the culture of the Isthmus was his talent to amuse audiences. His plays were exported from U'delph and performed by troupes throughout the Isthmus. They were a worthwhile offering, so he had always thought, though he had never quite taken himself seri-ously as a playwright, despite his success. Cheering people, making them laugh—that was valuable in a very basic way.

But this, here, was more important. His fight against the Felk in Callah. It was possible he would be remembered for it . . . but he would be remembered as the Minstrel, not as Bryck of U'delph. That suited him perfectly. He no longer was Bryck of U'delph, after all. There was no U'delph. And the man he had been was equally lost.

When the performance was done and Tyber was taking

his grandiose bows, Bryck again circulated with his cap, just for show. As before he refused to accept any money when it was offered. Twice, however, members of the crowd seized his hand and asked, in sharp urgent whispers, how they could join the Broken Circle.

He had no ready answer and felt the fool for not anticipating this situation. Of *course* more of these people would want to join up with the movement. Some would be impulsive about it, others more serious. The Broken Circle would inevitably have to accept new recruits. How Bryck could make use of those extra numbers was something he had to give serious thought to.

He and Tyber dispersed hurriedly this time. Bryck was satisfied that he could travel Callah's streets in this costume, behind this face paint, and go unrecognized by the Felk patrols. But the day was waning. It was time to get back to the Circle's base before curfew.

As they were striding along, Bryck chanced to glance up and to his left. By now he had a good sense of Callah's layout. He knew what he would see, peeking out between intervening buildings, before he looked. It was the Registry. The seat of the Felk occupational government.

Bryck's steps slowed, stopped. The great white structure was some distance off. Its tall wide walls caught the dwindling rays of sunlight.

"What's wrong?" Tyber asked, glancing back.

Bryck shook his head. Nothing was wrong. The Broken Circle was becoming real. It *was* real, in fact. If more recruits enlisted, its reality would only increase. And Bryck had just had a thought as to how to use those potential new members.

He gave Tyber a pat on the arm, and the two men headed onward.

•   •   •

HE EXPLAINED HIS ambition to the rest of the Broken Circle that evening. It was still something of a marvel to him how they all deferred to him, hung on his words. He was truly the leader here. The Minstrel.

It didn't matter that he *wasn't* a minstrel, that he didn't even have a vox-mellifluous anymore. He, too, was a player in this piece.

They liked his plan. They agreed that new members to the Circle would help realize it. Later, they discussed means of recruitment, how to weed out the useless from the worthwhile.

These rooms didn't afford a great deal of privacy for their more than a dozen occupants, but Bryck still had the most comfortable berth, partitioned off from the others by a decorative screen that was painted with birds in flight above a lush grassy field. He had often spent some while at bedtime staring at those images, waiting for his mind to slow and slacken so that he could sleep.

Tonight as he lay on his bunk, drained by the minor magical efforts of the day, there came a soft rapping on the screen. He had washed away the paint from his face.

"Who is it?" he murmured.

Quentis peeked her head around the edge. Her amber eyes blinked. "I'm not waking you?"

He shook his head, making to sit up, though he was quite comfortable where he was. Beyond the screen the room was dim, lit only by the light of a single candle. The noise of the workshops on the other side of the wall had gone still watches ago.

"Don't get up," she said. Her voice was quiet, edged huskily. She wore clothes he had seen her wear before, though now the front of her garment was loosened. Not enough to be flagrant; but too much flesh exposed to entirely ignore.

She was Bryck's age, and her face showed those winters. But it was still a comely face. And she had been the one who had saved him when he was first on the run from killing that Felk soldier.

"What do you want, Quentis?" he heard himself asking, his own words faint, uncertain.

She stepped around the screen but did not approach his bunk. She was regarding him intently. There was something sad in her eyes, he thought. And perhaps something needy.

"I want to know if there is anything *you* want," she finally said.

Bryck felt his heart beating hard, the blood rushing. It was an almost adolescent anxiety, an uneasiness and excitement that was unmistakably sexual.

So much had died within him. So much, he presumed, that would never live again. Nonetheless he felt a stirring, but it was so odd, so out of place, so alien. He had not known a woman since the last time he and his wife, Aaysue, had made love. It wasn't something he thought about.

He wasn't sure he could even imagine himself being with another woman . . .

"There's nothing I want," he said at last. Frail words. Helpless words.

But Quentis accepted them, and she nodded her acknowledgment and turned and went, even as Bryck caught the shine sparkling her amber eyes. When he felt the wetness on his cheeks, it took him a moment to realize that he, too, had shed tears.

RAVEN
(3)

"THE INFORMANTS FROM the many various individual units in your battalion will submit reports to you," Raven explained, "and you will pass on any relevant information to me."

"Informants?" the officer asked. "You mean spies, right?"

"I mean," Raven said, "that in every unit of this great army there is one soldier who is, above all the others, most loyal to General Weisel. One who would gladly lay down his or her life to protect him. I have sought out these individuals one by one, and am still doing so."

"Sounds like quite a task," the officer said.

"It is. But when it is complete there will be a vast network in place, one that I can use to monitor any serious dissent in the ranks."

The officer mulled it over, then nodded. "Essentially, you're getting the soldiers to spy on themselves."

Raven was mildly annoyed. She didn't much like that word, *spy*. Then she shrugged. "If you want to see it that way."

"I think it's a marvelous idea, to be honest. When you first told me you were the new Military Security chief, I had uneasy thoughts about rank-and-file soldiers being suddenly arrested for muttering a single complaint about army life. I imagined agents scuttling about everywhere, keeping everyone on edge. But that's not what you have in mind, is it?"

Raven shook her blond-haired head. "No. Specifically, General Weisel doesn't want to foster that sort of environment for his troops. But keeping an eye out for any genuinely mutinous attitudes is only prudent. Particularly after that assassination attempt."

The officer nodded, gravely now. "Yes. And that poor girl who I hear died in his place. I can't remember her name. She must have been quite brave."

"I would say she was," Raven said.

She dismissed the officer and met with a few more. That network was indeed falling into place. It would be as effective as the structure that had assured the loyalty of the students at the Academy, without putting anyone through the undue stresses of such harsh discipline. She was pleased with the progress she was making in her new important position. She hoped Weisel would be pleased as well.

The general, of course, was busy with the occupation of Trael. Or at least select members of his senior staff were, those who had handled the occupations of Callah, Windal, and Sook. A governor would have to be appointed for Trael, and a garrison assigned to the captured city, though maybe these things had already been seen to.

Raven hadn't met with the general since that surprising and glorious occasion the night before the invasion, when she and Weisel had . . . had . . . she still blushed a little to think about it, despite her experiences with this new body. Certainly she had always found the general attractive. He was handsome enough and had also shown her the sort of attention she couldn't seem to get from Matokin.

When he had seduced her, it was still a shock, though a pleasant one. He was a masterful lover. Even Vadya had remarked on it. He was as decisive and forceful in bed as he was on a battlefield.

She was still using the name Raven. No one in the field here would recognize the face of Lady Vadya, courtesan of Felk. Raven, after all, was a common enough name. Her recent promotion from liaison officer to head of Military Security had been very well timed, she noted. As far as anybody knew, Raven was a plump homely girl who had died saving the general's life, and this new Raven, so elegant and beautiful, was someone else entirely.

It had been explained to her that resurrection magic was a secret Matokin wanted kept. She wasn't to go about telling anyone that she was sharing this living vessel with another person's consciousness.

The bulk of the army was presently encamped just south of Trael, while fresh conscripts from that city were processed and given a fast course in soldiering.

Now was a good time to report to Matokin and Abraxis, back at Felk. Raven sought out the Far Speak mage Berkant. Like Weisel, he knew the full truth of her identity. She had contacted the wizard previously, whenever she needed to make private communications with Lord Matokin.

He ushered her into his tent. "Sit and wait," he said. "I'll arrange it."

Raven sat. She watched Berkant take up a piece of fabric, squeezing it, concentrating. A moment later, all expression washed from his face.

"Raven, what do you have to report?" Berkant's lips moved, and it was his voice that spoke, but the tone was different. Raven knew that Matokin himself was originating these words and passing them on, via the Far Speak magic.

"Lord Matokin," she said, "there have been some interesting developments . . ."

She went on to quickly detail her promotion and what the goals of the newly formed Military Security were. She demurely omitted the tryst she and Weisel had shared. It was something, she knew, that she should report but somehow she couldn't bring herself to do so. The event had been too private. Too special.

Matokin, speaking through Berkant, cut her off. "*Military* Security?" he barked. "What is he playing at? I never authorized any such agency. Does he think he can have an independent bureau, separate and autonomous from Internal Security, just because he wants it? The audacity!"

Raven was taken aback. She swallowed. "I, uh, didn't consider the implications—"

"Oh, I don't blame you, Raven. In fact, you did exactly the proper thing by accepting the position. Weisel imagines he can run the army like it's his own sovereign state? Let him try. Now we have you as the chief of his security corps. And you belong to us." Berkant, face still slack, let out an eerie laugh.

"Yes, Lord," Raven said, obediently.

"Carry on then, Raven. Lord Abraxis will find all this most amusing."

Berkant's hand opened, and the piece of fabric dropped

out of it. The mage's eyes cleared. Raven reflexively thanked him for his time and exited the tent.

She was deep in thought. Matokin had said, *You belong to us.* Raven discovered, somewhat to her surprise, that she didn't like the way that sounded. Maybe it was just too bluntly stated. Maybe it hit too close to home. No one wanted to be owned by another person, even if that person was the most powerful man in the empire. Even if Matokin was her father. She wanted to be a part of him, yes, but . . .

It was complicated.

I think you're simply feeling the first real stirrings of independence, Raven.

Raven acknowledged the quiet, steady voice of wisdom and experience within her.

Perhaps I am, Raven conceded.

It's all a part of growing up, Vadya added.

Raven considered that a moment. She was nearly two tenwinters old. She had thought of herself as an adult for some while now. It was possible she had been mistaken.

It's . . . difficult.

Growing up always is, Vadya said.

THOUGH VADYA HAD willingly ceded physical control of her body to Raven, that body still had its physical memories intact. It moved with a natural grace that Raven didn't need to consciously exert.

Even so, she had learned more than a thing or two about gait, deportment, and general appearance. Despite the relative hardships of being out here in the field, Raven was managing to maintain her appearance. She already had this borrowed beauty, to be sure, but with the application of a little consistent hygiene she could make herself look truly stunning.

Cleanliness had never meant much to her before. Her mother had once hoped she would flower into a beauty. But it hadn't happened. The body she had been born into simply wasn't made that way. Now, however, she had surpassed any expectations of loveliness her mother could have ever entertained about her daughter.

Perhaps someday she would return to the village of her birth, to show her mother what she had become, to show all those horrid people there who had been so cruel to her . . .

No. There was no going back. No one would recognize her. No one would believe that she was the same Raven, not even her mother.

In point of fact, she *wasn't* the same Raven. Not at all. She was a blond beauty who held a key position of power in the new Felk Empire. She was caught in an intrigue between the two most powerful players in that empire, Matokin and Weisel.

One man was her father. The other was her lover. Could things get more interesting than that?

She felt an odd pang of guilt and realized that it was over her reporting to Matokin about Weisel's activities. But that was what she was supposed to do. Matokin had assigned her the task, and she was compelled, because of her loyalty, to obey.

But what of her loyalty to Weisel? Surely the general would not be pleased if he discovered that she was spying for Matokin. Then again, maybe he already knew. Both those men were very complex, very shrewd. It might be that Raven was merely a piece in a game being played between them.

She shook her head. Even if that were true, she had sufficient will and determination to make her own destiny.

Raven returned to her tent. She had a private one now, as an officer. She received a few more visits from various company commanders and explained to them how the informant system would work. All the officers were at least willing to go along with it. Some were enthusiastic about it.

She did the same thing with commanding mages from the magic-using units. She noticed that these wizards, though still reflexively wary, were more relaxed than they were when she had first joined this army. That had to be due to Weisel's ecumenical policies that didn't exclude these magicians from any of the benefits enjoyed by the regular troops.

Night was falling. Raven had been prepared to report to General Weisel all day regarding the headway she was making in getting Military Security set up and operating. But she had received no summons.

Instead, she settled down to write up a report. The general could look it over at his leisure.

You're disappointed that you haven't heard from him? Vadya asked.

Raven frowned. *What makes you ask that?*

Just a feeling . . .

I thought we weren't supposed to be able to feel each other's feelings, not unless they're very strong. That gave Raven sudden pause. Was she actually so concerned that General Weisel hadn't summoned her? Was it because she had developed passionate feelings for him after that one unexpected night?

That was childish. She shook her head sharply.

Vadya, I have a great respect for you, but kindly do not fill my head with such nonsense.

As you wish.

Raven finished writing her report, then summoned a

messenger to take it to General Weisel. The messenger was a young man, nearly still a boy, with soft eyes and hair the same color as hers. Raven noticed his eyes lingering on her.

Her lips twisted slightly. "Do you find me attractive, soldier?"

He gaped, not knowing quite what to do. In the end, it was probably his youthful urges that decided for him. "Y-yes. You're very beautiful." He gulped, uncertain if he'd gone too far.

"I suppose you'd like to feel this body, to taste these lips, wouldn't you?" She hovered a step closer to him, watching his face flush.

He was very uncomfortable, but also very obviously aroused. "Oh y-yes. I would . . ."

Raven's features suddenly hardened, and she spat, "Well, fraternization between officers and enlisted personnel is forbidden. After you deliver that to the general, go put yourself on report." She spun away, hearing the befuddled messenger exit the tent.

She smiled to herself.

Did you enjoy that? asked Vadya.

I did. What of it?

Now, don't be terse. There's no reason you shouldn't enjoy the power that comes with this body. Believe me, I know what it can do.

Raven sat down in her chair, suddenly tired. Today had been a long and active day.

Tell me something, Vadya, Raven said.

Do you want to know about the many men I've slept with? Vadya asked.

No, Raven said firmly. *I would very much like to know*

why you agreed to be my host. She waited. Vadya had avoided this question once already.

I think you're ready to hear it now, she finally said.

Raven listened eagerly.

Vadya said, *I recognized that you were in a position of significant power. You are balanced between the emperor and the general. You can affect both men, without exposing yourself to the direct rigors of visible power. There is truly nothing worse than being the one in command, Raven. You have to answer for your mistakes, and the more power you have, the bigger those mistakes will be. But, if you're only the whispering advisor, the unofficial consultant . . .*

Raven blinked. "Then you can make your moves without anyone being aware you are the source," she said aloud, in wonder.

Not even the person you are manipulating, Vadya added with some satisfaction.

It was a shocking revelation. *Then your loyalty to Matokin is—* Raven started.

Is very real, Vadya finished, firmly. *I believe in Matokin's aim to unite the Isthmus. But he will make mistakes. All men do. I've seen it happen, over and over. They bumble and fumble.*

But you know better? Raven asked, dubiously.

I know differently. I am a special sort of woman, Raven, and therefore you are as well. I know the carnal secrets of many men. I know how they think. I know how they compete with each other, even when cooperation would serve everyone better. I know their jealousies, their stupidities. I know that Matokin distrusts Weisel and that Weisel has misgivings about Matokin. I know this because it must *be. They are both men.*

Raven felt dazed. What Vadya said was of course true.

Raven knew firsthand. Raven was spying on Weisel for Lord Matokin, after all; and General Weisel had spoken what amounted to outright treason against the emperor.

How do you propose to use my . . . our . . . position to affect anything? Raven asked.

There was another silent pause. Then Vadya said, *If either man becomes a threat to the overall success of the empire, we will see that he dies. It's very simple.*

Raven closed her eyes. She pushed away Vadya's voice, pushed herself toward a quiet corner of their shared mind. She wanted only to retreat, to give herself time to absorb this.

At that moment, however, a messenger, different from the one before, asked for entry into her tent and told her that General Weisel wished to see her. It was by now rather late.

Raven straightened up her uniform and made for the general's well-guarded pavilion. She was passed through.

"General," she said, saluting, still in something of a daze.

Weisel gave her a smile. But there was something cold and morose about it. "Raven, you've lived all your life on this Isthmus, right?"

She blinked. "Where else would I live, sir?" She realized belatedly that her reply was a bit impertinent. The Northern and Southern Continents were, after all, well inhabited. But those cultures were so different from those of the Isthmus.

Weisel grunted. He was drinking something and looked like he had been drinking it awhile.

"What is it about the people of this Isthmus?" he wondered aloud.

"Sir?"

He fixed her with his eyes. "I mean, why don't they fight back? Why is it that all this army has ever met has been the most pitiful, most pathetic resistance in the history of warfare!"

He didn't wait for an answer. He ranted on like that for some time, asking rhetorical questions. He actually seemed upset about the lack of organized resistance his military had met. But that, Raven thought, made no sense.

You see? Vadya said as Raven patiently and silently listened to the general, knowing that afterward he would take her to his bed. *They look to make trouble for themselves when there is no trouble. We will have to watch this general.*

Yes, Raven conceded. *We will.*

RADSTAC

(3)

THE WORDS BECAME awkward in her mouth, too many, piling up, their corners bumping, so she revised them then and there. She sang the altered bridge, knowing as she heard herself croon the simpler improvised phrases that she had improved Aquint's words, while keeping their spirit.

That spirit was, of course, one of treason against the Felk, the masters of Callah.

Some of the tavern's patrons had vacated the premises immediately on hearing the nature of the songs she and Deo were performing. But the others had remained, huddling instinctively closer to the corner where they played, their eyes big, tongues anxiously licking lips as if to taste the taboo words.

Radstac thought the songs silly. Or at least trite. Deo was playing the serviceable melodies on that cumbersome vox-mellifluous, an Isthmus instrument, obviously a larger cousin to the more graceful musical implements of Southsoil.

He was certainly passable on the instrument. More than that actually. As with most things, so it seemed, Deo had a flair, a grinning gusto that was hopelessly charming, even while he was inhabiting this persona of an idiot. He kept up a dazed, mildly giddy expression, obviously happy with the music he was producing and the vocals Radstac was providing.

Radstac, for her part, had had no trouble maintaining the fiction of a maimed leg. Their pretenses excused them both from combat, in the eyes of anyone who observed them. Aquint would be pleased the ruses were working.

Aquint was plainly a dubious character. Internal Security agent he might be, yes . . . but he was no Felk fanatic. Radstac didn't sense in him *any* special loyalties, except to himself and possibly to his young companion, Cat. She had first thought the two were lovers, then had revised her opinion. They seemed more associates in crime.

She was uncertain what their ultimate game was, though most certainly they were playing one, probably against the Felk occupying Callah. And yet their efforts to capture the Broken Circle rebels did seem genuine, at least on the surface. But Aquint also seemed intent on maintaining his position, which would become moot when the rebels were in custody and the threat was through.

So Radstac had to be concerned how she herself fit into this game. Deo, too. Internal Security agent, so far, was a far better alternative to being arrested as the attempted assassin and accomplice of General Weisel.

She sang the song to its insipidly "inspiring" end. Vocal lessons had been a part of her upbringing. Such training was customary on the vastly more civilized Southern

Continent and specifically in the Republic of Dilloqi, her
home state. Hynñsy was the city of her birth, and there she
had learned about art and philosophy with the same vigor
with which she was taught practical matters. It was not the
Southsoil way to separate such elements of life.

The patrons of the tavern applauded Radstac's finely
modulated singing as well as the crowd-baiting revolutionary doggerel that she sang. Deo nodded a cheerful wit-
less bow at their audience.

She and Deo had followed Aquint's advice and, for the
most, had purloined their melodies from already existing
songs, replacing the lyrics with those Aquint had concocted. The songs were all very much alike, condemning
the Felk and celebrating native Callahan culture above all
else.

There had been several times when Radstac had to
furtively pinch her arm to keep herself from laughing in
the middle of what she was singing.

The elderly man and wife who owned the tavern had at
first been shocked and upset by the songs, more so when a
segment of their patrons immediately evacuated. But those
that had remained were apparently eating and especially
drinking enough to keep the proprietors content.

They had, however, quietly pulled to the tavern's shut-
ters and thrown the door's bolt.

The patrons clustered even closer now, scraping chairs
toward Radstac and Deo's corner. They murmured in an
excited hush. Radstac understood their anxious caution. If
the Felk patrols raided this place and learned the sort of
songs that were being played here, the consequences
would be dire. Only, there wouldn't be consequences. Not
for her and Deo. They were, after all, verifiable agents of
the Internal Security Corps, a bureau that evidently had

power over just about every other branch of the Felk Empire.

Besides, they had informed Colonel Jesile's office that they would be operating at this tavern until curfew today. They expected no interference. They had actually said this to the same pinch-faced officer who had made their arrival in Callah so difficult only a few days ago. Radstac had felt a mild satisfaction from that, though punching the man in the nose or leaving him a scar or two would have been even more gratifying.

Radstac paused to take a swallow from the jug of water sitting on the table next to her. She didn't drink wine. She did not drink spirits. If there was a faster way to turn a functional being into a driveling dimwit, she didn't know what it was.

Callah's tainted water had all been replaced, probably at some cost and inconvenience. But what the tactic implied was more disturbing than what the Broken Circle had actually accomplished; it insinuated that the rebels could wreak a much greater havoc if they so chose.

"Are you . . ." a woman with matted grey hair whispered, edging closer than the rest, her one good eye brightly alight. "Are you . . . friends of . . . of . . ."

Radstac finished her drink, set it down, waited. She herself would never live so long as to become a doddering husk like this creature. Radstac would not outlive her usefulness.

"Of . . . of . . . of . . ." The gibbering lips were pale and fine.

"Of *whom*?" Radstac barely managed not to growl it.

The good eye blinked solemnly. "Of the Minstrel." The crone clamped tight those thin lips after she'd said it, anxiety quivering her bony shoulders.

Behind her, the others huddling near were waiting for the answer.

The Minstrel was a folk legend, then, Radstac thought, shooting Deo a fast glance. He gave her a scarcely perceptible nod.

She studied the faces, noting that the entire room had gone quiet. At last she said, "Maybe we are friends of the Minstrel. But that doesn't mean we know him."

The patrons tried to absorb that. They had the same faces and demeanors one could find in any drinking establishment. Vaguely vacuous. Adult countenances reduced to the simplistic expressions of children. Emotions, too, were diminished in their complexity. It was why fights could start so easily when alcohol was liberally present. Anger was a hot and simple emotion, and it came readily to the surface when all the civilized checks were removed.

"Do you know anything about the uprising in Windal, then?" another asked, a small shrunken man who appeared to be accompanying the crone.

Windal. The name was familiar. Vaguely so. Some Isthmus city, presumably already conquered by the Felk. Rumors of an uprising there? It sounded like more of the inciting gossip from the Minstrel. In fact, hadn't she read of this very rumor in the report Aquint had first shown her?

"I don't know anything about that," Radstac said.

There was a small collective groan of disappointment.

Radstac hid an appreciative smile. She understood in that moment just how effectively and subtly the one called the Minstrel had spread dissent. These people were receiving no news whatsoever from beyond the borders of this city. So it was that a rousing story about an uprising in Windal couldn't be refuted. The Minstrel had no doubt plucked it entirely from his imagination, giving these downtrodden Callahans the very news they most wanted to hear—that someone somewhere was successfully resisting the Felk invaders.

"I *do* know," Radstac added, "that Governor Jesile and his whole garrison haven't been able to find the Minstrel. Or stop the Broken Circle from doing whatever they please."

They grinned at her for that. They slapped tables and applauded and ordered fresh drinks and congratulated each other for feats they themselves had nothing to do with. The tavern's owners looked pleased, too.

Deo was fiddling with the stringbox, snapping random chords. No one in their audience had questioned that someone so obviously mentally flawed could be so deft on the instrument. Deo made it look natural.

"Ish it time to play shome more?" he asked her in a giggly voice, his mouth slack and wet.

Radstac nodded. Deo started winding and plucking. It was a faster tempo, and she leapt on it, skimming the words off the tops of the musical undulations. Another drearily predictable tirade against Callah's interlopers. Aquint's hope was that these songs would attract members of the Broken Circle. After these tunes had circulated awhile, as they most certainly would, perhaps the rebels might approach her and Deo. Then they could make their arrests.

As Radstac sang, she was at the same time detached from her performance, thereby able to observe the audience closely. She watched them picking up the chorus, learning it, memorizing it, singing along with it. Yes, these silly songs would indeed circulate. But wouldn't they, in the course of being repeated and passed around, hopefully to be heard eventually by someone in the Broken Circle, wouldn't such songs inevitably incite certain thoughts and attitudes in these Callahans? Wouldn't they generate rebellious inclinations? Wouldn't they, despite Aquint's plan, actually do more damage to the Felk . . . and lend more aid to the rebels?

It wasn't her problem. She could go along with this charade of being an Internal Security agent for as long as necessary. At some point a means of escaping this city would present itself, and she and Deo would take it.

So she continued singing. And when the room turned very suddenly and very disconcertingly blue, she kept the song moving, digging her fingers into her legs and trying to control her pounding heartbeat. The urge, of course, was to get up and flee. Simply run. Actually *out*run. For what was coming for her was terrible. A great terrible beast that hunted her footsteps.

Deo sensed that something was wrong, but he was the only one. He cut short the song and turned to her.

How blue he was . . .

Radstac reached for the water jug, but her hand was wavering beyond her control. She returned it to her lap. The audience was applauding and cheering once more. The matted-haired old woman was the nearest one.

She would have to do. Radstac caught her good eye, motioned her even closer, and said in a tight, aching, very earnest voice, "I shall need some *mansìd* leaves. As quickly as possible."

THE POPULAR NARCOTIC in Callah, it seemed, were *phato* blossoms. These were pink and delicate, and they were smoked in a pipe and produced effects not entirely unlike those one could get from alcohol. Radstac had no interest in the drug. It was *mansìd* or nothing. And for a while it appeared she was going to have to settle for nothing.

She had chewed the final tiny rationed fragment of her last leaf two days ago. She had made efforts to replenish her supply, but all the likely places she visited had nothing to offer. Whatever drug dens there were in Callah had evidently been cleaned out during the Felk invasion. Legitimate narcotic trade had continued in the marketplaces awhile, but, she had learned, the supplies had dried up. There were no traders on the roads anymore. Nothing was getting into the city.

But addicts, Radstac knew, weathered all calamities. No matter what the circumstances, they could always find what they absolutely required.

Which meant that someone in Callah, some other user, had what she needed.

So various members of their audience, caught up in the spirit of revolutionary camaraderie, volunteered to help find her what she required. They scattered half-drunkenly out of the tavern, whistling and humming and muttering those songs she'd been singing.

Meanwhile, Radstac's world was blue.

She handled it. It was a very unsettling experience, but she had faced physical terrors on battlefields that would shrink most men and women just to hear of them. She remained in her chair and maintained a calm veneer, even as the lack of clarity engulfing everything around her deepened, so that the sense of things broke apart at a more profound level with nearly every passing moment.

She had certainly experienced this before. She came north habitually, traveling from the Southsoil to seek out the Isthmus's petty little wars, so to sell her sword to one side or the other. It never mattered who she fought for. She had survived many of those trifling skirmishes between Isthmus states.

What mattered was the procurement of her leaves. Fresh and potent. In quality, far beyond the dried specimens the trade caravans brought back home from the Isthmus. And while she was here, pursuing her mercenary livelihood, she enjoyed the awesome penetrating clarity that came from chewing *mansìd*.

But she did not remain here on this Isthmus year-round. Eventually she would return home, taking with her as much of her drug as would last before losing its potency. And, just as inevitably, those supplies would be gone, and she would undergo this same withdrawal. And she would handle it. And survive it. And live her life in Dilloqi without the daily stimulus of *mansìd*. Until it was time to once more go north.

Radstac was aware, in an increasingly abstract way, that Deo was by her side trying to comfort her, while maintaining his imbecilic pretense. She was finding herself less and less able to understand words. She still recognized them individually, but whenever someone spoke to her, she could barely manage to put them into a coherent order.

Even so, she sat and waited and did not behave in the way pathetic wretches who couldn't handle their addictions behaved.

When her leaf was finally procured and delivered to the tavern, she couldn't hold her hands still enough to get it to her mouth to bite off a piece. Deo held it for her. Deo, by now, was a shifting, erratic, almost ethereal presence who she could not quite identify any longer.

She bit away a quarter of the leaf and knew by the ache that sang through her teeth that it was of the proper potency. After that it was just a matter of waiting for the blue to recede and the clarity to assert itself. It happened quickly enough.

Radstac, with much composure, thanked her deliverer and counted out the necessary Felk scrip from her pocket to cover it. Next to her Deo was pale. He tried to lead her out of the tavern. But there was still half a watch before they needed to think about curfew, so Radstac sang another passel of songs and Deo accompanied on the vox-mellifluous. Once again their audience became enthralled and enthused. The songs took hold.

CRIERS WERE CALLING the first notice. Curfew in a quarter of a watch. She and Deo were on the streets, heading to their lodgings. Evening had brought an unpleasant snap to the air. A damp wind was blowing in irregular irritating gusts.

Between them was silence. Strained on Deo's part, uncomfortable, embarrassed, concerned. Radstac merely said nothing. From her deliverer she had learned where she could likely obtain more leaves.

The streets were emptying rapidly and orderly. These Callahans knew the rules of occupation, and they obeyed them. If not for the Broken Circle, this would surely be the model of a conquered city.

On a deserted stretch, just a short distance from their destination, Deo, taut and uneasy, suddenly erupted in a tense whisper, "When we find the rebels, I'm going to join them."

Radstac looked at him sidelong and wordlessly. They didn't speak again until they were indoors, up on the third level, in their shabby room.

She hadn't taken too large a bite from her leaf. The

mansìd had stabilized her, but the clarity wasn't so intense as to be distracting.

"Why?" she finally asked.

Deo propped the stringbox in a corner. "Because it could make a difference against the Felk."

"Like assassinating General Weisel might have?"

"It *might* have. It *would* have." His fists bunched at his sides.

"I know," she said. Her tone was flat, but she had meant it to sound softer. Instead of trying again, she crossed to him, put hands to his shoulders. At first his lips were unresponsive; then they did respond.

Later, after curfew was official, there came a knock on their door. Later still, they learned of the audacious feat the Broken Circle enacted that night.

PRAULTH

(3)

THERE WAS NO waiting this time, no lapse while she brooded over her place in the greater scheme of this war and this turning point in history. She heard the solid decisive foot-falls, turned, and there was Cultat's broad frame—broader still in armor—blocking the chamber's doorway.

"Thinker Praulth," he rumbled, red-and-gold-maned head in silhouette, "I wished to make our farewell a private one. Thank you for meeting me."

Praulth bowed; it was almost an involuntary action. It was an artifice on the premier's part. The man had a great control of language, of etiquette. By taking the humbler stance of thanking *her,* he was contrarily reaffirming his already more powerful position. A manipulator, this one. Surely a prerequisite for someone holding such a high po-litical office.

It never occurred to Praulth that Cultat might be sin-cerely thankful.

"We have very little time," Cultat said, striding inside, swinging shut the door behind him, "but enough, I think, to say what we will say."

"And what are we to say, Premier?" Praulth asked, her voice slightly edged. It was important she assert herself here.

The chamber was a small lounge in the same building where the Alliance conference had been held. It was expensively if indifferently furnished, and it smelled of disuse. Praulth was standing.

Cultat halted, rested his hand atop the sword at his belt; then began a slow circuit of the room, around the backs of the lush dusty furniture. A lone lamp burned. There was a painting on one wall of a nude woman sprawling on a leafy riverbank. Praulth hadn't noticed it until the premier passed before it.

"I would imagine," Cultat finally said, his tone now thoughtful, "that you will say your position in all these matters of war is unappreciated. Or *under*appreciated." The crags of his face shadowed his severe blue eyes.

Praulth gazed back at him, willing herself not to blink.

Cultat continued, "And I will say in reply that you are appreciated. Of course you are. When all this is done, I'll bestow some tawdry bauble on you and shower you with all the gaudy honors the Noble State of Petgrad has to offer, which won't mean much to you. As to what you'll say to that, I can't quite guess, since this grows increasingly speculative and abstract." He halted again. A wry smile moved under his beard. "But I'll wager I'm fairly accurate so far, yes?"

Praulth felt a tightness in her throat. She swallowed deliberately. "Without me you'd have nothing." It came hoarse and pained, but also audible and steady.

"We wouldn't have the Battle of Torran Flats."

"You wouldn't have my predictions about the Felk movements."

"True. We've had others—Petgradites, some who've studied wars with perhaps the same fervor you have, but not with the same total understanding. They've made their guesses, pored over the same maps you were receiving through Master Honnis in Febretree. They could not forecast with your success."

"No one can," Praulth said with a dire firmness.

"Again, true." Cultat didn't qualify the statement.

Her heart filled with pride, beating giddily. This was recognition. This was acknowledgment.

"But," Cultat added, "what do my words matter? Your place is in the chronicles that will make this war a history to be remembered above all others."

The Petgrad premier was still at the fringe of the chamber. Now he came toward the center, where Praulth stood beneath the lamp. His face, aged and robust all at once, came into glaring view. He came to a halt, looking down on her. Something had diluted the ruthlessness of his eyes. Perhaps fatigue. Perhaps wariness of the battle to come.

"Praulth," he said quite softly, "you *are* appreciated. You are necessary. You are crucial. I have sensed your discontent, and I respect it. How can I address it?"

Now she did blink. Repeatedly. She was taken aback. She turned her head. She hadn't expected this man—*this* man, this powerful man—to express such a keen awareness of her inner turmoils. How had he known? He was canny. That was how he'd sensed her thoughts. He needed her to be at her cooperative best before he took the assembling forces of the Alliance off to engage Dardas/Weisel on the Pegwithe Plains south of the city of Trael, which had of course fallen to the Felk.

His interest in her was self-serving. Yet his manner, the cast of his rugged features, made it seem sincere. He wanted from her what he wanted. It was nearly irrelevant that it was for a greater good, a *much* greater good. The defeat of the Felk. He was still manipulating her.

"I've been manipulated before, Premier," she said.

He wasn't fazed. He heaved a small weary chuckle. "Manipulated? Well, so have I, young Thinker. By my family, by the Noble Ministry, by the people of this state. Not once. Many times. It comes with the rank and the responsibility. Manipulation is a guiding force, *if* you're aware of it. And if you keep ahead of it. Can you keep ahead, Praulth?"

She thought of Xink. She thought of Honnis. She thought also of this premier. What exactly did she want from him anyway? What acknowledgment could he make that would satisfy her?

Praulth knew Cultat was departing this evening, a night ride with the Petgrad contingent. They would start making their way to the rendezvous site. The delegates who'd come to Petgrad had all returned or sent word to their home states and cities and villages for their forces to make for the gathering as well. There was no sure way to know precisely what numbers would finally assemble. Praulth of course would be kept scrupulously informed.

Using the intelligence provided by the Petgradite Far Speak scouts, she would oversee the first clash between the Alliance and the Felk. And if it went correctly, it would mean the end of this war.

Praulth lifted her chin. She met those blue eyes squarely.

"I want the rank of general," she said.

No flicker in the eyes. Nothing whatever to read on that astute intelligent face. What she was asking for could be considered a trifle or an outrageous demand. What, after all, did a title denote? But there was a sacredness about military conventions. They were almost fanatical, almost religious.

"Thinker Praulth" might not be remembered. But "General Praulth" stood a better chance, particularly since she intended to write this war's most definitive accounting.

Beneath a segmented breastplate Premier Cultat's hardy chest rose as he drew a deep breath. "I will see that the proper documents receive my approval before I leave," he said. Then he stepped past her, giving her his back as he strode from the chamber.

SHE WAS BREATHLESS and restless. Her and Xink's rooms were only a short distance away, but she turned in a random direction, following a wide street beneath the clouded night sky. It was cooler than when she'd arrived in Petgrad. It was coming into the heart of autumn, the season of fading, of dwindling. But this was *her* time of renewal. So it very much seemed.

Praulth hadn't dreamt of glories, not during her childhood in Dral Blidst. Her ambitions had involved only a deepening of her education, and those had led her directly to the University. Febretree was her refuge, a staunch fortress of learning, where intellect was celebrated above all else, where she could achieve and succeed and surpass. Where the very inclinations that had made her life so uncomfortable among her timber trade family here made her a fourth-phase student of first ranking, one with a very promising future.

She would have been content. She would have kept to her course and climbed from Thinker to Attaché. She would have striven, and one day she would have taken her rightful place as head of the University's historical war studies.

If Master Honnis hadn't chosen her to study the Felk war, if Xink had never appeared in her life, if Cultat hadn't brought her here to Petgrad . . .

How different her life would have been, how normal, how predictable. And what a waste if she had never achieved this new, more exciting identity.

General Praulth, chief strategist of the Alliance. It was a worthy title. Now she had to make certain that the Alliance defeated the Felk. History remembered the victors.

She had examined the recent reports of the conquest of Trael. The Felk had initially surrounded the city, like water in a rising river encircling a stone. But there was a delay before the actual invasion commenced. It was a curiosity. Cultat's scouts, however, attested to the lag, and Praulth trusted them for their accuracy.

She had puzzled over the anomaly. It vexed her. She could deduce no military advantage in the postponement, not unless General Weisel meant to provoke a surrender.

But it *wasn't* Weisel, she reminded herself unnecessarily. It was Dardas. And Dardas wouldn't have wasted time in this manner, wouldn't have allowed the people of Trael the courtesy of deliberating their surrender. Sook had successfully surrendered to the Felk, but only because they had done so preemptively, before the great enemy horde was at their borders.

Something else must have been afoot at Trael, Praulth had concluded. Some other military operation . . . perhaps some smaller action. And Dardas/Weisel had been awaiting the results before committing his forces to overrunning the city.

It barely made sense. At least, as far as it fit with Dardas's historical tactics. And there, of course, was the thought that was most disturbing. Perhaps it wasn't Dardas any longer. Maybe Cultat's godsdamned nephew *had* succeeded in assassinating Weisel, and thereby had killed off the brilliant war commander who was living a resurrected life within that body.

What that would mean, most catastrophically, was that Praulth's ingenious plan to reenact the Battle of Torran Flats would prove useless. A new Felk war leader wouldn't recognize the battle pattern. Wouldn't try to recreate one of Dardas's greatest Northland victories. Wouldn't fall into the trap that Praulth had devised, whereby the Alliance forces would move suddenly and decisively and hack the Felk army in two, which would almost certainly be a crippling blow.

Praulth had said nothing of this to Premier Cultat or anyone else, not even Xink. It meant, of course, that she was committing this newly formed Alliance to a strategy that might fail utterly. And if this Alliance was defeated, there would be no other force that could rise up against the Felk advance. This was the last desperate chance, before the Felk conquered their way southward, all the way to Febretree and Dral Blidst.

Then the Felk would possess all of the Isthmus.

She wouldn't allow it. Whatever her personal goals and her ambitions for her place in history, she had no desire to live under an invader's rule.

She had turned several corners, onto various streets, without giving her direction much thought. She paused now, looking over her surroundings, looking upward. The district's towers were still there, stark and looming and just a little bit sinister in the cloud-muted moonlight and the glow of the huge city.

But this particular street wasn't familiar. Around her were the monuments of municipal buildings, but at this late watch there was no activity within or among them. A wind sounded through the great gully of the street, whistling eerily. She had come to think of Petgrad as a place of constant bustle, but this patch of it at least was quite inert at the moment.

Praulth glanced all about. She saw no one.

Petgrad had changed over the past quarter-lune or so. She was peripherally aware of the disruptions and burdens the rash influx of refugees had caused. People were fleeing ahead of the Felk, streaming south. Petgrad, no doubt, looked like an obvious sanctuary, the greatest strongest city of the southern half of the Isthmus. Surely the Felk wouldn't dare go against it.

It was foolish thinking, but Praulth understood it. She also understood that Petgrad's food supplies weren't inexhaustible. Nor was its housing. Something on the order of thousands of war fugitives had crossed into the city in a disastrously short time. Native Petgradites were raising irate protests.

But that wasn't Praulth's concern. She was no desperate stray evading the war. She was *in* that war. Granted, she wasn't riding off with Cultat and the Petgrad contingent of the Alliance; she would never walk a battlefield or be put in physical harm's way. But her contribution was invaluable, and her sacrifice was noble. After all, she had foregone a promising academic career—

Praulth heard a ruckus, above the whistling of the night wind. The large buildings in this district weren't jammed together side by side. They were separated by alleyways, and along these refuse had accumulated, probably over a long time. More recent deposits of trash were evident, including slops and offal from whatever kitchens serviced these institutions.

She had halted nearby the mouth of one of these alleys. The commotion was coming from there. Sounds of somebody rooting among the rubbish. It was dark down there, and the noises abruptly set her heart speeding. Memories of being caught out late in Dral Blidst's woods, hurrying homeward, hearing unidentifiable animal sounds in the trees around her, scavengers tearing at wild meat, no doubt scenting her as well.

Praulth backed away. There was still no one else within sight. She looked skyward, trying to orient herself. She couldn't have wandered too far. She could get back to her rooms quickly enough. Surely she was no farther than a few streets away. Xink would be there waiting for her, and quite suddenly she wanted very much to see him.

But the ruckus from the dark alleyway increased, something heavy now being tumbled over on its side, and at last a voice, savage and unintelligible and enraged, rose in the darkness. It scarcely sounded human, and it put a terrible deep chill into Praulth that the night alone could not have managed. She felt eyes watching her from that alley.

Then she heard footfalls. Coming up that alleyway. And more of those furious gibbering cries.

Praulth turned and started to run; and before she'd made her first fleeing step, she knew that the thing in the alley *was* human, and that made it all the more frightening. She tried to draw breath to shout, but fear froze everything she needed to make the noise.

The creature from the alley smelled of the foul slops it had been scavenging. It overtook her and knocked her to the ground from behind and laid a terrible weight on her.

She heard and felt the fabric of her clothing being rent.

•   •   •

DARDAS THE CONQUEROR. Dardas the Fox. Dardas the Invincible. There was one other moniker that history had awarded the Northland war master. What was it?

Dardas the *Butcher.* Yes, that was right.

He had earned every one of those titles. Likely he had been known by many more, names whispered fearfully, conjuring up images of implacable bloodshed, a relentless army sweeping the cold bleak reaches of the Northern Continent . . . and Dardas commanding its every crushing move.

How many had been slain in his campaigns, in total? How many deaths was that one man responsible for? The number could never be counted. It could never be guessed. One might as readily number the drops of water necessary to fill a lake.

And that number was only growing. U'delph had been a slaughter. Surely other such atrocities awaited.

"Beauty?"

Dardas. Dardas. Undying Dardas. There, that was yet another name for him. But none would ever know him by it. Weisel would take the credit for Dardas's deeds in this modern age.

"What's happened?"

In Dardas's original life two hundred and fifty years ago, he had faced quite a few adversaries. He was hardly the only war commander the contentious Northern Continent had produced. He had contemporaries, some quite skilled. Some of those warlords raised armies and did battle and held off Dardas's advances . . . for a time. But none of those foes were remembered. They had all been pulverized by the legend that the Butcher had left indelibly behind.

"By the madness of the gods, Praulth, *what's happened to you?*"

To be remembered she had to defeat Dardas, even if he was only in the guise of General Weisel. Besides, when she wrote her history of this war, she could reveal the truth of things, fantastic though it was.

Xink was holding her, fussing over her torn clothes, making a useless nuisance of himself. Just draw me a bath, she told him. But he acted as if he hadn't heard.

Praulth was tired. She was cold. She hurt, here and there. She hurt within. But she had made it back to these rooms. When it had all finished, she had picked herself up from the street and come here.

Perhaps there was yet one more name for Dardas, she thought. Dardas the Rapist. For what was his invasion but the unwanted penetration of the Isthmus by the Felk army?

Just heat some water and fill the tub. I will wash myself. I will scrub myself. I will scour away every last thing that has been done to me, and it will not deter me, will not daunt me, will not stand between me and my victory over my rightful adversary.

But Xink, sobbing now, still didn't hear her.

AQUINT
(3)

THE SHOCK WAS so great that his first reaction was to laugh. He put his hands on his sides, put back his head, and guffawed, loud and long. It was just so . . . so . . . so *audacious!* By the gods, the nerve it must have taken.

"I think the joke's lost on me," Cat finally said, with his usual disapproval.

They were outside the Registry, looking up at the north face of the building.

"The cheek!" Aquint managed, bringing his laughter under control. "The grit, the fortitude. What is the matter with you, lad? Can't you appreciate the magnitude of this stunt?"

"You might want to appreciate it a little less loudly," the boy said, his eyes flickering around at the other people.

Naturally, the sight had gathered a crowd. There was a lot of pointing and excited muttered comments. It was causing quite a stir.

Soldiers from the garrison were keeping everybody

back, but dispersing the crowd wouldn't do much good. They would only reassemble a little farther away. Besides, the giant sigil could be seen from many streets away.

That obviously had been the whole idea behind it.

Aquint shook his head, wiping tears of laughter from his eyes.

"I'm stunned," he said.

"Then maybe you should try to act it," Cat said. "Laughter is a way of dealing with shock. You might give it a try sometime."

"I don't feel like laughing," the boy said.

Aquint sighed. "When do you? Lad, the younger you are when you sample the joys and merriments of life, the better your memories of your youth will be."

Cat gave him a flat look. "Will that include all the times I've almost starved in the streets? Or been beaten? Or nearly been stabbed to death because someone wanted what I had?"

Aquint shrugged. Sometimes, there was just no talking to the boy.

"Well, never mind," Aquint said, adopting a business-like tone. "What do you make of it?"

"Of what?" Cat asked, probably just to be difficult.

"What do you think, boy? That bold and enormous display there on the outer wall of the Registry. The giant circle with the slash through it, rendered in black paint. What do you make of it?"

Cat considered a moment, then said, blandly, "I'll bet the Broken Circle is responsible for it."

For a moment, Aquint was almost tempted to cuff the boy. Instead, he chuckled. "All right, Cat. Fun's over. Now, let's get to work. Come along."

It was early morning. The two of them had received an

urgent summons from Governor Jesile. Now Aquint understood what it was all about.

Evidently, sometime during the night, somebody had scaled the north outside wall of the Registry and painted the Broken Circle's emblem there on the white stone. Probably there had been more than one person involved in the stunt. What was truly remarkable was that it had been accomplished almost literally under the noses of the garrison, without raising the alarm.

And *that,* Aquint judged, took real daring. Whatever else, it was an admirable feat.

He and Cat went around to one of the Registry's other entrances. They made their way to Jesile's office.

Aquint expected to find the Felk governor ranting and furious. He was prepared to let Jesile vent his frustrations by barking orders and demanding that the Circle be brought in, *right now.*

Instead, Colonel Jesile was at his desk, immersed in paperwork, his hard face showing no special emotion. He glanced up when Aquint and Cat were admitted.

He didn't offer them seats, didn't say anything for a long, curiously blank moment. Then he said, conversationally, "I've been contemplating the particular placement."

Aquint blinked. "How's that, Governor?"

"They chose the north wall," Jesile said, as if pointing out something obvious.

"So they did," said Aquint.

"You don't find that significant?"

"More significant than the fact that the perpetrator or perpetrators managed the deed at all?" Aquint didn't see what the colonel was getting at.

Jesile drummed his fingers among the opened scrolls on his desk. "You're not a Felk native."

It wasn't a question but Aquint answered anyway, "No, I am not." Then he added, with just a slight edge to his voice, "I'm a Callahan by birth." It was information Jesile surely already knew.

"If you were of Felk," the governor said, "you'd understand why those rebel bleeders painted that offense on the *north* wall."

Suddenly, Aquint did understand. Felk was to the north. It was, in fact, the northernmost city-state of the Isthmus. The Broken Circle had no doubt chosen the northern face of the Registry deliberately for this operation, as a way of demonstrating their most poignant defiance.

"So they've got flair," Aquint finally said, realizing as he did that he was being as drolly aggravating as Cat had been with him earlier.

"Flair?" Jesile said, spearing Aquint with his eyes. For a moment he seemed on the edge of an angry retort. Then he said, maintaining his calm manner, "Very well. We'll agree they've got . . . flair. I hope you'll also agree that this crime cannot go unanswered."

Aquint, even with his first reaction of stunned laughter, had known this. He had feared it.

"You're quite right," he said to Jesile. He felt Cat giving him a long, subtle sidelong look.

Jesile nodded. "Good. There will have to be visible punitive measures. Can you, at this time, locate any members of the so-called Broken Circle, which is currently operating against the lawful Felk occupation of Callah?"

It was a withering, formal question, and Aquint almost sagged under the weight of it.

"No," he said at last, voice suddenly hoarse, "I can't."

Colonel Jesile nodded again. He made a notation on one of the scrolls on his desk.

"Very well," Jesile said. "I suggest that you and your associates in the Internal Security Corps continue—and perhaps, if I might advise, step up—your efforts to locate the rebel underground here in Callah. In the meantime, I am forced to take actions more aggressive and severe than I would normally be inclined to take. The matter is out of my hands. What occurred last night wasn't merely an act of vandalism. It was a formal declaration of war, as far as I'm concerned."

Aquint nearly interrupted, but caught himself and held silent, dreading what was coming.

"If these people of Callah don't want the peace we've brought them," Jesile said, "then they can experience the alternative. Ten citizens will be rounded up at random. They will be flogged at the top of the watch, starting today at midday, in the public square. At the start of each subsequent watch, they will receive another regulation flogging. It will continue until the ten victims are all dead . . . or until at least one member of the Broken Circle comes forward and surrenders to this command."

Jesile waved the back of his hand at Aquint and Cat.

"That's all. Dismissed."

The two of them exited the office, a numb silence between them.

THERE WAS NOTHING even remotely amusing about that giant symbol now. It glared down menacingly as Aquint led Cat quickly away from the Registry.

Aquint's thoughts were moving fast. He had anticipated that Jesile would react militantly. But he hadn't expected the Felk governor to take *these* measures. Ten innocent Callahans were going to be killed. They were going to be beaten to death. Aquint nurtured no illusions that any self-sacrificing member of the Broken Circle was going to actually come forward to stop it. Things didn't work that way.

He looked back, almost involuntarily, at the receding north wall of the Registry. Whoever had managed the escapade had surely used a rope secured to the roof. What that must have been like, dangling there in the night, slapping black paint against stone, swinging gradually across the wall to complete the huge circle and slash, all while the Registry guards milled about obliviously below.

Yes, a bold and audacious feat, Aquint brooded. And one that was going to have dire consequences.

"Who do these godsdamned rebels think they are?" he suddenly exploded, there in the street.

Cat cautioned him to keep his voice down.

Aquint continued, more quietly but just as intently, "This Broken Circle, what good do they think they're doing?"

"I believe they're rebelling against the Felk," Cat said.

Aquint ignored the droll tone this time. "They're rebelling, are they? Then they should *rebel*. What have they accomplished so far? They've killed one Felk soldier. One! And that was as likely an accident as a premeditated act. They're just stirring up trouble for everybody else."

"What would you have them do?" Cat asked.

Aquint glanced at the boy and saw that he wasn't being facetious now. He considered the lad's question.

He sighed, "I just wish they could find some way to resist the Felk that wouldn't . . . wouldn't . . ."

"Wouldn't cause any trouble," Cat supplied quietly.

It pointed out the ridiculousness of Aquint's argument. The Broken Circle was a rebel organization. You couldn't have rebellion without conflict, and conflict had inevitable repercussions.

They walked awhile in tense silence.

Finally Cat asked, "Where are we going?"

Aquint tasted something unpleasant in the back of his throat. From the moment Jesile had made his pronouncement about the public floggings, Aquint had known in his bones what he had to do. It was a ghastly thing. But it was also a lesser evil. He recalled his days of keeping the ledgers of the hauling company he had first gone to work for. He had juggled figures. He had made the numbers balance. It was a talent he had.

Now he was being indirectly saddled with this burden. He couldn't allow ten fellow Callahans to die . . . not when it was within his power to prevent those deaths.

"Where are we going?" Cat repeated.

They were some distance from the Registry by now. Aquint abruptly halted. He looked about, recognizing the street. There was a drug den of some sort hereabouts. Narcotics had never interested Aquint. Alcohol was so much simpler a recreational stimulant.

Drugs, he understood, were difficult to come by these days, what with the general suspension of trade and the closed roads between the cities. But Aquint wagered the den would still be operating in some shape or form.

He turned to Cat and laid a hand on the boy's bony shoulder.

"We're going to procure ourselves a rebel, Cat," he said solemnly.

DRUG ADDICTS COULD generally be relied on to abuse their habits, more so even than drunks with their liquor.

The place stank like a latrine. Aquint had gone in through

the front door, flashing a fistful of scrip notes and purporting to be a buyer. He named the first narcotic he could think of, *phato* blossoms, and was told he could purchase some inside.

The den smelled of more than just human waste and neglectful hygiene, of course. It smelled of a trap. Aquint was unarmed. He had never been much for weapons, anyway. Even during his stint in the Felk infantry, when he had helped in the slaughter of U'delph, he had felt no ease with a sword. Such an awkward implement.

U'delph . . . he still hated thinking about it. It was a disgrace, and he was ashamed he'd had any part in it.

Then again, *this* was pretty shameful as well. But it was also necessary, in order to save those ten innocent lives.

The man who had admitted Aquint now led him into a dimly lit cavernous room, where there were quite a number of people lying about in various states of stupefaction on the floor. Aquint breathed through his mouth, but that only caused him to taste the foul human stench.

"We have blossoms of high quality, my friend." The man grinned, teeth appearing in the dimness. "The more you spend, the better they will be."

Aquint was looking around. The specimens on display here were quite poor. Many were huddling under blankets, presumably to block out any and all traces of light. Aquint studied the bodies. Some looked half-starved. When one was only interested in the procurement and ingestion of one's preferred narcotic, then luxuries like food probably became a low priority.

It was disgusting. But Aquint kept up his search, ignoring the man standing beside him. Finally he crossed toward a figure who was sitting cross-legged and bare-chested, head lolling.

"Where are you going?" the man said behind him, startled.

Aquint looked down on the sitting figure. It was a male, relatively young, though still too old to have been swept up by the Felk conscription. He had a reasonably healthy muscle tone, with enough flesh on his bones that he didn't appear too sickly.

Mostly though there was something about the planes and angles of his face. His cheekbones were sharp, and his bleary eyes had a vaguely sinister cast. He *looked* like he might be a rebel. He would fulfill the role nicely.

"I'll take him," Aquint said. "How much do you want?"

The man had caught up to him. "What . . . ? But you wanted *phato* blossoms."

"I've changed my mind. I'll buy him instead. Here, take these. Is it enough?" Aquint stuffed notes into the man's hand.

"This isn't a brothel," the man said, summoning a faint righteous tone, even as he accepted Aquint's money. "But, perhaps two or three more bronze notes . . ."

Aquint handed them over. Then he reached down and hauled the sitting man up onto his feet. He moved bonelessly, head still lolling. Aquint started him back the way they had come, toward the front door.

"Just a moment," said the den's proprietor, hurrying after them. "I've changed my mind, too. He'll cost you an extra—*yeeowchhh!*"

Aquint had been expecting the shriek. Greed was a vile trait. Cat of course had crept in here ahead of Aquint, unseen in the dimness, and had watched out to make sure Aquint wasn't waylaid. If the proprietor had just let Aquint go without pressing him for more money, Cat wouldn't have had to jam that needle-shaped little knife he carried into the man's backside. The wound wouldn't be fatal, but it would allow Aquint to vacate the premises without any further bother.

Vacate he did, his arm around the addict's shoulders, propping him up and leading him onward on unsteady feet. Cat joined Aquint a moment later on the street, and they took the man back to their apartment.

The midday watch was approaching. He and Cat worked fast. They rustled up some decent clothing for the man. They groomed him until he looked relatively presentable. That was the easy part. All the while, the man remained only scarcely aware of his surroundings, eyes blinking in druggy stupor.

Aquint leaned close to him and said in a steady tranquil voice, "I am a member of the Broken Circle. I am a member of the Broken Circle. Say it. Say it back to me. I am a member of the Broken Circle. I am—"

Eventually, the man picked up the repetitious words and started to say them in a tiny mumble. Aquint persisted, saying the phrase clearly over and over again. The man followed suit, and the words became more distinct.

"I am a member of the Broken Circle," Aquint said. "I will say nothing else."

"I am a member of the Broken Circle. I will say nothing else." The man spoke it perfectly now, without a hint of slur.

They commandeered a wagon and horses and rode at a reckless speed toward the Registry. Their timing was close, very close. Jesile had already gathered his ten random victims.

Aquint led the man inside, Cat trailing. Aquint had bound the man's hands behind his back. When they reached

Jesile, Aquint gave the man a hard shove, and he tumbled to the floor.

"Here," Aquint said. "Ask him who he is."

Colonel Jesile looked at Aquint, then at the man on the floor. "Who are you?" he finally asked.

"I am a member of the Broken Circle," the addict said. "I will say nothing else."

Jesile nodded. "That's good work, Aquint. I hope you'll believe me when I say I would much rather put this guilty man to death than harm any innocent citizen of this city."

Aquint made no reply. He turned and exited, Cat following, leaving behind the single innocent man who would unknowingly sacrifice himself for the sake of ten others.

DARDAS
(3)

THE FRESH CONSCRIPTS from Trael were being absorbed into the ranks. Soon, it would be time to get this army moving again. Two targets were within striking distance, the city-states of Grat and Ompellus Prime.

Weisel was standing over a table where a map was spread. He was gazing down intently, brow furrowed as he concentrated.

They are both good choices, he finally said. *I'm having difficulty seeing how one might be better than the other to invade next.*

Within the Felk nobleman's skull, Dardas stifled a mental sigh.

The capture of Trael was a decisive move. It has, effectively, opened up the entire south portion of this Isthmus.

Weisel nodded. *I can see that.*

Dardas wondered if Weisel actually did. Then he continued, *Grat and Ompellus Prime lie to our west and east, respectively. They are of comparable size and population and could both most likely mount similar resistance to this army.*

So, there is no logical choice? Weisel asked.

The man expected war to be a thing of simple logic, Dardas thought darkly. As if it were a puzzle or a riddle that could be unraveled with the application of a formula.

If the choices are equal, Dardas said, *then it is wise to consider where either choice will lead. What happens after the conquest of Grat or Ompellus Prime?*

Weisel studied the map harder. There was no one else inside the pavilion, and Weisel had given orders not to be disturbed. He apparently wanted this time to absorb a lesson in warfare from Dardas. Dardas, for his part, was complying, though it was taxing his patience.

He could bear it, however. The day couldn't last forever, and when night came, things would be different. Weisel was still evidently blissfully unaware that Dardas was taking full control of this body while the Felk general's consciousness slept at night.

If we take Grat first . . .

Yes? Dardas prompted.

Then we will face the Rijjï Hills to the southwest of the city, Weisel went on, excited now.

And what would that mean? Dardas coaxed him along.

It's dangerous terrain, as far as moving an army through it. There are gullies and rivers, and no easy roads through. Whatever military Grat has could retreat into those hills. It would take a lot of effort to dislodge them.

So . . . ? Dardas said.

"So we take Ompellus Prime," Weisel said, aloud now, "then move south, make a lateral move west, and swing up at Grat so that they have nowhere to retreat to!"

Well done, General Weisel.

Weisel was as happy as a child, and that was fitting, Dardas thought. Even a child could have figured out which city was their next sensible target.

There was more to it than cold appraisal, however, and this was something that Dardas knew he could never teach the Felk noble, even if he had been inclined to try. Weisel had no war instincts. Armies and terrains and weather conditions were fluid things, and one often had to make adjustments in mid-stride, so to speak. There wasn't always time for cool, rational analysis. Sometimes one had to act from the gut, trusting oneself that a particular maneuver was the right one to make.

Two hundred and fifty years ago, Dardas had led his mighty army with instincts he had honed to gleaming sharpness all his life.

Your assistance has been valuable, Weisel now said.

Dardas replied, graciously, *You solved the problem on your own, General. I merely helped you to see it.*

With your aid, this war will be won.

Then what? But Dardas kept the thought to himself. Once more, Weisel had obviously not thought it through. Dardas knew that he himself would no longer be useful to Lord Matokin once this war was done. Apparently, Weisel was unaware that the same was true of him. Matokin would have no need of Weisel after the Isthmus was fully conquered.

Perhaps the Felk general planned to retire gracefully, ceding his position of power and importance, allowing the bureaucracies of the empire to replace the vigorous animation of the military. Perhaps Weisel was happily anticipating this. If so, he was an even greater fool than Dardas suspected.

A war commander was nothing without a war to sustain his existence.

Dardas had been giving a good deal of thought to his own peculiarly sustained existence. His resurrection was not entirely stable. It needed to be maintained through rejuvenation spells. He had already experienced one close call, when death had come to reclaim what had been taken from it. A mage had come from Felk, through the portals, and had brought Dardas back from the black brink.

But Matokin controlled that mage. Kumbat was his name, the same one who had evidently been responsible for resurrecting Raven inside the delectable body of Vadya.

How much better it would be for Dardas, how much more secure he would feel, if Mage Kumbat were under *his* control.

Weisel set his aide Fergon to summoning the senior staff, no doubt to unveil his grand plan for the conquest of Ompellus Prime. He would bask in his officers' accolades, feeling for that moment as if he truly was this army's legitimate leader.

Dardas wouldn't spoil his fun. It was best if Weisel was distracted by his "progress" in learning the craft of war. Meanwhile, Dardas had serious plans for tonight.

RAVEN WAS OBVIOUSLY expecting another session of torrid lovemaking. Dardas noted her flushed color, the quickness of her breath as her sublimely shaped breasts rose and fell. In her eyes was a lascivious glimmer that she didn't try to hide.

"Raven," Dardas said, "how good of you to join me."

"I serve at your pleasure, General," she said in that throaty purr as she sashayed across the length of the pavilion toward him.

It was very tempting to just seize her and toss her down onto the bed and mount her in that eager violent fashion she seemed to find so agreeable. But there were other matters of import to attend to tonight, and that night, like the day, wouldn't last forever.

When Weisel woke this would be his body again. Dardas didn't have the will or sway to successfully challenge his host full on. Not yet, anyway. Each night, however, Dardas tested his control to its limits. Maybe he could eventually unlock Weisel's command of this body.

Better still, of course, would be to eliminate the Felk nobleman's consciousness altogether. However, Dardas had no idea how or if that could be accomplished.

"We have work to do tonight," Dardas said to Raven.

She halted before him, angling her body just so, to give him a pleasing view of her outline. "What work would that be, General?" she asked in a mock-coy tone that was quite sensuous.

Dardas pushed aside his baser impulses and said, "Work for my chief of Military Security, Raven."

Raven straightened, the wanton light leaving her eyes. "Yes, General Weisel," she said, seriously now.

Dardas nodded. "You fully understand your authority as the head of Military Security, don't you?"

"I . . . believe so, General."

"You wield a great power, Raven. It supersedes even rank. You are this army's defense against treason."

Raven lifted her elegantly molded chin. "I shall do everything I can to live up to that."

"I know that." Dardas smiled. "But what if you were to receive information that a visiting dignitary, a high-ranking mage under Lord Matokin's command, was in fact a traitor to all of Felk?"

Raven blinked, but her expression didn't waver. "I would first want to know the source of this information," she said evenly.

Dardas nodded. It was a good answer.

He said, "*I* am the source, Raven."

"Then I would trust your word utterly, sir."

"Good." Dardas had been sitting. He rose now. "I have summoned this mage here. He will be arriving at any moment. He believes he is here on a . . . medical emergency."

Now a small frown pinched Raven's lips. "Medical?" she asked. "Is someone injured?"

"The mage in question," Dardas said, "is here to administer a rejuvenation spell."

Raven plainly recognized the term. But she looked confused.

"Administer it to whom?" she asked.

"Why"—Dardas blinked—"to you of course, my dear."

She digested that a brief moment, then nodded. "I am the bait then?"

"You are."

"And who is the quarry?"

"I think you may already know the answer to that," Dardas said, quietly and significantly.

Raven drew a long breath, then let it out. "Mage Kumbat . . ." she murmured.

"Correct."

"The wizard responsible for my resurrection," Raven said, stunned.

"Again, correct."

For a moment, she was lost in thought. Then she gathered herself and looked Dardas steadily in the eye. "What do you wish me to do with him when he arrives, General?"

Dardas smiled appreciatively. This girl was indeed

something special. He told her the plan. She nodded as she listened.

Raven saluted. "It will be done, sir."

He returned the salute. "I'm counting on you, Raven."

KUMBAT ARRIVED A short while later. He bustled into the tent after being passed through Weisel's personal guard. The wizard's black robe twirled as he looked all about, seeing only the general present. He frowned.

"General Weisel," Kumbat said, "I was told specifically to report to your tent. Where is Raven? The spell must be delivered as soon as possible."

Dardas stood casually, hands clasped easily behind him.

"Why the hurry, Mage Kumbat?" he asked.

Kumbat gaped. "By the sanity of the gods, General, you yourself know what she must be going through. It's a very traumatic experience. The rejuvenation spell will end her fear and discomfort. Now, please, where is she?"

He was a conscientious wizard at least, Dardas noted silently. Matokin himself had received the coded Far Speak communication in Felk and had ordered Kumbat hastily Far Moved here.

"Is it unusual that Raven should require the spell so soon after her resurrection?" Dardas asked, his manner still relaxed.

"Well, yes, I suppose, yes, but—" Kumbat fumbled. "The magic requires a great effort on my part, General. I must prepare and administer it."

"You see, that's interesting," Dardas said, ignoring the urgency of the situation. "I myself know so little about resurrection magic and rejuvenation spells that when you mention any minor aspect about them it's completely fresh news to me. It's very specialized magic, isn't it?"

Kumbat was blinking rapidly, totally off guard.

"It . . . it is," he said.

"There must be very few practitioners."

Kumbat swallowed, visibly. "There are only three in all the empire."

"And I'll wager you're the best of the lot, else Matokin wouldn't keep you so close at hand. Modesty be damned, Mage Kumbat, am I correct? Are you the best?"

The wizard was starting to look quite pale, contrasting sharply with the color of his robe.

"I . . . I am the most skilled at this particular form of magic." He did not say it proudly. In fact, he sounded rather regretful at the moment.

Dardas smiled. "I have come to understand that Far Movement magic—another specialized and taxing skill, but one more commonplace than yours—is somewhat dangerous to practice. Not long ago, I had a plan to use those portals as an offensive weapon. It was a rather ingenious application of the magic, but sadly my plan was . . . vetoed."

Kumbat retreated a step toward the flap of the pavilion. If he tried to flee he would have a short journey. Dardas had given orders to his guards to admit, but not to allow the mage to leave.

"As far as Matokin knows," Dardas said, "you're here tending to Raven. He'll no doubt expect you back in Felk after a plausible amount of time. I will see to it that the proper orders are issued to have you transported there by my Far Movement wizards. Only"—Dardas smiled wider— "you won't be arriving at the other end. Eventually, it will be concluded that you were unfortunately lost in transit. As

I said, Far Movement magic is evidently a somewhat dangerous practice."

Now Kumbat did turn to flee, but he didn't even make it to the flap. Raven rose from behind the trunk where she had been concealing herself, and seized the mage. Kumbat recoiled, fear bright in his eyes.

Raven said, "By the authority of Military Security, I hereby place you under arrest, Mage Kumbat. You will be detained here in this camp until such time as it is deemed fit to release you, or until further punitive measures will be taken against you."

Dardas resisted the urge to applaud. Even so, it was a magnificent performance on Raven's part. Here she was, arresting the very man who had brought her back to life. The irony tickled him.

But this wasn't an occasion for levity. He had already made the arrangements with the proper Far Speak and Far Movement wizards under his command to falsify Kumbat's return trip to Felk. Essentially, they would effect a blank delivery through the portals and later claim that they had transported Kumbat. Dardas had handpicked the two wizards, ones that Raven herself had reported as being especially loyal to him.

"But, but, but—" Kumbat sputtered. "What am I charged with?"

Dardas gestured to Raven.

She said, coldly, "Treason."

Then she led Kumbat away to specially prepared quarters. Kumbat was no Far Movement mage. He wouldn't be able to just conjure up a portal and step through and escape.

Alone in the pavilion now, Dardas yawned. The episode had been rather draining and this body had to rest sometime. He lay down on his bed, vaguely disappointed that

Raven wasn't joining him. In a short while, Matokin would contact him, demanding to know what had happened to Kumbat. Dardas would express bafflement and then later on regret for the apparent tragedy that had occurred.

Matokin might or might not believe the ruse. Almost certainly, however, he would send someone to investigate. Maybe Abraxis, chief of the Internal Security Corps. The few times Dardas had met Abraxis, he had been struck by the canniness and wiliness of the man.

It would be interesting to see what would happen when the chief of Internal Security met the chief of Military Security, especially since it would be on Raven's ground.

Now Dardas did allow himself a chuckle. He was enjoying himself. As complex and perilous as things had become, he was still participating in life. Two and a half centuries after his own death, and he was living his new life to its fullest! It was worth savoring every moment of it.

He was *still* Dardas the Invincible.

Soon, he would add the city-state of Ompellus Prime to his roster of conquests. After that, Grat would fall. This army would work farther and farther south, swallowing its enemies. But before it reached the southward extremity of the Isthmus, a worthy foe would surely rise to challenge him.

It had to happen. His instincts told him so. Wars were not fought like this, without any notable resistance. The laws of existence wouldn't allow it.

Dardas only hoped he wasn't mistaking his instincts for desperate, irrational hope.

Yes, Dardas the Invincible. He laughed a bit harder. With Kumbat as his captive, and with the mage's rejuvenating powers at his beck and call, invincible was precisely what he was.

BRYCK
(3)

"HE WAS AN innocent," Bryck said, cutting through the contesting voices.

He did not speak loudly, but this group still showed him deference. They quieted. They turned. They listened for what he had to say.

"They grabbed up some poor wretch," he continued. "And they declared him guilty of the crime. And they took him into the plaza and hacked his head off."

"But I *heard* him," Gelshiri said in that insistent adolescent tone. "I heard him say he was a part of the Broken Circle."

Tyber, leaning against the wall nearby where Bryck was sitting, shrugged. "The soldiers must've coerced him into saying it."

"How would they do that?" Ondak countered. "How do you compel someone condemned to death to do anything? What's left to threaten him with?"

"A less comfortable death," Tyber offered.

A valid point, Bryck noted silently.

"So . . ." one of the new recruits to the Circle said, somewhat timidly, "he wasn't, uh, one of us?"

"Definitely not," said Tyber.

"So he died," said the same recruit, a sinewy middle-yeared female named Scaullit, "for a crime, uh, that—"

"That he didn't commit," Tyber impatiently finished for her.

She lowered her eyes. "I was going to say, for a crime that . . . that Minst and I committed."

They were all gathered in the most spacious of the Circle's rooms, the full complement, including the four fresh faces, two of whom—Scaullit and Minst—had painted the sigil on the wall of the Registry during the night's darkest watches. Bryck hadn't entirely expected the brazen scheme to succeed, but the two eager new members of the Broken Circle had carried it off fearlessly, scaling their way stealthily up onto the Registry's roof, lowering themselves on ropes with buckets of paint in hand. They had been gloriously successful. The giant sigil was a thing of beauty.

They all fell into an uncomfortable silence. The plan had indeed succeeded. And some poor innocent had indeed paid the price.

Bryck could sense the others waiting for him to speak. It was a slow pressure, and he had gradually become aware that it was always present. This group relied on him. That amounted to more than the courtesy and respect they showed him; it meant he had to be the foundation for them, the voice of wisdom and reason. He was their *leader*.

"The innocent died," Bryck said. "But would anyone here rather it was one of you?"

"I'd rather it hadn't happened at all," Scaullit said softly. "Whoever he was, he was a fellow Callahan."

Bryck looked directly at her. "Then you wish you hadn't painted the sigil? That's what led to all the rest, after all. The activities of this Broken Circle will contribute to the miseries of the people of this city. We strike against the Felk, and they, unable to find any of us, make reprisals against ordinary citizens who have nothing to do with any of our operations. And yet, *they* are the very people we are fighting for. Didn't you realize all that, Scaullit? Hadn't any of you new people thought this through before you agreed to join us?" He looked around at the others. "Take the time. Right now. Think about it. Understand what it means to go against the Felk. Not just to yourselves, but to everyone else it will affect."

Bryck sat back. It was a performance of sorts. He had never acted in one of his own theatricals. While he had been quite skilled at creating words to fit into actors' mouths, he had never had any desire to speak them himself before an audience. Yet here he was, performing his part as the leader of the Broken Circle. He only hoped he was convincing in the role.

While he let the dramatic pause settle over the group, he furtively eyed Quentis sitting on a chair at the far side of the room. He hadn't forgotten the night she had visited him as he lay on his bunk, the night she had more or less offered herself to him. Bryck had relived the incident quite a number of times in his mind, redirecting the action, changing the words she said, changing the words he said. He had followed each altered scene to its conclusion, and though he was somewhat ashamed of himself for it, he had by now imagined in detail making love to Quentis more often than he would ever care to admit.

She gazed back now with her amber eyes. He could read nothing there, and it irked him. Did she still have feelings for him? Or had his one rejection spoiled everything? The puzzlement made a small agitation in his stomach.

Once, before he had married Aaysue, Bryck had enjoyed a reasonably libidinous young adulthood, one bolstered by the status and privilege of his noble bloodline and the wealth that accompanied it. In those long bygone days he had given little thought to specific matters of romance or carnal recreation. If one potential bed partner fell through, he glibly sought out the next. He couldn't recall ever seriously brooding over any individual female, no matter how alluring he might have found her at any given time. Not until he'd met Aaysue, in fact, had he given the possibility of love and true emotional depth any credence.

So why was it that now, when he was twice the age of that promiscuous lad, he should be experiencing such classically adolescent feelings as he was having toward Quentis?

Bryck blinked. He still had the full silent attention of the room, and he had been holding it until that silence had grown distinctly awkward.

He rallied. "If any of you new people can't accept the consequences of what we do," he said before his point was lost, "then now is the time to quit."

Again he looked over the new faces. He and Tyber had recruited them, picking ones that appeared able-bodied, intelligent, and committed.

"I will not quit," said Scaullit, tone firm now.

"Neither will I," Minst said. He was a thick-limbed male, with a hunched posture, but was evidently nimble enough to have scaled the Registry with Scaullit.

"The Felk took my sons," said the third one of the recruits. She was named Cancallo. "Whisked them off into that army. I don't know if I'll ever see them again. But I'll fight the Felk until my boys are back with me."

Bryck looked to the fourth new member. The man's eyes were wide, white showing all around their soft color. This was the one who had beseeched him and Tyber most ardently when the two of them had roved Callah's streets a second time in costume and face paint, furtively displaying the Circle's symbol. Bryck, circulating through the crowds that gathered to watch Tyber's juggling, had rekindled that false rumor about an uprising against the Felk in the neighboring city of Windal. Bryck had murmured about its success, about how the people were slaughtering the Felk, retaking their home.

This man had most wanted to become a part of the Broken Circle. His name was Setix.

Bryck could see now that Setix was having a change of heart.

"I—I . . ." the man fumbled as all eyes turned toward him. He squirmed under the pressure. Perspiration shone on his wide forehead. "I don't know if—I'm not—I—"

A quiet and implacable dread closed over Bryck. This at least was one eventuality he had foreseen and prepared himself for. Which wasn't going to make it any easier to deal with.

Setix was standing at the edge of the group. He came forward now, involuntarily it seemed. His hands shook at his sides.

"Do you wish to quit?" Bryck asked, the question flat, barely inflected.

Setix offered that same beseeching look as he had when he had asked to join the Circle. His mouth worked soundlessly a moment, then the words started to spill. "This is very difficult. I don't want to show any disrespect. But I didn't count on all this. On someone being killed for actions *we* did. Next time it could be me doing the thing that would lead the Felk to take another innocent life. That would make me a murderer of my own people. That's not what I bargained for. I hate the Felk. I want them driven from this place, from my home. But I just can't . . . I just don't . . . it doesn't seem right that—"

He blundered on awhile after that, the fragments of sentences piling up, choking him, until he was making only whimpering sounds.

Bryck stood. He didn't want to stand. He wanted very much to remain sitting, to give the necessary order and then look away while it was carried out. But even his most ludicrous comedies had their moments of pathos, and he knew how this needed to be played.

He had discussed this particular eventuality with Tyber. Though the man was fairly aged, he was the strongest, in body and perhaps spirit, among this company. Bryck caught his eyes.

"Take him," he ordered.

It was swifter than he could have imagined it. Bryck himself had taken a life, that luckless Felk soldier he'd killed in that alleyway with a single murderous blow. Death could happen very quickly. He knew this. But to watch it occur. To be the spectator. To see the knife drawn and slammed into the body, knowing it was going to happen and still barely able to follow the movements. *That* was what sucked the air out of Bryck's lungs.

Setix gasped. His final instants of life were filled with surprise at what he could only just be starting to comprehend was happening to him. Then, when Tyber had wrenched loose his blade, the body dropped heavily to the floor. It bled and did not move.

"He was in a position to betray us," Bryck said. "Our identities, our location. We could not afford that."

He waited. No one had anything to add to that. No one in the room contradicted him. His assertion was logical. The truth of it was as plain and unpleasant as the corpse that lay at everyone's feet.

"IT'S MY FAULT." Bile still burned his throat. "I should have chosen better."

Quentis put a hand to his arm. Bryck felt the warmth of it keenly, that peculiar human heat. But was it a caress or a neutral pat? He shook his head. He had just vomited, slipping outdoors to do so. Only Quentis had noticed. Setix's body was being disposed of. Bryck lingered near the doorway, shaded by the building's eaves.

"He *was* a danger. You were right." Quentis's tone was gentle.

Bryck spat into the dust. "Things are only going to get more dangerous. More violent. More murderous."

"We are all prepared for that," she said.

He looked into her eyes. Emotions roiled within him, out of the safe control in which he normally kept them. Setix's murder, necessity or not, had unsettled him at a fundamental level. It was actually more disturbing than when he'd personally killed that soldier. This time he had merely *ordered* it and stood there while his will was carried out.

"Do you understand that alone we can do nothing?" Bryck heard himself whisper.

Quentis blinked at him, a small furrow appearing between her brows.

He should not be divulging this. Even as a playwright

he had known not to reveal everything to the audience. Horrified, he felt his mouth moving, more words rasping out. "We can't go against the Felk. Our little group, stand against the full strength of the garrison? They have weapons and numbers and organization. And more so, they have the mental supremacy of having conquered this city. The people are beaten already. In order to rise against the Felk they have to feel they are *worthy* of the victory."

Quentis dropped her hand from his arm. He felt a small chill where her warmth had been.

"What are you saying?" she asked.

It was too late to retreat. Bryck had started this. Now he had to see it through. "Our only hope of victory against the Felk is to get the people of this city to rise up. Callah's civilian population vastly outnumbers the garrison. If everyone rose as one, the Felk would be crushed. As for what the Circle can do alone, it's negligible . . . except as an example to others. If they believe in us, they might believe in the uprising."

Quentis drew a long breath. Bryck watched her and admired the control she displayed. He realized that he had longed to confide in someone for some while, but he had denied himself. His war against the Felk, despite his having assumed leadership of the Broken Circle, still felt, more often than not, like a purely private endeavor. And he had felt the loneliness of that, even if he hadn't wanted to admit it.

"Fabrication," she said at last, with a soft note of wonder.

Bryck waited, wondering if anger would follow.

"If you create the falsehood and find ways to give it credibility . . ." Quentis went on, pondering aloud, "then you need only find others to believe in it as reality. And then it *is* real." Her amber eyes brightened. "So our goal is to make the people of Callah believe that the revolution is already under way. That they would be joining a movement already in full swing. It would be a kind of . . . of self-inducing momentum, wouldn't it?" She appeared quite taken with the notion.

Bryck nodded. "Yes. The Broken Circle represents hope. The last hope for freedom from the Felk these people will probably ever know."

She regarded him. Then she said solemnly, "Wherever you come from, Minstrel, and whoever you are, I am grateful for you."

It wouldn't have done to kiss her just then, not with the bilious taste of vomit still on his lips. But he wanted to, at that moment. Wanted very much to kiss this woman. Wanted all the warmth and passion that would come from that.

Instead, of course, he went back inside. One of the new recruits, Cancallo, the woman whose sons had been conscripted into the Felk army, was on her knees with a damp rag, scrubbing away Setix's bloodstains from the floor. The body itself was gone.

THERE WAS MUCH talk all around the city about the great sigil on the north wall of the Registry. Many people had noted the significance of its placement, which Bryck found gratifying. It was meant to symbolize full defiance of the Felk, who had invaded this city from the north.

The huge black symbol was already being painted over, naturally. The Felk had commandeered a work crew of Callahans to do the job, but even that wasn't going to lessen the impact, Bryck judged.

There were other operations for the Circle to undertake. They couldn't relax their efforts now. He had been candid with Quentis earlier. Things were only going to grow more violent and dangerous.

And eventually, hopefully, these people of Callah would follow the Broken Circle's lead and rise united against the Felk.

It was well past curfew. Bryck was in his bunk, behind his screen of painted birds in flight. He hadn't eaten, unwilling to risk vomiting again. As with most nights, sleep wasn't coming easily. He had tried repeatedly to clear his mind, but such efforts only seemed to spur his thoughts faster. He knew the only thing to do was to wait for physical fatigue to overcome the mental agitation.

After some long while he felt the first threads of dreams poking through his tiring consciousness. These were odd nonsensical intrusions that vanished the instant he focused his mind on them. Some he recognized fleetingly as memories, mostly from his distant past, incidents from his boyhood distorted and reshuffled into strange episodes.

It was dark in the room, and there were others in here, already sleeping. It might be time for the Circle to find new, bigger lodgings. Or perhaps they could spread their numbers out to different locations.

Inevitably an erotic image of Quentis surfaced in his dwindling thoughts. It was a fantasy Bryck had visualized before, often enough apparently for his mind to mistake it for a memory. It played out familiarly, and he felt a vague pang of shame for the arousal he was experiencing.

But when he distantly heard the screen around his bunk being softly jostled and felt the warm hands searching under his blanket, Bryck responded as he would in the fantasy, drawing the visiting body onto the bunk and pressing himself eagerly against it.

Until a sudden alarming thought cut through him.

"Quentis?" he breathed, his heart pounding in the darkness. "It is you, isn't it?"

"Yes," she said. "It's me." And her mouth closed tightly over his.

As the fantasy became reality, the fabrication became a true memory; and when she left his bunk later that night, after the full satisfaction of the event, Bryck clutched that memory and did not let go.

RAVEN
(4)

THE TWO AGENTS stared at her with cold eyes. Raven didn't flinch.

"We are officers in the Internal Security Corps," the taller of the two of them repeated. Then he added, with emphasis, "We report directly to Lord Abraxis."

"Show me your orders," Raven said, standing her ground. These two had appeared out of a portal just a few moments ago, without much warning. She had come as soon as she'd heard.

The shorter agent slapped a scroll grudgingly onto her palm. "And who are you to question us?"

She returned them a mild gaze, one full of the sort of passive sexual confidence that she had discovered unnerved so many men. It was as if she were allowing these males this glimpse of her beauty, deigning to let them stand in her presence, but if they thought for an instant they could attain her, in any fashion, she would cruelly crush their dreams.

"I am the chief of Military Security," she said, tone almost nonchalant.

"*Military* Security?" The tall one sniffed. "Yes, we've heard about you."

"Lord Abraxis made it quite clear to us that you have no official authority," said the shorter one.

"Did he?" Raven purred, taking her time reading the orders. She finished and handed back the scroll. "Well, what do you two want here in this camp?"

The two agents glanced at each other, incredulously.

"Didn't we just say you have no authority over us?" asked the short one.

"No." Raven shook her head. "You said *Abraxis* said Military Security has no authority over you. However, you two aren't in Felk now, or skulking about in some conquered city-state. This is the field. And it's my jurisdiction, whether you want to acknowledge it or not."

They gaped at her. Hers was a simple tactic. She was simply refusing to bow to these Internal Security officers, however rightful their authority might be. Weisel had almost certainly overstepped himself by creating his Military Security agency and appointing her as its head, but that didn't mean she was willing to cede her position just because these two had shown up.

"I ask again," she said. "What do you want here?"

They traded another uneasy glance. The tall one cleared his throat and said, somewhat contritely, "We're here to investigate the disappearance of Mage Kumbat."

"Surely you've heard the report we relayed to Lord Matokin, via Far Speak," Raven said.

"We have." The shorter one nodded.

"And? It was unclear that Kumbat was Far Moved from this location and failed to arrive at his destination?" Raven shrugged. "My understanding is that Far Movement magic isn't entirely trustworthy . . . though that's kept hushed up for obvious reasons."

"We've heard the report," the tall one said firmly. "But we are here to investigate, nonetheless. I hope, for your sake, that you don't intend to impede us in any way." His tone turned subtly threatening.

Raven didn't respond to it. She merely nodded. "Very well. The two of you will have the cooperation of Military Security, assuming you don't make nuisances of yourselves. Remember, this is military territory. These brave men and women and wizards have been fighting this war step-by-step, while types like you have probably been luxuriating back at the Palace. If you treat these soldiers and magicians respectfully, you'll have fewer problems. Understood?"

The two nodded mutely, plainly undone by her very convincing bluff.

Raven all but dismissed the pair and walked off.

That was well done, Vadya said.

Thank you. Raven, too, was proud.

She strode along, noting the preparations under way. Scuttlebutt had it that the army was going to move east, against the city-state of Ompellus Prime. It would probably happen soon, by the look of things.

Raven hadn't been officially informed, but, then again, she wasn't really a part of General Weisel's senior staff. Her position was unique. Evidently, Weisel didn't think she needed to be notified about the tactical movements of this army, and he was probably right in that judgment.

Besides, Weisel always seemed to call for her at night, receiving her alone in his pavilion. Those visits, of course, weren't all business.

Raven smiled to herself, even as she stifled a small

yawn. Weisel was a fine lover, but lack of sleep was taking its toll on her.

Even so, she was more than alert enough to carry out her duties, including the special one that Vadya had conceived—to keep an eye on both Weisel and Matokin, to see that neither man, through stubbornness or stupidity, sabotaged the efforts to establish an Isthmus-wide Felk Empire.

Of course, the arrest and subsequent cover-up of Mage Kumbat was certainly an unorthodox move on Weisel's part. Raven had appeared to accept Weisel's charge of treason against the powerful wizard at face value, but she had wondered what machinations were involved. Surely this was something she should report immediately to Lord Matokin.

Then why haven't you? Vadya asked.

Raven was startled. She hadn't been aware she had "spoken" the thought so that Vadya could hear it. Then again, their affinity was strong.

I want to know what General Weisel is doing before I report, Raven said.

Is that entirely wise? Vadya asked.

Maybe not. But there has to be a reason he wanted Kumbat.

It may merely be as I've warned, Vadya said. *Men like Weisel create trouble for themselves and those around them simply because it's their nature.*

Raven found that strangely annoying. She walked on. Finally, she reached the small guarded tent that was her destination. The guards saluted and held open the flap for her. She stepped inside.

Kumbat was bound and gagged, sitting in a chair. His bleary, frightened eyes opened wide at the sight of her. He made urgent muffled noises under the gag.

Weisel had decided to take no chances. Restrained like

this, the mage wouldn't easily be able to enact any magic. Raven regarded him a moment. Then she came forward.

"You'll keep your voice down?"

Kumbat nodded, head bobbing a bit wildly.

Raven unknotted the gag. She poured water into a cup from a jug and held it to the wizard's lips. He drank eagerly.

"Will you untie the rest of me?" he pleaded.

"No," Raven said. "But we can have a little time to talk."

The mage sighed, "Very well." He sounded defeated.

"Do you still deny the charges against you?" Raven asked.

"*Yes,*" Kumbat said emphatically. "I am no traitor."

"General Weisel thinks otherwise."

"Weisel is—" he started, then bit down on the words. He visibly gathered himself and said more evenly, "The general is mistaken. I serve the empire faithfully. I serve the emperor. Lord Matokin—"

"Lord Matokin is not the one accusing you of treason," Raven said.

"I have done nothing to make General Weisel think I am in any way disloyal."

"Perhaps you crossed him personally at some time?" Raven suggested. She had to find out why Weisel wanted to keep this mage in custody.

"Hardly," Kumbat said.

"You're so certain?"

"I have done nothing to offend or displease the general, at any time," the mage said. He added, in a grumble, "Quite the contrary, I've been of important service to him."

Raven took note of this last. "What service was that?"

But Kumbat was shaking his head, looking upset. "Raven, why are you doing this to me? *I* am the one responsible for your being among the living once more."

"I realize that, Mage Kumbat."

"Doesn't that earn me any favor or fidelity from you?" He was pleading once again. "I gave you back life!"

"Lower your voice," Raven warned, actually feeling a brief pang of guilt.

It was true of course that Kumbat had performed her resurrection. But he had only done so because Weisel had pressured Matokin into making it happen. Kumbat had merely been the tool.

"What service did you do for General Weisel?" she asked again.

The wizard pressed his lips together. "I . . . cannot say."

That interested Raven even more. "Did you bungle this service, perhaps? Did Weisel order your arrest as revenge against you?"

Plainly, the mage was reluctant to talk. But Raven judged that he didn't possess an especially strong will.

After a moment, Kumbat said, "General Weisel could have no complaints about the quality of my service."

Raven stooped slightly and peered directly into Kumbat's fearful eyes.

"You do understand that as head of Military Security, I hold your life very literally in my hands?" As she asked this, she gently cupped his face in her hands. Then she bent even lower and mashed her lips hard against his.

When she broke the kiss Kumbat sputtered violently. She stepped back and smiled. The combination of threat and sexuality was a potent one. He gasped for breath.

"Very well . . ." he muttered finally. "If I tell you what you want to know, what do I get in return?"

"You're hardly in a position to bargain."

"Nevertheless, I will not divulge without some compensation." He made a valiant effort to adopt a firm tone.

Raven shrugged. It was fair, after all.

"If you cooperate," she said, "I'll see that a message is relayed to Lord Matokin in Felk, one that says you are alive and well."

Distrust and hope warred on Kumbat's face. He gazed at Raven and finally said, "I want to trust you."

"And I want to know what secret you carry about General Weisel. I suggest you trust me. Your options at the moment are markedly limited."

Kumbat nodded grimly. It was patently true.

He gathered a long breath, then began, "General Weisel isn't entirely who you think he is." The tale the mage proceeded to tell was indeed a fascinating one.

RAVEN FAIRLY WANDERED in a daze.

Those two Internal Security agents would never locate Kumbat on their own. The tent was one among hundreds, and the guards were from Weisel's personal squad. Neither would the agents have any luck interrogating the wizards who had supposedly Far Moved Kumbat back to Felk; they were loyal to Weisel and would never betray the deception.

These weren't the thoughts that preoccupied Raven. She was still quite stunned by what Kumbat had told her. Naturally, she questioned the veracity of the mage's claims. But she could find no plausible reason why he would make up something so outrageous. More, there was a great deal of sense in what he asserted.

Kumbat claimed that he himself had effected the resurrection of the ancient Northland war commander Dardas. The vessel for him was Lord Weisel, a Felk nobleman with military aspirations.

I now understand why Weisel wants Kumbat close at hand, Raven mused.

Why is that? Vadya asked, catching the clearly formed thought.

It's so that Weisel doesn't have to rely on Matokin for his rejuvenation spells, Raven said. *Since the outset of this war my fath—Lord Matokin has deliberately kept the secrets of magic out of the general's reach. The very reason I was originally summoned from the Academy to serve Weisel was because he hoped to glean those secrets from me, not realizing that I knew little of the complex magic that interested him.*

You believe Weisel invented this charge of treason against Kumbat? Vadya asked.

Yes, Raven said, matter-of-factly.

So do I.

But, Raven continued, *I can understand his motives. I can even sympathize.*

Vadya's surprise was strong enough that Raven could actually feel it.

I don't know if you can grasp it, Raven said. *Existing as a . . . a passenger within the body of another person is very disconcerting.*

But you have virtually free rein, Vadya protested. *Is it not you controlling the movements of this body right now?*

Raven was walking. She deliberately halted, and there was no resistance at all to the commands she was giving.

Even so, Raven said, *the thought that my existence must be maintained from now on through the aid of magic is disturbing. I dread the eventuality of my first need for a rejuvenation spell.*

Indeed, the thought alone made her shudder slightly.

Are you going to report this to Matokin? Vadya asked.

When she had finished with Kumbat, Raven had replaced his gag and promised him she would get word to Lord Matokin. But she hadn't promised *when* she would do so. However, she couldn't see how she could make any delay.

Telling Matokin, though, would mean betraying General Weisel. Only, he wasn't Weisel! By the madness of the gods, she had been the eager bed partner of a man who had been dead for more than two hundredwinters.

Raven shuddered again, this time for a different reason.

Perhaps she should feel a kindredness with Dardas/Weisel. After all, she was in effect Raven/Vadya. And the general, whoever he actually was, had in fact shown her much trust and attention and fondness.

It was very confusing.

What's going on? Vadya asked.

Raven focused. It seemed there was a mounting activity around her. She frowned. It was widespread. She saw the troops stirring, heard the rumble of voices.

What's going on? Raven repeated Vadya's question.

After a few moments, it became clear. The horns sounded. The camp was being struck. The army was mobilizing. She guessed they were going to move against Ompellus Prime to the east.

Raven caught a soldier hurrying past.

"You there! Are we off to invade Ompellus Prime?"

The soldier shook his head. He looked excited and afraid all at once.

"No, the scouts have reported a force organizing to our south!"

Raven frowned again.

"There's another army coming to meet us! They say it's a big one!"

RADSTAC
(4)

SHE WAS PREPARED to kill Nievzê if the situation called for it. In fact, she had been ready to do so from the first moment he had appeared in their lives, knocking at their door after curfew, the same night the rebels had painted their emblem so conspicuously on the wall of the Registry.

Radstac had also been prepared to turn the renegade Felk magician over to Aquint. He was, after all, most certainly the type of individual who would interest the Internal Security Corps. What Nievzê was not, however, was a rebel in good standing with the local Broken Circle underground here in Callah, who were the only rebels that interested Radstac.

Deo's position on the matter was something entirely different.

"You were *encouraged* to turn your fellow students in as traitors?" he asked the wizard with that same note of excited incredulity.

Nievzê made a small rasp of a laugh. He tossed the gnawed rabbit bone onto his plate and proceeded to lick his fingers clean. "More like we were obliged to do so. I can barely describe the pressure we were under. Your loyalty was always suspect, no matter what you did, however true your allegiance to Matokin was. We took oaths, swearing our eternal devotion, and the next day we'd do the same thing all over again. It was a constant testing and affirming. It was brutal."

"This Academy of yours sounds like a dreadful place," Deo said. It was, by Radstac's count, the third time he'd said it.

She let out a short breath. "Then stop making him tell these horror stories."

Deo gave her a flat glance. Plainly he was enthralled by all this. Nievzê was a figure of wonder and mystery to him. He was a Felk wizard who had fabricated his own death and deserted his post before this war had even gotten under way. That he had fled to Callah was, in Radstac's opinion, a tactical error. But perhaps this unfaithful Felk magician had been unable to imagine the rapid success of his home state's military adventures. Callah had fallen to the Felk army less than a lune after he'd smuggled himself into the neighboring city.

Nievzê guzzled down another cup of wine. Deo filled it without making him ask.

She and Deo—entirely at Deo's insistence—were paying this hostel's proprietress the fee for the room in which Nievzê was now staying. The wizard's plans for escape had apparently not included setting aside enough funds to live comfortably once he reached his destination. Laina, the old woman who ran this house, was happy to receive the money.

It irked Radstac. They were paying for this deserter's lodging and board out of the money that Aquint was paying them to act as Internal Security agents. The money didn't quite stretch that far, particularly since Nievzê was consuming enough food and wine to fill the bellies of three men.

Granted, he did appear half-starved. His gaunt face was trimmed with greying stubble, and his eyes bulged from his skull. He was perhaps four tenwinters old, but looked older. He had a slight frame and wasn't especially tall. He was a man one wouldn't normally notice and a man who evidently didn't *want* to be noticed.

Nievzê's deceptions had been successful. When his fellow Felk had invaded this city-state, Nievzê wasn't recognized. To the occupiers he was just one more Callahan who was too old to absorb into the army. He had blended in with Callah's poorer inhabitants, eating scraps when he had to, sleeping where he could. This last hadn't been so bad during the summer, but as autumn deepened, it had grown more and more problematical.

Nievzê was very grateful for the room. He was also grateful for the food. And the wine. Deo seemed to be enjoying the man's perpetual expressions of gratitude as much as his stories of the inner workings of the Academy, which was some school for magic training in the city of Felk.

"So, you deserted because you were ill-treated at your school," Radstac said, putting a slight but hard edge to it. "I've got that right, don't I?"

"Radstac—" Deo started. But she returned him that same flat look, and he quieted with a shake of his head.

Nievzê took a more measured swallow of wine this time. He was aware of Radstac's animosity but was hardly in a position to take offense at it.

"Actually," he said, his tone civil, "it was after I had graduated."

"And what happens after a magic student graduates from your Academy?"

Nievzê made a breezy gesture with one hand. "Well, there are a number of possibilities. Matokin had uses for wizards in quite a few capacities, so . . ." He dropped his hand and his eyes. "After graduation you go into the army."

Radstac let her teeth show in her unnerving version of a grin. "So, really, you ran away because you didn't want to go to war."

He didn't lift his gaze. "Yes," he said simply.

Radstac shrugged. Despite her career as a mercenary, she had no strong opinion about deserters. Cowardice on a battlefield was a very understandable condition.

Nievzê's faked death had been one of opportunity, he'd said. An accident had occurred at the Academy on the same day he was scheduled to leave to join the ranks of the Felk army. A wizard with a particular forte for fire magic—and not enough control over her talent—had managed to incinerate herself and four others nearby. Nievzê, the first one on the scene, recognized that one of these was a visitor who had, at great peril, infiltrated the Academy to see his young lover, the fire producing magician. Nievzê seized the opportunity, knowing that no record of the young man's visit would exist. He stuffed a few of his own personal effects into the man's seared clothing, fled the scene, and later escaped over the Academy walls.

Deo looked embarrassed for Nievzê. Seeking to change the subject, he asked, "What sort of magic did you learn at the Academy?"

Nievzê finally looked up. "Actually it's only technique that you learn there. Some people have an innate talent for magic. Most don't. Whatever capabilities you have are all you'll ever possess. They can only be refined."

Deo nodded. "That's very interesting. So, what techniques were you taught?"

"I specialized in blood magic."

Radstac had accompanied Deo when he'd brought the food and wine to Nievzê's room, meaning only to make sure Deo didn't pass the man any more money. Now she was regretting coming along. Nievzê was an irrelevancy. He could do nothing to help them and was in fact only a burden. Radstac felt no especial sympathy for him or his plight. He had been resourceful enough to contrive his own death, but he'd been barely able to survive on the streets of Callah.

"Blood magic?" Deo's brows raised. "What's that?"

Nievzê pushed away his plate and settled back in his chair with his cup of wine. "Human blood has certain individual properties," he said, adopting an oratory tone. "These specific characteristics are very susceptible to magic. The blood can be influenced, so to speak. In a number of counterproductive ways."

"Fascinating. How does it work?"

"If I were to take a sample of your blood and dab it onto a cloth and store it," the wizard said, "then later, whenever I wished, I could cast a spell that would affect the living blood in *your* body. More, your physical proximity would have no effect on the magic. In essence, you could flee to the far end of the Isthmus, and I would still be able to reach you."

Deo gaped. Radstac, for the first time, shared some part of his astonishment.

"That's . . . diabolical," he breathed.

Nievzê nodded his agreement.

Radstac frowned. "But what is the practical application of this magic?"

They both turned to look at her. Radstac could see in Nievzê's eyes that he knew she wasn't trying to provoke him this time.

"It was a security measure," he said. "One dreamed up by a highly placed, politically powerful mage named Abraxis. You've heard of him?"

Radstac and Deo shook their heads. When Nievzê had shown up at their door after curfew, having followed them from the tavern where they'd played that night, the two of them had maintained the pretense of being anti-Felk troubadours. Deo dropped the charade of being mentally deficient, and Radstac didn't fake her limp around Nievzê, but otherwise the Felk deserter had no clue that they were actually working for Internal Security.

"Abraxis is a ruthless man," Nievzê continued, "and his commitment to the success of the empire is equally fearsome. He arranged for samples of blood to be taken from each and every student who entered the Academy. Some of those students completed their training there, and some did not. But only the successful emerged alive. So now Abraxis has—inside that little red bag he always has, they say—the blood specimens of every wizard in the entire military. It's meant to ensure the total loyalty of the army's magicians. None of them dares turn against the empire, no matter how powerful they might be individually."

Radstac had seen many wars in her day, petty though they were in comparison to *this* conflict. She had seen brutality. She had seen abundant bloodshed. But she had never imagined that magic could be perverted so, turned into such a vicious instrument.

She rose from the room's only other chair. Deo was sitting on the foot of the bed. The space was windowless and, if anything, even shabbier than their own quarters.

"We should go," she said to Deo. "We have to go play soon."

He nodded reluctantly and stood. Nievzê rose as well and said in that servilely thankful voice he seemed able to summon at will, "Once more I give you my humblest thanks for the kindness you've showed me. Your humane nature is inspiring."

Deo waved all this off. Back in Petgrad he had been renowned for his philanthropy. Radstac supposed it was simply his disposition that had led him to aid this wayward magician so generously. Nevertheless, Deo took the bottle of wine with them, Radstac noted, pleased.

They exited the room, made for the building's third level. Deo needed to collect his vox-mellifluous.

He paused on the groaning stairs, looked at her. "You think I'm being foolish for supporting that man?"

Radstac nearly answered with a curt and simple *yes*. But she reconsidered and went through the unfamiliar process of allowing for another person's feelings. She finally said, "Foolishly altruistic." She even spoke it in a softer tone.

Deo pressed a smile from his lips. He nodded. "He thought we were connected to the rebels that night he saw us play. He wanted to join up."

Radstac shrugged. That was far less remarkable, in her view, than the fact that Nievzê had scraped together on his own the price of a drink at that tavern. Apparently Nievzê had undergone a change of heart regarding fighting; now, after having lived under the Felk occupation, he was ready to join the rebels.

Deo leaned nearer. The stairwell was dim, but his blue

eyes seemed to have a light of their own at the moment. "A rebel wizard. Don't you think that would be a valuable asset in this movement against the Felk?"

"I thought we were working *for* the Felk," Radstac said with a tiny smirk.

"Aquint's playing his game, and I'm playing mine. Should I ask which game you're participating in?"

"Not if you ever want a feel of my flesh again in this lifetime," she said facetiously; and even so, she was remotely stung that Deo would question her loyalty even in jest. She still considered her contract to him operative.

"I think he'll be . . . useful," Deo said.

"And in the meantime you can keep him as a pet. Let's get your stringbox. We have songs of protest to perform and Callahan hearts to swell. Let's not disappoint anyone."

IT WAS CALLED "Callah Forever Free," and it was among their catchiest songs, the melody borrowed from a bawdy ballad that concerned the endowments of a certain young female of frivolous sexual fidelity. Radstac sang the substitute words, and Deo made the music, and the patrons in the tavern gathered close as if to a warming fire.

Everyone was enjoying the performance. Everyone was properly stirred.

But it was during the second chorus of "Callah Forever Free," which the audience took up with her, that one figure rose to his feet and shot an accusing finger and shouted, "Traitors!"

Deo continued winding the instrument's knob, but Radstac left off her singing, eyeing the man, more amused than startled. The patrons murmured among themselves. Radstac finally gestured to Deo, and the music went silent.

"Your treachery disgusts me!" the man roared.

Radstac took a swallow of water from the cup on the table next to her. The man was large, gruff of voice, but also rather aged, at least six tenwinters. Still, he was heavy across the shoulders, and his bearded face was contorted into a fierce visage.

"Why do you shay that?" Deo asked in that labored lisping voice. Radstac could feel his sudden tension, very much like someone ready to defend his lover from insult. She wanted to tell him not to take it personally.

"All your pretty prattling about how evil the Felk are. What good is it? Do you even know what you're talking about? Do you honestly believe conditions here in Callah are so bad now? I remember the times before they arrived. I remember how we were always wondering if *this* was the year we would go to war with Windal. Well, that's not likely to happen now, is it? Windal is under the same protective control as we are. One Felk city isn't going to attack another."

"Oh, Saigot, either sit down or go away," someone among the patrons said.

But Saigot wasn't done. Radstac doubted he had ever been a man who ceased talking before he'd said all he had to say.

"The Felk are probably still sweeping southward. We hear all kinds of rumors, of course. But if the Felk had been stopped—and who, I ask, could do *that*?—then I think we would know about it, even as isolated as we are. That means they are busy conquering more of the Isthmus. And I say that is the best thing that could happen!"

The patrons jeered, but no one stepped up to challenge Saigot directly. Radstac continued to watch and listen, interested. Here was a viewpoint she'd not yet encountered.

"I am a Callahan," Saigot went on. "Born and bred to this city and proud of it. But I am also an inhabitant of a greater state—that of the Isthmus itself. And that Isthmus has, for virtually all its history, been struggling and divided, teetering on the brink of internal destruction. Now the Felk will end all that. We will have *one* rule. We'll have final unity."

It was, Radstac thought, as articulately bombastic as the inane songs she sang. This Saigot was simply arguing the other extreme end of the political gamut.

"And so," he said, "I say you two are traitors. And anyone who listens to this treasonous music is a traitor."

Radstac set down her cup of water. The tavern was tensely silent as she stepped down from the small raised space in the corner. She was prepared for his bodily strength, not deceived into confidence by Saigot's age. But the big bearded man produced a knife from his coat and held it and swung it in a way that demonstrated he knew what to do with it. The appearance of the weapon made up Radstac's mind for her, of course. She and Deo would have lost considerable credibility if Saigot's accusations went unanswered. Now, she would have to do something more than merely batter him.

Deo said later that he barely saw the two prongs that flashed out of her left leather glove. Quite suddenly Saigot was holding the side of his face and howling and bleeding profusely. The other patrons were shocked and impressed.

One of them, a woman with amber-colored eyes, came to Radstac and Deo and said quietly that the Minstrel would want to meet them. She named a time and place for a rendezvous tomorrow, then she left the tavern.

PRAULTH
(4)

"THANK YOU, XINK."

"My pleasure, General Praulth."

She accepted the tallgreen tea, served in a delicate sunset pink ceramic cup, properly honeyed and at the very temperature she liked. She accepted Xink's ministrations, accepted his desperate need to care for her. She even accepted his apparent conviction that with enough coddling and nurturing he could undo all her wounds.

The deeper truth was that Praulth's wounds *were* healing, physically and in every other significant manner. Xink, however, had been damaged as well, and he seemed wholly unable to admit to this.

It was a dilemma, and a dire one, but it was also taking up precious space that she simply couldn't spare right now. Her ultimate purpose was coming to fruition, her day against Dardas. She had a war to consider, one that could permanently change the fabric of the Isthmus. That was where her concentration needed to be.

She sat among the tables that were atop the dais. The auditorium wasn't nearly so crowded and active as the last time she'd been here, but there were enough officials gathered to give the place an engaged atmosphere. Petgrad's Noble Ministry was not present.

The tables were still spread with maps and intelligence reports. Praulth was current on the movements of the Alliance army, which had assembled—and was still accumulating—on a wide prairie south of the fallen city of Trael. This area, she had learned, was called the Pegwithe Plains. The bulk of the forces were in place, though stray units continued to collect.

It might be generous on her part to regard this as the Alliance *army*. It was, quite literally, a hodgepodge of military companies of vastly unequal training and strength. Worse, these forces had had no time or opportunity to drill together in any manner. They would be tried and tested on their very first venture as a united military entity.

Holding them together was Cultat. And Praulth's plan to utilize the Battle of Torran Flats.

A desperate history being made . . .

The others here in the auditorium were secondary delegates who had remained in Petgrad and aides to these minor dignitaries. Praulth had brought Xink along in the capacity of her adjutant. He needed to be near her, and she understood that. Actually she felt very understanding toward him lately, a stark reversal from her previous attitude. She wasn't experiencing the hot reblooming of her onetime virginal love for him; rather, it was a calmer, more reasonable appreciation of his evident loyalty to her. He had, after all, stayed at her side despite the petty incivility and contempt with which she'd treated him too often since they had left Febretree.

Now, after all that had happened, Xink's deceptions didn't seem especially relevant. Even Xink working in cahoots with Master Honnis, blatantly manipulating her, didn't bother Praulth overmuch. Maybe Cultat had been correct; maybe manipulation wasn't so awful a crime.

She could certainly see the reasons for Honnis's artifices. Her old mentor had needed to be assured that she would stay entirely focused on the Felk war. Had he approached her openly, she might have hesitated, reluctant to risk the advancement of her academic career at the University. Xink had served as a distraction from her other studies.

Honnis had been right to do it. This war outweighed all other considerations. It occurred to Praulth, as she sipped her tea, that she wanted very much to tell Honnis that.

Merse was here in the auditorium as well. He sat alone, out in the seats, slouched, a brimmed hat on his head pulled low to shadow his weathered features. Praulth sensed that he wasn't asleep; rather, was watching this small assembly atop the dais, watching her in particular. He was there to receive and relay any messages from the Far Speak scouts observing the Felk and accompanying the Alliance forces. It had been nearly two full watches since he'd said anything.

She wondered briefly what Merse thought of her new title, then she dismissed the thought. What did it matter what the cantankerous Petgradite wizard thought? She was pleased with how Xink pronounced it: "General Praulth." Without any hint of irony. With the full respect the title merited.

Her gaze fell to the maps, but she already had every square memorized. The configuration for the Torran Flats gambit was carefully drawn out according to her instructions. From the reports so far received, it appeared the Alliance might just have sufficient numbers to carry this off successfully.

It was, for the moment, the quiet agony of wait and see.

This was the first time Praulth had come out of her rooms since the Incident. Xink, capering about in an unproductive panic, had finally summoned a physician that night, then officials of the local police. These latter were a pair of elderly officers who had remained behind while the Petgrad army rode off to gather with the Alliance forces. Petgrad's police force was a meager complement these days, the ranks dangerously thinned. It was why patrols of the streets had been reduced and why crimes of opportunity were on the increase. Add to that the catastrophic influx of refugees, many hungry and destitute, and the situation was well out of hand.

Praulth, following the professionally thorough examination by the Petgrad physician, had told the police she understood the dire state of things. She had by then recovered her voice. It was Xink who insisted repeatedly that the individual who'd assaulted her be apprehended. He demanded that no effort be spared. He invoked her prominent standing and her personal favor with Premier Cultat. The police promised to do everything possible, but Praulth had recognized that a single scavenger, even mentally unbalanced as he probably was, could likely elude capture in this vast city.

She didn't yet know if the Incident had left her pregnant. Certainly her assailant took none of the prudent precautions with which she was familiar with Xink. Again it was a matter of wait and see.

Did she feel wounded? Did she feel invaded, violated?

Naturally she did. The foul creature had robbed from her. He had knocked her to the ground and infiltrated her body in the most careless and hurtful fashion, indifferent to everything but the savage satisfaction of the moment. He had gibbered and ranted all the while, ugly broken fragments of speech propelled by repulsive breath.

But when the fast wrenching spasms had struck him, this violator let out a frail little whine, like the sound of a hurt puppy, and leaped to his feet and went running off in a mad scramble. It was very much as if that violent and rapid climax had taken with it every last shred of maddened courage the creature possessed.

Such was the conclusion Praulth had drawn in those first stinging instants after the Incident. Her attacker was weak, she told herself. Therefore, she would be strong. And thus she had picked herself up from the street and returned to her rooms, all on her own, without faltering, without even tears.

She had since cried, and it had served her as a release. Xink had certainly been generous enough with his own tears, almost to the point where she felt an inkling of that old reflexive irritation; but she'd checked that. There was no point in abusing him. He, however, was going to have to find his own way to come to terms with the Incident.

Praulth had dressed for today. She wore no uniform, though she had considered it; it was, after all, her privilege. Instead, she had picked meticulously through the clothes that had been provided with the rooms. It was quite a wardrobe. Eventually she had settled on a long coat of dark green that was trimmed with leather at the cuffs and collar. She chose a flattering shirt and trousers, accentuating with a knotted scarf of a deep red metallic fabric. She also picked out a pair of gleaming boots, ones that fit her to her knees and served to compliment the narrowness of her legs. She was very pleased with the ensemble. She was determined to wear it from here on out, for all public appearances. When she was remembered, when her portrait was painted and handed down with history, she would be dressed so. It would help seal the memory of her.

She didn't think these details trivial. Certainly they weren't as important as her prime purpose, but she had a clear and concise picture in her mind of the full sweep of her life from this point onward. Her place at the University, once the self-contained goal of her existence, would be in hindsight only an interlude, even if in her declining years she elected to return to Febretree to take up a lofty post among the faculty. It would be nothing too demanding, merely enough to keep her mind active. More of an excuse, in truth, to receive the excited visitations of burgeoning war scholars younger than she was now who would be eager to bask in her—

Merse, who Praulth was keeping furtively in her line of sight at all times, abruptly rose to his feet. In his hand he gripped an old bracelet she recognized as an article he used when he worked the Far Speak magic.

Her heart quickened. She sat up straighter. The ancillary diplomat from Q'ang, who had been keeping up a steady banal patter next to her, went silent, following her gaze.

"Is that—" he started.

Xink was on her other side, standing behind, acting every bit the attentive aide. She felt him edge forward, near enough that she heard his breathing.

Merse stood there a moment, silent, his features beneath the hat's brim hardened in concentration. Then it broke, and the disconnection was almost visible. He jammed the bracelet back into his coat and started up the aisle.

"The outer fringes of the armies have just come within sight of each other," the older, wiry-limbed man announced, not addressing anyone on the dais directly, which annoyed Praulth mildly. Clearly she was the personage of highest rank present.

The minor diplomats broke out into excited chatter. Praulth remained silent, stately, her eyes still on Merse. She had known from the scouts' reports that the Felk had mobilized, doubtlessly alerted to the Alliance forces by their own Far Speak scouts. The Felk had come to meet the Alliance, without any apparent hesitation.

Dardas, it seemed, wasn't about to shirk from a fight.

This would effectively be the very first battle of this war. As yet, the Felk had ably conquered cities and villages without meeting any special resistance. Even the infamous atrocity at U'delph had been merely a one-sided slaughter.

Premier Cultat was leading the Alliance in the field. Petgrad's respectably sized military was by far the single largest force among the Alliance's array, and so leadership fell naturally to the man most responsible for assembling that Alliance. Cultat knew how this reenactment of the Battle of Torran Flats needed to be conducted. Praulth had seen to it that he was fully versed on the placement of troops, the tactics, every military nuance of that original campaign. If it was carried out properly, Dardas would be lured into a fatally vulnerable position, allowing the Alliance to drive straight through the Felk.

If it was still Dardas leading that army . . .

"Merse," Praulth said, "approach, if you would."

He had halted at the foot of the aisle. Now Merse lifted his chin to give her a wry look. "What's it you want, Praulth?"

"That's *General* Praulth," Xink said, storming forward

a step, voice cracking off the auditorium's far walls, as the place had been acoustically designed for.

Merse let a subtle—and all the more infuriating for it—smile touch his lips. Praulth recalled the naked contempt he'd had for the students at the University. His view was that they should all be eagerly joining the Alliance. Perhaps he still regarded her as one of those "idlers."

But she would not respond childishly to his attitude. Her position called for a dignified bearing. She had survived the Incident. She would weather this man's opinions.

Praulth gently but pointedly waved Xink back. He was so . . . so *coiled* these days. His anger winding him up. It was his frustration that he hadn't been there to defend her. He wanted to assuage that futile anger by finding the culprit who had assaulted her (this was unlikely, the Petgrad police had said) and by protecting and tending to her every moment (this was becoming rather intrusive, but she was determined to let him do what he needed to do).

Merse stepped up onto the dais, taking his time, coming to the opposite side of the table where she sat.

"Was the information you received detailed?" she asked, voice level.

He shrugged. "Those are good scouts out there. What exactly do you mean?" She knew that those Far Speak scouts were members of Merse's own clan.

Praulth turned a map around and pushed it across the tabletop. "Could you show where the Felk units are starting to appear?"

Merse paused a moment, then removed his hat and dropped it beside the map. "Give me something to draw with," he said, stooping. Praulth passed him an implement. He sketched quickly and neatly, pushed the sheet back toward her. "There. That's what you want?"

Praulth looked at the advancing Felk array. She stared. She felt her eyes glazing. She felt herself entering that physically languid, mentally dynamic state that she had assumed so often before at the University.

Moments later she blinked her way back to the auditorium. A silence was focused on her. The Q'ang official was turned, watching her. Xink had crept back up beside her. Merse, too, was still standing before her, a frown creasing his leathery face.

"Where did you go?" he asked, quite softly now, and a small impressed smile replaced his frown as she watched.

It wasn't the first time she had startled others with the depth of her concentration. Fellow students at Febretree had told her it was like she was asleep with her eyes opened.

"It is what I do," she said. "It's how I concentrate."

Merse nodded, seeming to regard her anew. He gestured to the map. "What are you looking for?"

She met his eyes. "A signature," she finally said, adding nothing more.

Merse said, "I'll bring you any further communications." He stepped off the dais.

THE LARGE MUNICIPAL building that housed the auditorium was equipped with plumbing and indoor facilities. Xink followed when, later, she went to relieve herself.

"Xink . . ." she said, squelching a sharply edged barb; finally saying, "I can do this alone."

"I know." He halted there in the corridor outside the auditorium. His long dark hair fell around his face. He looked small, turned in on himself.

Praulth let out a small sigh. "Xink, you've got to come to grips. You can't be present for every single instant of my life from this moment onward. You can't safeguard me, not completely, not forever."

For a brief moment she thought he was going to start weeping, which *would* have annoyed her. Instead, he drew himself up straighter, took a step toward her. "I know," he repeated. "But what happened to you will never happen again. I swear that." His tone was hard, unyielding. But there was warmth there as well, compassion for her. He did still love her.

Praulth ignored the increasingly insistent pangs from her bladder. Immediately following the Incident it had hurt to urinate; since, however, the discomfort had eased.

"He's coming," she said.

Xink blinked, nonplussed.

"Dardas," she said. "I know it's still him. I *feel* him." Her lips tightened in a smile. The sketch Merse had made on that map had provided scant clues, just the outer shapes of the advance Felk companies. Yet . . . she had known. She wondered what old Honnis would say to her barely logical, acutely intuitive judgment.

Praulth turned away, hurrying a bit now, wanting to get back to the auditorium as fast as possible. She would stay there until this was done. He was coming. Dardas the Rapist. And she was ready for him.

AQUINT
(4)

HE ALMOST LET out a yelp and jumped to his feet, but restrained himself. Even so, his heart pounded as the shock of the news hit him.

Radstac was standing inside the doorway of the apartment. It was early morning and Aquint's head was doing its usual whirl whenever he was woken up at such an early watch. He ran a hand through his hair. Cat had heard her insistent knocking and had come to shake him out of bed.

Now, he was sitting in the outer room wondering if he had really heard her right. Cat stood off to one side. They had said little to each other since Aquint had handed over that innocent addict for Jesile to behead in the square.

"The Minstrel," Aquint finally said, his mouth feeling pasty and his eyes smarting. "He wants to meet you?"

Radstac, having said it once, didn't appear to feel the need to repeat herself. She gazed at him with those colorless eyes.

Aquint shook his head, marveling at the news. He had
sent out Radstac and Deo as bogus anti-Felk troubadours,
hoping against all reasonable hope that the Broken Circle
would be lured by their songs of rebellion. It had been a
desperate gamble, frankly, with longer odds than he ever
would have considered if this were a game of Dashes.

"Where and when is the rendezvous?" he asked.

Radstac recited it. Aquint glanced at Cat, who nodded.
They both knew where this location was, a number of
streets west of the city's central marketplace.

Finally, Aquint couldn't contain himself. He stood and
let out a hoarse but heartfelt whoop of happiness. The Minstrel! The troublemaker. The bleeder who had forced
Aquint to make a sacrifice of that wretched drug addict.

"We've still got several watches before it's scheduled,"
Aquint said. He clapped his hands together. Then he said,
"Wait. Why did you wait until now to report to me?"

"Curfew came," Radstac said.

Aquint waved a hand. "You're an Internal Security
agent. You don't have to worry about any of that. Haven't
I made that clear?"

"And if that Broken Circle contact observed us breaking curfew with total impunity?" Radstac asked.

Aquint considered and nodded. It was an excellent
point. He asked, "You're sure this person at the tavern said
the Minstrel himself wanted to meet with you?"

Radstac was sure. She managed to convey this without
speaking or nodding.

She certainly was a hard thing, Aquint thought. Those
facial scars didn't make her any more cuddly. Still, that
Deo fellow certainly seemed fond of her . . .

Aquint frowned. There was no obvious reason why
Deo should have accompanied her here this morning.

This message she was conveying didn't require the pair of them. Nonetheless, Deo's absence suddenly concerned Aquint.

"Where, may I ask, is Deo this morning?" Aquint asked, knowing by some instinct that he wasn't going to like the answer.

He was right.

Radstac said, just as tonelessly as before, "Deo has deserted his post. He decided he wants to join the rebels. He left me at that tavern and followed the woman out."

It was one shock too many this early in the day. Aquint fell back into his seat.

From his twirling thoughts, he grabbed a question. "Did Deo say anything to you before he went?"

"He asked me if I wanted to join the rebels with him."

"And you said . . . ?" Aquint prompted.

"I told him he was being an ass. I threatened to snap his arm if he talked anymore foolishness."

"What did he say?" Aquint asked.

"He didn't," said Radstac. "He went scurrying off."

Silent until now, Cat suddenly asked, "You didn't follow him?"

Radstac gave him a glance. Then she did something Aquint had never seen her do before. She looked embarrassed. She bit her lower lip and looked at the floor.

"I, uh, didn't," she hesitated. "Look, we're more than comrades, Deo and I. I didn't want him to do this stupid thing. But I just couldn't—I mean, what could I do? *Arrest* him?"

Aquint raised a hand. "All right, all right. I think I understand." He put the hand to his forehead. Now he had a renegade agent to worry about. "Do you think this rendezvous with the Minstrel will still be on?"

Radstac shrugged. "I don't know. The woman had already left the tavern. Deo may not have caught up to her."

Aquint drummed his fingers on the arm of the chair. "But let's assume he did. With his new set of loyalties, would he tell her you two were with Internal Security? If he wanted to warn the Minstrel away from the rendezvous today he would have to tell that woman *something*. Surely he knows we'll set a trap for the Minstrel." The thought still set Aquint tingling with anticipation.

"I'm sorry," Radstac said. "I don't know what he'll do. All this was very surprising to me."

He looked closer at her. Did she look . . . sad? That, too, was unprecedented. It certainly confirmed his suspicion that she and Deo were lovers.

Aquint was sorry to have lost one of his agents, especially like this. But if he had to lose one of these two, he was glad he still had Radstac working for him. He was also glad he didn't have to report these details to Abraxis. After all, Abraxis only wanted results.

And Aquint had damned well better start producing results. This was a choice assignment he had here in Callah. He definitely didn't want to find himself stripped of his position and sent back to that warehouse in Sook, or much worse, sent back into the field. Being a foot soldier had not agreed with him.

Also, he had Cat to think of.

Aquint rose to his feet, more deliberately this time.

"Very well," he said. "It's just the three of us. I don't want to bring Jesile's troops in on this just yet. We don't know how this is going to play out, but we do have a time and a place for the rendezvous. Radstac, you're going to be there. Understood?"

She understood it.

"Cat and I will be there, too," he went on, "but you won't see either of us. We'll observe what happens. Maybe nothing will happen. But it's just possible that the Minstrel *will* show up. We still have a decent description of him. If he's there today, he's ours."

HE AND CAT made their way to the rendezvous site well ahead of time. The place was an empty lot between two buildings, and it was fairly overgrown with weeds. The street it abutted wasn't a busy one.

Aquint had dressed in grubby clothes, along with a cloak with a hood. He hadn't bothered wearing his arm sling. It was drizzling. With the hood up, his face was hidden. He wanted himself and Cat to appear as nondescript as possible. This was a poorer district of Callah. Cat, too, had worn more ragged attire than usual.

Together they surveyed the scene for the best place to observe the empty lot.

Cat was humming softly to himself. Twice Aquint had caught a glimpse of the boy smiling secretly.

"Why're you so pleased?" Aquint asked.

"Because we might be capturing the Minstrel today," Cat blinked back innocently at him.

"I'm thinking it might be something else," Aquint said blandly.

The lad shrugged. "I guess one of those agents, at least, wasn't so good a pick."

For a moment, Aquint felt a stab of anger. This was Cat's jealousy over Deo and Radstac again. The boy had never liked those two intruding on his and Aquint's personal association.

Then Aquint reconsidered and let out a soft chuckle.

Admitting it when you were wrong wasn't always easy. And anyway, it was good that he and Cat were talking again. "Fine, lad. Deo turns out to have been a bad choice for an Internal Security agent."

"Perhaps a *very* bad choice," Cat mused aloud.

"Fine. Very bad. Now, stop gloating, and let's find ourselves a vantage point."

That place turned out to be a recessed doorway at the corner of one of the buildings. It was a crumbling pile, and Aquint guessed the place was abandoned. From here, he and Cat could observe the whole weedy lot.

The time for the rendezvous was creeping closer.

Today, Aquint was armed. He had a short Felk sword under his cloak. The hard length pressed against him, bringing him no comfort. He didn't like weapons any better than he ever had, but if the Minstrel did show up, things were liable to get sticky.

The possibility of capturing the Minstrel still put a thrill into Aquint. Handing the Minstrel over to Abraxis would be a boon to his career. It would surely mean he would be allowed to conduct his operations against the Broken Circle some while longer. The more time Aquint spent in Callah, the better. Occupied by the Felk or not, this was home and it was also far away from the war.

He and Cat waited, silently. The day's grey drizzle continued to sift down. Aquint watched the passersby in the street.

Finally, the time had come. Aquint glanced to his side and realized with a start that Cat had vanished. He shook his head. The boy had a knack for stealth that was almost eerie. Probably he had slipped off to his own vantage place, so that the two of them could watch the lot from more than one angle. Aquint probably should have thought of that himself. Wherever Cat was now, he was well hidden.

At that moment Aquint saw Radstac approaching, walking along with that affected limp. She came up to the edge of the lot and halted.

Aquint didn't watch her as she stood there waiting. Instead, he swept the area continuously with his eyes, his heart beating hard again. He looked for any male bearing any resemblance to the Minstrel's description. He took into account the many possible disguises the man might attempt. He also watched for the woman from the tavern, who Radstac had described very adequately.

As for other members of the Broken Circle who might show up today, they could be anybody.

Aquint put his hand into his cloak and gripped the short sword's hilt. He continued to study the scene keenly.

Radstac, apparently impatient, stepped out into the lot. Aquint muttered a silent curse. The instructions had been to remain still. She moved deeper into the weeds, looking around. As he'd promised, she didn't see him, and it was a near certainty that she wouldn't see Cat either.

No one else entered the lot. No one appeared to be lingering nearby the scene. Aquint sighed, disappointed. He hadn't had any right to expect much from this, but he had been hoping nonetheless.

Suddenly, Radstac, half obscured by the tall weeds, gave a yelp and dropped from view.

Aquint started, grip tightening on the sword handle. Had she merely tripped and fallen? Or, had someone been lying in ambush for her out in those weeds?

He hesitated. She didn't stand back up. Something was wrong. He didn't see Cat emerging from wherever his hiding place was to come to her aid. That wasn't surprising. Aquint gritted his teeth. Once he exposed himself, this operation was through. But Radstac had demonstrated loyalty, sticking to her assignment even though Deo had abandoned his. Aquint had to go make sure she was all right.

He broke from the recessed doorway at a fast trot. The ground was uneven, and the dirt had turned to mud. He nearly stumbled as he approached the spot where Radstac had fallen. With an unhappy grunt, he loosed his sword, swinging its unfamiliar weight.

Aquint cut a swath through a clump of weeds. With a final leap he came down on the place where Radstac had disappeared, expecting to find her lying on the ground. She wasn't there. He halted, stunned.

"Let go of that sword."

Aquint turned sharply, and squinted into the drizzling rain. Deo was standing about ten paces off, a crossbow against his shoulder, the bolt aimed directly at Aquint's chest.

"Let go of it," Deo repeated.

"Gods*damn* you," Aquint muttered.

"They may or they may not. Either way, you're running out of chances to drop that weapon peaceably, before I have to skewer you."

Aquint lowered the sword but didn't yet let it go. Hot anger welled up inside him. He glared venomously at Deo.

"You traitorous bleeder."

A hard smile touched Deo's mouth. "That's a word I've heard bandied around quite a bit lately. Traitor. A very flexible word, I think. Tell me, do you think it might just apply to you as well?"

The anger went suddenly white hot. Aquint wasn't one to let himself be provoked, but the insult cut too deep. Without thinking, he was raising the sword and taking a first step toward Deo.

Suddenly a hand locked over his wrist and a fist sailed in from the edge of his field of vision and smacked his jaw. It was just hard enough for him to loosen his grip and stagger back a step. The short sword was snatched from his hand.

When he turned, rubbing his jaw, he saw that Radstac now held it.

"Traitors . . ." Aquint said. He felt genuinely betrayed. After all, he had rescued this pair from whatever military disciplinary action awaited them after their unauthorized arrival here in Callah. He had entrusted these two with the responsibilities of Internal Security agents.

"You wanted to meet the Minstrel," Radstac said. "We're taking you to see him." From her pocket she pulled a strip of black cloth. *A blindfold,* Aquint thought.

Here in the middle of the lot, they were screened from the street by the weeds. No bystander was going to come to Aquint's rescue. He had no choice but to submit.

He saw the tiny flash of movement, but did not let his eyes betray it. Radstac was coming toward him with the blindfold. Deo was still holding the crossbow on him. Aquint had seen the figure moving behind Deo.

Radstac halted sharply, turned, and shouted, "Behind, on your right, low!"

With horror-wide eyes, Aquint watched Deo pivot tightly and fire the crossbow bolt. It twanged keenly, and Aquint heard the sound of the bolt striking something soft.

Radstac stuck the point of the sword against his ribs to keep him from running heedlessly toward Cat. Her hard, scarred face showed no emotion as she handed him the blindfold and told him to put it on. Numbly, he did so. She told him to pull up the cloak's hood once more, and he obeyed. She gripped one of his arms, and Deo came to take the other.

In lockstep they led him off. Aquint couldn't bring himself to ask if Cat was still alive.

DARDAS
(4)

ANTICIPATION AND GLEEFUL joy sharpened his senses to knife-edge keenness. Unfortunately, it was daylight and Weisel had control of the body, so there wasn't much Dardas could do to physically celebrate.

Still, the news of the rival army coming to meet them was absolutely thrilling.

This Isthmus was mustering up armed, organized resistance to the Felk conquest. Finally! Now, Dardas would have a genuine war to fight. And there was nothing better in life than war.

However, it seemed that it would probably take some convincing to persuade Weisel of that fact.

"I want reports, damnit!" Weisel snapped. "I want *current* reports!"

Fergon, his personal aide, winced. "Yes, General. The Far Speak scouts are sending them as quickly as—"

"Not quickly enough!" Weisel cut him off. "I want to

know what's happening with that army out there every single moment. Is that clear?"

"Very clear, General."

Weisel dismissed him curtly. Fergon saluted and hurried off on horseback.

Was it necessary to treat your aide so? Dardas asked. *Are you so fond of the boy?*

That's not the point. We will be going into battle almost certainly in the near future. As a general, you will be called upon not just for your military expertise—somehow Dardas managed to say this without laughing—*but for cool-headed reliability. Your officers and even your troops will want to know that their commander is calm, confident, and thinking clearly.*

Weisel drew a deep breath. Dardas could feel the man's anxiety. It was powerful. It had started the moment word had reached Weisel's tent about the enemy army.

At the moment, the vast Felk host was moving southward, just as that other army was moving north. Weisel was riding his strong, hardy horse, surrounded by the entourage of his personal guards. As customary, he was toward the rear of the Felk forces. It gave him a good view of the various companies arrayed ahead of him. They were on the broad, massive prairie south of the city of Trael.

For Dardas's part, he was quite pleased that they were finally outside of that damned tent of Weisel's. Since the assassination attempt, Weisel had barely set foot outside, and that pavilion had become something of a canvas prison. Now he had been forced outdoors, and the cool air was refreshing. The sight of all those troops was stirring. It was glorious to be alive.

I still need current intelligence, Weisel grumbled silently.

This Felk nobleman was going to be tested by this coming battle, and the outcome of that testing, Dardas judged, was rather foregone.

You will have that intelligence, Dardas assured him. *Better field intelligence than any war commander in history.*

Dardas could sense that this wasn't doing much to calm Weisel. Once things got started, once the two armies actually met, Dardas knew that the implementation of strategies and counterresponses would fall inevitably to him. Weisel would have no idea what he was doing when instantaneous decisions and positive action were called for.

Weisel would want his advice, and Dardas would give it. He would know how to meet this resistance, how to parry with various units, thrust with others. It was the merry dance of warfare. Dardas's instincts were honed. His talent for war was, literally, historic.

General Weisel would continue to defer to him as things heated up. Even without command of this body, Dardas would be the one leading this coming battle.

But who are they? Weisel asked suddenly. *This other army—it's too large to belong to any one state. Not even Petgrad could assemble something this large.*

It's an agglomeration, surely, Dardas said. *Various states banding together against a common enemy.*

That's very glib, General Dardas, Weisel said, sourly.

Dardas gave a mental shrug. It didn't especially matter to him where these rival troops had come from, though he was quite sure his theory was correct. He was simply happy that the natural order of existence had at last asserted itself and provided him a worthy foe.

At least, he hoped this was a worthy foe. If this army was a collection of diverse militaries, he hoped it was led by a creditable general.

Still, the reports so far received from the Felk scouts at the army's forefront showed that the rival array had some organizational integrity. Troops and cavalry weren't just blundering northward haphazardly.

We have advantages over this enemy, General Weisel.

Weisel held his horse at a steady trot. At least outwardly he was maintaining something of a stolid front, except for his outburst at Fergon. *Of course we do,* he agreed, not sounding entirely convinced.

Dardas pressed on, annoyed at having to prop up this creature of such hollow courage. *We have magic. We have a means to move ourselves great distances. We have wizards who can start fires remotely. We have instant communications. All these advantages have never been tested in actual battle. But it is unmistakable that these are crucial benefits.*

Of course, Weisel repeated, only slightly more confidently.

Dardas gave up for the moment, instead enjoying the sights around him. The grandeur of this army in motion was breathtaking. He found it quite moving. How nostalgic it was. He remembered so very vividly the days he'd led his Northland horde against the armies of rival warlords. Always it was a thrill. Always he saw his troops as extensions of himself, a great mass of power and brawn and weaponry, advancing implacably against all adversaries, conquering as he pleased.

Presently, they were still some appreciable distance from the army to their south. They might meet in the field today, though this would only happen in the waning watches of the day's light. More likely, they would move gradually into full mutual view, each slowing, arranging and rearranging their forward units, feeling each other out.

Actual contact might not occur until tomorrow, with the day's dawning.

And that day would be a memorable one, Dardas thought with keen anticipation.

Of course, it was possible to Far Move a few units into nearly direct contact with the other army right this moment. That might be interesting. Strike the first blow prematurely, even recklessly. Stories of U'delph's annihilation and the way the Felk had appeared from nowhere had doubtlessly circulated southward, inspiring fear. Dardas had made sure a few survivors from that city were set loose just for this purpose.

But Weisel would never agree to it. It was too bold. Weisel desperately wanted to be the heroic, dauntless general, but his basic nature was a cautious one. He would want to study their enemy before committing to anything, and this was, Dardas had to admit, the militarily prudent thing to do.

Besides, Dardas, too, wanted to gain a sense of this other army's leadership. He wanted a feel for his adversary's tactics. He wanted to "know" who he was fighting.

There was a company of wagons on their right, carrying food, supplies, and ordnance. One of those wagons, however, was secretly bearing a different cargo, the wizard Kumbat. He was still bound and gagged, as per Dardas's orders, and was being carefully guarded. Dardas was seeing to it that nothing happened to him. Raven had been instrumental in securing the mage, and Dardas was grateful to her for it.

That pair from the Internal Security Corps, who had arrived when the army was still encamped, had since returned to Felk, empty-handed and none the wiser. They couldn't very well continue their investigations while the army was heading into battle.

Kumbat would ensure Dardas's longevity, freeing him from whatever pressure Matokin might decide to exert on him. Actually, no longer needing to rely on the Felk emperor for those rejuvenation spells freed Dardas utterly. He could now do what he would, and Matokin could do nothing to threaten him.

Though this had already occurred to him, Dardas hadn't considered it so directly and fully. The realization filled him with a satisfied glow that was as powerful as Weisel's anxiety.

You seem pleased, Weisel observed.

Dardas clamped down on his emotions. Only the most potent could bleed over like that into his host's consciousness.

I am looking forward to the battle, Dardas said, quite honestly.

You don't . . . feel fear? Weisel asked a bit shyly.

Dardas didn't, but said, *Of course I feel fear. But it is a valuable fear. It is one that will keep you sharp, alert. One that will, contrarily, bolster your courage.*

Weisel let out a barely audible sigh. *That's a real army out there. It's not some pitiful little village we're going to simply run over on our way to our next victory.*

It's time this army faced a real challenge, Dardas said.

Why do you say that? Weisel asked suspiciously.

Dardas couldn't contain it any longer. *General Weisel, an army exists for specific purposes. It is the instrument through which a political entity, like your Felk Empire, can exert itself upon its rivals. An army can serve the will of any number of causes, whether they are worthy or monstrous. But that army, those soldiers, have purposes of their own. They have been trained relentlessly to perform in combat. If they are denied that opportunity too long it leads to serious trouble. Every fighter here, even those who would consider themselves the most craven, or the most inexperienced, longs in his or her heart to* fight. *They are starved for the taste of blood, for the chance to prove themselves in the greatest, truest sense. They need to battle an enemy. And now, finally, their moment is coming!*

Dardas's tirade seemed to echo in the mental air a moment. He wondered if he had gone too far. It might be that Weisel simply couldn't understand the code of battle and the righteousness of a soldier's bloodlust.

Weisel drew himself up straighter in the saddle. He set his jaw and firmed his features.

General Dardas, I will not disappoint these good soldiers.

For that moment, Dardas almost respected the Felk lord.

THE COMPANIES HALTED briefly and individually for their meals. Only the vanguard units stayed in steady motion, eating and taking water as they continued their advance toward the enemy army. Thus, the Felk military moved throughout the day.

Weisel received his reports, and Dardas studied them through his eyes. Slowly, the enemy was taking shape. That was indeed a sizable force out there. Its organization was growing more apparent as well. It was arrayed into separate companies, just as this Felk military was.

The map accompanying the report showed the clear delineations. Weisel pulled his horse to a brief stop as he concentrated on the map.

What do you propose we do, General Dardas?

Weisel was deferring to him. It was beginning already. Dardas was pleased.

We should continue the advance, he said. *There is still a watch or so of good daylight.*

We should attack them at night? Weisel asked, dubiously.

I don't think so. I don't think the other commander would want to either. We'll get a good look at each other, maybe make a few feints, just to test one another.

How do you know what that other army's commander will do? Weisel asked.

It's the militarily sensible thing to do, General Weisel. Dardas didn't add that already, from this relatively meager intelligence, he was gleaning a sense of how this enemy operated. In his time, two hundred and fifty years ago, he had possessed the uncanny talent for deciphering a foe's predilections and skills, and then of course working against that foe's weaknesses.

He would do the same with this enemy. But he would not crush this army, not completely. So long now he had waited for an enemy, some force to counter this Felk one, to justify this magnificent host of fighters and wizards. He wanted perpetual warfare. He couldn't have that if he had no enemies.

Dardas continued to hope that this opposite army had a commander of some skill directing it.

As the day wore on, the incoming reports became more detailed. By now Dardas could actually see the enemy through Weisel's eyes, straddling the flat horizon, filling the other end of the wide prairie. That army's numbers were impressive, though not quite equal to these Felk troops. Still, if this enemy had the talent for combat it would be a very respectable fight.

It was now clear, according to the scouts' observations, that this was indeed an agglomerated force. These troops wore widely varying uniforms, when they wore them at all. The forward companies appeared well armed. They bore swords, spears, pikes, crossbows; there were archers and cavalry and all the traditional components of a military.

Dardas wondered who had assembled it all. Surely there had to be one driving force behind it, some individual who had rallied these sundry armies, large and small. Then again, maybe the mass need had brought them all together, the intractable awareness that the Felk were coming to conquer these lands and that these people of the southern Isthmus had better do something if they wanted to prevent that.

The soldiers of that army would be defending their homes. That would make them fierce.

Dardas grinned.

What— Weisel started, sharply surprised.

Dardas realized that he himself had just caused that grin, had made the facial muscles move, all while Weisel was fully conscious.

He decided to effect innocence. *Is something wrong, General Weisel?*

I just— I thought— Oh, never mind. I think I'm just a little nervous.

I understand, Dardas said sympathetically.

This was an interesting development, but it could wait for later, for him to give it more attention. At the moment more reports were arriving.

Heeding Dardas's recommendation, Weisel had slowed the Felk advancement. The daylight was definitely waning by now, and a night battle wouldn't be wise. There was still a considerable gap between the two armies' front ranks.

Weisel halted his mount, as Fergon delivered the fresh

batch of field intelligence. He opened the map and studied it.

Dardas studied as well, of course. The enemy forces had solidified their positions noticeably from the last batch of scout reports. They were taking tactical shape now. Not that there had been any doubt about it, but this was definitely a hostile posture. This enemy *was* an enemy.

He continued to pore over the map. Those forces, arrayed as they were . . .

Excitement flooded suddenly through Dardas, and once more it had an effect on Weisel body, speeding the heart conspicuously.

What is it, General Dardas? Weisel asked, again aware of his emotional reaction. Was the barrier between their two consciousnesses breaking down somehow? There was no time to contemplate it.

Send your scouts east and west, Dardas said. *I feel quite certain they will find enemy units moving into flanking positions.*

You mean this is a trap? Weisel's fear sped his heart as well.

Yes, Dardas said, happily and confidently. *It is.* Once more Weisel's lips twitched in a Dardas-directed grin. *And I know how to turn that trap back on our enemy.*

BRYCK
(4)

THE CROSSBOW HAD been lifted—boldly—from beside a Felk soldier who'd dozed at his post. Gelshiri had perpetrated the theft, seizing the opportunity and the valuable weapon without hesitation. She was a believer in the cause, that one. Rebellion against the Felk. Liberation for Callah. She might not be the shiniest coin in the ante, but she had been wily enough to get away with the crossbow.

Bryck had considered staging this meeting in a shadowed place, where his face would be without feature. Or simply wearing his yellow and blue face paint. But the Felk had his description, a thorough one according to Deo and Radstac; so it made no difference what this Aquint saw, regardless of what they ultimately intended to do with him.

Let the enemy see my face finally and clearly, Bryck had concluded.

Deo, as it happened, was quite handy with the crossbow. Radstac, Deo claimed, was very able with edged weapons, to say nothing of her fists. That pair, both most unexpected additions to the Broken Circle, had already proven their worth with this apprehension and delivery of Aquint, the chief Internal Security agent in Callah. That such an organization existed was interesting news to Bryck. It meant the Felk recognized the need to deliberately maintain security within their expanding empire. Or it might mean that they were experiencing general resistance significant enough to justify the agency.

The latter was a welcome thought, even if it were just fantasy. Then again, who knew? Perhaps the people *were* rising in Windal after all, a fiction he had maintained for some while now.

Aquint, then, wasn't just working for the Felk. He was Bryck's direct adversary, more so even than the troops of Callah's garrison. Aquint's job was to seek out rebellion within the empire.

Well, he'd found it.

Ondak had scouted out this place. It was a granary that had burned a lune or so before the Felk incursion. The burning hadn't been total. The beams still stood, as did the walls, which were thick. Portions of the roof were gone, and the day's drizzle misted down through shafts of drab daylight.

The old ash made a grimy paste where it was wet, and the interior reeked still of the burning, of scorched grain and seared wood. But there was a corner where it was dry, and it was where Bryck waited while Aquint was brought inside.

Quentis waited with Bryck under the intact segment of roof. She gave him a reassuring look as they both heard the footsteps shuffling toward the granary's entryway. And

Bryck *was* reassured by that look. It meant that she had faith in him. It meant more than that probably, meant emotions and affections that he could not—would not—take for granted. Once, with Aaysue, he could have made assumptions; now . . .

He and Quentis had made love only the one time. So far. That was how it felt, that the first occasion would lead inevitably to others, that Quentis wanted it that way. The two of them might be at the start of something. But by the sanity of the gods, what did *he* want?

He didn't know. Or if he did, he wasn't telling himself what it was.

With a silent self-disgusted sigh and a somewhat strained return smile to Quentis, Bryck turned his attention toward the trio of figures entering the abandoned structure. The Circle had sentries watching the granary's perimeter, and Bryck had received warning that they were approaching. He had also been assured that they weren't being followed. He was pleased with the efficiency with which everyone was operating. The Broken Circle, it seemed, was becoming a tight, able little group.

As they picked their way over the interior rubble, Deo and Radstac pressing their blindfolded charge between them, Bryck's first impression of the Internal Security officer was of a man in a state of high dudgeon. His second impression was that this fellow Aquint wasn't afraid, not in the most obvious sense anyway. He was keeping cool, waiting to see what happened. Deo pulled back the hood of Aquint's cloak, and with a neat tug, undid the blindfold over the man's eyes. They had put it on him to make him less likely to offer up any resistance.

Radstac and Deo had led him here through a serpentine route of unused alleys. Now they let Aquint go, both stepping back, Deo's crossbow at the ready and Radstac no doubt set to pounce lethally if their erstwhile chief made an untoward move. Aquint blinked repeatedly but didn't lift a hand to rub his eyes.

Bryck gazed at him a long, silent moment. Water dripped in a tireless patter from the semi-demolished roof.

Aquint's pique finally won out over his cautious reserve. "You're the Minstrel." He said it, voice rasping over the name; he did not ask it.

Bryck stared levelly, standing a few paces off, glad now that he'd chosen to show this man his face. It felt proper. "Yes," he said.

"I've waited a long time to meet you," Aquint said, then let out a breath that deflated him noticeably. Just as quickly, he drew himself back up. There was fast calculation in the man's eyes. "If you wanted me dead, you'd have killed me back there. Like you did Cat."

Bryck couldn't quite check the frown that creased his brow or the flicker of his eyes toward Deo, standing behind on Aquint's right. According to the Circle's two new recruits, Cat was Aquint's deputy or some such. Deo lifted his shoulders slightly at Bryck.

"We would have already killed you," Bryck agreed. Aquint was looking for an edge in this somewhere, he sensed.

Aquint nodded, then deliberately folded his arms across his chest, adopting a nonchalant stance. "Then—and I'm just guessing here, of course—I suppose when you finish making whatever revolutionary speech you feel compelled to make to me, one who so insidiously collaborates with the hated Felk, you might get around to telling me what in all the bleeding gods you want from me."

This time Bryck managed to check a smile. It was an

impressive display of bravado, particularly under the circumstances. Bryck indulged himself with a glance toward Quentis, standing several steps away. In her amber eyes he again sought and found reassurance.

"We know about you what your two former agents know about you," Bryck said to Aquint, tone frank, not belligerent. "You've been assigned by Abraxis, a powerful Felk lord and mage, to seek out dissent in Callah. You like this assignment. You want to keep it as long as possible. You're not Felk yourself, and you have no genuine loyalty to the empire. But you'll go along with this, finding and arresting rebels here in Callah, so long as it serves your ends. You *are* a collaborator, but the Felk haven't won you over. You're interested only in your personal gain and well-being—and perhaps that of your youthful partner. You're not loyal to the Felk, because you have no loyalty to give."

It didn't appear to faze Aquint. But if he was the kind of man Bryck had just accused him of being, he wouldn't react to such an allegation. Bryck considered another course.

"Are you curious as to how your two associates so quickly became *our* confederates?" Bryck asked.

Aquint's lips moved sourly. He glanced behind at Deo. "I'm not entirely surprised about this one. From the start I sensed something weak in him." He turned about the other way, eyed Radstac. "But her—that is startling. I'm not disappointed, mind you. But I'd figured her for the smart one. And joining up with your wretched little band isn't a smart move." His gaze swung forward once more and settled wryly on Bryck. "You're going to be hunted down, however many of you there are, and Jesile's going to have your heads taken off. You and the gods know how many innocent Callahans. Yours is a sorry cause."

Behind him Radstac showed no response, but Deo's teeth bared in an ugly grimace.

Bryck nodded. "Well, now we've *both* made our speeches."

Aquint sniffed an involuntary laugh at that. They were equal adversaries. Perhaps that gave them all the common ground they needed to communicate. And Bryck did wish to communicate.

So he told Aquint how Radstac and Deo had joined with the Broken Circle.

It was, in the main, Quentis's doing. Rumors had spread about a new pair of troubadours in the city, ones very blatantly singing songs of dissent against the Felk. The songs themselves were spreading as well, rather infectious tunes with clever provocative lyrics, one or two of which Bryck nonetheless recognized as traditional songs that had been revamped to new purposes.

He dispatched Quentis to investigate. She had easily enough located the tavern where they were going to play last night—which led Bryck to wonder how this duo was operating with seeming impunity in a city where the Felk came down brutally on signs of defiance. But he wanted to meet these two. He had thoughts of persuading them to perform songs even more inflaming, calling directly for an uprising of the Callahan people. The giant sigil on the wall of the Registry—since painted over, of course—had had an effect. So had that execution in the square. The people were stirred.

Quentis had observed the performance, then approached the two musicians and proposed a rendezvous. Then she exited the tavern.

Deo followed her out. But Quentis wasn't alone. Ondak, her older cousin, had gone along and waited outside the establishment. When Deo eagerly rushed after her, Ondak stepped from his nook and seized the vox-mellifluous. Radstac had come out into the street pursuing Deo, but by then Ondak had a cleaver to his throat. It was sufficient to induce Radstac not to act hastily. Ondak quickly discovered that Deo wasn't the imbecile he was pretending to be. In fact, when the four withdrew off the street, it was found that the troubadours weren't at all what they seemed.

Deo confessed everything, immediately and earnestly; and added to it his avid desire to join the rebellion. Radstac claimed the same, though appeared to Quentis's eye to be merely following Deo's lead. Still, Quentis decided the strange pair should indeed meet the Minstrel—that night. This was too urgent to wait for the next day.

Bryck did meet the two. Deo was very convincing in his zealous desire to strike against the Felk. Convincing, too, were his reasons. He was a wayward member of Petgrad's royalty, one who wanted to make his own mark in this life. So fervent was his ambition that he'd attempted to assassinate General Weisel, the head of the Felk army. Radstac, it was revealed, was a Southsoil mercenary who was in Deo's employ.

It was too fantastic a tale to be any kind of sane covering story.

"So, after all this you contrived to capture me," Aquint said. He frowned his puzzlement. "Why?"

"You're an important figure," Bryck said.

"You could've made better use of your two new acquisitions." He didn't bother glancing behind at Deo and Radstac. "They could have gone into the Registry, with the proper access, and assassinated Governor Jesile."

"He'd be replaced. What good would that do?"

"About as much good as anything else your Broken Circle is liable to carry out."

"You don't think much of us."

"I don't."

Bryck nodded, accepting this. "What do you think of our aim, at least?"

"And it is?"

"To overthrow the Felk here in Callah, of course."

Aquint appeared to be measuring his thoughts. Finally he said, somewhat grudgingly, "To be rid of the Felk in Callah? Yes. A worthy goal." He added, with another hint of drollery, "Just between us, of course."

Bryck moved a step closer. A bead of moisture had gathered on the tip of Aquint's nose. It fell when he cocked his head. He was curious about this, Bryck judged.

"We might have an even greater goal," Bryck said quietly. "One that we could actually accomplish."

Aquint lifted a brow.

Bryck licked his lips. Aquint was their prisoner, but he might also be the key to all this. He and the renegade Felk wizard, Nievzê, the practitioner of blood magic, which Deo and Radstac had told Bryck about. The long odds chafed Bryck's bygone gambler's instincts. But this was no game.

"Can you lure Abraxis here to Callah?" Bryck asked Aquint. He suddenly found himself a bit breathless. "Because if you can . . . we might be able to end this entire war."

THERE INSIDE THE scorched granary, with the drizzle finally thickening into actual rain and bringing with it an even chillier damp, Bryck explained the plan. He listened detachedly to himself as he revealed it to Aquint, and to his own ears it sounded wild, imprudent, nearly preposterous and fascinating.

It wasn't something he had ever imagined as a possible objective for this Broken Circle. It was hugely ambitious, far beyond the relatively safe and contained scope of operating covertly against the Felk garrison here in Callah. That at least was a manageable feat, more or less.

But these instruments had been seemingly placed deliberately into Bryck's hands, like a miraculous round of Dashes, where every card and dice throw has gone in one's absolute favor. He *couldn't* ignore the astonishing combination of all this.

It seemed . . . ordained. Not that Bryck put any sincere stock in the workings of the gods. To do so would be to acknowledge that those gods had permitted the annihilation of U'delph.

At last he finished. Aquint had listened without interruption, which Bryck didn't take as a sign one way or the other. Rain dribbled down onto the gummy black ashes flooring the granary's exposed interior.

Bryck let Aquint digest it. He had explained the plan to the Internal Security agent in succinct terms, without any rhetoric. Aquint didn't need to be won away from the Felk. He, too, Bryck guessed, had done some gambling in his time. He would want to weigh the odds. He would consider the gain and the risk. Both were considerable.

Quentis sneezed. Bryck looked her way as she tightened her coat across her shoulders. She was another factor in all this. She had made contact with Radstac and Deo. She had felt the ring of sincerity in Deo's wish to join the rebellion. She fit into that wonderful assembly of semi-improbabilities that had produced this fabulous scheme.

Bryck gave her a soft, tiny, candid smile, remembering the feel of her against himself, remembering how fine it had felt, physically and on levels deeper than that. Quentis smiled back.

"I can bring Abraxis to Callah," Aquint said quite suddenly, in a tone that was almost comically conversational.

Bryck's head whipped back toward him. Behind, Deo stiffened noticeably. Radstac showed no reaction.

"You can?" Bryck heard himself ask dumbly.

A hardness came to Aquint's face. "Before we get down to that, however, you send someone back to that godsdamned lot where you waylaid me. You find Cat's body and bring it to me. I want my friend buried. Properly. Even though he probably wouldn't care about it. Understand?"

Bryck nodded. "It'll be done."

Aquint looked up at the jagged remains of the roof. "Now I'd like to get properly indoors. And if you could provide a cup of something with a little bite to it, so much the better. This has been quite a day."

RAVEN
(5)

ORDERS HAD COME for the halt, then for the scrambling reorganization of the lines. Something big was happening, on top of the very obvious magnitude of the enemy army they were now clearly facing in the last fading bits of daylight.

Torches were being fired all around. They lit among the enemy ranks, too, points of light neatly delineating those large opposite numbers. That was a sizable army. The massive, collective glow of torchlight beat back the emerging pinprick lights of the stars above.

Were they going to fight a night battle? From what Raven had overheard from the soldiers around her, this Felk army had never undertaken a major engagement at night during this whole campaign.

Then again, this army had never faced an enemy so large and evidently organized.

Raven's heart was racing, but not entirely from fear. This was undeniably exhilarating.

This will be Weisel's true test, Vadya said.

Raven had climbed off her horse. She looked around at the frenzied activity. *You mean Dardas's test.* She was still astonished by what she'd learned from Kumbat. Vadya, too, had been surprised to learn that Lord Weisel was the vessel for Dardas, a warlord of the Northern Continent who had been resurrected two and a half hundredwinters after his death.

I think Dardas passed his tests centuries before either of us was born, Vadya said. *But now, wearing the form of Weisel, he must vanquish a new enemy, with a new army. And if he succeeds, it will be Weisel who gets the credit.*

Raven nodded, slowly. Resurrection magic certainly made for strange conceptions about identity. She knew it only too well.

You still haven't reported to Matokin, Vadya said.

I don't see how I could find Berkant in all this tangle, Raven said, referring to the Far Speak wizard who had a direct line of communication to Lord Matokin in Felk.

You're not going to report Kumbat's abduction? Vadya asked.

Raven softly bit her lip. *I know I should . . .*

But? Vadya prompted.

Is that really the right thing to do? Raven blurted, then immediately regretted it. She hadn't meant to reveal her misgivings to Vadya so nakedly.

After a long silence in Raven's head, Vadya said, *Your loyalties are divided, between Matokin and Weisel—or is it Dardas?*

Raven lowered her eyes to the ground. *I do feel an allegiance to both men,* she admitted.

It's a tricky situation you're in, Vadya said.

I know.

Raven looked around. It was difficult to get an overall sense of what was happening. Troops appeared to be shifting into new patterns, companies rearranging themselves, presumably to engage this enemy. The wizards, in their black robes, were being mobilized as well.

Whatever was happening, it was being done quickly, and on a massive scale. Raven wasn't among the combatants. Actually, she wasn't sure where her place was just now. Maybe she should go check on Kumbat. But no, he was being securely guarded.

Perhaps you should report to the general, Vadya suggested.

Raven noticed how Vadya had avoided naming him. Maybe it was strange, even for her, to think of Weisel and Dardas existing within the confines of the same being.

It was a good idea though. Raven mounted her horse once again and swung it about. She had to pick her way carefully, with all the troops and equipment being moved about. Even amidst all this confusion, she was aware of those male stares that followed her everywhere. Her beauty was a radiant thing, as glorious and entrancing as a full moon.

She had a rough idea where she could find Dardas in this huge array of military might. He would be toward the rear, insulated from harm, and with a good commanding view of his army.

With that army halted and currently redeploying, the general had set up a very temporary base of operations. He was dismounted and standing with a few select members of his senior staff. They were gathered around a map-strewn table, and Dardas was pointing and speaking rapidly. His personal guard ringed the scene.

Raven reined her horse. The foot traffic was becoming too thick for her to navigate. For a moment, she sat and watched as the general gave his orders. He certainly appeared to be in his element. There was no hesitancy in his manner, no hints of self-doubt.

For so long now she had thought this man was Weisel, a Felk lord turned military leader. She had accepted Weisel as her superior, as one who treated her as a confidant. She had accepted him as a lover.

Now she knew her beliefs were awry. When she had made love to that man, it was actually *two* men. The thought was peculiarly unsettling. Peculiar, because when he had made love to her it was, in fact, to two women.

Raven hopped off her horse once more, shaking her head. Whatever the new dynamic, she supposed she could get used to it.

As she approached she began to realize that all wasn't actually right with the general. There was something strange in his body language. His movements were just slightly off. As she got near enough to see his face, she noticed that his expressions were somewhat exaggerated, the facial muscles pulling tautly, the eyes protruding from the skull.

With a start, Raven realized that this disturbing appearance reminded her sharply of when the general had experienced that strange paralysis just before . . . just before . . . she had been struck by that crossbow bolt.

She sucked in a breath. It was the first time since her resurrection that she had remembered the event so vividly. It was her own death, and she was *remembering* it!

Plainly, this wasn't the same kind of episode, whatever

was now happening to the general. But something odd was going on, she was sure. She sensed it.

The guards passed her through, and Raven edged unobtrusively up to the tight circle of senior officers gathered with Dardas around the maps.

Now she could hear him speaking. "The scouts confirm it! East and west, precisely like I said. They're flanking us. It's a very clever battle plan. They're making the best use of their numbers, hemming us in. They can do us real damage. Whoever's strategizing for that army, they have a genuine flair. I admire it."

Raven listened closely. It was the voice she was used to hearing, but it was pitched somewhat differently. It was strained, as if some struggle were going on behind the words. But that was mad. Or was it . . . ?

Nevertheless, Dardas carried on.

"I wouldn't normally recommend a night attack, but the surprise advantage will be considerable. I want those Far Movement mages in place as soon as possible."

"Yes, General Weisel," one of the senior officers said.

"They're to go out past both enemy flanks." Dardas's lips pulled in a tight grin.

"Understood, General," said the officer. "Two squads are moving the mages covertly into position right now. Both have Far Speak wizards with them, of course. They'll report when all is ready."

"Outstanding." Dardas sounded pleased. There was even a faint note of hysterical giddiness in his voice.

If the officers were aware that the general appeared distressed, they didn't show it. But Raven noted the odd, overwrought manner. Maybe, though, this was just how Dardas behaved when faced with an actual battle.

I don't think so, Vadya said.

Neither do I, Raven said, grimly.

Something was definitely wrong.

The same senior officer blinked at the general, smiled admiringly, and said, "You mean to outflank the enemy's flanks."

Dardas nodded. "That's correct."

"A brilliant strategy, sir."

"It's served me before."

"Sir?"

"Never mind." Dardas waved. "Report when the Far Movement mages are in place. In the meantime, continue to get the companies organized to be Moved through the portals. Dismissed."

The officers all saluted and dispersed. Dardas's eye now fell on Raven.

"Ah, Raven. Exciting, isn't this?" He swept an arm to encompass the whole, huge militaristic display around them.

"Yes . . . uh, General," she said, biting her lip again. She had to maintain a front for him. He was unaware that she knew his secret. "Very exciting, sir," she said, more firmly this time.

Dardas nodded and even that was exaggerated, a jerking movement.

"We're going to outflank the outflankers," he said, happily.

"I overheard, sir."

But Dardas was looking down at the maps on the table, not hearing her. "It's a nice tactic they've got, whoever they are. See how their forward companies are arranged? It's bait, pure and simple. They have deliberately placed a 'weakness' right there in the middle, this unit that's weaker than the others on either side of it. They want me to attack

there. It would draw our forces forward, toward that specific point. If I hadn't known in advance about the flanking maneuvers . . ."

"How *did* you know?" Again Raven was horrified to
hear herself blurt so tactlessly. So much for her stoic front.

Dardas looked up from the maps. There was a hot glint
in his eyes that seemed to pierce her.

"Oh," he said finally, "let's just say this particular sce-
nario has a kind of . . . familiarity about it." He let out a
chuckle that climbed sharply into the upper registers.

Raven felt a chill.

Has he gone mad? she wondered.

Perhaps not, Vadya said. *As Dardas, he must have
memories of past battles, a vast experience of war.*

Raven felt herself frowning. *Do you mean that this
might resemble something from two hundred and fifty
years ago, some battle he and his Northland army fought?*
It was a staggering thought, though perfectly logical.

Yes.

Amazing, Raven said.

"Fergon!" the general called abruptly.

The aide came scampering to his side, saluting, freckled
face flushed. "Yes, sir!"

Unexpectedly, Dardas clapped a comradely hand on the
junior officer's shoulder and said, "I want you to fetch a
drink for myself and this delectable creature here. We're
going to drink a toast to this war. Right away, Fergon!"

The young officer vanished. Raven had time only for a
veiled, dismayed look at the general, who was chuckling
anew, before Fergon returned with a bottle and two cups.
He neatly filled the cups, handed them over, and scurried
off once more.

Dardas lifted his cup, some of the dark liquor sloshing

over the brim, and said, "To the eternal strife, the unending play of might against might, the test of every fighter's valor, and the dread beauty of bloodshed. To our *war*!"

Raven held her cup numbly a moment, then hurriedly drank. Dardas gulped his heroically and tossed away the cup. Raven found herself looking down at the maps, at the confusing scrawls of troop movements. She saw the enemy flanks, to the east and west, moving to surround the Felk army.

Suddenly, she looked up. A terrible thought had occurred to her.

It was sharp enough that Vadya perceived it. *No,* she said, horrified. *You don't think . . . ?*

It's certainly possible, Raven said.

But you can't tell him, not without revealing that you know Weisel is the host body for Dardas.

Raven prepared herself grimly. *Then that's what I'll have to do. This is too important.*

Vadya raised more objections, but Raven deliberately shut them out.

"General Dardas," Raven said, clearly and levelly.

It took a moment for it to sink in, then the general froze. He turned and looked at her fully. The grin died on his face, replaced by a cold, penetrating stare.

"What?" he asked, too softly to be heard by anyone but her. "What did you call me?"

Raven drew a steadying breath. "I spoke to Mage Kumbat," she said, not hesitating now, but also speaking quietly, privately. No one else needed to hear this. "He told me. We are alike in this way, General. I am Raven, and yet I'm not. You are Dardas, yet you appear as Weisel."

He seemed to absorb the shock with admirable speed. He regarded her closely, shrewdly.

"Why are you saying this to me now?" he asked.

Without a waver, Raven said, "Because I believe I see a flaw in all this." She indicated the maps on the table.

Dardas's brows lifted. "Do you imagine you know something of military strategy that I don't?" He sounded incredulous, but there was a first hint of anger in his voice.

Raven trembled. She didn't want to invoke this man's ire.

"Tell me, General, is this similar to some battle you fought in your . . . your original lifetime?"

It felt to her as if she were asking a most intimate, most inappropriate question, and perhaps she was. But she stood her ground.

Dardas didn't answer. He frowned, looked puzzled, then annoyed, then seemed to coolly consider her question.

"As a matter of fact," he finally said, "it does."

Raven was biting her lip again. She forced herself to stop. "It is possible, General," she said, "that this particular battle—whatever it is—has been studied by the enemy. Dardas's exploits are quite famous, I understand. They're a matter of history. It is further possible that this enemy has recognized your style from previous actions during this war. They may believe you are copying Dardas's techniques of warfare, and so they might have, conceivably, restaged *this* battle, believing that you will react as you did in its original incarnation."

It drained her. She felt suddenly lightheaded.

Dardas's jaw had slowly unhinged. He gazed at her, stupefied now.

"You believe this is a trap within a trap?" he asked in a whisper. He waved a stiff hand at the maps.

Raven swallowed. "I strongly believe you must consider the possibility, sir." Inside her head, Vadya was utterly silent now.

Dardas shook his head, but not to negate what she had proposed. "If it's true, then I face an enemy far more worthy than I suspected." A soft, pleased smile played briefly on his lips. This time, the expression wasn't strained.

He took a step closer to her and brushed a finger along her sublime jawline, apparently not caring who saw this.

"This is excellent, Raven. You've proven invaluable to me. And of course you are correct, I am Dardas. In fact, I'm *more* Dardas than I was just half a watch ago. An internal shift has occurred. I believe that my host doesn't have the stomach for battle, in the end. He has . . . withdrawn. I am in command of this body. Do you understand?"

"I do, General," she said, firmly.

"That I can truly believe," he said. "But for the moment, you'll have to excuse me. I must call my senior staff back. If the Battle of Torran Flats can't be won one way, it can be won another."

RAVEN WANDERED A little distance off. She glanced back now and then at Dardas, watching him issuing new orders, his movements assured and natural now. Apparently his distress of earlier had been due to some sort of struggle or adjustment between himself and his host. Raven hadn't known such a thing could happen between people sharing a bodily vessel. She had certainly felt no such contention between herself and Vadya. She remarked on this silently to her own host.

I think we are unusually compatible, Vadya said.

Raven agreed. She was pleased with herself right now.

She had contributed something worthwhile. She had pointed out a possibility for disaster that Dardas himself had overlooked. It might not be too farfetched to say she had just saved the day.

Tell me something, Raven.

Yes? Despite the oncoming night's chill and the frenzy of activity around her, Raven felt a warm calm glow of satisfaction.

Do you love Matokin? Vadya asked. *As the father you believe him to be—do you love him?*

Raven blinked. She had never put it into such language. *I think I must,* she finally said. *If he is my father, I must love him.*

Vadya was silent a moment, then asked, *Do you love Dardas?*

As . . . ? Raven asked, prompting her.

As Dardas, Vadya said simply.

Raven considered. She looked at him now, a short distance away. He was bold, confident, powerful, full of ancient shrewdness and a curiously fresh zest for life.

How could I not love him? she said, finally.

Very well, Vadya said. *Then, for your sake, I hope that it never becomes necessary to kill either man. Or both.*

RADSTAC
(5)

IT WAS NEARLY a whole leaf she'd chewed, but the occasion was special, the need poignant. Not the addict's craving; not so much, at least. More, the needs of the moment. Sharpened senses, an acute alertness. Clarity. These things she needed.

Radstac walked side by side with Aquint, their pace steady and parallel. The pain in her teeth had peaked and passed, and the clear solid sense of things was emerging. She understood, in a profound way, the inner meanings of the patterns of traffic in the streets leading up to the Registry. She saw and comprehended the code of the sky in the lowering grey of the clouds overhead.

Sidelong, her peripheral vision stimulated and intense, she saw that Aquint despised her. It wasn't that she had betrayed him; his fealty to the Felk was quite flimsy. It was that she, by cooperating with the Broken Circle, had set in motion the events that had resulted in Cat being shot by

Deo's crossbow. *That* was something worthy of a grudge, in his mind.

She silently acknowledged the rightfulness of his enmity.

Cat, however, wasn't dead. Or at least probably wasn't. The Broken Circle's leader, the one called the Minstrel, had sent someone back to that lot to retrieve Cat's body, per Aquint's request. But the boy wasn't there. There were bloodstains on the scene and a confusion of footprints among the mud but nothing to explicitly tell the tale of what had happened. Had Cat merely been wounded, then staggered away? Had someone come upon his corpse and hauled it off?

Deo, as she well knew, was a most excellent shot with a crossbow; but even he was unsure if the bolt had hit the boy fatally. It had happened so fast, and Deo didn't have a combatant's instincts. Radstac's feeling was that the lad was still alive and licking his wounds. And very likely seeking out his partner this very moment. Certainly there was a bond between the two males; the staunch camaraderie of thieves was her guess.

It meant she had an eye out for Cat, as well as all the other potential dangers she was alert to. She had no complaints. She simply accepted the parameters of the mission.

This was, after all, what Deo wanted, and she was still in his employ. He wanted to play at being a rebel, just as before he had tried his hand at being an assassin. The latter hadn't worked out, though Radstac conceded that Deo had made a very fine effort at it.

As to this new role of anti-Felk rebel in this occupied city . . . today would likely tell if he was going to succeed. In truth, if this operation was accomplished, it would have consequences of almost unimaginable scope.

They came at the Registry through the marketplace. The

scene seemed brisk, but Radstac noted that very little actual transacting was taking place. The new higher taxes were evidently impacting the economy. Governor Jesile had thought he'd found a way to stabilize things after the counterfeiting debacle, which she had first read about in the report Aquint had given her and Deo when they were recruited. Instead, the Felk governor was probably worsening conditions overall—and certainly giving the people of Callah something more to grumble about.

Aquint, under the Minstrel's directions, had sent an official messenger to the Registry last night, bearing a communication meant for the garrison's Far Speak wizard. The message had since been relayed to Felk and acknowledged. Radstac was satisfied that Aquint hadn't planted some code in the communiqué that would lay a trap for herself and the others of the Broken Circle.

It wasn't too difficult to judge a person's character, particularly if *mansìd*-inspired clarity was involved. Aquint had a thief's heart, and his interests were almost entirely selfish. But he had no love for the Felk, especially those that had subjugated this city of his birth. He specifically didn't like this war because it interfered with the comforts of his life.

"I'd like to have my sword back before things happen," Radstac said as they approached one of the Registry's entrances.

Aquint gave her a glance. It was flat, indifferent, yet she knew it was full of loathing. "That won't be a problem."

They entered the large stone building. Radstac was no longer affecting her limp. It felt good to be moving about normally. Her balance was right, her reflexes at the ready. She was primed, just as though this were a battlefield and she was preparing to face an enemy.

She had never had an opinion regarding who she favored to win a particular war. It was a pointless frill for a mercenary. But perhaps she did have a conviction about this Felk war. After all, if the Felk did manage to conquer every other state of the Isthmus, then that unified Isthmus would no longer supply her with the reliable conflicts that allowed her to earn her livelihood. Certainly the Southsoil didn't produce enough wars to keep her employed. The Southern Continent, though a shadow of its former pre-Upheavals glory, was still too civilized to engage routinely in internal hostilities.

Also, she couldn't get her *mansìd* leaves anywhere but here.

Sentries immediately passed her and Aquint through, and they moved along chilly corridors. Radstac wondered if they would encounter that same fussy officer with the pinched lips who'd made things difficult for her and Deo when they first arrived in Callah.

Aquint led her into a room where a uniformed clerk appeared. His eyes moved rapidly between them, while his face remained bland.

"Describe the sword," Aquint said to her.

She did so, and the clerk went scurrying into a partitioned alcove, emerging a moment later bearing her sheathed combat sword. She took it, examined it, feeling that a piece of herself had been returned to her. It was nearly a sentimental experience.

She strapped it on, and Aquint led her out. The clerk had been nervous in their presence. The Registry's sentries, too, had betrayed an uneasiness. It was surely their status as Internal Security agents that prompted this reaction. Aquint had told her and Deo repeatedly that their positions overrode any normal military authority.

What measure of power, then, did this Abraxis wield? Aquint had said he was second in the empire only to Matokin. It was a formidable figure they were going to tangle with today.

They wound through a few more corridors, finally coming to a high-ceilinged chamber that Radstac recognized. A pair of robed mages was already present. They gave her and Aquint timid anxious glances. One of the wizards held a figurine of smooth purple glass in her hand, her thumb stroking it persistently. This was the Far Speak mage, Radstac concluded. Waiting for the word from Felk to open the arrival portal, which would be the job of the other wizard.

She and Aquint stood and waited. Aquint maintained a cool demeanor. For the first time Radstac spared a thought to wonder who this man had been before this war, before he had become so successful a collaborator. Surely he had engaged in some illicit enterprise. She couldn't quite imagine Aquint living an honest life. If she had to guess, she would say he'd been a black marketeer.

The message Aquint had sent to Felk had alerted Lord Abraxis that arrests of the key figures in the Callahan rebel underground were imminent. It also invited Abraxis to participate in the subsequent interrogations. Abraxis's reply indicated that he would accept the invitation.

The Far Speak wizard's grip on the glass figurine tightened, and her eyes closed. When she opened them and looked to her fellow magician, the Far Movement wizard started the busy process of conjuring the portal that linked to the one being opened at this same moment in the city of Felk.

Radstac was acutely conscious of the shifting energies in the room. She watched as the air in the center of the chamber wavered in a way that contradicted all natural

principles. Magic, though, she knew, was as natural as any
other precept of nature. It existed, as did those who had an
innate affinity to practice it.

It was only that those users could pervert magic to their
own unnatural ends that made it dangerous.

A figure—robed, tall, trim almost to the point of gaunt-
ness—emerged from the patch of disorderly air. He had a
confident stride, cold and expressionless eyes. He showed
no more response from materializing out of the portal than
he might have if he'd merely walked across this room.

From Abraxis's right shoulder hung a small red cloth
bag.

Aquint stepped forward and saluted. "Lord Abraxis,
welcome to Callah." The two wizards of the garrison huddled excitedly together, sneaking looks at the mage from
Felk. Radstac supposed that Abraxis was something of a
celebrity to these magicians.

"Have the arrests been made?" Abraxis asked bluntly.
There was no trace of friendliness in his voice. This was a
man who likely associated with no one but those of comparable status and power. Underlings were not to be frater-
nized with.

"I have been holding the order until your arrival,"
Aquint said.

"My time is very valuable. Why have you delayed?"

"I thought you would enjoy seeing the rebels' downfall
for yourself, Lord."

"I am interested in results, nothing more. I believe I've
made mention of that fact before."

Aquint didn't flinch from the cool edge of Abraxis's
tone. "You have, Lord. However, since you *are* here, and
the operation is set, perhaps . . ."

Abraxis's gaze shifted past Aquint, picking out Radstac

for the first time. His eyes dismissed her, and he looked again at Aquint. "Very well. I will observe. But I perceive that you are doing this to demonstrate to me how useful an agent you are. I don't especially object to that. However, if you fail in this, my disappointment will be proportionally dire."

Aquint took this without blinking. He escorted Abraxis back through the corridors, Radstac behind the two, palm atop her sword's pommel. Aquint mentioned that he had recruited other agents for this assignment, but Abraxis made no comment, evidently truly uninterested in the details.

They came out again into the marketplace that abutted the Registry. Aquint picked a path through the stalls and the bustle. They wound among the hagglers, the fast-handed merchants, the poorer patrons eyeing goods too costly for them. Quickly their tiny entourage was out of sight of the sentries at the Registry's entrance.

Ahead there was a stall with a red and yellow canvas awning. A large man with a brimmed hat pulled low over a blemished face was tending it. A few nondescript goods were on display.

Radstac let out a breath, drew another, slowly, smoothly. She fell a further deliberate step behind Aquint and Abraxis. As the pair reached the stall, she stooped and snapped the blade from her right kidskin boot. At the same moment, Tyber grabbed up a piece of pottery and stepped out from the stall, directly into Abraxis's path.

"Now, here's a person of obvious taste and refinement!" Tyber cried with the false merriment of a vendor. "Surely you, my friend, can appreciate the precious quality of this—this—this fine thing here in my hand! As to the price, well . . ."

Abraxis halted. Aquint stepped ahead to brush aside the impertinent merchant, but Tyber wasn't budging easily. Radstac moved forward, senses primed, the knife balanced in her hand.

"Were it not for the completely justified but gods-damned murderous taxes imposed by our righteous Felk visitors, I might be able to offer you a true bargain. Never-theless, you'll find the price I ask so astonishingly reason-able that a man as wise and perceptive as yourself will jump at—"

Radstac reached for the red carrying bag's strap. She would cut it, like a common sneak thief, and make off with the prize. Before she could reach the bag, however, Abraxis's tall bony frame stiffened, and the mage spun sharply about.

She had done nothing to betray herself. Her stealth had been impeccable. Magic. Some sort of protective spell cast over the bag. It made sense.

Abraxis's cold eyes came alive. Aquint was still pre-tending to hold off Tyber, who had cut short his spiel, see-ing that Radstac's gambit had failed.

Radstac saw it all with the honed clarity of *mansìd.* Abraxis brought a hand up out of his drab robe. The long fingers were splayed. His lips moved, rapidly, with much contorting. She still had the flat throwing blade in hand. She was in jeopardy. As with the casting of the Far Move-ment spell, she perceived now a fluctuation of abstract en-ergies in the air about the scene. Abraxis was about to loose on her some brand of destructive magic.

Tyber roughly shoved aside Aquint. His brimmed hat tumbled off his head. He had insisted on having a part in this today, despite the fact that, as Radstac had learned, he was already wanted by the garrison. Something about an attempted bribing of a Felk officer. The Minstrel, initially opposed to Tyber's participation, had eventually relented.

Lifting the piece of cheap pottery the full extension of his arm, Tyber brought it slamming down on Abraxis's skull. It shattered into unrecognizable shards, and the mage staggered heavily, mouth gaping in pain, interrupting whatever incantation he was reciting.

Tyber had done it without the least hesitation, once he'd seen that Radstac was in danger.

Abraxis stumbled a further step, doubled over, trying to stay on his feet. Radstac made a second grab at the bag, but the wizard twisted out of the way with surprising litheness. There was of course nothing for it. She was going to have to kill him. Already a commotion was growing around this scene, vendors and patrons looking to see what was happening. The tumult was going to call the attention of the Felk soldiers very soon.

Radstac would swing the blade up into Abraxis's abdomen, gutting the wizard. She saw he was already bleeding from his scalp, dark droplets flecking the ground. She planted her feet, seized a handful of his robe and cocked back her arm, muscles pulling taut.

At that moment Tyber's face erupted into flame. A sharp maddened shriek accompanied this, as Tyber reeled to one side, hands clawing at the licking tongues of fire that had appeared so suddenly and impossibly, without any combustion. He blundered hard into Aquint, who in turn crashed against the stall with the red and yellow awning, tumbling the rest of its wares to the ground.

Radstac smelled the terrible cooking meat on the air.

She swung with the blade, but the fire had been an effective distraction. Abraxis took advantage of it, twisting himself once again, so that the knife sliced through the robe's fabric, glancing off flesh, then bone, but not cutting deeply enough to bring the wizard down.

She knew that she was going to be the next thing to burst into flame. She let go of the blade, rather than trying to pull it out of the tangle of Abraxis's robe. Tyber fell, his head roaring with fire, as thick and bright as the head of a torch. He writhed and made more awful noises. Aquint was trying to scramble back onto his feet.

Abraxis was grimacing, but his lips were working again, his hands in motion. Radstac felt a heat gathering over her, harsh and dry and smothering. In another eye blink, she knew, she would be enveloped in the fiery magic.

The bolt struck Abraxis in his back, just to the left of his backbone. He reared up to his full height. Deo had smuggled the crossbow into the marketplace, wrapping it in a small rug. He had taken up a sniper's vantage near the edge of the market. Radstac hadn't expected that they would require his services. She had, frankly, foreseen this episode much differently from how it was turning out. A fast cut and run. Abraxis not knowing what was happening until it was too late. She had put much faith in her own abilities.

The heat around her was climbing. But she was faster than this magic. She had survived so very many battles by simply being faster than her enemies.

Her heavy combat sword seemed to leap eagerly from its sheath into her ready hands, an ominous weight, the blade glinting sinisterly. She swung it as she had swung it many times before, a hard clean hack, backed by her sinewy strength and the tenacity of her simple philosophy. Survive. Always survive. Beat the enemy, whoever it may be.

Radstac's blade caught the mage's throat just below the

ear. The metal went into the flesh, did not pause for the bone it met and came back out into the air, showering blood in a wide thick spray.

The head dropped to the ground, rolled wetly, came to a stop. The body held itself upright an instant, acting now without any directives, then collapsed gracelessly.

Radstac sheathed her sword and tore the red bag from the headless corpse's shoulder. With her other hand, she seized and wrenched Aquint onto his feet. His eyes were wide and horrified. On the ground, Tyber had gone silent.

It had all happened quite fast, as such things often did. But it was most certainly time to flee the scene.

Deo had already disappeared from the market. Radstac held the bag hard to herself as she and Aquint sprinted off. It was, quite possibly, the fate of the Felk war that was inside this bag. And Radstac found she did indeed have an opinion about that war.

PRAULTH
(5)

THESE WEREN'T MAPS of ancient engagements, celebrated by fastidious military scholars and studied with compulsive exactitude by University students. She had been one of those students, one of the most astute and promising, in fact. War studies had consumed the bulk of her intellectual interest. Master Honnis had been her caustic mentor, a man she had judged to be as intent and single-minded as herself. She had been wrong. Honnis had lived a life she knew nothing of, a life that included the active practicing of magic and participation in a vast scouting network that had kept track of this war since its inception.

Not faded brittle papers, these. Not testimonials of warfare that had occurred a hundredwinter and more before her birth, and which absorbed her strictly as an intellectual abstraction, without any true thought ever given to the unruly bloodshed and final human cost of the events.

No. *These* maps and intelligence reports spread before

her were very much alive. They were news of events occurring in the present and still unfolding, and very much
requiring her attention.

And like many things that occurred in the here and now,
these events were not going as planned.

Praulth was on her feet, staring down at the maps as
Merse delivered them, the ink still glistening. The Far
Speak magician was apparently receiving field intelligence
from a number of different sources, which was serving to
give Praulth a clearer picture of what was happening north
of this city of Petgrad.

The cluster of minor diplomats inhabiting the auditorium pressed near to get a look, sensing something important transpiring. Praulth's scarf of metallic red kept
swaying into her line of sight, and with a grunt of annoyance she unknotted it and tossed it behind her. Now, she
realized with clear understanding, wasn't the time to worry
about how she was going to look for any future portraits.

An ambassador's assistant from Ebzo jostled her left
elbow. "What's going on?" he wanted to know, eyes
squinting confusedly at the arrayed maps. "Is the Alliance
winning?"

Praulth felt the very uncharacteristic urge to backhand the
man across his balding skull. Instead she called, "Xink!"

He was at her side immediately. "General Praulth?"

"Clear any extraneous personnel. I need room to work."

It was a treat for Xink, being ordered to take some positive physical action on her behalf. He wasn't gentle about
clearing the curious from the auditorium's dais.

Praulth had remained vigilant here throughout the day
and now into the night. She had received the reports of initial visual contact between the Felk and Alliance forces.
Cultat had arrayed the aggregate army, which he led

according to Praulth's instructions. A "vulnerability" was placed among the front ranks, a company of noticeably weak strength, bait that Dardas was meant to recognize. Apparently he had, for the Alliance scouts had then reported that the Felk were moving small units east and west, presumably having discovered the Alliance's flanking gambits. These, too, were bait, however; and if Dardas had followed through, using (here Praulth adjusted for the magical capabilities of the Felk) Far Movement wizards to transport companies against the Alliance flankers, then the Felk army would have left itself susceptible to an attack that would have cut it in two.

But that wasn't what had happened.

Dardas had evidently abandoned his maneuvers against the Alliance's flanks. New strategies were arising, ones not documented in war studies texts that she knew from memory. Dardas was adapting. Dardas was strategizing in the present. Dardas would have to be engaged by an equal tactician.

"Tell me what's happening."

She looked up abruptly. Merse was standing on the opposite side of the table, plainly addressing her, though his eyes looked past her and weren't quite focused. His hand clutched the familiar-looking bracelet.

"Who's asking?"

"Cultat," Merse said. "I'm speaking to a scout here, and she is relaying the words to you. Praulth, time is crucial. What is happening?"

"The Felk aren't moving to outflank your forces," she said. "The trap has failed." She heard several gasps from the diplomats who had regrouped a safe distance from the dais. Xink, standing off to one side now, turned his head sharply toward her. The words felt like knives in her throat.

Merse gazed blankly and silently, merely a vessel at the moment waiting for more words to be poured into him. Praulth's fists bunched.

"So, there's to be no Battle of Torran Flats."

"No, Premier," Praulth said, struggling to keep her voice from choking. The trap had failed. *She* had failed. But this wasn't over yet. "We'll have to fight another battle."

In her mind she imagined the fearsome Petgradite premier astride his horse, officers from dozens of disparate states looking to him for victory, troops by the thousands trusting that they were in the capable military hands of the Alliance's leader. She imagined the night winds blowing, the stark moon overhead, the torches flickering and the arms and armored bodies creaking and clanging. An army waiting to act. And Cultat there at its heart.

He wouldn't despair, though. He wouldn't succumb to fear. Cultat was fierce, and he was a visionary. Without him no Alliance would ever have been assembled in the first place. And Praulth would not have the opportunity she now had, to engage Dardas in final decisive combat.

"Praulth . . ." Merse said; then, tone shifting, added, "General Praulth, I rely on you."

She looked away from Merse, down at the maps. With the speedy and meticulous intelligence she was receiving, she could keep abreast of this battle moment to moment. She could relay tactics to Cultat. She could fight the war from this very room, engage Dardas blow for blow. Her talent as a war scholar and, much more, her ability to apply that trenchant knowledge actively and effectively would determine victory or defeat for the Alliance, for the Isthmus.

Praulth didn't now pause to consider how this would affect her and her lofty future place in history. At the moment nothing seemed less important.

"Premier, mobilize your third and seventh companies. Fortify your weak strength unit in the forward rank. Bring up your cavalry on the eastward line. It's time for the Felk to meet their enemy."

A NIGHT BATTLEFIELD. She knew this, knew the armies would be engaging by torchlight, by star and moonlight. The images came to her, sidling in upon the cold and clear war logic that gripped her mind. She glimpsed the liquid spill of firelight over the armored bodies. She saw the melange of Alliance troops, their varying uniforms, assembled unlike the Felk for a cause of defense. Hold these lands against the sweeping invaders from the north. That was the unifying motive. And it had thrown together peoples who had, until very recently, been traditional antagonists. This Alliance . . . such a hodgepodge. How could it function?

Cultat was there. Nâ Niroki Cultat. Premier of Petgrad. He would hold the miscellany together. He would make them work as one. Praulth would be strategizing, yes; Praulth would be deciphering the enemy's movements and concocting the countering maneuvers. But Cultat would execute the reality of this battle, and without him, all her intellectual and tactical talent would be meaningless.

If she ever saw the premier alive again, she would tell this to him. She would say it quite humbly and sincerely.

Merse's hands were busy with a number of different trinkets, items well-handled and thereby impressed by whichever Far Speak operator he was currently linked to. Actually it seemed he was communicating with several at once, a feat that had to require some effort and skill. He remained on the dais with Praulth.

"Lateral move," Merse said. Sweat stood out on his forehead. "East . . . here. This company, *this*." He was stabbing at a map with his finger, indicating a specific Felk unit.

Praulth noted it. The maneuver resonated. It had many possible meanings—feint, supporting posture, outright assault. It was idiosyncratic of Dardas. This was how he fought. He put his forces into play and moved them about in unexpected patterns. He worked deep, weaving tactics inside tactics, confusing his opponents.

But Praulth's answering movement was clear to her. A unit of Alliance archers was nearby. They were to take positions. Whatever Dardas meant to do, the Felk company would be covered.

She told this to Merse. He relayed it.

The first actual combative contact between the armies had come. The Felk had made a thrust, a foray with a unit of infantry. It wasn't meant to break the Alliance lines. It was, to Praulth's eyes, the signal that this fight wouldn't wait for the daylight. Dardas was eager. Dardas had recognized the canny trap within the trap that had been laid, and he expressly wanted it known that he could not be fooled.

Such was how Praulth interpreted the gambit. The Felk infantry had been met. The clash was quick, casualties had resulted, and the Felk thrust was withdrawn. Blood was on the ground now. It wasn't going to be the last spilled tonight.

Those deaths weren't remote to her. They weren't as the lives lost in ancient battles that she read about, times so distantly past that whole generations had died off since.

Yet she didn't allow the thought of that newly shed blood to paralyze her. Soldiers would die tonight, members of this hastily amassed Alliance, and they would die in engagements that she had devised. But they had come together to fight off the Felk. They would supply whatever sacrifices needed to be made in this cause. Praulth owed them her best efforts, her keenest wits.

"Movement," Merse said. Xink had brought him a seat, and he had fallen heavily into it. He was presently clutching a small silver medallion looped with a thong of old leather. Praulth couldn't see what it was. "Middle ranks. A company is moving forward, toward the front."

Praulth noted the place on a map. Dardas was moving a unit forward from the rear. Cavalry? Infantry?

Wizards.

Merse's weathered features were tightened across the bones of his face. Abruptly he lurched to his feet, the movement violent. The chair clattered off the dais behind him. His hand opened, and the medallion bounced off the table and rolled out of sight.

His eyes widened and shot through Praulth. "My boy," he said, voice hoarse and slight. "He's gone."

A scout lost. A valuable Far Speak scout. But the pale and sudden loss on Merse's face was something else. This was the loss of one of his children, his *son*. How incalculable a loss was that?

"How did it happen?" Praulth asked. She reached a hand across the table, took Merse's wrist. She meant it to be forceful, to wrench him back from his shock, to delay it until there was time for it. Instead, her touch was gentle. She held him to comfort him.

Merse's jaw moved, tiny muscles bunching below the ear. Finally he said, "Fire."

"Fire?"

"His last word."

"Wizards," Praulth said.

Merse nodded solemnly.

The Felk fire magic had been used minimally during the war so far. The Felk had until now only been overrunning villages and invading cities. These were places they meant to occupy, and they wanted these sites left relatively undamaged. Surely fire magic had played a part in U'delph's razing, but here, on this battlefield, there was nothing to hold them back from full use of this offensive magic.

"Find out the range," she said, and now her fingers did tighten around Merse's wrist.

He wasn't drifting away entirely into the shock and sorrow that was his due. He straightened up and snatched an article from his pocket, gripping it fiercely, with an air of determination. He gave her a last sharp look before the link was established and said, "I won't fail you."

Praulth knew that he wouldn't.

He relayed the information to her. Apparently the fire producing magicians could only use their talents within a fairly limited range and at a finite intensity. They couldn't, for instance, hurl great clouds of fire across the prairie at the Alliance ranks. They seemed—Praulth assimilated the rapidly incoming reports—to be able to cause combustion only among the Alliance's most advanced units. Among these had been the one that included the Far Speak scout.

Even within that range the Felk wizards were limited, it seemed. That whole unit hadn't suddenly burst into flame. Instead, an individual here and there had suffered the horrible fate, while the person standing alongside went unscathed.

They could only pick out individual targets, then, like archers did.

"Tell Cultat to advance this unit of infantry," Praulth

said, pointing to a map. "Draw the wizards forward from the Felk ranks. Give them something to go after. Then send this company of cavalry—it's a strong company—on a northwestward tangent. They'll cut through the wizards before they can retreat. Go. *Go.*" Her hand thumped the table, but Merse was already passing it to the premier.

It was calculated sacrifice. Some of those infantry soldiers were going to die—and die as bait. But they would serve the greater cause.

It was a pure and painfully profound fact.

Praulth blinked and lifted her head. She quickly and unabashedly swiped a hand across her eyes, blinked more until the tears were gone. She caught a glimpse of the diplomats still watching raptly from the auditorium's aisles. They were silent, perhaps finally and truly aware that they were witnessing a moment of genuine history.

She noticed Xink, too, still standing to the side, still attending her. Ready to perform any task she set him to do. He was faithful. She saw that he had retrieved Merse's medallion from where it had fallen. She would need Xink, later, when all this was done. No matter what the outcome, she realized, she would survive this night and the following day. She was intimately involved in this war, but she wasn't bodily at risk. She had already faced her physical hardships, being assaulted and ravaged on Petgrad's streets. She had survived that.

When this momentous battle was through, Praulth would have Xink; and she would take her comfort there, and he would welcome her, because he still loved her . . . with a greater depth of authentic feeling than she perhaps deserved. But she *would* deserve it. Eventually, at least. She would right the wrongs between them, and their mutually inflicted wounds would heal.

Still gazing at him, she smiled, a small sweet curl of her lips. Xink smiled back.

Merse told her the infantry unit was drawing out the wizards. The Alliance soldiers were sustaining casualties, being picked off one by one, erupting into awful gouts of murderous flame.

"The cavalry," Praulth said. "*Now.*"

It happened for her on those maps, with every fresh bit of field intelligence that arrived and with every tactic she ordered. But the human cost was never far from her mind. Later, in the deep night, when the extraordinary and inexplicable event occurred, Praulth judged—gravely and sorrowfully—that the cost had been worth paying.

AQUINT
(5)

HE HAD DRIED flecks of blood in his hair and kept combing his fingers through it, trying to get it out. Abraxis wasn't the first person he'd seen killed, but it certainly was one of the most violent and sensational deaths he had ever witnessed, though Tyber's had been gruesomely spectacular, too.

Radstac definitely knew how to handle that sword of hers.

She and Aquint had fled the marketplace together. They had gone sprinting through streets and alleys, along a pre-planned route to shake off any pursuers. Though Aquint had heard the alarm being raised behind them, no Felk soldiers had followed.

Now they had met up at some rooms that were behind a row of smithies and woodworking shops.

Aquint looked around. He saw the Minstrel and the woman who had been with him at that burnt-out granary. A few of the others he recognized as belonging to the Broken Circle were here, plus one new face. It was thin, and wore grey stubble. Also present was Deo, of course.

"Tell me something," Aquint said, addressing the Minstrel. "Why did you move your operation here from that warehouse where you were?"

The Minstrel said nothing. Someone else spoke up, "How do you know about that?"

"It used to be *my* warehouse," Aquint said. "In another life. Isn't that ironic?"

"No one's in the mood for humor," a large elderly man said. Aquint vaguely remembered his name was Ondak. "We've lost a good man today."

That would be Tyber, of course, the one who'd gotten himself turned into a torch by Abraxis before Radstac took the wizard's head off. Aquint had known the old thief from bygone days.

"Funny," Aquint said. "I lost one yesterday."

Though his tone was nonchalant and sarcastic, the truth of what Aquint said still stung. He missed Cat terribly. He did have some cause to think the boy was still alive, but that meant trusting what these people had told him, that Cat's body wasn't there when they had gone back for it.

There was silence in the rooms. Then the Minstrel stepped forward.

"That's the bag?" he asked Radstac.

She had the small red bag under an arm. "Of course it is," she said curtly. Having decapitated a man a short while ago, she showed no obvious reaction.

"May I have it?" asked the Minstrel.

She tossed it toward him. But Aquint's hand flashed upward and caught it. He dangled it by its strap.

"There's something in here I need before you do whatever you think you're going to do," he said.

The Minstrel blinked. A murmur went through the others of the Broken Circle.

"What is it?" the Minstrel asked. It was a courtesy, since there were more than enough here to overpower Aquint and take the bag.

"When I was in the city of Sook," Aquint said, "I was assigned to the quartermaster. That's where Lord Abraxis came to recruit me. Never mind why he picked me. But when I accepted his offer to become an Internal Security agent, he did something curious."

They were waiting to hear. "What?" the Minstrel prompted him.

"Abraxis made a cut on my thumb," Aquint said, "and dabbed up the blood with a bit of cloth that he then put into . . . a bag."

"I thought it was just the wizards from that Academy place who had to give samples of their blood," Deo said. He had set down the crossbow with which he'd shot Abraxis in the back, before Radstac had finished him off.

Several heads turned toward the thin-faced one in the room Aquint didn't recognize, though he could now guess who he was. The man shrugged and said, "That is my understanding of it. Luckily, my own sample was disposed of after it was presumed I was dead. That is the standard procedure."

"It was Abraxis's measure," Aquint said. "His idea, to maintain discipline. Yes, all those magicians had to provide samples. But Abraxis told me that other, prominent figures throughout the empire were also included."

"And *you* are prominent?" Ondak asked scornfully.

"I was an Internal Security agent on a very important assignment."

"I like that you say 'was,'" the Minstrel said.

Aquint gave him a stony look. "What else would I say now?"

The Minstrel nodded. He considered, then said, gesturing, "This man here is named Nievzê. He is late of the Academy for magic in Felk. He's a deserter. He is also a skilled practitioner of blood magic. The whole point of today's operation, which cost us the life of our cherished colleague Tyber, was to secure Abraxis's bag of samples so that Nievzê here could . . . make use of them."

"I understand that," Aquint said sharply. It had been explained to him. "But before that happens, I need what's mine from this bag."

Silence came again. They might choose to simply ignore what he wanted. Aquint knew full well the enormous potential that this bag contained. Would these rebels pause in their plans to accommodate him—he, who had until very recently been hunting this same group, meaning to turn them over to the Felk?

Aquint wished he'd had the chance to say good-bye to Cat before everything had gone so wrong.

The Minstrel looked to Nievzê. "Can you find his individual sample among all the others?"

"There'll be hundreds," Nievzê said, aghast.

"Answer my question."

The wizard thought, finally scratched at his stubbly face, and said, "It *can* be done. But—"

"Do it," the Minstrel said, in a voice that brooked no defiance.

Aquint, still holding the bag by its strap, now handed it directly to the Minstrel. He, in turn, passed it to Nievzê.

"I will need a fresh sample of his blood," the wizard grumbled. "Then I will have to match it to one of these in here. Oh, it'll be a bother."

He opened the bag, and Aquint caught a glimpse of the many, many bits of blood-blotted cloth jammed inside. Doubtlessly Abraxis had had some magical means to quickly and accurately identify each and every sample in there. But Abraxis was gone. It was up to this deserter magician from Felk.

Aquint submitted to the new sample. Nievzê took it unhappily and went off into the next room for privacy while he worked. Aquint sat down to wait. The Minstrel wordlessly pulled a chair near and sat with him. The others quietly retreated.

THEY HEARD THE criers.

"What watch is it?" Aquint asked, glancing up. He had sunk into a dull reverie, wondering mostly about Cat and remembering their good times with maudlin hindsight.

These rooms had only a few windows, and those were shuttered up tight. But lines of daylight still showed around the edges.

"It's an early curfew," the Minstrel said.

"That's not good," someone muttered ominously.

"What did you expect?" Aquint said tartly. "An important official from Felk, the number two man in this whole bleeding empire, was beheaded today just outside the Registry. Remember what happened after that one soldier was murdered?" He directed this poignantly at the Minstrel.

"I remember," the Minstrel said, without inflection.

"I'll bet you do. Well, let's all try to imagine how the garrison is going to respond to *this*." Aquint listened a moment to the criers outside calling for the clearing of the streets. "Governor Jesile has no doubt contacted Felk by now. It's a safe guess that Matokin is none too happy."

"It'll be worse than last time?" a youngish girl said, looking like she didn't quite grasp the whole situation.

Aquint gave her an offhand glance. The Minstrel had killed that garrison soldier, and for a while after that incident Callah had been subjected to the full brutality of the garrison. The Felk soldiers had entered homes randomly, assaulted citizens, seeking the murderer of one of their own, and doing a good deal of damage in the process.

"That's another safe guess," Aquint finally said to the girl. She looked uneasy.

"Don't worry, Gelshiri," the Minstrel said reassuringly.

The other members of the Circle had come back into this room, apparently rallying around their leader.

"But we *should* be worrying, shouldn't we?" Ondak said. "There will be a citywide search—for you and you." He pointed to Aquint and Radstac, respectively.

Radstac stood with her arms folded, no emotion on that scarred face. Aquint knew enough to realize she was the most dangerous one here. He wondered if the rest of these people knew it.

"The Felk will tear this city apart!" Ondak continued, voice rising.

"Calm yourself," Deo said. He was avoiding looking Aquint in the eye. Aquint had certainly not forgotten that he had been the one to shoot Cat with that crossbow.

"We should have Nievzê cast that blood magic spell right now, while we can," somebody said.

"It's a very complicated spell," the Minstrel said. "It will take some while to perform it."

"Then let's get it started!" said Ondak.

The Minstrel glanced toward the next room, where the wizard was still murmuring mysteriously over the contents of Abraxis's bag. "Nievzê hasn't yet found Aquint's blood sample."

"It's too late for that!"

"I said, calm down, Ondak," Deo said, more sharply.

The Minstrel nodded. He looked around the room. "This man lured Abraxis here in the first place. Without him we wouldn't have that bag. If Nievzê casts that spell with Aquint's sample still among . . ." He shook his head. "No. Aquint has earned that much from us. I'll hear no more about it."

They all quieted, the matter dropped. Aquint didn't quite give the Minstrel a grateful look, but he was impressed by the man's authority.

The wait continued.

A passing commotion was heard now and then, in the distance, as night fell. Tension mounted among the group. Finally one among them, asking the Minstrel's permission first, crept stealthily outside for a look around. He returned a moment later, somewhat white-faced.

"What did you see, Minst?" asked the girl, Gelshiri.

"There must be many more Felk soldiers in this city now than there have been since Callah's invasion," the one named Minst said. "I saw a company of them, several streets distant. It looked like *hundreds*."

The Broken Circle members absorbed that with varying degrees of apprehension.

"Jesile probably had troops Far Moved in," Aquint said. "Or maybe Matokin ordered it."

His eyes flickered around at the surrounding faces. Now that danger was looming, would they change their minds about waiting for Nievzê to locate his sample among the contents of that bag?

"Gods," Ondak said. "*Listen* to that."

There was a great rumble nearing, booted feet pounding Callah's streets, the rattle of arms. Voices cried out as— presumably—houses were being entered by the soldiers and the inhabitants forced outside.

It would be worse than the last time the Felk had acted so. In fact, the Felk might be slaughtering Callahans indiscriminately, as a reprisal for Abraxis's grisly death. However, Matokin would also know about the bag. He would understand how important it was to get it back.

The Minstrel rose to his feet. "Nievzê, are you nearly done? Time is growing short."

From the next room, the wizard said, "I'm working as fast as this can be done. I'm trying—" He sounded slightly hysterical.

The tumult outside was growing closer still. Deo picked up the crossbow and laid a bolt in its groove. The Broken Circle members exchanged grim looks amongst themselves. Radstac put her hand almost casually to the pommel of her sword.

There was suddenly the sound of someone moving about on the roof overhead. The footsteps were soft, but the old rafters creaked nonetheless. Grit sifted down from the ceiling.

"They're on top of us!" Ondak said in a raspy, frightened whisper, ducking his head instinctively.

Aquint finally stood from his seat. This wasn't right. Why would the garrison bother climbing atop the roof?

In the corner of the room's ceiling, a hinged hatchway abruptly came open to reveal a space just large enough to accommodate a person. Aquint hadn't noticed the hatch before. If the expressions of surprise on the faces of the others were any measure, no one else had known it was there either.

When Cat ducked his fair-haired head down through the hole, Aquint was gripped simultaneously with shock, joy, and a strange feeling that the boy's reappearance just now was somehow inevitable.

"Are you hurt?" Aquint asked, hurrying toward the corner, grinning broadly up at his young friend.

"Being shot with a crossbow isn't as much fun as you'd think," Cat said, an uncharacteristic try at humor.

Aquint wanted to whoop with laughter. But there wasn't time.

"Can we get away from here over the roof?" he asked.

Cat, head hanging upside down, nodded. "You'll want to get moving fast."

"I have it!" Nievzê suddenly cried out, then came hurrying into the room. He brandished two bloodstained bits of cloth, one the sample that Aquint had just surrendered, the other evidently the one Abraxis had taken from him back in Sook.

Aquint stepped forward. He seized the two pieces of bloodied cloth.

"You're sure?" he asked the wizard, intently.

The man with the grey stubble nodded. "I was trained in this magic. It's what I know."

Aquint continued to search the gaunt face, looking for signs of treachery.

"You will have to trust him, Aquint," said the Minstrel, behind him.

Aquint realized that this was true. He pocketed the blood samples.

"Let's go, let's go!" Ondak was urging, wrestling a chair toward the corner. He hopped atop it, then levered his grunting weight up into the hatchway.

One by one, they swiftly evacuated the rooms. When

Aquint finally rolled out onto the roof, he felt the bite of the night air. He heard the large Felk patrol nearing in the street below.

"Keep your heads down," the Minstrel whispered. He was standing by the hatch, making sure everyone got out. Aquint went ahead, catching up to Cat, wanting to put his arms around the boy, but knowing that would only make the lad uncomfortable. He settled for slapping him cheerily on the back.

"I knew you weren't dead," Aquint said, half-lying.

Cat gave him a look that, briefly, was warm and welcoming. Then the boy grimaced and resumed his more normal, stoic expression. He said, "I was able to track you to that granary, then to here." Then he said, pointing, "We're going this way."

Aquint followed, seeing how Cat moved a bit awkwardly, a hand to his side. He hoped the boy's wound wasn't too serious. This rooftop connected to the roofs over the row of craft shops, and these led some distance away from the approaching patrol. The Broken Circle members came after them, everyone hunkered low, moving quickly and stealthily. Nievzê was among them, Abraxis's red bag clutched tightly to him.

Frightened voices rose from the street, as people were turned out of doors. If their group could get off these rooftops at the far end, Aquint judged, they could stay ahead of the patrols, long enough to find someplace where Nievzê could cast his elaborate blood magic spell.

And after that . . . what? After that, this whole war might be over. It was a delirious, intoxicating, exciting thought, one Aquint couldn't help but entertain, no matter that his pragmatic instincts told him not to wholly trust this plan.

"You! Up there! Hold!"

Aquint looked back, dread closing over him. The Broken Circle members were rushing toward the roofs' far end, but somebody must have gotten careless. Now the patrol had spotted them.

"Hurry!" Cat said. He had apparently used a ladder to get up onto the rooftops in the first place. It was still leaning against the building's eaves. Gelshiri bounded down it. Ondak followed her over the side immediately. But there wasn't enough time to get everyone down that way.

The Minstrel was still toward the rear. Deo, with his crossbow, was with him. Radstac had reached Aquint near the edge. She looked back now, saw Deo, and reversed course.

"Radstac, don't!" Aquint called, forgetting for the moment that she was partly responsible for Cat being shot.

Cat grabbed Aquint's sleeve. "Come *on*," the lad said.

He was right, of course. "Everybody jump!" Aquint said to the others, all vying for a chance at the ladder.

As if to demonstrate, Cat nodded and vaulted fearlessly over the edge of the roof. It was a fair distance to the street below, but most would probably survive the fall with a minimum of broken bones.

Aquint took a last look behind. Deo, aiming at the street, fired off his crossbow, then fit it with another bolt. Radstac had drawn her sword. That woman who'd been with the Minstrel at the granary, the one with the amber eyes, was with him now, at his side.

Nievzê suddenly stepped in front of Aquint. "I'm frightened!" the wizard said, voice quivering.

Aquint roughly seized Nievzê's arm. "Come with me, *friend.* We still need you to work your magic."

With that, Aquint leapt from the roof, carrying the magic-using Felk deserter down with him.

DARDAS

(5)

LIFE PUMPED STRONGLY through his veins. Life was there with every breath that moved in and out of his lungs. He surged with it, with its vitality, with its exuberance. He was *alive,* in every sense.

This was truly the medium of Dardas's life. Finally, this Felk war was delivering what he needed most—an enemy. So far, that enemy appeared to be worthy. There was definitely a tactical intelligence to that opposite army's movements, and in its replies to Dardas's feints and probes. That wasn't some mass of disorganized, armed rabble facing his army out there. Someone, or some*ones,* over there had a knack for military strategies.

Dardas couldn't keep the grin off his face as the field intelligence reports continued to flow in. Never before, in his days of conquering the Northern Continent, had he had such speedy information available to him. He could know within moments how the enemy was responding to a particular thrust. He could have his orders relayed instantly to the various units he wished to mobilize. It was fantastic.

Dardas still had no real explanation as to why Weisel had so suddenly withdrawn from their dual consciousness, leaving Dardas with full command of this body once more. It may very well have been the intense fear the Felk noble had felt. Maybe strong negative emotions weakened one's hold on the shared host body, especially when faced with the equally powerful emotions of joy and expectation that Dardas was experiencing.

He didn't have time to bandy about the theory. At the moment, he was just glad Weisel was out of the way.

Dardas noticed Raven lingering on the periphery of where he'd set up his temporary base of operations. She had performed an invaluable service for him by pointing out the possibility, which he hadn't considered, that this enemy might have studied his ancient strategies. It was conceivable that Raven, with that one bit of advice, had saved this army countless casualties. Dardas couldn't imagine rewarding her enough, once this was done. Perhaps someday he would elevate her to the status of his permanent consort. After all, she knew his secret, knew he was Dardas. He would want her close to him.

The Battle of Torran Flats . . . that was why it had looked so familiar. It had been a great victory of his, and apparently history had recorded and remembered it. If he had acted as he had during that original battle, surely this enemy would have sprung some cunning trap. Maybe his whole army would have been slaughtered, the ferocity of his warriors and the might of his mages notwithstanding.

By now, there had been several, relatively small engagements between the two armies. First blood had been spilled, and Dardas fancied he could smell it on the night wind, the scent bitter and coppery and . . . stimulating.

As yet, however, the all-out clash between the armies hadn't commenced. Dardas had wondered if this enemy would show signs of shying from a nighttime battle. But each of his exploratory thrusts had been met with decisive force, to say nothing of the wily, bold move that had drawn out a unit of his fire-working wizards. Those casualties had been high, but his army could absorb the losses.

Of course, when things *really* got under way Dardas had several resources he could tap that would vastly increase his advantage. Those Far Movement mages were certainly going to earn their pay. Dardas had a number of strong, compact units of fighters scattered throughout his forces, with Far Movement and Far Speak wizards attached. He planned to use these for fast disruptive attacks, keeping them in almost constant motion through the portals, stabbing the enemy with short vicious jabs.

This Isthmus plain would be glutted red with blood before the sun rose.

Fergon delivered the fresh intelligence. Dardas looked it over and grinned anew.

"Send forward this cavalry company, here," he pointed to one of the maps on the table before him. One of his senior officers acknowledged the order and relayed it to a nearby Far Speak wizard.

The rhythm of battle was building. He could feel it. Soon, the full force of the two armies' front ranks would be sent against each other. Dardas keenly anticipated it. For the moment, though, he would continue with these jockeying maneuvers, studying how the enemy responded.

"Sir?"

Dardas looked up. Fergon was there again, but without a report in hand.

"What is it?" he asked. He would be very annoyed if the junior officer wanted to make mention of his father again, who Lord Weisel had known socially in Felk.

"It's Berkant, General," Fergon said. "He says he has a message from Emperor Matokin, an urgent one."

"Is there any other kind?" Dardas grunted. He looked past his aide and saw the wizard standing back some distance, waiting. "Very well. Bring him."

Fergon fetched the wizard, who appeared remarkably calm, despite the night's uproar. Then Fergon and the other officers withdrew out of earshot, giving the two privacy.

"Battle doesn't faze you, eh, Berkant?"

"I am not among your combatant magicians, General."

Dardas gave the wizard a nod. "As you might guess, I am extraordinarily engaged at the moment. I rely on your assurance that this communication is crucially important."

"It is, General." Berkant had his familiar shred of fabric in hand.

"Proceed," Dardas said.

Berkant fell swiftly into the seeming stupor. A moment later, with unfocused eyes, he said, "General, I am told you are facing an opponent army."

"That's true, Lord Matokin." As always, communicating in this fashion was mildly eerie but Dardas had adapted to many strange things over the past few lunes. "I am confident we will be victorious against this—"

"I am confident, too, General," Matokin said through the conduit that was Berkant. "I have had confidence in you from the start. You were chosen very carefully."

Compliments from Matokin? Dardas wondered. Surely the great Felk lord hadn't contacted him just to say this.

"Thank you, Lord," he said, concealing his puzzled frown, though he still didn't know if Matokin could see as well as hear through Berkant.

"Everything regarding you has been handled very carefully, General . . . *Weisel.*" There was no mistaking the ironic emphasis. "In fact, when you originally arrived here in Felk, before you even assumed your duties as commander of the Felk army, I made sure a token of your loyalty remained here with me. I keep it with me at all times, which turns out to have been a fortunate precaution. The idea was Lord Abraxis's, may the gods give him peace. I wouldn't take any credit away from him."

Whatever ploy this was, Matokin was at least getting to the point. Dardas waited grimly.

"Blood magic is an invaluable tool for maintaining discipline among the many wizards that have been so meticulously trained at our Academy here," Matokin's words continued from Berkant's mouth. "When I founded that Academy, and set in motion this unifying war, I fully understood the vast power and great delicacy of what I was letting loose into this world. Magic has, in the distant past of both the Northern and Southern Continents, been the cause of untold distress. Its misuse, in fact, was the root of the Great Upheavals."

Dardas blinked. The Upheavals were an ancient chaotic period of history that had occurred long before his original life, even. They had led to the fall of the mighty empires that had once ruled Northland and Southsoil.

Matokin was saying that *magic* was responsible?

"But," the Felk lord went on, "I will not allow that to happen again. I control magic in this world. I was born with a tremendous natural talent. I am also endowed with a perfect vision for the future of this Isthmus. Nothing will frustrate that plan. Nothing . . . and no one."

Dardas didn't cringe. Cringing wasn't in his nature. Matokin had powers, yes, but Dardas was a force to be reckoned with in his own right.

"What is it you want, Lord Matokin?" Dardas spoke it with a blunt edge in his voice.

"I want Mage Kumbat returned to Felk."

Dardas was silent a long moment. Finally he said, "And if I refuse?"

"I appreciate your not vacillating and still pretending Kumbat disappeared between portals."

"And I appreciate your appreciation," Dardas said curtly. "Tell me what you intend to do if I refuse to release Mage Kumbat."

"I believe I've made myself as clear as I need to, General. I have what I need, right here with me, to snuff you out like the flame of candle. Blood magic is potent, and very effective."

"Is that all you can threaten me with?" Dardas asked, adopting a milder tone now. Matokin could have obtained whatever measure of blood was necessary when Dardas was still insensible immediately following his resurrection.

"All?" There was a note of surprise in Berkant's voice.

"Yes. Is that all? Do you honestly expect me to believe that you would kill me right at the moment when you require my talents and services the most?" Dardas allowed himself a chuckle. "You say you've been told about the enemy army. No doubt you are aware of its size. Without me to command this Felk military, that other army could, conceivably, tear through this one, and thereby end your dreams of uniting the Isthmus under Felk rule."

Dardas savored the moment. It had chafed him from the start, being under Matokin's thumb, having to answer to someone "superior" to himself. Matokin may have indeed been the one to set this war into motion, but without Dardas's command of the army, that war of conquest would have remained an unfulfilled vision. The failed dream of a delusional, power-mad mind.

He waited for Matokin's reply. He would not surrender Kumbat. Kumbat was *his*. The mage would provide rejuvenation spells whenever Dardas needed them. Perhaps the wizard could even find a way to permanently expunge Weisel's presence from this vessel.

Berkant's face remained slack. A slow frown touched Dardas's lips. Was something wrong?

Abruptly, a muscle twitched violently in Berkant's cheek. The wizard's unfocused eyes widened, and he gulped in air. His whole body shuddered.

Just as suddenly, Berkant's eyes came into sharp focus, fixing intently on Dardas. His hand shot out and seized the front of Dardas's uniform. Some vehement emotion spilled across his features. He was either frightened, or furious, or in great pain.

"Help . . ." Berkant panted, as Dardas moved to break the man's hold on him. Was this Matokin's doing? Had the Felk ruler somehow directed Berkant to attack him? But that made no sense, not if Matokin's threat about blood magic was real. Maybe it wasn't.

Another great shudder went through Berkant. He suddenly stiffened, then collapsed utterly, hitting the ground with a heavy thud.

Dardas looked down at the body, stunned. Fergon rushed to Dardas's side.

"General, are you—"

"I'm fine. See if he's alive."

Fergon knelt and felt Berkant's throat, then his chest.

"He's dead, sir," Fergon said.

Dardas shook his head. "It was quite sudden." Then again, he mused, that was how death came sometimes— swiftly and inexplicably.

"I'll get him out of your way, General," Fergon said, summoning two of Dardas's personal guard to haul the body away. How quickly it had become an object, Dardas noted, something to be removed to allow freer movement for the living.

The episode had taken up a relatively large amount of time, considering the urgency of the battle his army was engaged in.

"Fergon! I need fresh field reports."

His aide scrambled to comply. Dardas glanced and saw Raven once again. He'd forgotten about her. She appeared now to be in a daze of some sort. She staggered where she was standing, and nearly fell.

Dardas motioned her over to him. She came, blinking, footsteps unsure.

"What's wrong with you?" he asked.

"I . . . I . . . I . . . General, it's—" She could barely make coherent sounds. Her lovely face was pale with shock.

He took her shoulders and leaned close to her. "Raven, what's happened to you?"

"Raven?" she murmured, forlornly. Then she shook her head. Tears were welling up in her eyes. "No. No Raven. Raven's gone. Just . . . *gone*. She just suddenly . . . I can't explain . . . I—"

Something cold and hard closed over Dardas's chest. "What do you mean she's gone?" he asked.

She blinked some more. "I'm just Vadya now. Raven's not with me anymore." The tears overflowed and streaked her face. "She wanted to tell . . . her father . . . wanted to tell him . . ."

Dardas turned away. Fergon was there. He, too, looked distressed.

"General," his aide said, "the Far Speak wizards—they, uh, sir, uh—"

"Godsdamnit, what's happened?" Dardas barked, but somewhere inside he already knew.

"They're dead, sir," Fergon said hoarsely. He turned and gestured.

Dardas saw the dark-robed shapes on the ground, a short distance off. His other officers were milling around the scene, unsettled, upset.

Had Matokin done this? If so, the man was insane.

Dardas called to his guards. "You and you and you and you," he said, pointing out each in turn. "You're going to be my messengers. Get yourselves some fast horses." He pointed out another group. "You four, scatter through the ranks. Find out if there's a magician left alive in this army. Go!"

They jumped to obey, and that was somewhat reassuring. But if this was as widespread as Dardas feared, then panic would be rippling through his army. His regular troops, his officers and soldiers, would have just witnessed the sudden and simultaneous deaths of the wizards they had fought alongside, and come to grudgingly respect, these past lunes. It would be like a shock to the body; and that body, his army, would be stunned from the trauma, and would be vulnerable while it tried to recover itself.

If the strategic intelligence behind the enemy army's movements realized the Felk army's sudden vulnerability, it could be disastrous. Dardas had to be pragmatic about this. He had to assume the enemy would thrust at them when they were weakest.

It was what he would do.

If every wizard under his command was indeed dead, then he was without his special advantages. But he was still Dardas the Butcher, and he would still demonstrate to any opponent how he had earned that title.

Dardas vaulted atop his map-strewn table. This plain was very flat and with so many torches burning among the ranks of both armies, he could see quite a distance.

There they were. The enemy. He saw the clumps of troops and horses. Dardas was indifferent to the ideologies that separated their two forces. The Felk wanted total conquest; this amalgamated army plainly meant to defend their homelands against that; whereas Dardas only wanted war. For him, it was a simple case of physical law. War required resistance. He had to have something to overcome, in order to justify his own existence. Without an enemy, he was incomplete.

But this might be more than he'd bargained for.

The word came back to him that every last wizard in the Felk ranks had apparently died, without outward cause, at precisely the same instant. As he'd suspected, panic was indeed running rampant through his army. Dardas was now without Far Movement mages to transport his forces, without Far Speak wizards to relay field intelligence or make contact with distant parts of the Isthmus. He had even lost Kumbat, who he'd gone to such lengths to acquire. Which brought up an interesting point.

What would happen to him, Dardas, the next time he required a rejuvenation spell?

Dardas climbed down from the table. The enemy had

evidently seen the agitation in their ranks. They were moving now against the Felk. He had seen the forward ranks charging.

"Fergon," he said. "Bring my sword."

The aide delivered it, and Dardas strapped it on. His senior officers were gathered, their faces fearful.

"My fellows," Dardas said, his tone quiet and serious, "we are warriors, all. In our hearts is the longing to fight. Now is our time."

He called for his horse. He gave his last general orders, to be relayed through the ranks.

Attack. Attack the enemy.

Dardas glanced a last time at the dazed woman who had been a vessel for Raven. He thought of his own fellow occupant within this body, poor piteous Lord Weisel, who had imagined an exalted role for himself in this war.

Weisel, ironically, would be remembered, no matter if this night ended in obliteration for the Felk army.

Dardas's teeth bared as he rode toward the front ranks, drawing and swinging his sword overhead, rallying his fighters, letting them see him, leading and inspiring them, calling them to the only true glory that life could ever offer.

BRYCK
(5)

AT THAT MOMENT of ultimate crisis, when the soldiers spotted them atop that roof, he, curiously enough, had only one concern in mind—Quentis's safety.

Deo had fired off one bolt from his crossbow. Bryck watched as he slapped the weapon to his shoulder a second time, a fresh bolt in place, grinning as he worked the trigger.

"*Got* him!"

No matter how accurate a shot it had been, Bryck noted silently, it couldn't make nearly enough of a difference. Not with the number of armed Felk in the street below, now alerted to their position above.

Quentis was by Bryck's side. Radstac, sword in hand, had joined Deo. The others of the Broken Circle, including Aquint and Nievzê, had made their escape off the far lip of the rooftops, Bryck saw with a distant shudder of relief. It was of course crucial that the blood magic wizard got away, so to perform his spell.

But still Bryck's only real priority was getting Quentis out of danger.

Below, the soldiers were charging toward the buildings that held the Circle's rooms and the craft workshops, looking for access to the roofs. They would find it. The patrol was very large, bigger than the entire original garrison put together. Aquint had been correct; reinforcements had obviously been Far Moved to Callah.

Also in the streets were the Callahans that the soldiers had turned out from their homes. Several of these were prone on the ground. Bryck saw blood.

It'll be worse than last time? Gelshiri had wondered.

The last time the Felk had run rampant through the city, it had been because of Bryck's inadvertent murder of a garrison soldier. This time a Felk mage of great political importance lay dead. These soldiers had probably received their orders from high up the chain of command. They wouldn't be concerned with the niceties Governor Jesile had tried to observe while occupying this city for the Felk.

Callah's streets would be wet with blood before sunrise.

These thoughts flashed through Bryck's mind, not eclipsing his concerns for Quentis's safety. He seized her hand. Her returning grip was strong.

Deo's crossbow gave another sharp twang, and another Felk soldier dropped in the street.

"We're going to run!" Bryck said to Radstac and Deo.

Radstac was studying the terrain below. "Too late," she said, clearly and calmly.

And it was, of course. He wanted to say some last thing to these two; both had been instrumental in this desperate and supremely important Broken Circle operation. But Deo was busy with another bolt, and Radstac wouldn't waste her attention listening.

"Thank you," he whispered. It was lost in the general tumult.

He turned, with Quentis, and they raced across the rooftops, over onto those atop the shops. The Felk clogged this street as well. Bryck hunkered low, pulling down Quentis, then dropped to his knees. His fingers clawed the squared sections of a particular roof.

"What're you doing?" Quentis asked, imitating his actions anyway, fingertips probing the edges of the squares.

"Looking for a trap door." Bryck was scrabbling hard now, trying not to let his fear overwhelm him. The roar from below was growing louder, more violent. He hoped the others were making good their escape.

Suddenly his fingers found a groove, and he pried upward. The hatch came free. No hinge, just a loose segment of roof. Beneath was an invitingly dark hole. No doubt the Felk would break into all these shops, but maybe they could hide themselves down there somewhere, somehow—

"What *is* that?" Quentis asked.

Bryck lifted his head from the hole. The turmoil was louder still, and it had taken on some new quality, it seemed. Quentis, on one knee, was trying to peer cautiously over the roof edge.

"Be careful," Bryck said, grabbing for her again.

She instead took his hand and drew him near. She was not one to panic, he knew, and in that moment he appreciated that trait fully.

Together they looked down on the street. The Felk soldiers were no longer alone.

Bryck felt a wave of such strong emotion that at first he was wholly unable to identify it. His eyes widened, and his breath went still in his chest. His fingers tightened around Quentis's hand, until his bones ground against hers.

They came in a gathering wave. Bryck saw individuals joining the mass, and by the time they actually came into contact with the patrol, the numbers were substantial. They brandished improvised weaponry, mostly objects that would serve as bludgeons. The added noise was the general cry of battle, a high taut note, a collective voice of frustration and fury. These people had suffered enough under their occupiers. They had withstood the conquest of their city, and they had acquiesced to the laws of their conquerors. But surrender wasn't enough apparently. Tonight the Felk had come once more into their homes, and the violation and violence was, finally, too much.

And so the Callahans were rising.

Even with these numbers they weren't going to have an easy time of it. The Felk were professionally armed. They were troops drawn possibly from Felk itself or some other occupied city, but as likely had been culled from the active ranks in the field. These soldiers almost certainly had combat experience of some sort. It was unlikely many of these Callahans did.

The Felk cut into them, without hesitation or mercy. Bryck was still holding's Quentis's hand, still overwhelmed with feeling. But what *was* it he was feeling?

"Should we help?" Quentis was asking.

Pride, Bryck realized. He felt pride for these people. At long last they were doing as he'd hoped. He had created for them a fictional revolution, one that had become, by increments, real. Now these people of Callah were giving it its final authenticity.

Yet even under the sway of such powerful emotions, Bryck's prime concern was still Quentis's safety.

"We've done enough," he said, pulling her toward the

opening in the roof. An arrow or crossbow bolt streaked past her shoulder, perilously close.

Quentis dropped her legs into the hole, swung by her hands planted on either side and shot her eyes up at him. "You're coming, too, aren't you?"

"I am." Another missile whisked past, just overhead.

She disappeared into the dark. He barely heard her landing over the uproar. He didn't have time for a look back at Radstac and Deo. He just went down into the very relative safety of the empty shop below, hoping fervently that these Callahans had success with their uprising.

THE ISTHMUS, BRYCK later learned, became once again a very large place that night. As large as it had been before the advent of Far Movement and Far Speak magic. Distances were once more their normal and natural scope. If three days of horseback travel were required to traverse two points, then that was just how it had to be done once again. No more portals. No more wizards to make them appear.

However, Bryck and many others in the city of Callah had concerns of a more immediate nature.

For a quarter-lune the fight for Callah's freedom splashed blood into the streets. The patrol that Bryck and Quentis saw that first night weren't the only Felk reinforcements transported into the city. Quite a large company had been ordered in, to recover Abraxis's bag of blood samples and to crush the evident rebel element in the city. But now no further reinforcements would arrive; and no Felk could be Far Moved to safety.

As the uprising carried on, growing bloodier by the watch, it also drew more participants. More Callahans joined their fellows. They saw an opportunity to be rid of the Felk. They saw the moment of their revenge against their oppressors. Some no doubt simply succumbed to the frenzy of the bloodthirsty spectacle.

The Callahans fought the Felk, neighborhood by neighborhood, street by street. The natives grew more organized. As they recovered weapons from the fallen soldiers, they became better armed. It was war. It was a second chance. Callah had fallen too easily the first time to these invaders from the north.

There were no more curfews, no more public floggings, no rules of any kind that these occupiers could enforce any longer. Eventually the Felk retreated toward the Registry, and eventually the rebels—so many now—surrounded that building from every side. A siege ensued.

Rumors circulated wildly in the city that the Felk, everywhere throughout the Isthmus, had suffered a crippling blow. Their wizards, all of them and all at once, had been struck mysteriously with death. No one could say where the rumor had originated, but it was evident that no Far Movement magicians were currently operating within Callah.

With the surviving soldiers barricaded in the Registry and veritable droves of Callahans encircling the site, Governor Jesile prudently announced the garrison's surrender. He came to a window to do so. The mob hurled stones and obscenities. They had several times tried unsuccessfully to set fire to the combustible parts of the building.

Despite the furor and carnage, Bryck and Quentis had little trouble staying out of the chaos after that first night. They had hunkered there inside that shut up shop, listening to the violence outside, holding tightly to each other. Time became fluid, imprecise, and that ambiguity was its own special sort of fright.

But the time did pass, and the battle did drift away, and the Felk didn't trample their way into the shop. Bryck and Quentis stayed there until morning, until the primitive comforts of light and warmth returned. When they emerged, they saw the bodies, smelled the blood. Radstac and Deo weren't among the corpses. Bryck found himself thinking suddenly and very vividly of Setix, the man who had changed his mind about joining the Broken Circle and who Bryck had ordered killed. He couldn't regret the necessity of that act, but it was one more death, and there was so much death.

He wiped his eyes. Revenge against the Felk. For so long it had been the only motive urging his life forward, allowing him to go on living, rather than choosing to join Aaysue and his children. It was a good motive. The Felk deserved their destruction. But a better reason for living was perhaps the desire to live for something, for someone.

He and Quentis went to ground. And stayed there.

Later they learned of the rebel actions against the Felk, of the standoff at the Registry. Someone emerged from the mobs surrounding the building, someone of calm and reason and extreme pragmatism, and a negotiation between the two parties followed. What resulted was Jesile's agreement to submit himself to a beheading, with the understanding that the remaining soldiers would lay down their arms and be treated to thorough floggings, after which they would be set free.

Jesile, the erstwhile Felk governor of Callah, was by all accounts quietly heroic about his fate. The crowds that gathered to see him dispatched didn't cheer, either before or after the deed.

When later on the bloody-backed soldiers were turned loose, the people of Callah found themselves faced with the business of ruling their own city once more. It was, to the surprise of many, a daunting challenge.

It was at this time that Bryck and Quentis at last emerged from hiding. They walked the streets of the stunned city. People were trying to resume their normal lives, but for the lunes since war had come, the concept of normalcy had shifted radically. Callah was still an isolated city. They had no news of the war. They had learned from the former garrison soldiers that the wizards in residence at the Registry had indeed all died suddenly and inexplicably.

These Callahans were of course the dregs left behind after the Felk conscription efforts, the very young and the oldish. It now fell to them to reestablish a local government. Foodstuffs still had to be transported in from the city-state's surrounding farmland. A police force needed to be recruited. The Callahan economy had to be stabilized, and the Felk-issued scrip eliminated.

Bryck didn't involve himself in any of these matters. He accompanied Quentis back to her home, where she'd lived with her cousin Ondak before joining the Broken Circle. The house had been broken into and ransacked, but it hadn't been burned, as some parts of Callah had. Ondak wasn't there. She and Bryck settled in together, cleaning the place up, and waited and watched as the city reclaimed itself.

Bryck had noted the Broken Circle's sigil freshly drawn and slashed on many surfaces throughout the city. He heard also songs being sung, those revolutionary verses that Deo and Radstac had been spreading in the taverns.

There were lean times in the days that followed. Irregular supplies of food meant hunger, and that led to panic in some, violence in others. The new self-regulating Callahan government had to deal with these problems. Bryck and

Quentis merely survived, concerning themselves with their small personal needs.

They eventually met up with Aquint, who, it turned out, had been the one to negotiate the garrison's surrender at the Registry. Cat was with him, naturally, and the two were busily involved in some enterprise that neither would speak of directly.

"Have you seen Ondak?" Quentis asked.

"No," Aquint said. "But I know where Radstac is."

"Nievzê was able to cast his spell, evidently," Bryck said.

Aquint nodded. "We found a safe place that night. I watched him. It was . . . fascinating. It drained him almost to death. I wonder if its effect was as widespread as he claimed."

"I have to believe it was. I think we all have to believe that."

They didn't talk any further about the Broken Circle. Aquint planned to remain in Callah. If Bryck and Quentis intended to do the same, they would all have to meet for a drink some evening, Aquint said. Then they parted.

Bryck and Quentis sought out Radstac at the room she'd taken. Her left leg was bandaged, but if the wound was causing her pain, she didn't show it.

"Deo's dead," she said in that hard flat voice of hers. She seemed indifferent to Bryck and Quentis's company. "He fought with enthusiasm, and he died with his eyes open. I'll be going south in a few days. When I reach Pet-grad, I'll tell his family about him."

"Then what will you do?" Bryck asked.

Radstac regarded him with eyes that were almost color-less. "Keep going south. I'm going home. I'm done with your Isthmus." Something moved underneath that ac-cented voice, something hinting at a sorrow that might or might not have been profound. They left her there in that room.

Eventually word of the outside did reach Callah, in that way before Far Speak that news had always traveled. There was unfettered movement on Isthmus roads once again, as there hadn't been in some while. Travelers and traders and returning soldiers brought the word. The Felk war was done. The Felk themselves were done, as would-be conquerors. Their wizards were all dead, and their army had met with a mixed force of southern Isthmus militaries that had smashed the Felk at what was being called the Battle of Pegwithe Plains.

The one responsible for uniting those various armies against the Felk, the premier of Petgrad, had died in the fighting, it was said, as had the general of the Felk army. There was no reliable word of what had happened to the Felk ruler, Matokin, but he was evidently no longer in power in that northern city.

This news reached Bryck and Quentis in the same manner it did everyone else in Callah, and along with everyone else they celebrated the war's end.

Bryck found himself quite comfortable with Quentis and their living arrangements. They were lovers and, more, had settled into an easy daily rhythm with one another. It was emotional as well as physical. They had learned each other's basic predilections and day by day worked out the more niggling details of their relationship. It occurred to Bryck after Callah's major crises had been alleviated by its new government that he had no intention of leaving the city. Certainly there was no U'delph to go back to; but more than that he had a fondness for Callah now that he hadn't had before. These people had risen up against their oppressors. They had proven their character.

He went unrecognized as the leader of the Broken Circle, of course. Very few had ever seen his face, and the few original members of that group who he encountered did not give him away. People spoke of the Broken Circle often, but already these were becoming fanciful stories and romantic exaggerations, precursors of folklore.

It was generally assumed, even by the least devout, that the gods had had a hand in the war's ending. The deaths of all those wizards was surely proof of that. More, it was proof that those gods had not been on the side of the Felk.

"I'd like to ask you something," Quentis said one day. They were at home. Her old vendor cart had been lost, but she'd had a new one built. She and Bryck took turns pushing it through the streets, peddling an assortment of small wares. Callah's population had been reinvigorated by the return of the surviving native men and women who'd been conscripted into the Felk army.

Bryck was sitting comfortably in the forward room that got light through its windows in the later watches of the day. This house was snug, but he had helped make repairs to it. He was considering planting a fruit tree in the plot of dirt out front, when this encroaching winter was over.

"What's that?" he asked, turning an eye toward Quentis. He knew already by the subtly grave tone that she had something of import on her mind.

Quentis pressed her lips together thoughtfully. Her amber eyes took on a frank cast. After a moment of silence she finally asked, "What *is* your name?"

Bryck was dumbstruck. He had been "the Minstrel" for so long, he'd grown used to it. Yet how had he neglected to tell Quentis his actual name during this entire past lune? The thought tickled him comically, appealing to some dormant vein of humor, which had once run much nearer the surface.

He kept himself from smiling, knowing that Quentis was being quite serious.

"I am Bryck."

"Bryck?" She seemed to be tasting the name.

"Yes. Bryck of U'delph."

Those eyes blinked slowly. A glimmer came to them, and her expression shifted. "Not the playwright? *Chicanery by Moonlight. Glad of Nothing.* Not that Bryck of U'delph?"

"Well . . . yes." He felt a curious embarrassment that he couldn't quite explain to himself.

Quentis regarded him through another longer silence. At last she said, "I've always admired your work."

Now he did smile at her, with a true warmth he hadn't felt for far too long.

NOW AVAILABLE

First in a brand-new series from
New York Times bestselling author
Robert Asprin and Eric Del Carlo

WARTORN

The people of Isthmus live between two great
kingdoms: the Northland and the Southern
Continent. Now the Northland is on the move as
the city-state of Felk, under the control of the
magician Matoken, begins a campaign of battle
against its neighbor.

This is an epic journey of hope, magic,
tragedy, and war.

0-441-01235-3

**Available wherever books are sold or at
penguin.com**